TO
MY WIFE
BLESS HER

Jill the Reckless

By
P. G. WODEHOUSE

BARRIE & JENKINS
COMMUNICA - EUROPA

© P. G. Wodehouse 1920

First published in 1921 by
Herbert Jenkins Ltd

This edition published in 1978 by
Barrie and Jenkins Ltd
24 Highbury Crescent London N5 1RX

ISBN 0 257 65969 2

Printed and bound in Great Britain by
REDWOOD BURN LIMITED
Trowbridge & Esher

CONTENTS

★ 1 ★

The Family Curse

I

FREDDIE ROOKE gazed coldly at the breakfast-table. Through a gleaming eye-glass he inspected the revolting object which Barker, his faithful man, had placed on a plate before him.

"Barker!" His voice had a ring of pain.

"Sir?"

"What's this?"

"Poached egg, sir."

Freddie averted his eyes with a silent shudder.

"It looks just like an old aunt of mine," he said. "Remove it!"

He got up, and, wrapping his dressing-gown about his long legs, took up a stand in front of the fireplace. From this position he surveyed the room, his shoulders against the mantelpiece, his calves pressing the club fender. It was a cheerful oasis in a chill and foggy world, a typical London bachelor's breakfast-room. The walls were a restful grey, and the table, set for two, a comfortable arrangement in white and silver.

"Eggs, Barker," said Freddie solemnly, "are the acid test!"

"Yes, sir?"

"If, on the morning after, you can tackle a poached egg, you are all right. If not, not. And don't let anybody tell you otherwise."

"No, sir."

Freddie pressed the palm of his hand to his brow, and sighed.

"It would seem, then, that I must have revelled a trifle whole-heartedly last night. I was possibly a little blotto. Not whiffled, perhaps, but indisputably blotto. Did I make much noise coming in?"

"No, sir. You were very quiet."

"Ah! A dashed bad sign!"

Freddie moved to the table, and poured himself a cup of coffee.

"The cream jug is to your right, sir," said the helpful Barker.

"Let it remain there. *Café noir* for me this morning. As *noir* as it can jolly well stick!" Freddie retired to the fireplace and sipped delicately. "As far as I can remember, it was Ronny Devereux' birthday or something . . . "

"Mr. Martyn's, I think you said, sir."

"That's right. Algy Martyn's birthday, and Ronny and I were the guests. It all comes back to me. I wanted Derek to roll along and join the festivities—he's never met Ronny—but he gave it a miss. Quite right! A chap in his position has responsibilities. Member of Parliament and all that. Besides," said Freddie earnestly, driving home the point with a wave of his spoon, "he's engaged to be married. You must remember that, Barker!"

"I will endeavour to, sir,"

"Sometimes," said Freddie dreamily, "I wish I were engaged to be married. Sometimes I wish I had some sweet girl to watch over me and . . . No, I don't, by Jove. It would give me the utter pip! Is Sir Derek up yet, Barker?"

"Getting up, sir."

"See that everything is all right, will you? I mean as regards the foodstuffs and what not. I want him to make a good breakfast. He's got to meet his mother this morning at Charing Cross. She's legging it back from the Riviera."

"Indeed, sir?"

Freddie shook his head.

"You wouldn't speak in that light, careless tone if you knew her! Well, you'll see her to-night. She's coming here to dinner."

"Yes, sir."

"Miss Mariner will be here, too. A foursome. Tell Mrs. Barker to pull up her socks and give us something pretty ripe. Soup, fish, all that sort of thing. *She* knows. And let's have a stoup of malvoisie from the oldest bin. This is a special occasion!"

"Her ladyship will be meeting Miss Mariner for the first time, sir?"

"You've put your finger on it! Absolutely the first time on this or any stage! We must all rally round and make the thing a success."

"I am sure Mrs. Barker will strain every nerve, sir." Barker moved to the door, carrying the rejected egg, and stepped aside to allow a tall, well-built man of about thirty to enter. "Good morning, Sir Derek."

"Morning, Barker."

Barker slid softly from the room. Derek Underhill sat down at the table. He was a strikingly handsome man, with a strong, forceful face, dark, lean and cleanly shaven. He was one of those men whom a stranger would instinctively pick out of a crowd as worthy of note. His only defect was that his heavy eyebrows gave him at times an expression which was a little forbidding. Women, however, had never been repelled by it. He was very popular with women, not quite so popular with men—always excepting Freddie Rooke, who worshipped him. They had been at school together, though Freddie was the younger by several years.

"Finished, Freddie ?" asked Derek.

Freddie smiled wanly.

"We are not breakfasting this morning," he replied. "The spirit was willing, but the jolly old flesh would have none of it. To be perfectly frank, the Last of the Rookes has a bit of a head."

"Ass!" said Derek.

"A bit of sympathy," said Freddie, pained, "would not be out of place. We are far from well. Some person unknown has put a threshing-machine inside the old bean and substituted a piece of brown paper for our tongue. Things look dark and yellow and wobbly!"

"You shouldn't have overdone it last night."

"It was Algy Martyn's birthday," pleaded Freddie.

"If I were an ass like Algy Martyn," said Derek, "I wouldn't go about advertising the fact that I'd been born. I'd hush it up!"

He helped himself to a plentiful portion of kedgeree. Freddie watching him with repulsion mingled with envy. When he began to eat, the spectacle became too poignant for the sufferer, and he wandered to the window.

"What a beast of a day!"

It was an appalling day. January, that grim month, was treating London with its usual severity. Early in the morning a bank of fog had rolled up off the river, and was deepening from pearly white to a lurid brown. It pressed on the window-pane like a blanket, leaving dark, damp rivulets on the glass.

"Awful!" said Derek,

"Your mater's train will be late."

"Yes. Damned nuisance. It's bad enough meeting trains in any case, without having to hang about a draughty station for an hour."

"And it's sure, I should imagine," went on Freddie, pursuing his train of thought, "to make the dear old thing pretty tolerably ratty, if she has one of those slow journeys." He pottered back to the fireplace, and rubbed his shoulders reflectively against the mantelpiece. "I take it that you wrote to her about Jill ?"

"Of course. That's why she's coming over, I suppose. By the way, you got those seats for that theatre to-night ?"

"Yes. Three together and one somewhere on the outskirts. If it's all the same to you, old thing, I'll have the one on the outskirts."

Derek, who had finished his kedgeree and was now making himself a blot on Freddie's horizon with toast and marmalade, laughed.

"What a rabbit you are, Freddie! Why on earth are you so afraid of mother ?"

Freddie looked at him as a timid young squire might have gazed upon St. George when the latter set out to do battle with the dragon. He was of the amiable type which makes heroes of its friends. In the old days when he had fagged for him at Winchester he had thought Derek the most wonderful person in the world, and this view he still retained. Indeed, subsequent events had strengthened it. Derek had done the most amazing things since leaving school. He had had a brilliant career at Oxford, and now, in the House of Commons, was already looked upon by the leaders of his party as one to be watched and encouraged. He played polo superlatively well, and was a fine shot. But of all his gifts and qualities the one that extorted Freddie's admiration in its intensest form was his lion-like courage as exemplified by his behaviour in the present crisis. There he sat, placidly eating toast and marmalade, while the boat-train containing Lady Underhill already sped on its way from Dover to London. It was like Drake playing bowls with the Spanish Armada in sight.

"I wish I had your nerve!" he said awed. "What I should be feeling, if I were in your place and had to meet your mater after telling her that I was engaged to marry a girl she had never seen, I don't know. I'd rather face a wounded tiger!"

"Idiot!" said Derek placidly.

"Not," pursued Freddie, "that I mean to say anything in the least derogatory and so forth to your jolly old mater, if you understand me, but the fact remains she scares me pallid. Always has, ever since the first time I went to stay at your place when I was a kid. I can still remember catching her eye the morning I happened by pure chance to bung an apple through her bedroom window, meaning to let a cat on the sill below have it in the short ribs. She was at least thirty feet away, but, by Jove, it stopped me like a bullet!"

"Push the bell, old man, will you? I want some more toast."

Freddie did as he was requested, with growing admiration.

"The condemned man made an excellent breakfast," he murmured. "More toast, Barker," he added, as that admirable servitor opened the door. "Gallant! That's what I call it. Gallant!"

Derek tilted his chair back.

"Mother is sure to like Jill when she sees her," he said.

"*When* she sees her! Ah! But the trouble is, young feller-me-lad, that she *hasn't* seen her! That's the weak spot in your case, old companion. A month ago she didn't know of Jill's existence. Now, you know and I know that Jill is one of the best and brightest. As far as we are concerned, everything in the good old garden is lovely. Why, dash it, Jill and I were children together. Sported side by side on the green, and what not. I remember Jill, when she was twelve, turning the garden hose on me and knocking about seventy-five per cent off the market value of my best Sunday suit. That sort of thing forms a bond, you know, and I've always felt that she was a corker. But your mater's got to discover it for herself. It's a dashed pity, by Jove, that Jill hasn't a father or a mother or something of that species to rally round just now. They would form a gang. There's nothing like a gang! But she's only got that old uncle of hers. A rummy bird. Met him?"

"Several times. I like him."

"Oh, he's a genial old buck all right. A very bonhomous lad. But you hear some pretty queer stories about him if you get among people who knew him in the old days. Even now I'm not so dashed sure I should care to play cards with him. Young Threepwood was telling me only the other day that the old boy took thirty quid off him at picquet as clean as a whistle. And Jimmy Monroe, who's on the Stock Exchange, says he's frightfully busy these times buying margins or whatever it is chappies do down in the City. Margins. That's the word. Jimmy made me buy some myself on a thing called Amalgamated Dyes. I don't understand the procedure exactly, but Jimmy says it's a sound egg and will do me a bit of good. What was I talking about? Oh, yes, old Selby. There's no doubt he's quite a sportsman. But till you've got Jill well established, you know, I shouldn't enlarge on him too much with the mater."

"On the contrary," said Derek, "I shall mention him at the first opportunity. He knew my father out in India."

"Did he, by Jove! Oh, well, that makes a difference."

Barker entered with the toast, and Derek resumed his breakfast.

"It may be a little bit awkward," he said, "at first, meeting mother. But everything will be all right after five minutes."

"Absolutely! But, oh, boy! that first five minutes!" Freddie gazed portentously through his eye-glass. Then he seemed to be undergoing some internal struggle, for he gulped once or twice. " That first five minutes!" he said, and paused again. A moment's silent self-communion, and he went on with a rush. "I say, listen. Shall I come along, too ?"

"Come along ?"

"To the station. With you."

"What on earth for ?"

"To see you through the opening stages. Break the ice, and all that sort of thing. Nothing like collecting a gang, you know. Moments when a feller needs a friend and so forth. Say the word, and I'll buzz along and lend my moral support."

Derek's heavy eyebrows closed together in an offended frown, and seemed to darken his whole face. This unsolicited offer of assistance hurt his dignity. He showed a touch of the petulance which came now and then when he was annoyed, to suggest that he might not possess so strong a character as his exterior indicated.

"It's very kind of you," he began stiffly.

Freddie nodded. He was acutely conscious of this himself.

"Some fellows," he observed, "would say 'Not at all!' I suppose. But not the Last of the Rookes! For, honestly, old man, between ourselves, I don't mind admitting that this *is* the bravest deed of the year, and I'm dashed if I would do it for anyone else."

"It's very good of you, Freddie . . ."

"That's all right. I'm a Boy Scout, and this is my act of kindness for to-day."

Derek got up from the table.

"Of course you mustn't come," he said. "We can't form a sort of debating society to discuss Jill on the platform at Charing Cross."

"Oh, I would just hang around in the offing, shoving in an occasional tactful word."

"Nonsense!"

"The wheeze would simply be to . . ."

"It's impossible."

"Oh, very well," said Freddie, damped. "Just as you say, of course. But there's nothing like a gang, old son, nothing like a gang!"

II

Derek Underhill threw down the stump of his cigar, and grunted irritably. Inside Charing Cross Station business was proceeding as usual. Porters wheeling baggage-trucks moved to and fro like Juggernauts. Belated trains clanked in, glad to get home, while others, less fortunate, crept reluctantly out through the blackness and disappeared into an inferno of detonating fog-signals. For outside the fog still held. The air was cold and raw and tasted coppery. In the street traffic moved at a funeral pace, to the accompaniment of hoarse cries and occasional crashes. Once the sun had worked its way through the murk and had hung in the sky like a great red orange, but now all was darkness and discomfort again, blended with that odd suggestion of mystery and romance which is a London fog's only redeeming quality.

The fog and the waiting had had their effect upon Derek. The resolute front he had exhibited to Freddie at the breakfast-table had melted since his arrival at the station, and he was feeling nervous at the prospect of the meeting that lay before him. Calm as he had appeared to the eye of Freddie and bravely as he had spoken, Derek, in the recesses of his heart, was afraid of his mother. There are men—and Derek Underhill was one of them

—who never wholly emerge from the nursery. They may put away childish things and rise in the world to affluence and success, but the hand that rocked their cradle still rules their lives.

Derek turned to begin one more walk along the platform, and stopped in mid-stride, raging. Beaming over the collar of a plaid greatcoat, all helpfulness and devotion, Freddie Rooke was advancing towards him, the friend that sticketh closer than a brother. Like some loving dog, who, ordered home sneaks softly on through alleys and by-ways, peeping round corners and crouching behind lamp-posts, the faithful Freddie had followed him after all. And with him, to add the last touch to Derek's discomfiture, were those two inseparable allies of his, Ronny Devereux and Algy Martyn.

"Well, old thing," said Freddie, patting Derek encouragingly on the shoulder, "here we are after all! I know you told me not to roll round and so forth, but I knew you didn't mean it. I thought it over after you had left, and decided it would be a rotten trick not to cluster about you in your hour of need. I hope you don't mind Ronny and Algy breezing along too. The fact is, I was in the deuce of a funk—your jolly old mater always rather paralyses my nerve-centres, you know—so I roped them in. Met 'em in Piccadilly, groping about for the club, and conscripted 'em both, they very decently consenting. We all toddled off and had a pick-me-up at that chemist chappie's at the top of the Haymarket, and now we're feeling full of beans and buck, ready for anything. I've explained the whole thing to them, and they're with you to the death! Collect a gang, dear boy, collect a gang! That's the motto. There's nothing like it!"

"Nothing!" said Ronny.

"Absolutely nothing!" said Algy.

"We'll just see you through the opening stages," said Freddie, "and then leg it. We'll keep the conversation general, you know."

"Stop it getting into painful channels," said Ronny.

"Steer it clear," said Algy, "of the touchy topic."

"That's the wheeze," said Freddie. "We'll . . . Oh, golly! There's the train coming in now!" His voice quavered, for not even the comforting presence of his two allies could altogether sustain him in this ordeal. But he pulled himself together with a manful effort. "Stick it, old beans!" he said doughtily. "Now is the time for all good men to come to the aid of the party!"

"We're here!" said Ronny Devereux.

"On the spot!" said Algy Martyn.

III

The boat-train slid into the station. Bells rang, engines blew off steam, porters shouted, baggage-trucks rattled over the platform. The train began to give up its contents, now in ones and twos, now in a steady stream. Most of the travellers seemed limp and exhausted, and were pale with the pallor that comes of a choppy Channel crossing. Almost the only exception to the general condition of collapse was the eagle-faced lady in the brown ulster, who had taken up her stand in the middle of the platform and was haranguing a subdued little maid in a voice that cut the gloomy air like a steel knife. Like the other travellers, she was pale, but she bore up resolutely. No one could have told from Lady Underhill's demeanour that the solid platform seemed to heave beneath her feet like a deck.

Derek approached, acutely conscious of Freddie, Ronny, and Algy, who were skirmishing about his flank.

"Well, mother! So there you are at last!"

"Well, Derek!"

Derek kissed his mother. Freddie, Ronny, and Algy shuffled closer, like leopards. Freddie, with the expression of one who leads a forlorn hope, moved his Adam's apple briskly up and down several times, and spoke.

"How do you do, Lady Underhill?"

"How do you do, Mr. Rooke?"

Lady Underhill bowed stiffly and without pleasure. She was not fond of the Last of the Rookes. She supposed the Almighty had had some wise purpose in creating Freddie, but it had always been inscrutable to her.

"Like you," mumbled Freddie, "to meet my friends. Lady Underhill. Mr. Devereux."

"Charmed," said Ronny affably.

"Mr. Martyn."

"Delighted," said Algy with old-world courtesy.

Lady Underhill regarded this mob-scene with an eye of ice.

"How do you do?" she said. "Have you come to meet some-body?"

"I—er—we—er—why—er——" This woman always made

Freddie feel as if he were being disembowelled by some clumsy amateur. He wished that he had defied the dictates of his better nature and remained in his snug rooms at the Albany, allowing Derek to go through this business by himself. "I—er—we—er—came to meet *you*, don't you know!"

"Indeed! That was very kind of you!"

"Oh, not at all."

"Thought we'd welcome you back to the old homestead," said Ronny beaming.

"What could be sweeter?" said Algy. He produced a cigar-case, and extracted a formidable torpedo-shaped Havana. He was feeling delightfully at his ease, and couldn't understand why Freddie had made such a fuss about meeting this nice old lady. "Don't mind if I smoke, do you? Air's a bit raw to-day. Gets into the lungs."

Derek chafed impotently. These unsought allies were making a difficult situation a thousand times worse. A more acute observer than young Mr. Martyn, he noted the tight lines about his mother's mouth and knew them for the danger-signal they were. Endeavouring to distract her with light conversation, he selected a subject which was a little unfortunate.

"What sort of crossing did you have, mother?"

Lady Underhill winced. A current of air had sent the perfume of Algy's cigar playing about her nostrils. She closed her eyes, and her face turned a shade paler. Freddie, observing this, felt quite sorry for the poor old thing. She was a pest and a pot of poison, of course, but all the same, he reflected charitably, it was a shame that she should look so green about the gills. He came to the conclusion that she must be hungry. The thing to do was to take her mind off it till she could be conducted to a restaurant and dumped down in front of a bowl of soup.

"Bit choppy, I suppose, what?" he bellowed, in a voice that ran up and down Lady Underhill's nervous system like an electric needle. "I was afraid you were going to have a pretty rough time of it when I read the forecast in the paper. The good old boat wobbled a bit, eh?"

Lady Underhill uttered a faint moan. Freddie noticed that she was looking deucedly chippy, even chippier than a moment ago.

"It's an extraordinary thing about that Channel crossing," said Algy Martyn meditatively, as he puffed a refreshing cloud. "I've known fellows who could travel quite happily everywhere else in the world—round the Horn in sailing-ships and all that sort of thing—yield up their immortal soul crossing the Channel! Absolutely yield up their immortal soul! Don't know why. Rummy, but there it is!"

"I'm like that myself," assented Ronny Devereux. "That dashed trip from Calais gets me every time. Bowls me right over. I go aboard, stoked to the eyebrows with sea-sick remedies, swearing that this time I'll fool 'em, but down I go ten minutes after we've started and the next thing I know is somebody saying, 'Well, well! So this is Dover!' "

"It's exactly the same with me," said Freddie, delighted with the smooth, easy way the conversation was flowing. "Whether it's the hot, greasy smell of the engines . . ."

"It's not the engines," contended Ronny Devereux. "Stands to reason it can't be. I rather like the smell of engines. This station is reeking with the smell of engine-grease, and I can drink it in and enjoy it." He sniffed, luxuriantly. "It's something else."

"Ronny's right," said Algy cordially. "It isn't the engines. It's the way the boat heaves up and down and up and down and up and down . . ." He shifted his cigar to his left hand in order to give with his right a spirited illustration of a Channel steamer going up and down and up and down and up and down. Lady Underhill, who had opened her eyes, had an excellent view of the performance, and closed her eyes again quickly.

"Be quiet!" she snapped.

"I was only saying . . ."

"Be quiet!"

"Oh, rather!"

Lady Underhill wrestled with herself. She was a woman of great will-power and accustomed to triumph over the weaknesses of the flesh. After a while her eyes opened. She had forced herself, against the evidence of her senses, to recognize that this was a platform on which she stood and not a deck.

There was a pause. Algy, damped, was temporarily out of action, and his friends had for the moment nothing to remark.

"I'm afraid you had a trying journey, mother," said Derek. "The train was very late."

"Now, *train*-sickness," said Algy, coming to the surface again, "is a thing lots of people suffer from. Never could understand it myself."

"I've never had a touch of train-sickness," said Ronny.

"Oh, I have," said Freddie. "I've often felt rotten on a train. I get floating spots in front of my eyes and a sort of heaving sensation, and everything kind of goes black . . ."

"Mr. Rooke!"

"Eh?"

"I should be greatly obliged if you would keep those confidences for the ear of your medical adviser."

"Freddie," intervened Derek hastily, "my mother's rather tired. Do you think you could be going ahead and getting a taxi?"

"My dear old chap, of course! Get you one in a second. Come along, Algy. Pick up the old waukeesis, Ronny."

And Freddie, accompanied by his henchmen, ambled off, well pleased with himself. He had, he felt, helped to break the ice for Derek and had seen him safely through those awkward opening stages. Now he could totter off with a light heart and get a bite of lunch.

Lady Underhill's eyes glittered. They were small, keen, black eyes, unlike Derek's which were large and brown. In their other features the two were obviously mother and son. Each had the same long upper lip, the same thin, firm mouth, the prominent chin which was a family characteristic of the Underhills, and the jutting Underhill nose. Most of the Underhills came into the world looking as though they meant to drive their way through life like a wedge.

"A little more," she said tensely, "and I should have struck those unspeakable young men with my umbrella. One of the things I have never been able to understand, Derek, is why you should have selected that imbecile Rooke as your closest friend."

Derek smiled tolerantly.

"It was more a case of him selecting *me*. But Freddie is quite a good fellow really. He's a man you've got to know."

"*I* have not got to know him, and I thank heaven for it!"

"He's a very good-natured fellow. It was decent of him to put me up at the Albany while our house was let. By the way, he has some seats for the first night of a new piece this evening. He suggested that we might all dine at the Albany and go on to the theatre." He hesitated a moment "Jill will be there," he said,

and felt easier now that her name had at last come into the talk.
"She's longing to meet you."

"Then why didn't she meet me?"

"Here, do you mean? At the station? Well, I—I wanted you
to see her for the first time in pleasanter surroundings."

"Oh!" said Lady Underhill shortly.

It is a disturbing thought that we suffer in this world just as
much by being prudent and taking precautions as we do by
being rash and impulsive and acting as the spirit moves us. If
Jill had been permitted by her wary fiancé to come with him to
the station to meet his mother it is certain that much trouble
would have been avoided. True, Lady Underhill would probably
have been rude to her in the opening stages of the interview,
but she would not have been alarmed and suspicious; or, rather,
the vague suspicion which she had been feeling would not have
solidified, as it did now into definite certainty of the worst. All
that Derek had effected by his careful diplomacy had been to
convince his mother that he considered his bride-elect something
to be broken gently to her.

She stopped and faced him.

"Who is she?" she demanded. "Who is this girl?"

Derek flushed.

"I thought I made everything clear in my letter."

"You made nothing clear at all."

"By your leave!" chanted a porter behind them, and a baggage-
truck clove them apart.

"We can't talk in a crowded station," said Derek irritably.
"Let me get you to the taxi and take you to the hotel. . . . What
do you want to know about Jill?"

"Everything. Where does she come from? Who are her people?
I don't know any Mariners."

"I haven't cross-examined her," said Derek stiffly. "But I
do know that her parents are dead. Her father was an American."

"American!"

"Americans frequently have daughters, I believe."

"There is nothing to be gained by losing your temper," said
Lady Underhill with steely calm.

"There is nothing to be gained, as far as I can see, by all this
talk," retorted Derek. He wondered vexedly why his mother
always had this power of making him lose control of himself.
He hated to lose control of himself. It upset him, and blurred

that vision which he liked to have of himself as a calm, important man superior to ordinary weaknesses. "Jill and I are engaged, and there is an end to it."

"Don't be a fool," said Lady Underhill, and was driven away by another baggage-truck. "You know perfectly well," she resumed, returning to the attack, "that your marriage is a matter of the greatest concern to me and to the whole of the family."

"Listen, mother!" Derek's long wait on the draughty platform had generated an irritability which overcame the deep-seated awe of his mother which was the result of years of defeat in battles of the will. "Let me tell you in a few words all that I know of Jill, and then we'll drop the subject. In the first place, she is a lady. Secondly, she has plenty of money . . ."

"The Underhills do not need to marry for money."

"I am not marrying for money!"

"Well, go on."

"I have already described to you in my letter—very inadequately, but I did my best—what she looks like. Her sweetness, her lovableness, all the subtle things about her which go to make her what she is, you will have to judge for yourself."

"I intend to!"

"Well, that's all, then. She lives with her uncle, a Major Selby . . ."

"Major Selby? What regiment?"

"I didn't ask him," snapped the goaded Derek. "And in the name of heaven, what does it matter? If you are worrying about Major Selby's social standing, I may as well tell you that he used to know father."

"What! When? Where?"

"Years ago. In India, when father was at Simla."

"Selby? Selby? Not Christopher Selby?"

"Oh, you remember him?"

"I certainly remember him! Not that he and I ever met, but your father often spoke of him."

Derek was relieved. It was abominable that this sort of thing should matter, but one had to face facts, and, as far as his mother was concerned, it did. The fact that Jill's uncle had known his dead father would make all the difference to Lady Underhill.

"Christopher Selby!" said Lady Underhill reflectively. "Yes! I have often heard your father speak of him. He was the man who gave your father an I.O.U. to pay a card debt, and redeemed it with a cheque which was returned by the bank!"

"What!"

"Didn't you hear what I said? I will repeat it, if you wish."

"There must have been some mistake."

"Only the one your father made when he trusted the man."

"It must have been some other fellow."

"Of course!" said Lady Underhill satirically. "No doubt your father knew hundreds of Christopher Selbys!"

Derek bit his lip.

"Well, after all," he said doggedly, "whether it's true or not . . ."

"I see no reason why your father should not have spoken the truth."

"All right. We'll say it *is* true, then. But what does it matter? I am marrying Jill, not her uncle."

"Nevertheless, it would be pleasanter if her only living relative were not a swindler! . . . Tell me, where and how did you meet this girl?"

"I should be glad if you would not refer to her as 'this girl.' The name, if you have forgotten it, is Mariner."

"Well, where did you meet Miss Mariner?"

"At Prince's. Just after you left for Mentone. Freddie Rooke introduced me."

"Oh, your intellectual friend Mr. Rooke knows her?"

"They were children together. Her people lived next to the Rookes in Worcestershire."

"I thought you said she was an American."

"I said her father was. He settled in England. Jill hasn't been in America since she was eight or nine."

"The fact," said Lady Underhill, "that the girl is a friend of Mr. Rooke is no great recommendation."

Derek kicked angrily at a box of matches which someone had thrown down on the platform.

"I wonder if you could possibly get it into your head, mother, that I want to marry Jill, not engage her as an under-housemaid. I don't consider that she requires recommendations, as you call them. However, don't you think the most sensible thing is for you to wait till you meet her at dinner to-night, and then you can form your own opinion? I'm beginning to get a little bored by this futile discussion."

"As you seem quite unable to talk on the subject of this girl without becoming rude," said Lady Underhill, "I agree with you. Let us hope that my first impression will be a favourable one. Experience has taught me that first impressions are everything."

"I'm glad you think so," said Derek, "for I fell in love with Jill the very moment I saw her!"

IV

Barker stepped back and surveyed with modest pride the dinner-table to which he had been putting the finishing touches. It was an artistic job and a credit to him.

"That's that!" said Barker, satisfied.

He went to the window and looked out. The fog which had lasted well into the evening, had vanished now, and the clear night was bright with stars. A distant murmur of traffic came from the direction of Piccadilly.

As he stood there, the front-door bell rang, and continued to ring in little spurts of sound. If character can be deduced from bell-ringing, as nowadays it apparently can be from every other form of human activity, one might have hazarded the guess that whoever was on the other side of the door was determined, impetuous, and energetic.

"Barker!"

Freddie Rooke pushed a tousled head, which had yet to be brushed into the smooth sleekness that made a delight to the public eye, out of a room down the passage.

"Sir?"

"Somebody ringing."

"I heard, sir. I was about to answer the bell."

"If it's Lady Underhill, tell her I'll be in in a minute."

"I fancy it is Miss Mariner, sir. I think I recognize her touch."

He made his way down the passage to the front-door, and opened it. A girl was standing outside. She wore a long grey fur coat, and a filmy hood covered her hair. As Barker opened the door, she scampered in like a grey kitten.

"Brrh! It's cold!" she exclaimed. "Hullo, Barker!"

"Good evening, miss."

"Am I the last or the first or what?"

Barker moved to help her with her cloak.

"Sir Derek and her ladyship have not yet arrived, miss. Sir Derek went to bring her ladyship from the Savoy Hotel. Mr. Rooke is dressing in his bedroom and will be ready very shortly."

The girl had slipped out of the fur coat, and Barker cast a swift glance of approval at her. He had the valet's unerring eye for a thoroughbred, and Jill Mariner was manifestly that. It showed in her walk, in every move of her small, active body, in the way she looked at you, in the way she talked to you, in the little tilt of her resolute chin. Her hair was pale gold, and had the brightness of colouring of a child's. Her face glowed, and her grey eyes sparkled. She looked very much alive.

It was this liveliness of hers that was her chief charm. Her eyes were good and her mouth, with its small, even teeth, attractive, but she would have laughed if anybody had called her beautiful. She sometimes doubted if she were even pretty. Yet few men had met her and remained entirely undisturbed. She had a magnetism. One hapless youth, who had laid his heart at her feet and had been commanded to pick it up again, and endeavoured subsequently to explain her attraction (to a bosom friend over a mournful bottle of the best in the club smoking-room) in these words: "I don't know what it is about her, old man, but she somehow makes a feller feel she's so damned *interested* in a chap, if you know what I mean." And though not generally credited in his circle with any great acuteness, there is no doubt that the speaker had achieved something approaching a true analysis of Jill's fascination for his sex. She was interested in everything Life presented to her notice, from a Coronation to a stray cat. She was vivid. She had sympathy. She listened to you as though you really mattered. It takes a man of tough fibre to resist these qualities. Women, on the other hand, especially of the Lady Underhill type, can resist them without an effort.

"Go and stir him up," said Jill, alluding to the absent Mr. Rooke. "Tell him to come and talk to me. Where's the nearest fire? I want to get right over it and huddle."

"The fire's burning nicely in the sitting-room, miss."

Jill hurried into the sitting-room, and increased her hold on Barker's esteem by exclaiming rapturously at the sight that greeted her. Barker had expended time and trouble over the sitting-room. There was no dust, no untidiness. The pictures all hung straight; the cushions were smooth and unrumpled; and a fire of exactly the right dimensions burned cheerfully in the grate, flickering cosily on the small piano by the couch, on the deep leather arm-chairs which Freddie had brought with him from Oxford, that home of comfortable chairs, and on the photographs that studded the walls. In the centre of the mantel-piece, the place of honour, was the photograph of herself which she had given Derek a week ago.

"You're simply wonderful, Barker! I don't see how you manage to make a room so cosy!" Jill sat down on the club fender that guarded the fireplace, and held her hands over the blaze. "I can't understand why men ever marry. Fancy having to give up all this!"

"I am gratified that you appreciate it, miss. I did my best to make it comfortable for you. I fancy I hear Mr. Rooke coming now."

"I hope the others won't be long. I'm starving. Has Mrs. Barker got something very good for dinner?"

"She has strained every nerve, miss."

"Then I'm sure it's worth waiting for. Hullo, Freddie."

Freddie Rooke, resplendent in evening dress, bustled in, patting his tie with solicitous fingers. It had been right when he had looked in the glass in his bedroom, but you never know about ties. Sometimes they stay right, sometimes they wriggle up sideways. Life is full of these anxieties.

"I shouldn't touch it," said Jill. "It looks beautiful, and, if I may say so in confidence, is having a most disturbing effect on my emotional nature. I'm not at all sure I shall be able to resist it right through the evening. It isn't fair of you to try to alienate the affections of an engaged young person like this."

Freddie squinted down, and became calmer.

"Hullo, Jill, old thing. Nobody here yet?"

"Well, I'm here—the *petite* figure seated on the fender. But perhaps I don't count."

"Oh, I didn't mean that, you know."

"I should hope not, when I've bought a special new dress just to fascinate you. A creation I mean. When they cost as much as this one did, you have to call them names. What do you think of it?"

Freddie seated himself on another section of the fender, and regarded her with the eye of an expert. A snappy dresser, as the technical term is, himself, he appreciated snap in the outer covering of the other sex.

"Topping!" he said spaciously. "No other word for it. All wool and a yard wide. Precisely as mother makes it. You look like a thingummy."

"How splendid. All my life I've wanted to look like a thingummy, but somehow I've never been able to manage it."

"A wood-nymph!" exclaimed Freddie, in a burst of un-wonted imagery. He looked at her with honest admiration. "Dash it, Jill, you know, there's something about you! You're —what's the word?—you've got such small bones."

"Ugh! I suppose it's a compliment, but how horrible it sounds! It makes me feel like a skeleton!"

"I mean to say, you're—you're dainty!"

"That's much better."

"You look as if you weighed about an ounce an a half. You look like a bit of thistledown! You're a little fairy princess, dash it!"

"Freddie! This is eloquence!" Jill raised her left hand, and twiddled a ringed finger ostentatiously. "Er—you *do* realize that I'm bespoke, don't you, and that my heart, alas, is another's? Because you sound as if you were going to propose."

Freddie produced a snowy handkerchief, and polished his eye-glass. Solemnity descended on him like a cloud. He looked at Jill with an earnest, paternal gaze.

"That reminds me," he said. "I wanted to have a bit of a talk with you about that—being engaged and all that sort of thing. I'm glad I got you alone before the Curse arrived."

"Curse? Do you mean Derek's mother? That sounds cheerful and encouraging."

"Well, she is, you know," said Freddie earnestly. "She's a bird! It would be idle to deny it. She always puts the fear of God into me. I never know what to say to her."

"Why don't you try asking her riddles?"

"It's no joking matter," persisted Freddie, his amiable face overcast. "Wait till you meet her! You should have seen her at the station this morning. You don't know what you're up against!"

"You make my flesh creep, Freddie. What am I up against?"

Freddie poked the fire scientifically, and assisted it with coal.

"It's this way," he said. "Of course, dear old Derek's the finest chap in the world."

"I know that," said Jill softly. She patted Freddie's hand with a little gesture of gratitude. Freddie's devotion to Derek was a thing that always touched her. She looked thoughtfully into the fire, and her eyes seemed to glow in sympathy with the glowing coals. "There's nobody like him!"

"But," continued Freddie, "he always has been frightfully under his mother's thumb, you know."

Jill was conscious of a little flicker of irritation.

"Don't be absurd, Freddie. How could a man like Derek be under anybody's thumb?"

"Well, you know what I mean!"

"I don't in the least know what you mean."

"I mean, it would be rather rotten if his mother set him against you."

Jill clenched her teeth. The quick temper which always lurked so very little beneath the surface of her cheerfulness was stirred. She felt suddenly chilled and miserable. She tried to tell herself that Freddie was just an amiable blunderer who spoke without sense or reason, but it was no use. She could not rid herself of a feeling of foreboding and discomfort. It had been the one jarring note in the sweet melody of her love-story, this apprehension of Derek's regarding his mother. The Derek she loved was a strong man, with a strong man's contempt for other people's criticism; and there had been something ignoble and fussy in his attitude regarding Lady Underhill. She had tried to feel that the flaw in her idol did not exist. And here was Freddie Rooke, a man who admired Derek with all his hero-worshipping nature, pointing it out independently. She was annoyed, and she expended her annoyance, as women will do, upon the innocent bystander.

"Do you remember the time I turned the hose on you, Freddie," she said, rising from the fender, "years ago, when we were children, when you and that awful Mason boy—what was his name? Wally Mason—teased me?" She looked at the unhappy Freddie with a hostile eye. It was his blundering words that had spoiled everything. "I've forgotten what it was all about, but I know that you and Wally infuriated me and I turned the garden hose on you and soaked you both to the skin. Well, all I want to point out is that, if you go on talking nonsense about Derek and his mother and me, I shall ask Barker to bring

me a jug of water, and I shall empty it over you! Set him against
me! You talk as if love were a thing any third party could come
along and turn off with a tap! Do you suppose that, when two
people love each other as Derek and I do, that it can possibly
matter in the least what anybody else thinks or says, even if it is
his mother? I haven't got a mother, but suppose Uncle Chris
came and warned me against Derek . . ."

Her anger suddenly left her as quickly as it had come. That
was always the way with Jill. One moment she would be raging;
the next, something would tickle her sense of humour and restore
her instantly to cheerfulness. And the thought of dear, lazy old
Uncle Chris taking the trouble to warn anybody against anything
except the wrong brand of wine or an inferior make of cigar
conjured up a picture before which wrath melted away. She
chuckled, and Freddie, who had been wilting on the fender,
perked up.

"You're an extraordinary girl, Jill. One never knows when
you're going to get the wind up."

"Isn't it enough to make me get the wind up, as you call it,
when you say absurd things like that?"

"I meant well, old girl!"

"That's the trouble with you. You always do mean well. You
go about the world meaning well till people fly to put themselves
under police protection. Besides, what on earth could Lady
Underhill find to object to in me? I've plenty of money, and I'm
one of the most charming and attractive of Society belles. You
needn't take my word for that, and I don't suppose you've
noticed it, but that's what Mr. Gossip in the *Morning Mirror*
called me when he was writing about my getting engaged to
Derek. My maid showed me the clipping. There was quite a
long paragraph, with a picture of me that looked like a Zulu
chieftainess taken in a coal-cellar during a bad fog. Well, after
that, what could anyone say against me? I'm a perfect prize!
I expect Lady Underhill screamed with joy when she heard the
news and went singing all over her Riviera villa."

"Yes," said Freddie dubiously. "Yes, yes, oh, quite so,
rather!"

Jill looked at him sternly.

"Freddie, you're concealing something from me! You *don't*
think I'm a charming and attractive Society belle! Tell me
why not and I'll show you where you are wrong. Is it my face

you object to, or my manners, or my figure? There was a young
bride of Antigua, who said to her mate, 'What a pig you are!'
Said he, 'Oh, my queen, is it manners you mean, or do you
allude to my fig-u-ar?' Isn't my figuar all right, Freddie?"

"Oh, *I* think you're topping."

"But for some reason you're afraid that Derek's mother won't
think so. Why won't Lady Underhill agree with Mr. Gossip?"

Freddie hesitated.

"Speak up!"

"Well, it's like this. Remember, I've known the old devil . . ."

"Freddie Rooke! Where do you pick up such expressions? Not
from me!"

"Well, that's how I always think of her! I say I've known her
ever since I used to go and stop at their place when I was at
school, and I know exactly the sort of things that put her back
up. She's a what-d'you-call-it. I mean to say, one of the old
school, don't you know. And you're so dashed impulsive, old
girl. You know you are! You are always saying things that come
into your head."

"You can't say a thing unless it comes into your head."

"You know what I mean," Freddie went on earnestly, not to
be diverted from his theme. "You say rummy things and you do
rummy things. What I mean to say is, you're impulsive."

"What have I ever done that the sternest critic could call
rummy?"

"Well, I've seen you with my own eyes stop in the middle of
Bond Street and help a lot of fellows shove along a cart that had
got stuck. Mind you, I'm not blaming you for it . . ."

"I should hope not. The poor old horse was trying all he
knew to get going, and he couldn't quite make it. Naturally, I
helped."

"Oh, I know. Very decent and all that, but I doubt if Lady
Underhill would have thought a lot of it. And you're so dashed
chummy with the lower orders."

"Don't be a snob, Freddie."

"I'm not a snob," protested Freddie, wounded. "When I'm
alone with Barker—for instance—I'm as chatty as dammit. But
I don't ask waiters in public restaurants how their lumbago is."

"Have you ever had lumbago?"

"No."

"Well, it's a very painful thing, and waiters get it just as badly as dukes. Worse, I should think, because they're always bending and stooping and carrying things. Naturally one feels sorry for them."

"But how do you ever find out that a waiter has *got* lumbago?"

"I ask him, of course."

"Well, for goodness' sake," said Freddie, "if you feel the impulse to do that sort of thing to-night, try and restrain it. I mean to say, if you're curious to know anything about Barker's chilblains, for instance, don't enquire after them while he's handing Lady Underhill the potatoes! She wouldn't like it."

Jill uttered an exclamation.

"I knew there was something! Being so cold and wanting to rush in and crouch over a fire put it clean out of my head. He must be thinking me a perfect beast!" She ran to the door. "Barker! Barker!"

Barker appeared from nowhere.

"Yes, miss?"

"I'm so sorry I forgot to ask before. How are your chilblains?"

"A good deal better, miss, thank you."

"Did you try the stuff I recommended?"

"Yes, miss. It did them a world of good."

"Splendid!"

Jill went back into the sitting-room

"It's all right," she said reassuringly. "They're better."

She wandered restlessly about the room, looking at the photographs, then sat down at the piano and touched the keys. The clock on the mantelpiece chimed the half-hour. "I wish to goodness they would arrive," she said.

"They'll be here pretty soon, I expect."

"It's rather awful," said Jill, "to think of Lady Underhill racing all the way from Mentone to Paris and from Paris to Calais and from Calais to Dover and from Dover to London simply to inspect me. You can't wonder I'm nervous, Freddie."

The eye-glass dropped from Freddie's eye.

"Are *you* nervous?" he asked, astonished.

"Of course I'm nervous. Wouldn't you be in my place?"

"Well, I should never have thought it."

"Why do you suppose I've been talking such a lot? Why do you imagine I snapped your poor, innocent head off just now? I'm terrified inside, terrified!"

"You don't look it, by Jove!"

"No, I'm trying to be a little warrior. That's what Uncle Chris always used to call me. It started the day when he took me to have a tooth out, when I was ten. 'Be a little warrior, Jill!' he kept saying. 'Be a little warrior!' And I was." She looked at the clock. "But I shan't be if they don't get here soon. The suspense is awful." She strummed the keys. "Suppose she *doesn't* like me, Freddie! You see how you've scared me."

"I didn't say she wouldn't. I only said you'd got to watch out a bit."

"Something tells me she won't. My nerve is oozing out of me." Jill shook her head impatiently. "It's all so vulgar! I thought this sort of thing only happened in the comic papers and in music-hall songs. Why, it's just like that song somebody used to sing." She laughed. "Do you remember? I don't know how the verse went, but . . .

John took me round to see his mother,
                              his mother,
                              his mother!
And when he'd introduced us to each other,
    She sized up everything that I had on.
She put me through a cross-examination:
I fairly boiled with aggravation:
    Then she shook her head,
    Looked at me and said:
'Poor John! Poor John!'

Chorus, Freddie! Let's cheer ourselves up! We need it!"

John took me round to see his mother . . .!

"His m-o-o-other!" croaked Freddie. Curiously enough, this ballad was one of Freddie's favourites. He had rendered it with a good deal of success on three separate occasions at village entertainments down in Worcestershire, and he rather flattered himself that he could get about as much out of it as the next man. He proceeded to abet Jill heartily with gruff sounds which he was under the impression constituted what is known in musical circles as " singing seconds".

"His mo-o-other!" he growled with frightful scorn.

"And when he'd introduced us to each other . . ."

"O-o-o-other!"

"She sized up everything that I had on!"

"Pom-*pom*-pom!"

"She put me through a cross-examination . . ."

Jill had thrown her head back, and was singing jubilantly at the top of her voice. The appositeness of the song had cheered her up. It seemed somehow to make her forebodings rather ridiculous, to reduce them to absurdity, to turn into farce the gathering tragedy which had been weighing upon her nerves.

> Then she shook her head,
> Looked at me and said:
> 'Poor John!' . . .

"Jill," said a voice at the door. "I want you to meet my mother!"

"Poo-oo-oor John!" bleated the hapless Freddie, unable to check himself.

"Dinner," said Barker the valet, appearing at the door and breaking a silence that seemed to fill the room like a tangible presence, "is served!"

★ 2 ★

The First Night at the Leicester

I

THE front-door closed softly behind the theatre-party. Dinner was over, and Barker had just been assisting the expedition out of the place. Sensitive to atmosphere, he had found his share in the dinner a little trying. It had been a strained meal and what he liked was a clatter of conversation and everybody having a good time and enjoying themselves.

"Ellen!" called Barker, as he proceeded down the passage to the empty dining-room. "Ellen!"

Mrs. Barker appeared out of the kitchen, wiping her hands. Her work for the evening, like her husband's, was over. Presently what is technically called a "useful girl" would come in to wash up the dishes, leaving the evening free for social intercourse. Mrs. Barker had done well by her patrons that night, and now she wanted a quiet chat with Barker over a glass of Freddie Rooke's port.

"Have they gone, Horace?" she asked, following him into the dining-room.

Barker selected a cigar from Freddie's humidor, crackled it against his ear, smelt it, clipped off the end, and lit it. He took the decanter and filled his wife's glass, then mixed himself a whisky-and-soda.

"Happy days!" said Barker. "Yes, they've gone!"

"I didn't see her ladyship."

"You didn't miss much! A nasty, dangerous specimen, *she* is! 'Always merry and bright,' I don't think. I wish you'd have had my job of waiting on 'em, Ellen, and me been the one to stay in the kitchen safe out of it all. That's all I say! It's no treat to *me* to 'and the dishes when the atmosphere's what you might call electric. I didn't envy them that *vol-au-vent* of yours, Ellen, good as it smelt. Better a dinner of 'erbs where love is than a stalled ox and 'atred therewith," said Barker, helping himself to a walnut.

"Did they have words ?"

Barker shook his head impatiently.

"That sort don't have words, Ellen. They just sit and goggle."

"How did her ladyship seem to hit it off with Miss Mariner, Horace ?"

Barker uttered a dry laugh.

"Ever seen a couple of strange dogs watching each other sort of wary ? That was them! Not that Miss Mariner wasn't all that was pleasant and nice-spoken. She's all right, Miss Mariner is. She's a little queen. It wasn't her fault the dinner you'd took so much trouble over was more like an evening in the Morgue than a Christian dinner-party. She tried to help things along best she could. But what with Sir Derek chewing his lip 'alf the time and his mother acting about as matey as a pennorth of ice-cream, she didn't have a chance. As for the guv'nor—well, I wish you could have seen him, that's all. You know, Ellen, sometimes I'm not altogether easy in my mind about the guv'nor's mental balance. He knows how to buy cigars, and you tell me his port is good—I never touch it myself—but sometimes he seems to me to go right off his onion. Just sat there, he did, all through dinner, looking as if he expected the good food to rise up and bite him in the face, and jumping nervous when I spoke to him. It's not my fault," said Barker, aggrieved. "*I* can't give gentlemen warning before I ask 'em if they'll have sherry or hock. I can't ring a bell or toot a horn to show 'em I'm coming. It's my place to bend over and whisper in their ear, and they've no right to leap about in their seats and make me spill good wine. (You'll see the spot close by where you're sitting, Ellen. Jogged my wrist, he did!) I'd like to know why people in the spear of life which these people are in can't behave themselves rational, same as we do. When we were walking out and I took you to have tea with my mother, it was one of the pleasantest meals I ever ate. Talk about 'armony! It was a love-feast!"

"Your ma and I took to each other right from the start, Horace," said Mrs. Barker softly. "That's the difference."

"Well, any woman with any sense would take to Miss Mariner. If I told you how near I came to spilling the sauce-boat accidentally over that old fossil's head, you'd be surprised, Ellen. She just sat there brooding like an old eagle. If you ask my opinion, Miss Mariner's a long sight too good for her precious son!"

"Oh, but Horace! Sir Derek's a baronet!"

"What of it? Kind 'earts are more than coronets and simple faith than Norman blood, aren't they?"

"You're talking Socialism, Horace."

"No, I'm not. I'm talking sense. I don't know who Miss Mariner's parents may have been—I never enquired—but anyone can see she's a lady born and bred. But do you suppose the path of true love is going to run smooth, for all that? Not it! She's got a 'ard time ahead of her, that poor girl!"

"Horace!" Mrs. Barker's gentle heart was wrung. The situation hinted at by her husband was no new one—indeed, it formed the basis of at least fifty per cent of the stories in the True Heart Novelette Series, of which she was a determined reader—but it had never failed to touch her. "Do you think her ladyship means to come between them and wreck their romance?"

"I think she means to have a jolly good try."

"But Sir Derek has his own money, hasn't he? I mean it's not like when Sir Courtenay Travers fell in love with the milk-maid and was dependent on his mother, the Countess, for everything. Sir Derek can afford to do what he pleases, can't he?"

Barker shook his head tolerantly. The excellence of the cigar and the soothing qualities of the whisky-and-soda had worked upon him, and he was feeling less ruffled.

"You don't understand these things," he said. "Women like her ladyship can talk a man into anything and out of anything. I wouldn't care, only you can see the poor girl is mad over the feller. What she finds attractive in him, I can't say, but that's her own affair."

"He's very handsome, Horace, with those flashing eyes and that stern mouth," argued Mrs. Barker.

Barker sniffed.

"Have it your own way," he said. "It's no treat to *me* to see his eyes flash, and if he'd put that stern mouth of his to some better use than advising the guv'nor to lock up the cigars and trouser the key, I'd be better pleased. If there's one thing I can't stand," said Barker, "it's not to be trusted!" He lifted his cigar and looked at it censoriously. "I thought so! Burning all down one side. They will do that if you light 'em careless. Oh, well," he continued, rising and going to the humidor, "there's plenty more where that came from. Out of evil cometh good," said Barker philosophically. "If the guv'nor hadn't been in such a overwrought state to-night, he'd have remembered not to leave the key in the keyhole. Help yourself to another glass of port, Ellen, and let's enjoy ourselves!"

II

When one considers how full of his own troubles, how weighed down with the problems of his own existence the average play-goer generally is when he enters a theatre, it is remarkable that dramatists ever find it possible to divert and entertain whole audiences for a space of several hours. As regards at least three of those who had assembled to witness its opening performance, the author of "Tried by Fire," at the Leicester Theatre, undoubtedly had his work cut out for him.

It has perhaps been sufficiently indicated by the remarks of Barker, the valet, that the little dinner at Freddie Rooke's had not been an unqualified success. Searching the records for an adequately gloomy parallel to the taxi-cab journey to the theatre which followed it, one can only think of Napoleon's retreat from Moscow. And yet even that was probably not conducted in dead silence.

The only member of the party who was even remotely happy was, curiously enough, Freddie Rooke. Originally Freddie had obtained three tickets for "Tried by Fire." The unexpected arrival of Lady Underhill had obliged him to buy a fourth, separated by several rows from the other three. This, as he had told Derek at breakfast, was the seat he proposed to occupy himself.

It consoles the philosopher in this hard world to reflect that, even if man is born to sorrow as the sparks fly upward, it is still possible for small things to make him happy. The thought of being several rows away from Lady Underhill had restored Freddie's equanimity like a tonic. It thrilled him like the strains of some grand, sweet anthem all the way to the theatre. If Freddie Rooke had been asked at that moment to define happiness in a few words, he would have replied that it consisted in being several rows away from Lady Underhill.

The theatre was nearly full when Freddie's party arrived. The Leicester Theatre had been rented for the season by the newest theatrical knight, Sir Chester Portwood, who had a large following; and, whatever might be the fate of the play in the final issue, it would do at least one night's business. The stalls were ablaze with jewellery and crackling with starched shirt-fronts; and expensive scents pervaded the air, putting up a stiff battle with the plebeian peppermint that emanated from the pit. The boxes were filled, and up in the gallery grim-faced patrons of the drama, who had paid their shillings at the door and intended to get a shilling's worth of entertainment in return, sat and waited stolidly for the curtain to rise.

The lights shot up beyond the curtain. The house-lights dimmed. Conversation ceased. The curtain rose. Jill wriggled herself comfortably into her seat, and slipped her hand into Derek's. She felt a glow of happiness as it closed over hers. All, she told herself, was right with the world.

All, that is to say, except the drama which was unfolding on the stage. It was one of those plays which start wrong and never recover. By the end of the first ten minutes there had spread through the theatre that uneasy feeling which comes over the audience at an opening performance when it realizes that it is going to be bored. A sort of lethargy had gripped the stalls. The dress-circle was coughing. Up in the gallery there was grim silence.

Sir Chester Portwood was an actor-manager who had made his reputation in light comedy of the tea-cup school. His numerous admirers attended a first night at his theatre in a mood of comfortable anticipation, assured of something pleasant and frothy with a good deal of bright dialogue and not too much plot.

To-night he seemed to have fallen a victim to that spirit of ambition which intermittently attacks actor-managers of his class, expressing itself in an attempt to prove that, having established themselves securely as light comedians, they can, like the lady reciter, turn right around and be serious. The one thing which the London public felt that it was safe from in a Portwood play was heaviness, and "Tried by Fire" was grievously heavy. It was a poetic drama, and the audience, though loath to do anybody an injustice, was beginning to suspect that it was written in blank verse.

The acting did nothing to dispel the growing uneasiness. Sir Chester himself, apparently oppressed by the weightiness of the occasion and the responsibility of offering an unfamiliar brand of goods to his public, had dropped his customary debonair method of delivering lines and was mouthing his speeches. It was good gargling, but bad elocution. And, for some reason best known to himself, he had entrusted the role of the heroine to a doll-like damsel with a lisp, of whom the audience disapproved sternly from her initial entrance.

It was about half-way through the first act that Jill, whose attention had begun to wander, heard a soft groan at her side. The seats which Freddie Rooke had bought were at the extreme end of the seventh row. There was only one other seat in the row, and, as Derek had placed his mother on his left and was sitting between her and Jill, the latter had this seat on her right. It had been empty at the rise of the curtain, but in the past few minutes a man had slipped silently into it. The darkness prevented Jill from seeing his face, but it was plain that he was suffering, and her sympathy went out to him. His opinion of the play so obviously coincided with her own.

Presently the first act ended, and the lights went up. There was a spatter of insincere applause from the stalls, echoed in the dress-circle. It grew fainter in the upper circle, and did not reach the gallery at all.

"Well?" said Jill to Derek. "What do you think of it?"

"Too awful for words," said Derek sternly.

He leaned forward to join the conversation which had started between Lady Underhill and some friends she had discovered in the seats in front; and Jill, turning, became aware that the man on her right was looking at her intently. He was a big man with rough, wiry hair and a humorous mouth. His age appeared to be somewhere in the middle twenties. Jill, in the brief moment in which their eyes met, decided that he was ugly, but with an ugliness that was rather attractive. He reminded her of one of those large, loose, shaggy dogs that break things in drawing-rooms but make admirable companions for the open road. She had a feeling that he would look better in tweeds in a field than in evening dress in a theatre. He had nice eyes. She could not distinguish their colour, but they were frank and friendly.

All this Jill noted with her customary quickness, and then she looked away. For an instant she had had an odd feeling that somewhere she had met this man or somebody very like him before, but the impression vanished. She also had the impression that he was still looking at her, but she gazed demurely in front of her and did not attempt to verify the suspicion.

Between them, as they sat side by side, there inserted itself suddenly the pinkly remorseful face of Freddie Rooke. Freddie, having skirmished warily in the aisle until it was clear that Lady Underhill's attention was engaged elsewhere, had occupied a seat in the row behind which had been left vacant temporarily by an owner who liked refreshment between the acts. Freddie was feeling deeply ashamed of himself. He felt that he had per-petrated a bloomer of no slight magnitude.

"I'm awfully sorry about this," he said penitently. "I mean, roping you in to listen to this frightful tosh! When I think I might have got seats just as well for any one of half a dozen topping musical comedies, I feel like kicking myself with some vim. But, honestly, how was I to know? I never dreamed we were going to be let in for anything of this sort. Portwood's plays are usually so dashed bright and snappy and all that. Can't think what he was doing, putting on a thing like this. Why, it's blue round the edges!"

The man on Jill's right laughed sharply.

"Perhaps," he said, "the chump who wrote the piece got away from the asylum long enough to put up the money to produce it."

If there is one thing that startles the well-bred Londoner and throws him off his balance, it is to be addressed unexpectedly by a stranger. Freddie's sense of decency was revolted. A voice from the tomb could hardly have shaken him more. All the traditions to which he had been brought up had gone to solidify his belief that this was one of the things which didn't happen.

Absolutely it wasn't done. During an earthquake or a shipwreck and possibly on the Day of Judgment, yes. But only then. At other times, unless they wanted a match or the time or something, chappies did not speak to fellows to whom they had not been introduced. He was far too amiable to snub the man, but to go on with this degrading scene was out of the question. There was nothing for it but flight.

"Oh, ah, yes," he mumbled. "Well," he added to Jill, "I suppose I may as well be toddling back. See you later and so forth."

And with a faint "Good-bye-ee!" Freddie removed himself, thoroughly unnerved.

Jill looked out of the corner of her eye at Derek. He was still occupied with the people in front. She turned to the man on her right. She was not the slave to etiquette that Freddie was. She was much too interested in life to refrain from speaking to strangers.

"You shocked him!" she said dimpling.

"Yes. It broke Freddie all up, didn't it!"

It was Jill's turn to be startled. She looked at him in astonishment.

"Freddie?"

"That *was* Freddie Rooke, wasn't it? Surely I wasn't mistaken?"

"But—do you know him? He didn't seem to know you."

"These are life's tragedies. He has forgotten me. My boyhood friend!"

"Oh, you were at school with him?"

"No. Freddie went to Winchester, if I remember. I was at Haileybury. Our acquaintance was confined to the holidays. My people lived near his people in Worcestershire."

"Worcestershire!" Jill leaned forward excitedly. "But I used to live near Freddie in Worcestershire myself when I was small. I knew him there when he was a boy. We must have met!"

"We met all right."

Jill wrinkled her forehead. That odd familiar look was in his eyes again. But memory failed to respond. She shook her head.

"I don't remember you," she said. "I'm sorry."

"Never mind. Perhaps the recollection would have been painful."

"How do you mean, painful?"

"Well, looking back, I can see that I must have been a very unpleasant child. I have always thought it greatly to the credit of my parents that they let me grow up. It would have been so easy to have dropped something heavy on me out of a window. They must have been tempted a hundred times, but they refrained. Yes, I was a great pest around the home. My only redeeming point was the way I worshipped *you!*"

"What!"

"Oh, yes. You probably didn't notice it at the time, for I had a curious way of expressing my adoration. But you remain the brightest memory of a chequered youth."

Jill searched his face with grave eyes, then shook her head again.

"Nothing stirs?" asked the man sympathetically.

"It's too maddening! Why does one forget things?" She reflected. "You aren't Bobby Morrison?"

"I am not. What is more, I never was!"

Jill dived into the past once more and emerged with another possibility.

"Or—Charlie—Charlie what was it?—Charlie Field?"

"You wound me! Have you forgotten that Charlie Field wore velvet Lord Fauntleroy suits and long golden curls? My past is not smirched with anything like that."

"Would I remember your name if you told me?"

"I don't know. I've forgotten yours. Your surname, that is. Of course, I remember that your Christian name was Jill. It has always seemed to me the prettiest monosyllable in the language." He looked at her thoughtfully. "It's odd how little you've altered in looks. Freddie's just the same, too, only larger. And he didn't wear an eye-glass in those days, though I can see he was bound to later on. And yet I've changed so much that you can't place me. It shows what a wearing life I must have led. I feel like Rip van Winkle. Old and withered. But that may be just the result of watching this play."

"It is pretty terrible, isn't it?"

"Worse than that. Looking at it dispassionately, I find it the extreme, ragged, outermost edge of the limit. Freddie had the correct description of it. He's a great critic."

"I really do think it's the worst thing I have ever seen."

"I don't know what plays you have seen, but I feel you're right."

"Perhaps the second act's better," said Jill optimistically.

"It's worse. I know that sounds like boasting, but it's true. I feel like getting up and making a public apology."

"But . . . Oh!"

Jill turned scarlet. A monstrous suspicion had swept over her.

"The only trouble is," went on her companion, "that the audience would undoubtedly lynch me. And, though it seems improbable just at the present moment, it may be that life holds some happiness for me that's worth waiting for. Anyway, I'd rather not be torn limb from limb. A messy finish! I can just see them rending me asunder in a spasm of perfectly justifiable fury. 'She loves me!' Off comes a leg 'She loves me not!' Off comes an arm. No, I think on the whole I'll lie low. Besides, why should I care? Let 'em suffer. It's their own fault. They *would* come!"

Jill had been trying to interrupt the harangue. She was greatly concerned.

"Did you *write* the play?"

The man nodded.

"You are quite right to speak in that horrified tone. But between ourselves and on the understanding that you don't get up and denounce me, I did."

"Oh, I'm so sorry!"

"Not half so sorry as I am, believe me!"

"I mean, I wouldn't have said . . ."

"Never mind. You didn't tell me anything I didn't know." The lights began to go down. He rose. "Well, they're off again. Perhaps you will excuse me? I don't feel quite equal to assisting any longer at the wake. If you want something to occupy your mind during the next act, try to remember my name."

He slid from his seat and disappeared. Jill clutched at Derek.

"Oh, Derek, it's too awful. I've just been talking to the man who wrote this play, and I told him it was the worst thing I had ever seen!"

"Did you?" Derek snorted. "Well, it's about time somebody told him!" A thought seemed to strike him. "Why, who is he? I didn't know you knew him."

"I don't. I don't even know his name."

"His name, according to the programme, is John Grant. Never heard of him before. Jill, I wish you would not talk to people you don't know," said Derek with a note of annoyance in his voice. "You can never tell who they are."

"But . . ."

"Especially with my mother here. You must be more careful."

The curtain rose. Jill saw the stage mistily. From childhood up, she had never been able to cure herself of an unfortunate sensitiveness when sharply spoken to by those she loved. A rebuking world she could face with a stout heart, but there had always been just one or two people whose lightest word of censure could crush her. Her father had always had that effect upon her, and now Derek had taken his place.

But if there had only been time to explain . . . Derek could not object to her chatting with a friend of her childhood, even if she had completely forgotten him and did not remember his name even now. John Grant? Memory failed to produce any juvenile John Grant for her inspection.

Puzzling over this problem, Jill missed much of the beginning of the second act. Hers was a detachment which the rest of the audience would gladly have shared. For the poetic drama, after a bad start, was now plunging into worse depths of dullness. The coughing had become almost continuous. The stalls, supported by the presence of large droves of Sir Chester's personal friends, were struggling gallantly to maintain a semblance of interest, but the pit and gallery had plainly given up hope. The critic of a weekly paper of small circulation, who had been shoved up in the upper circle, grimly jotted down the phrase "apathetically received" on his programme. He had come to the theatre that night in an aggrieved mood, for managers usually put him in the dress-circle. He got out his pencil again. Another phrase had occurred to him, admirable for the opening of his article, "At the Leicester Theatre," he wrote, "where Sir Chester Portwood presented 'Tried by Fire', dullness reigned supreme. . . ."

But you never know. Call no evening dull till it is over. However uninteresting its early stages may have been, that night was to be as animated and exciting as any audience could desire—a night to be looked back to and talked about. For just as the critic of *London Gossip* wrote those damning words on his programme, guiding his pencil uncertainly in the dark, a curious yet familiar odour stole over the house.

The stalls got it first, and sniffed. It rose to the dress-circle, and the dress-circle sniffed. Floating up, it smote the silent gallery. And, suddenly, coming to life with a single-midned abruptness, the gallery ceased to be silent.

"Fire!"

Sir Chester Portwood, ploughing his way through a long peech, stopped and looked apprehensively over his shoulder. The girl with the lisp, who had been listening in a perfunctory manner to the long speech, screamed loudly. The voice of an unseen stage-hand called thunderously to an invisible "Bill" to cummere quick. And from the scenery on the prompt side there curled lazily across the stage a black wisp of smoke.

"Fire! Fire! Fire!"

"Just," said a voice at Jill's elbow, "what the play needed!" The mysterious author was back in his seat again.

★ 3 ★

Jill and the Unknown Escape

I

IN these days when the authorities who watch over the welfare of the community have taken the trouble to reiterate encouragingly in printed notices that a full house can be emptied in three minutes and that all an audience has to do in an emergency is to walk, not run, to the nearest exit, fire in the theatre has lost a good deal of its old-time terror. Yet it would be paltering with the truth to say that the audience which had assembled to witness the opening performance of the new play at the Leicester was entirely at its ease. The asbestos curtain was already on its way down, which should have been reassuring: but then asbestos curtains never look the part. To the lay eye they seem just the sort of thing that will blaze quickest. Moreover, it had not yet occurred to the man at the switchboard to turn up the house-lights, and the darkness was disconcerting.

Portions of the house were taking the thing better than other portions. Up in the gallery a vast activity was going on. The clatter of feet almost drowned the shouting. A moment before it would have seemed incredible that anything could have made the occupants of the gallery animated, but the instinct of self-preservation had put new life into them.

The stalls had not yet entirely lost their self-control. Alarm was in the air, but for the moment they hung on the razor-edge

between panic and dignity. Panic urged them to do something
sudden and energetic; dignity counselled them to wait. They,
like the occupants of the gallery, greatly desired to be outside,
but it was bad form to rush and jostle. The men were assisting
the women in their cloaks, assuring them the while that it was
"all right" and that they must not be frightened. But another curl
of smoke had crept out just before the asbestos curtain completed
its descent, and their words lacked the ring of conviction. The
movement towards the exits had not yet become a stampede,
but already those with seats nearest the stage had begun to feel
that the more fortunate individuals near the doors were infernally
slow in removing themselves.

Suddenly, as if by mutual inspiration, the composure of the
stalls began to slip. Looking from above, one could have seen a
sort of shudder run through the crowd. It was the effect of every
member of that crowd starting to move a little more quickly.

A hand grasped Jill's arm. It was a comforting hand, the hand
of a man who had not lost his head. A pleasant voice backed up
its message of reassurance.

"It's no good getting into that mob. You might get hurt.
There's no danger; the play isn't going on."

Jill was shaken; but she had the fighting spirit and hated to
show that she was shaken. Panic was knocking at the door of
her soul, but dignity refused to be dislodged.

"All the same," she said, smiling a difficult smile, "it would
be nice to get out, wouldn't it?"

"I was just going to suggest something of that very sort." said
the man beside her. "The same thought occurred to me. We
can stroll out quite comfortably by our own private route.
Come along."

Jill looked over her shoulder. Derek and Lady Underhill were
merged into the mass of refugees. She could not see them. For
an instant a little spasm of pique stung her at the thought that
Derek had deserted her. She groped her way after her companion, and presently they came by way of a lower box to the
iron pass-door leading to the stage.

As it opened, smoke blew through, and the smell of burning
was formidable. Jill recoiled involuntarily.

"It's all right," said her companion. "It smells worse than it
really is. And, anyway, this is the quickest way out."

They passed through on to the stage, and found themselves

in a world of noise and confusion compared with which the
auditorium which they had left had been a peaceful place. Smoke
was everywhere. A stage-hand, carrying a bucket, lurched past
them, bellowing. From somewhere out of sight on the other side
of the stage there came a sound of chopping. Jill's companion
moved quickly to the switchboard, groped, found a handle, and
turned it. In the narrow space between the corner of the prosce-
nium and the edge of the asbestos curtain lights flashed up: and
simultaneously there came a sudden diminution of the noise from
the body of the house. The stalls, snatched from the intimidating
spell of the darkness and able to see each other's faces, discovered
that they had been behaving indecorously and checked their
struggling, a little ashamed of themselves. The relief would be
only momentary, but, while it lasted, it postponed panic.

"Go straight across the stage," Jill heard her companion say,
"out along the passage and turn to the right, and you'll be at the
stage-door. I think, as there seems no one else around to do it,
I'd better go out and say a few soothing words to the customers.
Otherwise they'll be biting holes in each other."

He squeezed through the narrow opening in front of the
curtain.

"Ladies and gentlemen!"

Jill remained where she was, leaning with one hand against
the switchboard. She made no attempt to follow the directions
he had given her. She was aware of a sense of comradeship, of
being with this man in this adventure. If he stayed, she must
stay. To go now through the safety of the stage-door would be
abominable desertion. She listened, and found that she could
hear plainly in spite of the noise. The smoke was worse than
ever, and hurt her eyes, so that the figures of the theatre-firemen,
hurrying to and fro, seemed like Brocken spectres. She slipped a
corner of her cloak across her mouth, and was able to breathe
more easily.

"Ladies and gentlemen, I assure you that there is absolutely no
danger. I am a stranger to you, so there is no reason why you
should take my word, but fortunately I can give you solid proof.
If there were any danger, *I* wouldn't be here. All that has
happened is that the warmth of your reception of the play has
set a piece of scenery alight. . . ."

A crimson-faced stage-hand, carrying an axe in blackened
hands, roared in Jill's ear.

"'Op it!" shouted the stage-hand. He cast his axe down with a clatter. "Can't you see the place is afire?"

"But—but I'm waiting for . . ." Jill pointed to where her ally was still addressing an audience that seemed reluctant to stop and listen to him.

The stage-hand squinted out round the edge of the curtain.

"If he's a friend of yours, miss, kindly get 'im to cheese it and get a move on. We're clearing out. There's nothing we can do. It's got too much of an 'old. In about another two ticks the roof's going to drop on us."

Jill's friend came squeezing back through the opening.

"Hullo! Still here?" He blinked approvingly at her through the smoke. "You're a little soldier! Well, Augustus, what's on your mind?"

The simple question seemed to take the stage-hand back.

"Wot's on my mind? I'll tell you wot's on my blinking mind . . ."

"Don't tell me. Let me guess. I've got it! The place is on fire!"

The stage-hand expectorated disgustedly. Flippancy at such a moment offended his sensibilities.

"We're 'opping it," he said.

"Great minds think alike! *We* are hopping it, too."

"You'd better! And damn quick!"

"And, as you suggest, damn quick. You think of everything!"

Jill followed him across the stage. Her heart was beating violently. There was not only smoke now, but heat. Across the stages little scarlet flames were shooting, and something large and hard, unseen through the smoke, fell with a crash. The air was heavy with the smell of burning paint.

"Where's Sir Chester Portwood?" enquired her companion of the stage-hand, who hurried beside them.

"'Opped it!" replied the other briefly, and coughed raspingly as he swallowed smoke.

"Strange," said the man in Jill's ear, as he pulled her along. "This way. Stick to me. Strange how the drama anticipates life! At the end of Act Two there was a scene where Sir Chester had to creep sombrely out into the night, and now he's gone and done it! Ah!"

They had stumbled through a doorway and were out in a narrow passage, where the air, though tainted, was comparatively fresh. Jill drew a deep breath. Her companion turned to the stage-hand and felt in his pocket.

"Here." A coin changed hands. "Go and get a drink. You need it after all this."

"Thank you, sir."

"Don't mention it. You've saved our lives. Suppose you hadn't come up and told us, and we had never noticed there was a fire!" He turned to Jill. "Here's the stage-door. Shall we creep sombrely out into the night?"

The guardian of the stage-door was standing in the entrance of his little hutch, plainly perplexed. He was a slow thinker and a man whose life was ruled by routine, and the events of the evening had left him uncertain how to act.

"Wot's all this about a fire?" he demanded.

Jill's friend stopped.

"A fire?" He looked at Jill. "Did *you* hear anything about a fire?"

"They all come bustin' past 'ere yelling there's a fire," persisted the door-man.

"By George! Now I come to think of it, you're perfectly right! There *is* a fire! If you wait here a little longer you'll get it in the small of the back. Take the advice of an old friend who means you well and vanish. In the inspired words of the lad we've just parted from, 'op it!"

The stage-door man turned this over in his mind for a space.

"But I'm supposed to stay 'ere till eleven-thirty and lock up!" he said. "That's what I'm supposed to do. Stay 'ere till eleven-thirty and lock up! And it ain't but ten forty-five now."

"I see the difficulty," said Jill's companion thoughtfully. "Well, Casabianca, I'm afraid I don't see how to help you. It's a matter for your own conscience. I don't want to lure you from the burning deck; on the other hand, if you stick on here you'll most certainly be fired on both sides . . . But, tell me. You spoke about locking up something at eleven-thirty. What are you supposed to lock up?"

"Why, the theatre."

"Then that's all right. By eleven-thirty there won't *be* a theatre. If I were you, I should leave quietly and unostentatiously now. To-morrow, if you wish it, and if they've cooled off sufficiently, you can come and sit on the ruins. Good night!"

II

Outside, the air was cold and crisp. Jill drew her warm cloak closer. Round the corner there was noise and shouting. Fire-engines had arrived. Jill's companion lit a cigarette.

"Do you wish to stop and see the conflagration?" he asked.

Jill shivered. She was more shaken than she had realized.

"I've seen all the conflagration I want."

"Same here. Well, it's been an exciting evening. Started slow I admit, but warmed up later! What I seem to need at the moment is a restorative stroll along the Embankment. Do you know, Sir Chester Portwood didn't like the title of my play. He said 'Tried by Fire' was too melodramatic. Well, he can't say now it wasn't appropriate."

They made their way towards the river, avoiding the street which was blocked by the crowds and the fire-engines. As they crossed the Strand, the man looked back. A red glow was in the sky.

"A great blaze!" he said. "What you might call—in fact what the papers *will* call—a holocaust. Quite a treat for the populace."

"Do you think they will be able to put it out?"

"Not a chance. It's got too much of a hold. It's a pity you hadn't that garden-hose of yours with you, isn't it?"

Jill stopped, wide-eyed.

"Garden-hose?"

"Don't you remember the garden-hose? I do! I can feel that clammy feeling of the water trickling down my back now!"

Memory, always a laggard by the wayside that redeems itself by an eleventh-hour rush, raced back to Jill. The Embankment turned to a sunlit garden, and the January night to a July day. She stared at him. He was looking at her with a whimsical smile. It was a smile which, pleasant to-day, had seemed mocking and hostile on that afternoon years ago. She had always felt then that he was laughing at her, and at the age of twelve she had resented laughter at her expense.

"You surely can't be Wally Mason!"

"I was wondering when you would remember."

"But the programme called you something else—John something."

"That was a cunning disguise. Wally Mason is the only
genuine and official name. And, by Jove! I've just remembered
yours. It was Mariner. By the way,"—he paused for an almost
imperceptible instant—"is it still ?"

⋆ 4 ⋆

The Last of the Rookes Takes a Hand

I

JILL was hardly aware that he had asked her a question. She
was suffering that momentary sense of unreality which
comes to us when the years roll away and we are thrown abruptly
back into the days of our childhood. The logical side of her mind
was quite aware that there was nothing remarkable in the fact
that Wally Mason, who had been to her all these years a boy
in an Eton suit, should now present himself as a grown man.
But for all that the transformation had something of the effect
of a conjuring-trick. It was not only the alteration in his appearance that startled her: it was the amazing change in his personality.
Wally Mason had been the *bête noire* of her childhood. She had
never failed to look back at the episode of the garden-hose with
the feeling that she had acted well, that—however she might
have strayed in those early days from the straight and narrow
path—in that one particular crisis she had done the right thing.
And now she had taken an instant liking for him. Easily as she
made friends, she had seldom before felt so immediately drawn
to a strange man. Gone was the ancient hostility, and in its place
a soothing sense of comradeship. The direct effect of this was
to make Jill feel suddenly old. It was as if some link that joined
her to her childhood had been snapped.

She glanced down the Embankment. Close by, to the left,
Waterloo Bridge loomed up, dark and massive against the steel-
grey sky. A tram-car, full of home-bound travellers, clattered
past over rails that shone with the peculiarly frost-bitten gleam
that seems to herald snow. Across the river everything was dark
and mysterious, except for an occasional lamp-post and the dim
illumination of the wharves. It was a depressing prospect, and
the thought crossed her mind that to the derelicts whose nightly

resting-place was a seat on the Embankment the view must seem even bleaker than it did to herself. She gave a little shiver. Somehow this sudden severance from the old days had brought with it a forlorness. She seemed to be standing alone in a changed world.

"Cold?" said Wally Mason.

"A little."

"Let's walk."

They moved westwards. Cleopatra's Needle shot up beside them, a pointing finger. Down on the silent river below, coffin-like row-boats lay moored to the wall. Through a break in the trees the clock over the Houses of Parliament shone for an instant as if suspended in the sky, then vanished as the trees closed in. A distant barge in the direction of Battersea wailed and was still. It had a mournful and foreboding sound. Jill shivered again. It annoyed her that she could not shake off this quite uncalled-for melancholy, but it withstood every effort. Why she should have felt that a chapter, a pleasant chapter, in the book of her life had been closed, she could not have said, but the feeling lingered.

"Correct me if I am wrong," said Wally Mason, breaking a silence that had lasted several minutes, "but you seem to me to be freezing in your tracks. Ever since I came to London I've had a habit of heading for the Embankment in times of mental stress, but perhaps the middle of winter is not quite the moment for communing with the night. The Savoy is handy, if we stop walking away from it. I think we might celebrate this reunion with a little supper, don't you?"

Jill's depression disappeared magically. Her mercurial temperament asserted itself.

"Lights!" she said. "Music!"

"And food! To an ethereal person like you that remark may seem gross, but I had no dinner."

"You poor dear! Why not?"

"Just nervousness."

"Why, of course." The interlude of the fire had caused her to forget his private and personal connection with the night's events. Her mind went back to something he had said in the theatre. "Wally——" She stopped, a little embarrassed. "I suppose I ought to call you Mr. Mason, but I've always thought of you . . ."

"Wally, if you please, Jill. It's not as though we were strangers.

I haven't my book of etiquette with me, but I fancy that about eleven gallons of cold water down the neck constitutes an introduction. What were you going to say?"

"It was what you said to Freddie about putting up money. Did you really?"

"Put up the money for that ghastly play? I did. Every cent. It was the only way to get it put on."

"But why . . . ? I forget what I was going to say!"

"Why did I want it put on? Well, it does seem odd, but I give you my honest word that until to-night I thought the darned thing a masterpiece. I've been writing musical comedies for the last few years, and after you've done that for a while your soul rises up within you and says, 'Come, come, my lad! You can do better than this!' That's what mine said, and I believed it. Subsequent events have proved that Sidney the Soul was pulling my leg!"

"But—then you've lost a great deal of money?"

"The hoarded wealth, if you don't mind my being melodramatic for a moment, of a lifetime. And no honest old servitor who dangled me on his knee as a baby to come along and offer me his savings! They don't make servitors like that in America, worse luck. There is a Swedish lady who looks after my simple needs back there, but instinct tells me that, if I were to approach her on the subject of loosening up for the benefit of the young master, she would call a cop. Still, I've gained experience, which they say is just as good as cash, and I've enough money left to pay the bill, at any rate, so come along."

In the supper-room of the Savoy Hotel there was, as anticipated, food and light and music. It was still early, and the theatres had not yet emptied themselves, so that the big room was as yet but half full. Wally Mason had found a table in the corner, and proceeded to order with the concentration of a hungry man.

"Forgive my dwelling so tensely on the bill-of-fare," he said, when the waiter had gone. "You don't know what it means to one in my condition to have to choose between *poulet en casserole* and kidneys *à la maître d'hôtel*. A man's cross-roads!"

Jill smiled happily across the table at him. She could hardly believe that this old friend with whom she had gone through the perils of the night and with whom she was now about to feast was the sinister figure that had cast a shadow on her childhood.

He looked positively incapable of pulling a little girl's hair—as no doubt he was.

"You always were greedy," she commented. "Just before I turned the hose on you, I remember you had made yourself thoroughly disliked by pocketing a piece of my birthday cake."

"Do you remember that?" His eyes lit up and he smiled back at her. He had an ingratiating smile. His mouth was rather wide, and it seemed to stretch right across his face. He reminded Jill more than ever of a big, friendly dog. "I can feel it now—all squashy in my pocket, inextricably mingled with a catapult, a couple of marbles, a box of matches, and some string. I was quite the human general store in those days. Which reminds me that we have been some time settling down to an exchange of our childish reminiscences, haven't we?"

"I've been trying to realize that you are Wally Mason. You have altered so."

"For the better?"

"Very much for the better! You were a horrid little brute. You used to terrify me. I never knew when you were going to bound out at me from behind a tree or something. I remember your chasing me for miles, shrieking at the top of your voice!"

"Sheer embarrassment! I told you just now how I used to worship you. If I shrieked a little, it was merely because I was shy. I did it to hide my devotion."

"You certainly succeeded. I never even suspected it."

Wally sighed.

"How like life! I never told my love, but let concealment like a worm i' the bud . . ."

"Talking of worms, you once put one down my back!"

"No, no," said Wally in a shocked voice. "Not that! I was boisterous, perhaps, but surely always the gentleman."

"You did! In the shrubbery. There had been a thunderstorm and . . ."

"I remember the incident now. A mere misunderstanding. I had done with the worm, and thought you might be glad to have it."

"You were always doing things like that. Once you held me over the pond and threatened to drop me into the water—in the winter! Just before Christmas. It was a particularly mean thing to do, because I couldn't even kick your shins for fear you would let me fall. Luckily Uncle Chris came up and made you stop."

"You considered that a fortunate occurrence, did you?" said
Wally. "Well, perhaps from your point of view it may have been.
I saw the thing from a different angle. Your uncle had a whangee
with him. My friends sometimes wonder what I mean when I
say that my old wound troubles me in frosty weather. By the
way, how is your uncle?"

"Oh, he's very well. Just as lazy as ever. He's away at present,
down at Brighton."

"He didn't strike me as lazy," said Wally thoughtfully.
"Dynamic would express it better. But perhaps I happened to
encounter him in a moment of energy. Ah!" The waiter had
returned with a loaded tray. "The food! Forgive me if I seem a
little distrait for a moment or two. There is man's work before
me!"

"And later on, I suppose, you would like a chop or something
to take away in your pocket?"

"I will think it over. Possibly a little soup. My needs are very
simple these days."

Jill watched him with a growing sense of satisfaction. There
was something boyishly engaging about this man. She felt at
home with him. He affected her in much the same way as did
Freddie Rooke. He was a definite addition to the things that
went to make her happy.

She liked him particularly for being such a good loser. She
had always been a good loser herself, and the quality was one
which she admired. It was nice of him to dismiss from his
conversation—and apparently from his thoughts—that night's
fiasco and all that it must have cost him. She wondered how much
he had lost. Certainly something very substantial. Yet it seemed
to trouble him not at all. Jill considered his behaviour gallant,
and her heart warmed to him. This was how a man ought to
take the slings and arrows of outrageous fortune.

Wally sighed contentedly, and leaned back in his chair.

"An unpleasant exhibition!" he said apologetically. "But
unavoidable. And, anyway, I take it that you prefer to have me
well-fed and happy about the place than swooning on the floor
with starvation. A wonderful thing, food! I am now ready to
converse intelligently on any subject you care to suggest. I
have eaten rose-leaves and am no more a golden ass, so to speak.
What shall we talk about?"

"Tell me about yourself."

"There is no nobler topic. But what aspect of myself do you wish me to touch on? My thoughts, my tastes, my amusements, my career, or what? I can talk about myself for hours. My friends in New York often complain about it bitterly."

"New York?" said Jill. "Oh, then you live in America?"

"Yes. I only came over here to see that darned false alarm of a play of mine put on."

"Why didn't you put it on in New York?"

"Too many of the lads of the village know me over there. This was a new departure, you see. What the critics in those parts expect from me is something entitled 'Wow! Wow!' or 'The Girl from Yonkers.' It would have unsettled their minds to find me breaking out in poetic drama. They are men of coarse fibre and ribald mind and they would have been funny about it. I thought it wiser to come over here among strangers, little thinking that I should sit in the next seat to somebody I had known all my life."

"But when did you go to America? And why?"

"I think it must have been four—five—well, quite a number of years after the hose episode. Probably you didn't observe that I wasn't still around, but we crept silently out of the neighbourhood round about that time and went to live in London." His tone lost its lightness momentarily. "My father died, you know, and that sort of broke things up. He didn't leave any too much money, either. Apparently we had been living on rather too expensive a scale during the time I knew you. At any rate, I was more or less up against it until your father got me a job in an office in New York.

"My father!"

"Yes. It was wonderfully good of him to bother about me. I didn't suppose he would have known me by sight, and, even if he had remembered me, I shouldn't have imagined that the memory would have been a pleasant one. But he couldn't have taken more trouble if I had been a blood-relation."

"That was just like father," said Jill softly.

"He was a prince."

"But you aren't in the office now?"

"No. I found I had a knack of writing verses and things, and I wrote a few vaudeville songs. Then I came across a man named Bevan at a music publisher's. He was just starting to write music, and we got together and turned out some vaudeville sketches, and then a manager sent for us to fix up a show that was dying on the road and we had the good luck to turn it into a success, and after that it was pretty good going. George Bevan got married the other day. Lucky devil!"

"Are you married?"

"No."

"You were faithful to my memory?" said Jill with a smile.

"I was."

"It can't last," said Jill, shaking her head. "One of these days you'll meet some lovely American girl and then you'll put a worm down her back or pull her hair or whatever it is you do when you want to show your devotion, and . . . What are you looking at? Is something interesting going on behind me?"

He had been looking past her out into the room.

"It's nothing," he said. "Only there's a statuesque old lady about two tables back of you who has been staring at you, with intervals for refreshment, for the last five minutes. You seem to fascinate her."

"An old lady?"

"Yes. With a glare! She looks like Dunsany's Bird of the Difficult Eye. Count ten and turn carelessly round. There, at that table. Almost behind you."

"Good Heavens!" exclaimed Jill.

She turned quickly round again.

"What's the matter? Do you know her? Somebody you don't want to meet?"

"It's Lady Underhill! And Derek's with her!"

Wally had been lifting his glass. He put it down rather suddenly.

"Derek?" he said.

"Derek Underhill. The man I'm engaged to marry."

There was a moment's silence.

"Oh!" said Wally thoughtfully. "The man you're engaged to marry? Yes, I see!"

He raised his glass again, and drank its contents quickly.

II

Jill looked at her companion anxiously. Recent events had caused her completely to forget the existence of Lady Underhill. She was always so intensely interested in what she happened to

be doing at the moment that she often suffered these temporary
lapses of memory. It occurred to her now—too late, as usual—
that the Savoy Hotel was the last place in London where she
should have come to supper with Wally. It was the hotel where
Lady Underhill was staying. She frowned. Life had suddenly
ceased to be careless and happy, and had become a problem-
ridden thing, full of perplexity and misunderstandings.

"What shall I do?"

Wally Mason started at the sound of her voice. He appeared
to be deep in thoughts of his own.

"I beg your pardon?"

"What shall I do?"

"I shouldn't be worried."

"Derek will be awfully cross."

Wally's good-humoured mouth tightened almost imper-
ceptibly.

"Why?" he said. "There's nothing wrong in your having
supper with an old friend."

"N-no," said Jill doubtfully. "But . . ."

"Derek Underhill," said Wally reflectively. "Is that Sir
Derek Underhill, whose name one's always seeing in the
papers?"

"Derek is in the papers a lot. He's an M.P. and all sorts of
things."

"Good-looking fellow. Ah, here's the coffee."

"I don't want any, thanks."

"Nonsense. Why spoil your meal because of this? Do you
smoke?"

"No, thanks."

"Given it up, eh? Daresay you're wise. Stunts the growth
and increases the expenses."

"Given it up?"

"Don't you remember sharing one of your father's cigars with
me behind the haystack in the meadow? We cut it in half. I
finished my half, but I fancy about three puffs were enough for
you. Those were happy days!"

"That one wasn't! Of course I remember it now. I don't
suppose I shall ever forget it."

"The thing was my fault, as usual. I recollect I dared you."

"Yes. I always took a dare."

"Do you still?"

"What do you mean?"

Wally knocked the ash off his cigarette.

"Well," he said slowly, "suppose I were to dare you to get up and walk over to that table and look your fiancé in the eye and say, 'Stop scowling at my back hair! I've a perfect right to be supping with an old friend!'—would you do it?"

"Is he?" said Jill startled.

"Scowling? Can't you feel it on the back of your head?" He drew thoughtfully at his cigarette. "If I were you I should stop that sort of thing at the source. It's a habit that can't be discouraged in a husband too early. Scowling is the civilized man's substitute for wife-beating."

Jill moved uncomfortably in her chair. Her quick temper resented his tone. There was a hostility, a hardly veiled contempt in his voice which stung her. Derek was sacred. Whoever criticised him, presumed. Wally, a few minutes before a friend and an agreeable companion, seemed to her to have changed. He was once more the boy whom she had disliked in the old days. There was a gleam in her eyes which should have warned him, but he went on.

"I should imagine that this Derek of yours is not one of our leading sunbeams. Well, I suppose he could hardly be, if that's his mother and there is anything in heredity."

"Please don't criticise Derek," said Jill coldly.

"I was only saying . . ."

"Never mind. I don't like it."

A slow flush crept over Wally's face. He made no reply, and there fell between them a silence that was like a shadow. Jill sipped her coffee miserably. She was regretting that little spurt of temper. She wished she could have recalled the words. Not that it was the actual words that had torn asunder this gossamer thing, the friendship which they had begun to weave like some fragile web: it was her manner, the manner of the princess rebuking an underling. She knew that, if she had struck him, she could not have offended Wally more deeply. There are some men whose ebullient natures enable them to rise unscathed from the worst snub. Wally, her intuition told her, was not that kind of man.

There was only one way of mending the matter. In these clashes of human temperaments, these sudden storms that spring up out of a clear sky, it is possible sometimes to repair the damage, if the psychological moment is resolutely seized, by talking rapidly and with detachment on neutral topics. Words have made the rift, and words alone can bridge it. But neither Jill nor her companion could find words, and the silence lengthened grimly. When Wally spoke, it was in the level tones of a polite stranger.

"Your friends have gone."

His voice was the voice in which, when she went on railway journeys, fellow-travellers in the carriage enquired of Jill if she would prefer the window up or down. It had the effect of killing her regrets and feeding her resentment. She was a girl who never refused a challenge, and she set herself to be as frigidly polite and aloof as he.

"Really?" she said. "When did they leave?"

"A moment ago." The lights gave the warning flicker that announces the arrival of the hour of closing. In the momentary darkness they both rose. Wally scrawled his name across the bill which the waiter had insinuated upon his attention. "I suppose we had better be moving?"

They crossed the room in silence. Everybody was moving in the same direction. The broad stairway leading to the lobby was crowded with chattering supper-parties. The light had gone up again.

At the cloak-room Wally stopped.

"I see Underhill waiting up there," he said casually. "To take you home. I suppose. Shall we say good-night? I'm staying in the hotel."

Jill glanced towards the head of the stairs. Derek was there. He was alone. Lady Underhill presumably had gone up to her room in the elevator.

Wally was holding out his hand. His face was stolid and his eyes avoided hers.

"Good-bye," he said.

"Good-bye," said Jill.

She felt curiously embarrassed. At this last moment hostility had weakened, and she was conscious of a desire to make amends. She and this man had been through much together that night, much that was perilous and much that was pleasant. A sudden feeling of remorse came over her.

"You'll come and see us, won't you?" she said a little wistfully. "I'm sure my uncle would like to meet you again."

"It's very good of you," said Wally, "but I'm afraid I shall be going back to America at any moment now."

Pique, that ally of the devil, regained its slipping grip upon Jill.

"Oh? I'm sorry," she said indifferently. "Well, good-bye, then."

"Good-bye."

"I hope you have a pleasant voyage."

"Thanks."

He turned into the cloak-room, and Jill went up the stairs to join Derek. She felt angry and depressed, full of a sense of the futility of things. People flashed into one's life and out again. Where was the sense of it?

III

Derek had been scowling, and Derek still scowled. His eyebrows were formidable, and his mouth smiled no welcome at Jill as she approached him. The evening, portions of which Jill had found so enjoyable, had contained no pleasant portions for Derek. Looking back over a lifetime whose events had been almost uniformly agreeable, he told himself that he could not recall another day which had gone so completely awry. It had started with the fog. He hated fog. Then had come that meeting with his mother at Charing Cross, which had been enough to upset him by itself. After that, rising to a crescendo of unpleasantness, the day had provided that appalling situation at the Albany, the recollection of which still made him tingle; and there had followed the silent dinner, the boredom of the early part of the play, the fire at the theatre, the undignified scramble for the exits, and now this discovery of the girl whom he was engaged to marry supping at the Savoy with a fellow he didn't remember ever having seen in his life. All these things combined to induce in Derek a mood bordering on ferocity. His birth and income, combining to make him one of the spoiled children of the world, had fitted him ill for such a series of catastrophes. He received Jill with frozen silence and led her out to the waiting taxi-cab. It was only when the cab had started on its journey that he found relief in speech.

"Well," he said, mastering with difficulty an inclination to raise his voice to a shout, "perhaps you will kindly explain?"

Jill had sunk back against the cushions of the cab. The touch of his body against hers always gave her a thrill, half pleasurable, half frightening. She had never met anybody who affected her in this way as Derek did. She moved a little closer, and felt for his hand. But, as she touched it, it retreated—coldly. Her heart sank. It was like being cut in public by somebody very dignified.

"Derek, darling!" Her lips trembled. Others had seen this side of Derek Underhill frequently, for he was a man who believed in keeping the world in its place, but she never. To her he had always been the perfect, gracious knight. A little too perfect, perhaps, a trifle too gracious, possibly, but she had been too deeply in love to notice that. "Don't be cross!"

The English language is the richest in the world, and yet somehow in moments when words count most we generally choose the wrong ones. The adjective "cross" as a description of his Jove-like wrath that consumed his whole being jarred upon Derek profoundly. It was as though Prometheus, with the vultures tearing his liver, had been asked if he were piqued.

"Cross!"

The cab rolled on. Lights from lamp-posts flashed in at the windows. It was a pale, anxious little face that they lit up when they shone upon Jill.

"I can't understand you," said Derek at last. Jill noticed that he had not yet addressed her by her name. He was speaking straight out in front of him as if he were soliloquising. "I simply cannot understand you. After what happened before dinner to-night, for you to cap everything by going off alone to supper at a restaurant, where half the people in the room must have known you, with a man . . ."

"You don't understand!"

"Exactly! I said I did not understand." The feeling of having scored a point made Derek feel a little better. "I admit it. Your behaviour is incomprehensible. Where did you meet this fellow?"

"I met him at the theatre. He was the author of the play."

"The man you told me you had been talking to? The fellow who scraped acquaintance with you between the acts?"

"But I found out he was an old friend. I mean, I knew him when I was a child."

"You didn't tell me that."

"I only found it out later."

"After he had invited you to supper! It's maddening!" cried Derek, the sense of his wrongs surging back over him. "What do you suppose my mother thought? She asked me who the man with you was. I had to say I didn't know! What do you suppose she thought?"

It is to be doubted whether anything else in the world could have restored the fighting spirit to Jill's cowering soul at that moment; but the reference to Lady Underhill achieved this miracle. That deep mutual antipathy which is so much more common than love at first sight had sprung up between the two at the instant of their meeting. The circumstances of that meeting had caused it to take root and grow. To Jill, Derek's mother was by this time not so much a fellow human being whom she disliked as a something, a sort of force, that made for her unhappiness. She was a menace and a loathing.

"If your mother had asked me that question," she retorted with spirit, "I should have told her that he was the man who got me safely out of the theatre after you . . ." She checked herself. She did not want to say the unforgivable thing. "You see," she said more quietly, "you had disappeared. . . ."

"My mother is an old woman," said Derek stiffly. "Naturally I had to look after her. I called to you to follow."

"Oh, I understand. I'm simply trying to explain what happened. I was there all alone, and Wally Mason . . ."

"Wally!" Derek uttered a short laugh, almost a bark. "It got to Christian names, eh?"

Jill set her teeth.

"I told you I knew him as a child. I always called him Wally then."

"I beg your pardon. I had forgotten."

"He got me out through the pass-door on to the stage and through the stage-door."

Derek was feeling cheated. He had the uncomfortable sensation that comes to men who grandly contemplate mountains and see them dwindle to molehills. The apparently outrageous had shown itself in explanation nothing so out-of-the-way after all. He seized upon the single point in Jill's behaviour that still constituted a grievance.

"There was no need for you to go to supper with the man!" Jove-like wrath had ebbed away to something deplorably like a querulous grumble. "You should have gone straight home.

You must have known how anxious I would be about you."

"Well, really, Derek, dear! You didn't seem so very anxious! You were having supper yourself quite cosily."

The human mind is curiously constituted. It is worthy of record that, despite his mother's obvious disapproval of his engagement, despite all the occurrences of this dreadful day, it was not till she made this remark that Derek Underhill first admitted to himself that, intoxicate his senses as she might, there was a possibility that Jill Mariner was not the ideal wife for him. The idea came and went more quickly than breath upon a mirror. It passed, but it had been. There are men who fear repartee in a wife more keenly than a sword. Derek was one of these. Like most men of single outlook, whose dignity is their most precious possession, he winced from an edged tongue.

"My mother was greatly upset," he replied coldly. "I thought a cup of soup would do her good. And, as for being anxious about you, I telephoned to your home to ask if you had come in."

"And when," thought Jill, "they told you I hadn't, you went off to supper!"

She did not speak the words. If she had an edged tongue, she had also the control of it. She had no wish to wound Derek. Whole-hearted in everything she did, she loved him with her whole heart. There might be specks upon her idol—that its feet might be clay she could never believe—but they mattered nothing. She loved him.

"I'm so sorry, dear," she said. "So awfully sorry! I've been a bad girl, haven't I ?"

She felt for his hand again, and this time he allowed it to remain stiffly in her grasp. It was like being grudgingly recognized by somebody very dignified who had his doubts about you but reserved judgment.

The cab drew up at the door of the house in Ovingdon Square which Jill's Uncle Christopher had settled upon as a suitable address for a gentleman of his standing. Jill put up her face to be kissed, like a penitent child.

"I'll never be naughty again!"

For a flickering instant Derek hesitated. The drive, long as it was, had been too short wholly to restore his equanimity. Then the sense of her nearness, her sweetness, the faint perfume of

her hair, and her eyes, shining softly in the darkness so close
to his own, overcame him. He crushed her to him.

Jill disappeared into the house with a happy laugh. It had
been a terrible day, but it had ended well.

"The Albany," said Derek to the cabman.

He leaned back against the cushions. His sense were in a
whirl. The cab rolled on. Presently his exalted mood vanished
as quickly as it had come. Jill absent always affected him
differently from Jill present. He was not a man of strong
imagination, and the stimulus of her waned when she was not
with him. Long before the cab reached the Albany the frown
was back on his face.

IV

Arriving at the Albany, he found Freddie Rooke lying on his
spine in a deep arm-chair. His slippered feet were on the mantelpiece, and he was restoring his wasted tissues with a strong
whisky-and-soda. One of the cigars which Barker, the valet, had
stamped with the seal of his approval was in the corner of his
mouth. The *Sporting Times*, with a perusal of which he had
been soothing his fluttered nerves, had fallen on the floor beside
the chair. He had finished reading, and was now gazing peacefully
at the ceiling, his mind a perfect blank. There was nothing the
matter with Freddie.

"Hullo, old thing," he observed as Derek entered. "So you
buzzed out of the fiery furnace all right? I was wondering how
you had got along. How are you feeling? I'm not the man I was!
These things get the old system all stirred up! I'll do anything
in reason to oblige and help things along and all that, but to be
called on at a moment's notice to play Shadrach, Meshach, and
Abednego rolled into one, without rehearsal or make-up, is a
bit too thick! No, young feller-me-lad! If theatre fires are going
to be the fashion this season, the Last of the Rookes will sit
quietly at home and play solitaire. Mix yourself a drink of
something, old man, or something of that kind. By the way,
your jolly old mater. All right? Not even singed? Fine! Make
a long arm and gather in a cigar."

And Freddie, having exerted himself to play the host in a
suitable manner, wedged himself more firmly into his chair and
blew a cloud of smoke.

Derek sat down. He lit a cigar, and stared silently at the fire. From the mantelpiece Jill's photograph smiled down, but he did not look at it. Presently his attitude began to weigh upon Freddie. Freddie had had a trying evening. What he wanted just now was merry prattle, and his friend did not seem disposed to contribute his share. He removed his feet from the mantelpiece and wriggled himself sideways, so that he could see Derek's face. Its gloom touched him. Apart from his admiration for Derek, he was a warm-hearted young man, and sympathized with affliction when it presented itself for his notice.

"Something on your mind, old bean?" he enquired delicately.

Derek did not answer for a moment. Then he reflected that, little as he esteemed the other's mentality, he and Freddie had known each other a long time, and that it would be a relief to confide in some one. And Freddie, moreover, was an old friend of Jill and the man who had introduced him to her.

"Yes," he said.

"I'm listening, old top," said Freddie. "Release the film."

Derek drew at his cigar, and watched the smoke as it curled to the ceiling.

"It's about Jill."

Freddie signified his interest by wriggling still further sideways.

"Jill, eh?"

"Freddie, she's so damned impulsive!"

Freddie nearly rolled out of his chair. This, he took it, was what writing-chappies called a coincidence.

"Rummy you should say that," he ejaculated. "I was telling her exactly the same thing myself only this evening." He hesitated. "I fancy I can see what you're driving at, old thing. The watchword is 'What ho, the mater!' yes, no? You've begun to get a sort of idea that if Jill doesn't watch her step, she's apt to sink pretty low in the betting, what? I know exactly what you mean! You and I know all right that Jill's a topper. But one can see that to your jolly old mater only judging by first impressions, and the meeting not having come off quite as scheduled. . . .I say, old man," he broke off, "fearfully sorry and all that about that business. You know what I mean! Wouldn't have had it happen for the world. I take it the mater was a trifle peeved? Not to say perturbed and chagrined? I seemed to notice it at dinner."

"She was furious, of course. She did not refer to the matter when we were alone together, but there was no need to. I knew what she was thinking."

Derek threw away his cigar. Freddie noted this evidence of an overwrought soul with concern.

"The whole thing," he conceded, "was a bit unfortunate." Derek began to pace the room.

"Freddie."

"On the spot, old man."

"Something's got to be done."

"Absolutely!" Freddie nodded solemnly. He had taken this matter greatly to heart. Derek was his best friend, and he had always been extremely fond of Jill. It hurt him to see things going wrong. "I'll tell you what, old bean. Let *me* handle this binge for you."

"You ?"

"Me! The Final Rooke!" He jumped up, and leaned against the mantelpiece. "I'm the lad to do it. I've known Jill for years. She'll listen to me. I'll talk to her like a Dutch uncle and make her understand the general scheme of things. I'll take her out to tea to-morrow and slang her in no uncertain voice! Leave the whole thing to *me*, laddie!"

Derek considered.

"It might do some good," he said.

"Good ?" said Freddie. "It's *it*, dear boy! It's a wheeze! You toddle off to bed and have a good sleep. I'll fix the whole thing for you!"

⋆ 5 ⋆

Lady Underhill Receives a Shock

I

THERE are streets in London into which the sun seems never to penetrate. Some of these are in fashionable quarters, and it is to be supposed that their inhabitants find an address which looks well on note-paper a sufficient compensation for the gloom that goes with it. The majority, however, are in the mean neighbourhoods of the great railway termini, and appear to offer no compensation whatever. They are lean, furtive streets, grey as the January sky with a sort of arrested decay. They smell of cabbage and are much prowled over by vagrom cats. At night they are empty and dark, and a stillness broods on them, broken only by the cracked tingle of an occasional piano playing one of the easier hymns, a form of music to which the dwellers in the dingy houses are greatly addicted. By day they achieve a certain animation through the intermittent appearance of women in aprons, who shake rugs out of the front doors or, emerging from areas, go down to the public-house on the corner with jugs to fetch the supper-beer. In almost every ground-floor window there is a card announcing that furnished lodgings may be had within. You will find these streets by the score if you leave the main thoroughfares and take a short cut on your way to Euston, to Paddington, or to Waterloo. But the dingiest and deadliest and most depressing lie round about Victoria. And Daubeny Street, Pimlico, is one of the worst of them all.

On the afternoon following the events recorded, a girl was dressing in the ground-floor room of Number Nine, Daubeny Street. A tray bearing the remains of a late breakfast stood on the rickety table beside a bowl of wax flowers. From beneath the table peered the green cover of a copy of *Variety*. A grey parrot in a cage by the window cracked seed and looked out into the room with a satirical eye. He had seen all this so many times before—Nelly Bryant arraying herself in her smartest clothes to go out and besiege agents in their offices off the Strand. It happened every day. In an hour or two she would came back as usual, say "Oh, Gee!" in a tired sort of voice, and then Bill the parrot's day proper would begin. He was a bird who liked the sound of his own voice, and he never got the chance of a really sustained conversation till Nelly returned in the evening.

"Who cares ?" said Bill, and cracked another seed.

If rooms are an indication of the characters of their occupants, Nelly Bryant came well out of the test of her surroundings. Nothing can make a London furnished room much less horrible than it intends to be, but Nelly had done her best. The furniture, what there was of it, was of that lodging-house kind which resembles nothing else in the world. But a few little touches here and there, a few instinctively tasteful alterations in the general scheme of things, had given the room almost a cosy air. Later on, with the gas lit, it would achieve something approaching homeliness. Nelly, like many another nomad, had taught herself to accomplish a good deal with poor material. On tour in America, she had sometimes made even a bedroom in a small hotel tolerably comfortable, than which there is no greater achievement. Oddly, considering her life, she had a genius for domesticity.

To-day, not for the first time, Nelly was feeling unhappy. The face that looked back at her out of the mirror at which she was arranging her most becoming hat was weary. It was only a moderately pretty face, but loneliness and underfeeding had given it a wistful expression that had charm. Unfortunately, it was not the sort of charm which made a great appeal to the stout, whisky-nourished men who sat behind paper-littered tables, smoking cigars, in the rooms marked "Private" in the offices of theatrical agents. Nelly had been out of a "shop" now for many weeks—ever since, in fact, "Follow the Girl" had finished its long run at the Regal Theatre.

"Follow the Girl," an American musical comedy, had come over from New York with an American company, of which Nelly had been a humble unit, and, after playing a year in London and some weeks in the number one towns, had returned to New York. It did not cheer Nelly up in the long evenings in Daubeny Street to reflect that, if she had wished, she could have gone home with the rest of the company. A mad impulse had seized her to try her luck in London, and here she was now, marooned.

"Who cares ?" said Bill.

For a bird who enjoyed talking he was a little limited in his remarks and apt to repeat himself.

"I do, you poor fish!" said Nelly, completing her manœuvres with the hat and turning to the cage. "It's all right for you—you have a swell time with nothing to do but sit there and eat seed—but how do you suppose I enjoy tramping around looking for work and never finding any ?"

She picked up her gloves. "Oh, well!" she said. "Wish me luck!"

"Good-bye, boy!" said the parrot, clinging to the bars.

Nelly thrust a finger into the cage, and scratched his head.

"Anxious to get rid of me, aren't you ? Well, so long."

"Good-bye, boy!"

"All right, I'm going. Be good!"

"Woof-woof-woof!" barked Bill the parrot, not committing himself to any promises.

For some moments after Nelly had gone he remained hunched on his perch, contemplating the infinite. Then he sauntered along to the seed-box and took some more light nourishment. He always liked to spread his meals out, to make them last longer. A drink of water to wash the food down, and he returned to the middle of the cage, where he proceeded to conduct a few intimate researches with his beak under his left wing. After which he mewed like a cat, and relapsed into silent meditation once more. He closed his eyes and pondered on his favourite problem—Why was he a parrot? This was always good for an hour or so, and it was three o'clock before he had come to his customary decision that he didn't know. Then, exhausted by brainwork and feeling a trifle hipped by the silence of the room, he looked about him for some way of jazzing existence up a little. It occurred to him that if he barked again it might help.

"Woof-woof-woof!"

Good as far as it went, but it did not go far enough. It was not real excitement. Something rather more dashing seemed to him to be indicated. He hammered for a moment or two on the floor of his cage, ate a mouthful of the newspaper there, and stood with his head on one side, chewing thoughtfully. It didn't taste as good as usual. He suspected Nelly of having changed his *Daily Mail* for the *Daily Express* or something. He swallowed the piece of paper, and was struck by the thought that a little climbing exercise might be what his soul demanded. (You hang on by your beak and claws and work your way up to the roof. It sounds tame, but it's something to do.) He tried it. And, as he gripped the door of the cage it swung open. Bill the parrot now perceived that this was going to be one of those days. He had not had a bit of luck like this for months.

For a while he sat regarding the open door. Unless excited by outside influences, he never did anything in a hurry. Then proceeding cautiously, he passed out into the room. He had been out there before, but always chaperoned by Nelly. This was something quite different. It was an adventure. He hopped on to the window-sill. There was a ball of yellow wool there, but he had lunched and could eat nothing. He cast around in his mind for something to occupy him, and perceived suddenly that the world was larger than he had supposed. Apparently there was a lot of it outside the room. How long this had been going on he did not know, but obviously it was a thing to be

investigated. The window was open at the bottom, and just
outside the window were what he took to be the bars of another
and larger cage. As a matter of fact they were the railings which
afforded a modest protection to Number Nine. They ran the
length of the house, and were much used by small boys as a
means of rattling sticks. One of these stick-rattlers passed as Bill
stood there looking down. The noise startled him for a moment,
then he seemed to come to the conclusion that this sort of thing
was to be expected if you went out into the great world and that
a parrot who intended to see life must not allow himself to be
deterred by trifles. He crooned a little, and finally, stepping in a
stately way over the window-sill, with his toes turned in at right
angles, caught at the top of the railing with his beak, and proceeded to lower himself. Arrived at the level of the street, he
stood looking out.

A dog trotted up, spied him, and came to sniff.

"Good-bye, boy!" said Bill chattily.

The dog was taken aback. Hitherto, in his limited experience,
birds had been birds and men men. Here was a blend of the
two. What was to be done about it? He barked tentatively, then,
finding that nothing disastrous ensued, pushed his nose between
two of the bars and barked again. Anyone who knew Bill could
have told him that he was asking for it, and he got it. Bill leaned
forward and nipped his nose. The dog started back with a howl
of agony. He was learning something new every minute.

"Woof-woof-woof!" said Bill sardonically.

He perceived trousered legs, four of them, and, cocking his
eye upwards, saw that two men of the lower orders stood before
him. They were gazing down at him in the stolid manner peculiar
to the proletariat of London in the presence of the unusual. For
some minutes they stood drinking him in, then one of them
gave judgment.

"It's a parrot!" He removed a pipe from his mouth and
pointed with the stem. "A perishin' parrot, Erb."

"Ah!" said Erb, a man of few words.

"A parrot," proceeded the other. He was seeing clearer into
the matter every moment. "That's a parrot, that is, Erb. My
brother Joe's wife's sister had one of 'em. Come from abroad,
they do. My brother Joe's wife's sister 'ad one of 'em. Red-'aired
gel she was. Married a feller down at the Docks. *She* 'ad one of
'em. Parrots they're called."

He bent down for a closer inspection, and inserted a finger through the railings. Erb abandoned his customary taciturnity and spoke words of warning.

"Tike care 'e don't sting yer, 'Enry!"

Henry seemed wounded.

"Woddyer mean, sting me? I know all abart parrots, I do. My brother Joe's wife's sister 'ad one of 'em. They don't 'urt yer, not if you're kind to 'em. You know yer pals when you see 'em, don't yer, mate?" he went on, addressing Bill, who was contemplating the finger with one half-closed eye.

"Good-bye, boy," said the parrot, evading the point.

"Jear that?" cried Henry delightedly. " 'Goo'-bye, boy!, 'Uman they are!"

" 'E'll 'ave a piece out of yer finger," warned Erb the suspicious.

"Wot, 'im?" Henry's voice was indignant. He seemed to think that his reputation as an expert on parrots had been challenged. " 'E wouldn't 'ave no piece out of my finger."

"Bet yer a narf-pint 'e would 'ave a piece out of yer finger," persisted the sceptic.

"No blinkin' parrot's goin' to 'ave no piece of no finger of mine! My brother Joe's wife's sister's parrot never 'ad no piece out of no finger of mine!" He extended the finger further and waggled it enticingly beneath Bill's beak. "Cheerio, matey!" he said winningly. "Polly want a nut?"

Whether it was mere indolence or whether the advertised docility of that other parrot belonging to Henry's brother's wife's sister had caused him to realize that there was a certain standard of good conduct for his species one cannot say; but for a while Bill merely contemplated temptation with a detached eye.

"See!" said Henry.

"Woof-woof-woof!" said Bill.

"*Wow-Wow-Wow*'" yapped the dog, suddenly returning to the scene and going on with the argument at the point where he had left off.

The effect on Bill was catastrophic. Ever a high-strung bird, he lost completely the repose which stamps the caste of Vere de Vere and the better order of parrot. His nerves were shocked, and, as always under such conditions, his impulse was to bite blindly. He bit, and Henry—one feels sorry for Henry: he was a well-meaning man—leaped back with a loud howl.

"That'll be 'arf a pint," said Erb, always the business man.

There was a lull in the rapid action. The dog, mumbling softly to himself, had moved away again and was watching affairs from the edge of the sidewalk. Erb, having won his point, was silent once more. Henry sucked his finger. Bill, having met the world squarely and shown it what was what, stood where he was, whistling nonchalantly.

Henry removed his finger from his mouth. "Lend the loan of that stick of yours, Erb," he said tensely.

Erb silently yielded up the stout stick which was his inseparable companion. Henry, a vastly different man from the genial saunterer of a moment ago, poked wildly through the railings. Bill, panic-stricken now and wishing for nothing better than to be back in his cosy cage, shrieked loudly for help. And Freddie Rooke, running round the corner with Jill, stopped dead and turned pale.

"Good God!" said Freddie.

II

In pursuance of his overnight promise to Derek, Freddie Rooke had got in touch with Jill through the medium of the telephone immediately after breakfast, and had arranged to call at Ovingdon Square in the afternoon. Arrived there, he found Jill with a telegram in her hand. Her Uncle Christopher, who had been enjoying a breath of sea-air down at Brighton, was returning by an afternoon train, and Jill had suggested that Freddie should accompany her to Victoria, pick up Uncle Chris, and escort him home. Freddie, whose idea had been a *tête-à-tête* involving a brotherly lecture on impetuosity, had demurred but had given way in the end; and they had set out to walk to Victoria together. Their way had lain through Daubeny Street, and they turned the corner just as the brutal onslaught on the innocent Henry had occurred. Bill's shrieks, which were of an appalling timbre, brought them to a halt.

"What is it?" cried Jill.

"It sounds like a murder!"

"Nonsense!"

"I don't know, you know. This is the sort of street chappies are murdering people in all the time."

They caught sight of the group in front of them, and were reassured. Nobody could possibly be looking so aloof and distrait as Erb if there were a murder going on.

"It's a bird!"

"It's a jolly old parrot. See it? Just inside the railings."

A red-hot wave of rage swept over Jill. Whatever her defects —and already this story has shown her far from perfect—she had the excellent quality of loving animals and blazing into fury when she saw them ill-treated. At least three draymen were going about London with burning ears as the result of what she had said to them on discovering them abusing their patient horses. Zoologically, Bill the parrot was not an animal, but he counted as one with Jill, and she sped down Daubeny Street to his rescue —Freddie, spatted and hatted and trousered as became the man of fashion, following disconsolately, ruefully aware that he did not look his best sprinting like that. But Jill was cutting out a warm pace, and he held his hat on with one neatly-gloved hand and did what he could to keep up.

Jill reached the scene of battle, and, stopping, eyed Henry with a baleful glare. We, who have seen Henry in his calmer moments and know him for the good fellow he was, are aware that he was more sinned against than sinning. If there is any spirit of justice in us, we are pro-Henry. In his encounter with Bill the parrot, Henry undoubtedly had right on his side. His friendly overtures, made in the best spirit of kindliness, had been repulsed. He had been severely bitten. And he had lost half a pint of beer to Erb. As impartial judges we have no other course before us than to wish Henry luck and bid him go to it. But Jill, who had not seen the opening stages of the affair, thought far otherwise. She merely saw in Henry a great brute of a man poking at a defenceless bird with a stick.

She turned to Freddie, who had come up at a gallop and was wondering why the deuce this sort of thing happened to him out of a city of six millions.

"Make him stop, Freddie!"

"Oh, I say, you know, what?"

"Can't you see he's hurting the poor thing? Make him leave off! Brute!" she added to Henry (for whom one's heart bleeds), as he jabbed once again at his adversary.

Freddie stepped reluctantly up to Henry, and tapped him on the shoulder. Freddie was one of those men who have a rooted idea that a conversation of this sort can only be begun by a tap on the shoulder.

"Look here, you know, you can't do this sort of thing, you know!" said Freddie.

Henry raised a scarlet face.

" 'Oo are *you*?" he demanded.

This attack from the rear, coming on top of his other troubles, tried his restraint sorely.

"Well——" Freddie hesitated. It seemed silly to offer the fellow one of his cards. "Well, as a matter of fact, my name's Rooke . . ."

"And who," pursued Henry, "arsked *you* to come shoving your ugly mug in 'ere?"

"Well, if you put it that way . . ."

" 'E comes messing abart," said Henry complainingly, addressing the universe, "and interfering in what don't concern 'im and mucking around and interfering and messing abart. . . . Why," he broke off in a sudden burst of eloquence, "I could eat two of you for a relish wiv me tea, even if you 'ave got white spats!"

Here Erb, who had contributed nothing to the conversation, remarked "Ah!" and expectorated on the sidewalk. The point, one gathers, seemed to Erb well taken. A neat thrust, was Erb's verdict.

"Just because you've got white spats," proceeded Henry, on whose sensitive mind these adjuncts of the costume of the well-dressed man about town seemed to have made a deep and unfavourable impression, "you think you can come mucking around and messing abart and interfering and mucking around. This bird's bit me in the finger, and 'ere's the finger, if you don't believe me—and I'm going to twist 'is ruddy neck, if all the perishers with white spats in London come messing abart and mucking around, so you take them white spats of yours 'ome and give 'em to the old woman to cook for your Sunday dinner!"

And Henry, having cleansed his stuff'd bosom of that perilous stuff which weighs upon the heart, shoved the stick energetically once more through the railings.

Jill darted forward. Always a girl who believed that, if you want a thing well done, you must do it yourself, she had applied to Freddie for assistance merely as a matter of form. All the time she had felt that Freddie was a broken reed, and such he had proved himself. Freddie's policy in this affair was obviously to rely on the magic of speech, and any magic his speech might have had was manifestly offset by the fact that he was wearing white spats and that Henry, apparently, belonged to some sort of league or society which had for its main object the discouragement of white spats. It was plainly no good leaving the conduct of the campaign to Freddie. Whatever was to be done must be done by herself. She seized the stick and wrenched it out of Henry's hand.

"Woof-woof-woof!" said Bill the parrot.

No dispassionate auditor could have failed to detect the nasty ring of sarcasm. It stung Henry. He was not normally a man who believed in violence to the gentler sex outside a clump on the head of his missus when the occasion seemed to demand it; but now he threw away the guiding principles of a lifetime' and turned on Jill like a tiger.

"Gimme that stick!"

"Get back!"

"Here I say, you know!" said Freddie.

Henry, now thoroughly overwrought, made a rush at Jill; and Jill, who had a straight eye, hit him accurately on the side of the head.

"Goo!" said Henry, and sat down.

And then, from behind Jill, a voice spoke.

"What's all this?"

A stout policeman had manifested himself from empty space.

"This won't do!" said the policeman.

Erb, who had been a silent spectator of the fray, burst into speech.

"She 'it 'im!"

The policeman looked at Jill. He was an officer of many years' experience in the Force, and time had dulled in him that respect for good clothes which he had brought with him from Little-Sudbury-in-the-Wold in the days of his novitiate. Jill was well dressed, but, in the stirring epoch of the Suffrage disturbances, the policeman had been kicked on the shins and even bitten by ladies of an equally elegant exterior. Hearts, the policeman knew, just as pure and fair may beat in Belgrave Square as in the lowlier air of Seven Dials, but you have to pinch them just the same when they disturb the peace. His gaze, as it fell upon Jill, red-handed as it were with the stick still in her grasp, was stern.

"Your name, please, and address, miss?" he said.

A girl in blue with a big hat had come up, and was standing staring open-mouthed at the group. At the sight of her Bill the parrot uttered a shriek of welcome. Nelly Bryant had returned, and everything would now be all right again.

"Mariner," said Jill, pale and bright-eyed. "I live at Number Twenty-two, Ovingdon Square."

"And yours, sir?"

"Mine? Oh, ah, yes. I see what you mean. Rooke, you know. F. L. Rooke. I live at the Albany and all that sort of thing."

The policeman made an entry in his notebook.

"Officer," cried Jill, "this man was trying to kill that parrot and I stopped him. . . ."

"Can't help that, miss. You 'adn't no right to hit a man with a stick. You'll 'ave to come along."

"But, I say, you know!" Freddie was appalled. This sort of thing had happened to him before, but only on Boat-Race Night at the Empire, where it was expected of a chappie. "I mean to say!"

"And you, too, sir. You're both in it."

"But . . ."

"Oh, come along, Freddie," said Jill quietly. "It's perfectly absurd, but it's no use making a fuss."

"That," said the policeman cordially, "is the right spirit!"

III

Lady Underhill paused for breath. She had been talking long and vehemently. She and Derek were sitting in Freddie Rooke's apartment at the Albany, and the subject of her monologue was Jill. Derek had been expecting the attack, and had wondered why it had not come before. All through supper on the previous night, even after the discovery that Jill was supping at a near-by table with a man who was a stranger to her son, Lady Underhill had preserved a grim reticence with regard to her future daughter-in-law. But to-day she had spoken her mind with all the energy which comes of suppression. She had relieved herself with a flow of words of all the pent-up hostility that had been growing within her since that first meeting in this same room. She had talked rapidly, for she was talking against time. The Town

Council of the principal city in Derek's constituency in the north of England had decided that to-morrow morning should witness the laying of the foundation stone of their new Town Hall, and Derek as the sitting member was to preside at the celebration. Already Barker had been dispatched to telephone for a cab to take him to the station, and at any moment their conversation might be interrupted. So Lady Underhill made the most of what little time she had.

Derek listened gloomily, scarcely rousing himself to reply. His mother would have been gratified could she have known how powerfully her arguments were working on him. That little imp of doubt which had vexed him in the cab as he drove home from Ovingdon Square had not died in the night. It had grown and waxed more formidable. And now, aided by this ally from without, it had become a Colossus straddling his soul. Derek looked frequently at the clock, and cursed the unknown cabman whose delay was prolonging the scene. Something told him that only flight could serve him now. He never had been able to withstand his mother in one of her militant moods. She seemed to numb his faculties. Other members of his family had also noted this quality in Lady Underhill, and had commented on it bitterly in the smoking-rooms of distant country-houses at the hour when men meet to drink the final whisky-and-soda and unburden their souls.

Lady Underhill, having said all she had to say, recovered her breath and began to say it again. Frequent iteration was one of her strongest weapons. As her brother Edwin, who was fond of homely imagery, had often observed, she could talk the hind-leg off a donkey.

"You must be mad, Derek, to dream of handicapping yourself at this vital stage of your career with a wife who not only will not be a help to you, but must actually be a ruinous handicap. I am not blaming you for imagining yourself in love in the first place, though I really should have thought that a man of your strength and character would . . . However, as I say, I am not blaming you for that. Superficially, no doubt, this girl might be called attractive. I do not admire the type myself, but I suppose she has that quality—in my time we should have called it boldness—which seems to appeal to the young men of to-day. I could imagine her fascinating a weak-minded imbecile like your friend Mr. Rooke. But that you . . . Still, there is no need to go into

that. What I am trying to point out is that in your position, with
a career like yours in front of you—it's quite certain that in a
year or two you will be offered some really big and responsible
position—you would be insane to tie yourself to a girl who seems
to have been allowed to run perfectly wild, whose uncle is a
swindler . . ."

"She can't be blamed for her uncle."

. . . . Who sups alone with strange men in public restaurants. . . ."

"I explained that."

"You may have explained it. You certainly did not excuse it
or make it a whit less outrageous. You cannot pretend that you
really imagine that an engaged girl is behaving with perfect
correctness when she allows a man she has only just met to
take her to supper at the Savoy, even if she did know him slightly
years and years ago. It is very idyllic to suppose that a childhood
acquaintance excuses every breach of decorum, but I was
brought up to believe otherwise. I don't wish to be vulgar, but
what it amounts to is that this girl was having supper—supper!
In my days girls were in bed at supper-time!—with a strange
man who picked her up at a theatre!"

Derek shifted uneasily. There was a part of his mind which
called upon him to rise up and challenge the outrageous phrase
and demand that it be taken back. But he remained silent. The
imp-Colossus was too strong for him. She is quite right, said
the imp. That is an unpleasant but accurate description of what
happened. He looked at the clock again, and wished for the
hundredth time that the cab would come. Jill's photograph
smiled at him from beside the clock. He looked away, for, when
he found his eyes upon it, he had an odd sensation of baseness,
as if he were playing some one false who loved and trusted him.

"Well, I am not going to say any more," she said, getting up
and buttoning her glove. "I will leave you to think it over. All
I will say is that, though I only met her yesterday, I can assure
you that I am quite confident that this girl is just the sort of
harum-scarum so-called 'modern' girl who is sure some day to
involve herself in a really serious scandal. I don't want her to
be in a position to drag you into it as well. Yes, Barker, what is
it? Is Sir Derek's cab here?"

The lantern-jawed Barker had entered softly, and was standing
deferentially in the doorway. There was no emotion on his face

beyond the vague sadness which a sense of what was correct made him always wear like a sort of mask when in the presence of those of superior station.

"The cab will be at the door very shortly, m'lady. If you please, Sir Derek, a policeman has come with a message."

"A policeman?"

"With a message from Mr. Rooke."

"What do you mean?"

"I have had a few words of conversation with the constable, sir," said Barker sadly, "and I understand from him that Mr. Rooke and Miss Mariner have been arrested."

"Arrested! What are you talking about?"

"Mr. Rooke desired the officer to ask you to be good enough to step round and bail them out!"

The gleam in Lady Underhill's eye became a flame, but she controlled her voice.

"Why were Miss Mariner and Mr. Rooke arrested, Barker?"

"As far as I can gather, m'lady, Miss Mariner struck a man in the street with a stick, and they took both her and Mr. Rooke to the Chelsea Police Station."

Lady Underhill glanced at Derek, who was looking into the fire.

"This is a little awkward, Derek," she said suavely. "If you go to the police-station, you will miss your train."

"I fancy, m'lady, it would be sufficient if Sir Derek were to dispatch me with a cheque for ten pounds."

"Very well. Tell the policeman to wait a moment."

"Very good, m'lady."

Derek roused himself with an effort. His face was drawn and gloomy. He sat down at the writing-table, and took out his cheque-book. There was silence for a moment, broken only by the scratching of the pen. Barker took the cheque and left the room.

"Now, perhaps," said Lady Underhill, "you will admit that I was right!" She spoke in almost an awed voice, for this occurrence at just this moment seemed to her very like a direct answer to prayer. "You can't hesitate now! You *must* free yourself from this detestable entanglement!"

Derek rose without speaking. He took his coat and hat from where they lay on a chair.

"Derek! You will! Say you will!"

Derek put on his coat.

"Derek!"

"For heaven's sake, leave me alone, mother. I want to think."

"Very well. I will leave you to think it over, then." Lady Underhill moved to the door. At the door she paused for a moment, and seemed about to speak again, but her mouth closed resolutely. She was a shrewd woman, and knew that the art of life is to know when to stop talking. What words have accomplished, too many words can undo.

"Good-bye."

"Good-bye, mother."

"I'll see you when you get back?"

"Yes. No. I don't know. I'm not certain when I shall return. I may go away for a bit."

The door closed behind Lady Underhill. Derek sat down again at the writing-table. He wrote a few words on a sheet of paper, then tore it up. His eye travelled to the mantelpiece. Jill's photograph smiled happily down at him. He turned back to the writing-table, took out a fresh piece of paper, thought for a few moments, and began to write again.

The door opened softly.

"The cab is at the door, Sir Derek," said Barker.

Derek addressed an envelope, and got up.

"All right. Thanks. Oh, Barker, stop at a district-messenger office on your way to the police-station, and have this sent off at once."

"Very good, Sir Derek," said Barker.

Derek's eyes turned once more to the mantelpiece. He stood looking for an instant, then walked quickly out of the room.

⋆ 6 ⋆

Uncle Chris Bangs the Table

I

A TAXI-CAB stopped at the door of Number Twenty-two, Ovingdon Square. Freddie Rooke emerged, followed by Jill. While Freddie paid the driver, Jill sniffed the afternoon air happily. It had turned into a delightful day. A westerly breeze, springing up in the morning, had sent the thermometer up with a run and broken the cold spell which had been gripping London. It was one of those afternoons which intrude on the bleakness of winter with a false but none the less agreeable intimation that Spring is on its way. The sidewalks were wet underfoot, and the gutters ran with thawed snow. The sun shone exhilaratingly from a sky the colour of a hedge-sparrow's egg.

"Doesn't everything smell lovely, Freddie," said Jill, "after our prison-life!"

"Topping!"

"Fancy getting out so quickly! Whenever I'm arrested, I must always make a point of having a rich man with me. I shall never tease you about that fifty-pound note again."

"Fifty-pound note?"

"It certainly came in handy to-day!"

She was opening the door with her latch-key, and missed the sudden sagging of Freddie's jaw, the sudden clutch at his breast-pocket, and the look of horror and anguish that started into his eyes. Freddie was appalled. Finding himself at the police-station penniless with the exception of a little loose change, he had sent that message to Derek, imploring assistance, as the only alternative to spending the night in a cell, with Jill in another. He had realized that there was a risk of Derek taking the matter hardly, and he had not wanted to get Jill into trouble, but there seemed nothing else to do. If they remained where they were overnight, the thing would get into the papers, and that would be a thousand times worse. And if he applied for aid to Ronny Devereux or Algy Martyn or anybody like that all London would know about it next day. So Freddie, with misgivings, had sent the message to Derek, and now Jill's words had reminded him that there was no need to have done so. Years ago he had read somewhere or heard somewhere about some chappie who always buzzed around with a sizeable banknote stitched into his clothes, and the scheme had seemed to him ripe to a degree. You never knew when you might find yourself short of cash and faced by an immediate call for the ready. He had followed the chappie's example. And now, when the crisis had arrived, he had forgotten—absolutely forgotten!—that he had the dashed thing on his person at all.

He followed Jill into the house, groaning in spirit, but thankful that she had taken it for granted that he had secured their release

in the manner indicated. He did not propose to disillusion her.
It would be time enough to take the blame when the blame
came along. Probably old Derek would simply be amused and
laugh at the whole bally affair like a sportsman. Freddie
cheered up considerably at the thought.

Jill was talking to the parlourmaid whose head had popped
up over the banisters flanking the stairs that led to the kitchen.

"Major Selby hasn't arrived yet, miss."

"That's odd. I suppose he must have taken a later train."

"There's a lady in the drawing-room, miss, waiting to see him.
She didn't give any name. She said she would wait till the major
came. She's been waiting a goodish while."

"All right, Jane. Thanks. Will you bring up tea?"

They walked down the hall. The drawing-room was on the
ground floor, a long, dim room that would have looked like a
converted studio but for the absence of bright light. A girl was
sitting at the far end by the fireplace. She rose as they
entered.

"How do you do?" said Jill. "I'm afraid my uncle has not
come back yet . . . ."

"Say!" cried the visitor. "You *did* get out quick!"

Jill was surprised. She had no recollection of ever having seen
the other before. Her visitor was a rather pretty girl, with a sort
of jaunty way of carrying herself which made a piquant contrast
to her tired eyes and wistful face. Jill took an immediate liking
to her. She looked so forlorn and pathetic.

"My name's Nelly Bryant," said the girl. "That parrot belongs
to me."

"Oh, I see."

"I heard you say to the cop that you lived here, so I came
along to tell your folks what had happened, so that they could
do something. The maid said that your uncle was expected any
minute, so I waited."

"That was awfully good of you."

"Dashed good," said Freddie.

"Oh, no! Honest, I don't know how to thank you for what
you did. You don't know what a pal Bill is to me. It would have
broken me all up if that plug-ugly had killed him."

"But what a shame you had to wait so long."

"I liked it."

Nelly Bryant looked about the room wistfully. This was the

sort of room she sometimes dreamed about. She loved its subdued light and the pulpy cushions on the sofa.

"You'll have some tea before you go, won't you?" said Jill,
switching on the lights.

"It's very kind of you."

"Why, hullo!" said Freddie. "By Jove! I say! We've met
before, what?"

"Why, so we have!"

"That lunch at Oddy's that young Threepwood gave, what?"

"I wonder you remember."

"Oh, I remember. Quite a time ago, eh? Miss Bryant was in
that show. 'Follow the Girl,' Jill, at the Regal."

"Oh, yes. I remember you took me to see it."

"Dashed odd meeting again like this!" said Freddie. "Really
rummy!"

Jane, the parlourmaid, entering with tea, interrupted his
comments.

"You're American, then?" said Jill interested. "The whole
company came from New York, didn't they?"

"Yes."

"I'm half American myself, you know. I used to live in New
York when I was very small, but I've almost forgotten what it
was like. I remember a sort of overhead railway that made an
awful noise. . . ."

"The Elevated!" murmured Nelly devoutly. A wave of home-
sickness seemed to choke her for a moment.

"And the air. Like champagne. And a very blue sky."

"Yes," said Nelly in a small voice.

"I shouldn't half mind popping over to New York for a bit,"
said Freddie, unconscious of the agony he was inflicting. "I've
met some very sound sportsmen who came from there. You
don't know a fellow named Williamson, do you?"

"I don't believe I do."

"Or Oakes?"

"No."

"That's rummy! Oakes has lived in New York for years."

"So have about seven million other people," interposed Jill.
"Don't be silly, Freddie. How would you like somebody to ask
of you if you knew a man named Jenkins in London?"

"I *do* know a man named Jenkins in London," replied Freddie
triumphantly.

Jill poured out a cup of tea for her visitor, and looked at the clock.

"I wonder where Uncle Chris has got to," she said. "He ought to be here by now. I hope he hasn't got into any mischief among the wild stockbrokers down at Brighton."

Freddie laid down his cup on the table and uttered a loud snort.

"Oh, Freddie, darling!" said Jill remorsefully. "I forgot! Stockbrokers are a painful subject, aren't they!" She turned to Nelly. "There's been an awful slump on the Stock Exchange to-day, and he got—what was the word, Freddie?"

"Nipped!" said Freddie with gloom.

"Nipped!"

"Nipped like the dickens!"

"Nipped like the dickens!" Jill smiled at Nelly. "He had forgotten all about it in the excitement of being a jail-bird, and I went and reminded him."

Freddie sought sympathy from Nelly.

"A silly ass at the club named Jimmy Monroe told me to take a flutter in some rotten thing called Amalgamated Dyes. You know how it is, when you're feeling devilish fit and cheery and all that after dinner, and somebody sidles up to you and slips his little hand in yours and tells you to do some fool thing. You're so dashed happy you simply say 'Right-ho, old bird! Make it so!' That's the way I got had!"

Jill laughed unfeelingly.

"It will do you good, Freddie. It'll stir you up and prevent you being so silly again. Besides, you know you'll hardly notice it. You've much too much money as it is."

"It's not the money. It's the principle of the thing. I hate looking a frightful chump."

"Well, you needn't tell anybody. We'll keep it a secret. In fact, we'll start at once, for I hear Uncle Chris outside. Let us dissemble. We are observed! . . . Hullo, Uncle Chris!"

She ran down the room, as the door opened, and kissed the tall, soldierly man who entered.

"Well, Jill, my dear."

"How late you are. I was expecting you hours ago."

"I had to call on my broker"

"Hush! Hush!"

"What's the matter?"

"Nothing, nothing. . . . We've got visitors. You know Freddie Rooke, of course?"

"How are you, Freddie, my boy?"

"Cheerio!" said Freddie. "Pretty fit?"

"And Miss Bryant," said Jill.

"How do you do?" said Uncle Chris in the bluff, genial way which, in his younger days, had charmed many a five-pound note out of the pockets of his fellow-men and many a soft glance out of the eyes of their sisters, their cousins, and their aunts.

"Come and have some tea," said Jill. "You're just in time."

"Tea? Capital!"

Nelly had subsided shyly into the depths of her big armchair. Somehow she felt a better and a more important girl since Uncle Chris had addressed her. Most people felt like that after encountering Jill's Uncle Christopher. Uncle Chris had a manner. It was not precisely condescending, and yet it was not the manner of an equal. He treated you as an equal, true, but all the time you were conscious of the fact that it was extraordinarily good of him to do so. Uncle Chris affected the rank and file of his fellow-men much as a genial knight of the Middle Ages would have affected a scurvy knave or varlet if he had cast aside social distinctions for a while and hobnobbed with the latter in a tavern. He never patronized, but the mere fact that he abstained from patronizing seemed somehow impressive.

To this impressiveness his appearance contributed largely. He was a fine, upstanding man, who looked less than his forty-nine years in spite of an ominous thinning of the hair which he tended and brushed so carefully. He had a firm chin, a mouth that smiled often and pleasantly beneath the closely-clipped moustache, and very bright blue eyes which met yours in a clear, frank, honest gaze. Though he had served in his youth in India, he had none of the Anglo-Indian's sun-scorched sallowness. His complexion was fresh and sanguine. He looked as if he had just stepped out of a cold tub—a misleading impression, for Uncle Chris detested cold water and always took his morning bath as hot as he could get it.

It was his clothes, however, which, even more than his appearance, fascinated the populace. There is only one tailor in London, as distinguished from the ambitious mechanics who make coats and trousers, and Uncle Chris was his best customer. Similarly, London is full of young fellows trying to get along by the manufacture of foot-wear, but there is only one boot-maker in the true meaning of the word—the one who supplied Uncle Chris. And, as for hats, while it is no doubt a fact that you can get at plenty of London shops some sort of covering for your head which will keep it warm, the only hatter—using the term in its deeper sense—is the man who enjoyed the patronage of Major Christopher Selby. From foot to head, in short, from further South to extremest North, Uncle Chris was perfect. He was an ornament to his surroundings. The Metropolis looked better for him. One seems to picture London as a mother with a horde of untidy children, children with made-up ties, children with wrinkled coats and baggy trouser-legs, sighing to herself as she beheld them, then cheering up and murmuring with a touch of restored complacency, "Ah, well, I still have Uncle Chris!"

"Miss Bryant is American, Uncle Chris," said Jill.

Uncle Chris spread his shapely legs before the fire, and glanced down kindly at Nelly.

"Indeed?" He took a cup of tea and stirred it. "I was in America as a young man."

"Whereabouts?" asked Nelly eagerly.

"Oh, here and there and everywhere. I travelled considerably."

"That's how it is with me," said Nelly, overcoming her diffidence as she warmed to the favourite topic. "I guess I know most every town in every State, from New York to the last one-night stand. It's a great old country, isn't it?"

"It is!" said Uncle Chris. "I shall be returning there very shortly." He paused meditatively. "Very shortly indeed."

Nelly bit her lip. It seemed to be her fate to-day to meet people who were going to America.

"When did you decide to do that?" asked Jill.

She had been looking at him, puzzled. Years of association with Uncle Chris had enabled her to read his moods quickly, and she was sure that there was something on his mind. It was not likely that the others had noticed it, for his manner was as genial and urbane as ever. But something about him, a look in his eyes that came and went, an occasional quick twitching of his mouth, told her that all was not well. She was a little troubled, but not greatly. Uncle Chris was not the sort of man to whom grave tragedies happened. It was probably some mere trifle which she could smooth out for him in five minutes, once they were alone together, She reached out and patted his sleeve affectionately. She was fonder of Uncle Chris than of anyone in the world except Derek.

"The thought," said Uncle Chris, "came to me this morning, as I read my morning paper while breakfasting. It has grown and developed during the day. At this moment you might almost call it an obsession. I am very fond of America. I spent several happy years there. On that occasion I set sail for the land of promise, I admit, somewhat reluctantly. Of my own free will I might never have made the expedition. But the general sentiment seemed so strongly in favour of my doing so that I yielded to what I might call a public demand. The willing hands for my nearest and dearest were behind me, pushing, and I did not resist them. I have never regretted it. America is a part of every young man's education. You ought to go there, Freddie."

"Rummily enough," said Freddie, "I was saying just before you came in that I had half a mind to pop over. Only it's rather a bally fag, starting. Getting your luggage packed and all that sort of thing."

Nelly, whose luggage consisted of one small trunk, heaved a silent sigh. Mingling with the idle rich carried its penalties.

"America," said Uncle Chris, "taught me poker, for which I can never be sufficiently grateful. Also an exotic pastime styled Craps—or, alternatively, 'rolling the bones'—which in those days was a very present help in time of trouble. At Craps, I fear, my hand in late years has lost much of its cunning. I have had little opportunity of practising. But as a young man I was no mean exponent of the art. Let me see," said Uncle Chris meditatively. "What was the precise ritual ? Ah! I have it, 'Come, little seven!' "

" 'Come, eleven!' " exclaimed Nelly excitedly.

" 'Baby . . .' I feel convinced that in some manner the word baby entered into it."

" 'Baby needs new shoes!' "

" 'Baby needs new shoes!' Precisely!"

"It sounds to me," said Freddie, "dashed silly."

"Oh, no!" cried Nelly reproachfully.

"Well, what I mean is, there's no sense in it, don't you know."

"It is a noble pursuit," said Uncle Chris firmly. "Worthy of the great nation that has produced it. No doubt, when I return to America, I shall have opportunities of recovering my lost skill."

"You aren't returning to America," said Jill. "You're going to stay safe at home like a good little uncle. I'm not going to have you running wild all over the world at your age."

"Age?" declaimed Uncle Chris. "What is my age? At the present moment I feel in the neighbourhood of twenty-one, and Ambition is tapping me on the shoulder and whispering 'Young man, go West!' The years are slipping away from me, my dear Jill—slipping so quickly that in a few minutes you will be wondering why my nurse does not come to fetch me. The wander-lust is upon me. I gaze around me at all this prosperity in which I am lapped," said Uncle Chris, eyeing the arm-chair severely, "all this comfort and luxury which swaddles me, and I feel staggered. I want activity. I want to be braced!"

"You would hate it," said Jill composedly. "You know you're the laziest old darling in the world."

"Exactly what I am endeavouring to point out. I *am* lazy. Or, I was till this morning."

"Something very extraordinary must have happened this morning. I can see that."

"I wallowed in gross comfort. I was what Shakespeare calls a 'fat and greasy citizen'!"

"Please, Uncle Chris!" protested Jill. "Not while I'm eating buttered toast!"

"But now I am myself again."

"That's splendid."

"I have heard the beat of the off-shore wind," chanted Uncle Chris, "and the thresh of the deep-sea rain. I have heard the song—How long! how long! Pull out on the trail again!"

"He can also recite 'Gunga Din,'" said Jill to Nelly. "I really must apologize for all this. He's usually as good as gold."

"I believe I know how he feels," said Nelly softly.

"Of course you do. You and I, Miss Bryant, are of the gipsies of the world. We are not vegetables like young Rooke here."

"Eh, what?" said the vegetable, waking from a reverie. He had been watching Nelly's face. Its wistfulness attracted him.

"We are only happy," proceeded Uncle Chris, "when we are wandering."

"You should see Uncle Chris wander to his club in the

morning," said Jill. "He trudges off in a taxi, singing wild gipsy songs, absolutely defying fatigue."

"That," said Uncle Chris, "is a perfectly justified slur. I shudder at the depths to which prosperity has caused me to sink." He expanded his chest. "I shall be a different man in America. America would make a different man of *you*, Freddie."

"I'm all right, thanks!" said that easily satisfied young man.

Uncle Chris turned to Nelly, pointing dramatically.

"Young woman, go West! Return to your bracing home, and leave this enervating London! You . . ."

Nelly got up abruptly. She could endure no more.

"I believe I'll have to be going now," she said. "Bill misses me if I'm away long. Good-bye. Thank you ever so much for what you did."

"It was awfully kind of you to come round," said Jill.

"Good-bye, Major Selby."

"Good-bye."

"Good-bye, Mr. Rooke."

Freddie awoke from another reverie.

"Eh? Oh, I say, half a jiffy. I think I may as well be toddling along myself. About time I was getting back to dress for dinner and all that. See you home, may I, and then I'll get a taxi at Victoria. Toodle-oo, everybody."

Freddie escorted Nelly through the hall and opened the front door for her. The night was cool and cloudy and there was still in the air that odd, rejuvenating suggestion of Spring. A wet fragrance came from the dripping trees.

"Topping evening!" said Freddie conversationally.

"Yes."

They walked through the square in silence. Freddie shot an appreciative glance at his companion. Freddie, as he would have admitted frankly, was not much of a lad for the modern girl. The modern girl, he considered, was too dashed rowdy and exuberant for a chappie of peaceful tastes. Now, this girl, on the other hand, had all the earmarks of being something of a topper. She had a soft voice. Rummy accent and all that, but nevertheless a soft and pleasing voice. She was mild and unaggressive, and these were qualities which Freddie esteemed. Freddie, though this was a thing he would not have admitted, was afraid of girls, the sort of girls he had to take down to dinner and dance with and so forth. They were too dashed clever, and always seemed to be waiting for a chance to score off a fellow. This one was not like that. Not a bit. She was gentle and quiet and what not.

It was at this point that it came home to him how remarkable quiet she was. She had not said a word for the last five minutes. He was just about to break the silence, when, as they passed under a street lamp, he perceived that she was crying—crying very softly to herself, like a child in the dark.

"Good God!" said Freddie appalled. There were two things in life with which he felt totally unable to cope—crying girls and dog-fights. The glimpse he had caught of Nelly's face froze him into a speechlessness which lasted until they reached Daubeny Street and stopped at her door.

"Good-bye," said Nelly.

"Good-bye-ee!" said Freddie mechanically. "That's to say, I mean to say, half a second!" he added quickly. He faced her nervously, with one hand on the grimy railings. This wanted looking into. When it came to girls trickling to and fro in the public streets, weeping, well, it was pretty rotten and something had to be done about it. "What's up?" he demanded.

"It's nothing. Good-bye."

"But, my dear old soul," said Freddie, clutching the railing for moral support, "it *is* something. It must be! You might not think it, to look at me, but I'm really rather a dashed shrewd chap, and I can *see* there's something up. Why not give me the jolly old scenario and see if we can't do something?"

Nelly moved as if to turn to the door, then stopped. She was thoroughly ashamed of herself.

"I'm a fool!"

"No, no!"

"Yes, I am. I don't often act this way, but, oh, gee! hearing you all talking like that about going to America, just as if it was the easiest thing in the world, only you couldn't be bothered to do it, kind of got me going. And to think I could be there right now if I wasn't a bonehead!"

"A bonehead?"

"A simp. I'm all right as far up as the string of near-pearls, but above that I'm reinforced concrete."

Freddie groped for her meaning.

"Do you mean you've made a bloomer of some kind?"

"I pulled the worst kind of bone. I stopped on in London

when the rest of the company went back home, and now I've got to stick."

"Rush of jolly old professional engagements, what?"

Nelly laughed bitterly.

"You're a bad guesser. No, they haven't started to fight over me yet. I'm at liberty, as they say in the *Era*."

"But, my dear old thing," said Freddie earnestly, "if you've nothing to keep you in England, why not pop back to America? I mean to say, home-sickness is the most dashed blighted thing in the world. There's nothing gives one the pip to such an extent. Why, dash it, I remember staying with an old aunt of mine up in Scotland the year before last and not being able to get away for three weeks or so, and I raved—absolutely gibbered —for the sight of the merry old metrop. Sometimes I'd wake up in the night, thinking I was back at the Albany, and, by Jove, when I found I wasn't I howled like a dog! You take my tip, old soul, and pop back on the next boat."

"Which line?"

"How do you mean, which line? Oh, I see, you mean which line? Well . . . well . . . I've never been on any of them, so it's rather hard to say. But I hear the Cunard well spoken of, and then again some chappies swear by the White Star. But I should imagine you can't go far wrong, whichever you pick. They're all pretty ripe, I fancy."

"Which of them is giving free trips? That's the point."

"Eh? Oh!" Her meaning dawned upon Freddie. He regarded her with deep consternation. Life had treated him so kindly that he had almost forgotten that there existed a class which had not as much money as himself. Sympathy welled up beneath his perfectly fitting waistcoat. It was a purely disinterested sympathy. The fact that Nelly was a girl and in many respects a dashed pretty girl did not affect him. What mattered was that she was hard up. The thought hurt Freddie like a blow. He hated the idea of anyone being hard up.

"I say!" he said. "Are you broke?"

Nelly laughed.

"Am I? If dollars were doughnuts, I wouldn't even have the hole in the middle."

Freddie was stirred to his depths. Except for the beggars in the streets, to whom he gave shillings, he had not met anyone for years who had not plenty of money. He had friends at his

clubs who frequently claimed to be unable to lay their hands on
a bally penny, but the bally penny they wanted to lay their
hands on generally turned out to be a couple of thousand pounds
for a new car.

"Good God!" he said.

There was a pause. Then, with a sudden impulse, he began
to fumble in his breast-pocket. Rummy how things worked out
for the best, however scaly they might seem at the moment. Only
an hour or so ago he had been kicking himself for not having
remembered that fifty-pound note, tacked on to the lining of his
coat, when it would have come in handy at the police-station. He
now saw that Providence had had the matter well in hand. If
he had remembered it and coughed it up to the constabulary
then, he wouldn't have had it now. And he needed it now. A
mood of quixotic generosity had surged upon him. With swift
fingers he jerked the note free from its moorings and displayed it
like a conjurer exhibiting a rabbit.

"My dear old thing," he said. "I can't stand it! I absolutely
cannot stick it at any price! I really must insist on your trousering
this. Positively!"

Nelly Bryant gazed at the note with wide eyes. She was
stunned. She took it limply, and looked at it under the dim light
of the gas-lamp over the door.

"I couldn't!" she cried.

"Oh, but really! You must!"

"But this is a fifty-pound!"

"Absolutely! It will take you back to New York, what? You
asked which line was giving free trips. The Freddie Rooke Line
by Jove, sailings every Wednesday and Saturday! I mean,
what?"

"But I can't take two hundred and fifty dollars from you!"

"Oh, rather. Of course you can."

There was another pause.

"You'll think——" Nelly's pale face flushed. "You'll think
I told you all about myself just—just because I wanted to . . ."

"To make a touch? Absolutely not! Rid yourself of the jolly
old supposition entirely. You see before you, old thing, a chappie
who knows more about borrowing money than any man in
London. I mean to say, I've had my ear bitten more often than
anyone, I should think. There are sixty-four ways of making a
touch—I've had them all worked on me by divers blighters here

and there—and I can tell any of them with my eyes shut. I know you weren't dreaming of any such thing."

The note crackled musically in Nelly's hand.

"I don't know what to say!"

"That's all right."

"I don't see why . . . Gee! I wish I could tell you what I think of you!"

Freddie laughed amusedly.

"Do you know," he said, "that's exactly what the beaks—the masters, you know—used to say to me at school."

"Are you sure you can spare it?"

"Oh, rather."

Nelly's eyes shone in the light of the lamp.

"I've never met anyone like you before. I don't know how . . ."

Freddie shuffled nervously. Being thanked always made him feel pretty rotten.

"Well, I think I'll be popping," he said. "Got to get back and dress and all that. Awfully glad to have seen you, and all that sort of rot."

Nelly unlocked the door with her latchkey, and stood on the step.

"I'll buy a fur-wrap," she said, half to herself.

"Great wheeze! I should!"

"And some nuts for Bill!"

"Bill?"

"The parrot."

"Oh, the jolly old parrot! Rather! Well, cheerio!"

"Good-bye . . . You've been awfully good to me."

"Oh, no," said Freddie uncomfortably. "Any time you're passing . . ."

"Awfully good . . . Well, good-bye."

"Toodle-oo!"

"Maybe we'll meet again some day."

"I hope so. Absolutely!"

There was a little scurry of feet. Something warm and soft pressed for an instant against Freddie's cheek, and, as he stumbled back, Nelly Bryant skipped up the steps and vanished through the door.

"Good God!"

Freddie felt his cheek. He was aware of an odd mixture of embarrassment and exhilaration,

From the area below a slight cough sounded. Freddie turned sharply. A maid in a soiled cap, worn coquettishly over one ear, was gazing intently up through the railings. Their eyes met. Freddie turned a warm pink. It seemed to him that the maid had the air of one about to giggle.

"Damn!" said Freddie softly, and hurried off down the street. He wondered whether he had made a frightful ass of himself, spraying bank-notes all over the place like that to comparative strangers. Then a vision came to him of Nelly's eyes as they had looked at him in the lamp-light, and he decided—no, absolutely not. Rummy as the gadget might appear, it had been the right thing to do. It was a binge of which he thoroughly approved. A good egg!

II

Jill, when Freddie and Nelly left the room, had seated herself on a low stool, and sat looking thoughtfully into the fire. She was wondering if she had been mistaken in supposing that Uncle Chris was worried about something. This restlessness of his, this desire for movement, was strange in him. Hitherto he had been like a dear old cosy cat, revelling in the comfort which he had just denounced so eloquently. She watched him as he took up his favourite stand in front of the fire.

"Nice girl," said Uncle Chris. "Who was she?"

"Somebody Freddie met," said Jill diplomatically. There was no need to worry Uncle Chris with details of the afternoon's happenings.

"Very nice girl." Uncle Chris took out his cigar-case. "No need to ask if I may, thank goodness." He lit a cigar. "Do you remember, Jill, years ago, when you were quite small, how I used to blow smoke in your face?"

Jill smiled.

"Of course I do. You said that you were training me for marriage. You said that there were no happy marriages except where the wife didn't mind the smell of tobacco. Well, it's lucky as a matter of fact, for Derek smokes all the time."

Uncle Chris took up his favourite stand against the fireplace.

"You're very fond of Derek, aren't you, Jill?"

"Of course I am. You are, too, aren't you?"

"Fine chap. Very fine chap. Plenty of money, too. It's a

great relief," said Uncle Chris, puffing vigorously. "A thundering relief." He looked over Jill's head down the room. "It's fine to think of you happily married, dear, with everything in the world that you want."

Uncle Chris' gaze wandered down to where Jill sat. A slight mist affected his eyesight. Jill had provided a solution for the great problem of his life. Marriage had always appalle d him, but there was this to be said for it, that married people had daughters. He had always wanted a daughter, a smart girl he could take out and be proud of; and fate had given him Jill at precisely the right age. A child would have bored Uncle Chris—he was fond of children, but they made the deuce of a noise and regarded jam as an external ornament—but a delightful little girl of fourteen was different. Jill and he had been very close to each other since her mother had died, a year after the death of her father, and had left her in his charge. He had watched her grow up with a joy that had a touch of bewilderment in it—she seemed to grow so quickly—and had been fonder and prouder of her at every stage of her tumultuous career.

"You're a dear," said Jill. She stroked the trouser-leg that was nearest. "How *do* you manage to get such a wonderful crease ? You really are a credit to me!"

There was a momentary silence. A shade of embarrassment made itself noticeable in Uncle Chris' frank gaze. He gave a little cough, and pulled at his moustache.

"I wish I were, my dear," he said soberly. "I wish I were. I'm afraid I'm a poor sort of a fellow, Jill."

Jill looked up.

"What do you mean ?"

"A poor sort of a fellow," repeated Uncle Chris. "Your mother was foolish to trust you to me. Your father had more sense. He always said I was a wrong 'un."

Jill got up quickly. She was certain now that she had been right, and that there was something on her uncle's mind.

"What's the matter, Uncle Chris ? Something's happened. What is it ?"

Uncle Chris turned to knock the ash off his cigar. The movement gave him time to collect himself for what lay before him. He had one of those rare volatile natures which can ignore the blows of fate so long as their effects are not brought home by visible evidence of disaster. He lived in the moment, and, though matters had been as bad at breakfast-time as they were now, it was not till now, when he confronted Jill, that he had found his cheerfulness affected by them. He was a man who hated ordeals, and one faced him now. Until this moment he had been able to detach his mind from a state of affairs which would have weighed unceasingly upon another man. His mind was a telephone which he could cut off at will, when the voice of Trouble wished to speak. The time would arrive, he had been aware, when he would have to pay attention to that voice, but so far he had refused to listen. Now it could be evaded no longer.

"Jill."

"Yes ?"

Uncle Chris paused again, searching for the best means of saying what had to be said.

"Jill, I don't know if you understand about these things, but there was what is called a slump on the Stock Exchange this morning. In other words . . ."

Jill laughed.

"Of course I know all about that," she said. "Poor Freddie wouldn't talk about anything else till I made him. He was terribly blue when he got here this afternoon. He said he had got 'nipped' in Amalgamated Dyes. He had lost about two hundred pounds, and was furious with a friend of his who had told him to buy margins."

Uncle Chris cleared his throat.

"Jill, I'm afraid I've got bad news for you. I bought Amal-gamated Dyes, too." He worried his moustache. "I lost heavily, very heavily."

"How naughty of you! You know you oughtn't to gamble."

"Jill, you must be brave. I—I—well, the fact is—it's no good beating about the bush—I lost everything! Everything!"

"Everything ?"

"Everything! It's all gone! All fooled away. It's a terrible business. This house will have to go."

"But—but doesn't the house belong to me ?"

"I was your trustee, dear." Uncle Chris smoked furiously. "Thank heaven you're going to marry a rich man!"

Jill stood looking at him, perplexed. Money, as money, had never entered into her life. There were things one wanted which had to be paid for with money, but Uncle Chris had always looked after that. She had taken them for granted.

"I don't understand," she said.

And then suddenly she realized that she did, and a great wave of pity for Uncle Chris flooded over her. He was such an old dear. It must be horrible for him to have to stand there, telling her all this. She felt no sense of injury, only the discomfort of having to witness the humiliation of her oldest friend. Uncle Chris was bound up inextricably with everything in her life that was pleasant. She could remember him, looking exactly the same, only with a thicker and wavier crop of hair, playing with her patiently and unwearied for hours in the hot sun, a cheerful martyr. She could remember sitting up with him when she came home from her first grown-up dance, drinking cocoa and talking and talking and talking till the birds outside sang the sun high up into the sky and it was breakfast time. She could remember theatres with him, and jolly little suppers afterwards; expeditions into the country, with lunches at queer old inns; days on the river, days at Hurlingham, days at Lord's, days at the Academy. He had always been the same, always cheerful, always kind. He was Uncle Chris, and he would always be Uncle Chris, whatever he had done or whatever he might do. She slipped her arm in his and gave it a squeeze.

"Poor old thing!" she said.

Uncle Chris had been looking straight out before him with those fine blue eyes of his. There had been just a touch of sternness in his attitude. A stranger, coming into the room at that moment, would have said that here was a girl trying to coax her blunt, straightforward, military father into some course of action of which his honest nature disapproved. He might have been posing for a statue of Rectitude. As Jill spoke, he seemed to cave in.

"Poor old thing?" he repeated limply.

"Of course you are! And stop trying to look dignified and tragic! Because it doesn't suit you. You're much too well dressed."

"But, my dear, you don't understand! You haven't realized!"

"Yes, I do. Yes, I have!"

"I've spent all your money—*your* money!"

"I know! What does it matter?"

"What does it matter! Jill, don't you hate me?"

"As if anyone could hate an old darling like you!"

Uncle Chris threw away his cigar, and put his arms around Jill.

For a moment a dreadful fear came to her that he was going to cry. She prayed that he wouldn't cry. It would be too awful. It would be a memory of which she could never rid herself. She felt as though he were someone extraordinarily young and unable to look after himself, someone she must soothe and protect.

"Jill," said Uncle Chris, choking, "you're—you're—you're a little warrior!"

Jill kissed him and moved away. She busied herself with some flowers, her back turned. The tension had been relieved, and she wanted to give him time to recover his poise. She knew him well enough to be sure that, sooner or later, the resiliency of his nature would assert itself. He could never remain long in the depths.

The silence had the effect of making her think more clearly than in the first rush of pity she had been able to do. She was able now to review the matter as it affected herself. It had not been easy to grasp, the blunt fact that she was penniless, that all this comfort which surrounded her was no longer her own. For an instant a kind of panic seized her. There was a bleakness about the situation which made one gasp. It was like icy water dashed in the face. Realization had almost the physical pain of life returning to a numbed limb. Her hands shook as she arranged the flowers, and she had to bite her lip to keep herself from crying out.

She fought panic eye to eye, and beat it down. Uncle Chris, swiftly recovering by the fireplace, never knew that the fight had taken place. He was feeling quite jovial again now that the unpleasant business of breaking the news was over, and was looking on the world with the eye of a debonair gentleman-adventurer. As far as he was concerned, he told himself, this was the best thing that could have happened. He had been growing old and sluggish in prosperity. He needed a fillip. The wits by which he had once lived so merrily had been getting blunt in their easy retirement. He welcomed the opportunity of matching them once more against the world. He was remorseful as regarded Jill, but the optimist in him, never crushed for long, told him that Jill would be all right. She would step from the sinking ship to the safe refuge of Derek Underhill's wealth and position, while he went out to seek a new life. Uncle Chris' blue eyes gleamed with a new fire as he pictured himself in this new life. He felt like a hunter setting out on a hunting expedition. There were always adventures and the spoils of war for the man with brains to find them and gather them in. But it was a mercy that Jill had Derek. . . .

Jill was thinking of Derek, too. Panic had fled, and a curious exhilaration had seized upon her. If Derek wanted her now, it would be because his love was the strongest thing in the world. She would come to him like the beggar-maid to Cophetua.

Uncle Chris broke the silence with a cough. At the sound of it, Jill smiled again. She knew it for what it was, a sign that he was himself again.

"Tell me, Uncle Chris," she said, "just how bad is it? When you said everything was gone, did you really mean everything, or were you being melodramatic? Exactly how do we stand?"

"It's dashed hard to say, my dear. I expect we shall find there are a few hundreds left. Enough to see you through till you get married. After that it won't matter." Uncle Chris flicked a particle of dust off his coat-sleeve. Jill could not help feeling that the action was symbolical of his attitude towards life. He flicked away life's problems with just the same airy carelessness. "You mustn't worry about me, my dear. I shall be all right. I have made my way in the world before, and I can do it again. I shall go to America and try my luck there. Amazing how many opportunities there are in America. Really, as far as I am concerned, this is the best thing that could have happened. I have been getting abominably lazy. If I had gone on living my present life for another year or two, why, dash it, I honestly believe I should have succumbed to some sort of senile decay. Positively I should have got fatty degeneration of the brain! This will be the making of me."

Jill sat down on the lounge and laughed till there were tears in her eyes. Uncle Chris might be responsible for this disaster, but he was certainly making it endurable. However greatly he might be deserving of censure, from the standpoint of the sterner morality, he made amends. If he brought the whole world crashing in chaos about one's ears, at least he helped one to smile among the ruins.

"Did you ever read 'Candide,' Uncle Chris?"

" 'Candide'?" Uncle Chris shook his head. He was not a great reader, except of the sporting press.

"It's a book by Voltaire. There's a character in it called

Doctor Pangloss, who thought that everything was for the best in this best of all possible worlds."

Uncle Chris felt a touch of embarrassment. It occurred to him that he had been betrayed by his mercurial temperament into an attitude which, considering the circumstances, was perhaps a trifle too jubilant. He gave his moustache a pull, and reverted to the minor key.

"Oh, you mustn't think that I don't appreciate the terrible, the criminal thing I have done! I blame myself," said Uncle Chris cordially, flicking another speck of dust off his sleeve. "I blame myself bitterly. Your mother ought never to have made me your trustee, my dear. But she always believed in me, in spite of everything, and this is how I have repaid her." He blew his nose to cover a not unmanly emotion. "I wasn't fitted for the position. Never become a trustee, Jill. It's the devil, is trust money. However much you argue with yourself, you can't—dash it, you simply can't believe that it's not your own, to do as you like with. There it sits, smiling at you, crying 'Spend me! Spend me!' and you find yourself dipping—dipping—till one day there's nothing left to dip for—only a far-off rustling—the ghosts of dead banknotes. That's how it was with me. The process was almost automatic. I hardly knew it was going on. Here a little—there a little. It was like snow melting on a mountain-top. And one morning—all gone!" Uncle Chris drove the point home with a gesture. "I did what I could. When I found that there were only a few hundreds left, for your sake I took a chance. All heart and no head! There you have Christopher Selby in a nutshell! A man at the club, a fool named—I've forgotten his damn name—recommended Amalgamated Dyestuffs as a speculation. Monroe, that was his name, Jimmy Monroe. He talked about the future of British Dyes now that Germany was out of the race, and . . . well, the long and short of it was that I took his advice and bought on margin. Bought like the devil. And this morning Amalgamated Dyestuffs went all to blazes. There you have the whole story!"

"And now," said Jill, "comes the sequel!"

"The sequel?" said Uncle Chris breezily. "Happiness, my dear, happiness! Wedding bells and—and all that sort of thing!" He straddled the hearth-rug manfully, and swelled his chest out. He would permit no pessimism on this occasion of rejoicing. "You don't suppose that the fact of your having lost your money

—that is to say—er—of *my* having lost your money—will affect a splendid young fellow like Derek Underhill? I know him better than to think that! I've always liked him. He's a man you can trust! Besides," he added reflectively, "there's no need to tell him! Till after the wedding, I mean. It won't be hard to keep up appearances here for a month or so."

"Of course we must tell him!"

"You think it wise?"

"I don't know about it being wise. It's the only thing to do. I must see him to-night. Oh, I forgot. He was going away this afternoon for a day or two."

"Capital! It will give you time to think it over."

"I don't want to think it over. There's nothing to think about."

"Of course, yes, of course. Quite so."

"I shall write him a letter."

"Write, eh?"

"It's easier to put what one wants to say in a letter."

"Letters," began Uncle Chris, and stopped as the door opened. Jane, the parlourmaid, entered, carrying a salver.

"For me?" asked Uncle Chris.

"For Miss Jill, sir."

Jill took the note off the salver.

"It's from Derek."

"There's a messenger-boy waiting, miss," said Jane. "He wasn't told if there was an answer."

"If the note is from Derek," said Uncle Chris, "it's not likely to want an answer. You said he left town to-day."

Jill opened the envelope.

"Is there an answer, miss?" asked Jane, after what she considered a suitable interval. She spoke tenderly. She was a great admirer of Derek, and considered it a pretty action on his part to send notes like this when he was compelled to leave London.

"Any answer, Jill?"

Jill seemed to rouse herself. She had turned oddly pale.

"No, no answer, Jane."

"Thank you, miss," said Jane, and went off to tell the cook that in her opinion Jill was lacking in heart. "It might have been a bill instead of a love-letter," said Jane to the cook with indignation, "the way she read it. *I* like people to have a little feeling!"

Jill sat turning the letter over and over in her fingers. Her face was very white. There seemed to be a big, heavy leaden something inside her. A cold hand clutched her throat. Uncle Chris, who at first had noticed nothing untoward, now began to find the silence sinister.

"No bad news, I hope, dear?"

Jill turned the letter between her fingers.

"Jill, is it bad news?"

"Derek has broken off the engagement," said Jill in a dull voice. She let the note fall to the floor, and sat with her chin in her hands.

"What!" Uncle Chris leaped from the hearth-rug, as though the fire had suddenly scorched him. "What did you say?"

"He's broken it off."

"The hound!" cried Uncle Chris. "The blackguard! The—the—I never liked that man! I never trusted him!" He fumed for a moment. "But—but—it isn't possible. How can he have heard about what's happened? He couldn't know. It's—it's—it isn't possible!"

"He doesn't know. It has nothing to do with that."

"But . . ." Uncle Chris stooped to where the note lay. "May I . . .?"

"Yes, you can read it if you like."

Uncle Chris produced a pair of reading-glasses, and glared through them at the sheet of paper as though it were some loathsome insect.

"The hound! The cad! If I were a younger man," shouted Uncle Chris, smiting the letter violently, "if I were . . . Jill! My dear little Jill!"

He plunged down on his knees beside her, as she buried her face in her hands and began to sob.

"My little girl! Damn that man! My dear little girl! The cad! The devil! My own darling little girl! I'll thrash him within an inch of his life!"

The clock on the mantelpiece ticked away the minutes. Jill got up. Her face was wet and quivering, but her mouth had set in a brave line.

"Jill, dear!"

She let his hand close over hers.

"Everything's happening all at once this afternoon, Uncle Chris, isn't it!" She smiled a twisted smile. "You look so funny!

Your hair's all rumpled, and your glasses are over on one side!"

Uncle Chris breathed heavily through his nose.

"When I meet that man . . ." he began portentously.

"Oh, what's the good of bothering! It's not worth it! Nothing's worth it!" Jill stopped and faced him, her hands clenched. "Let's get away! Let's get right away! I want to get right away, Uncle Chris! Take me away! Anywhere! Take me to America with you! I must get away!"

Uncle Chris raised his right hand, and shook it. His reading-glasses, hanging from his left ear, bobbed drunkenly.

"We'll sail by the next boat! The very next boat, dammit! I'll take care of you, dear. I've been a blackguard to you, my little girl. I've robbed you, and swindled you. But I'll make up for it, by George! I'll make up for it! I'll give you a new home, as good as this, if I die for it. There's nothing I won't do! Nothing! By Jove!" shouted Uncle Chris, raising his voice in a red-hot frenzy of emotion, "I'll work! Yes, by Gad, if it comes right down to it, I'll work!"

He brought his fist down with a crash on the table where Derek's flowers stood in their bowl. The bowl leaped in the air and tumbled over, scattering the flowers on the floor.

★ 7 ★

Jill Catches the 10.10

I

IN the lives of each one of us, as we look back and review them in retrospect, there are certain desert wastes from which memory winces like some tired traveller faced with a dreary stretch of road. Even from the security of later happiness we cannot contemplate them without a shudder.

It took one of the most competent firms in the metropolis four days to produce some sort of order in the confusion resulting from Major Selby's financial operations; and during those days Jill existed in a state of being which could be defined as living only in that she breathed and ate and comported herself outwardly like a girl and not a ghost.

Boards announcing that the house was for sale appeared against the railings through which Jane the parlourmaid conducted her daily conversations with the tradesmen. Strangers roamed the rooms eyeing and appraising the furniture. Uncle Chris, on whom disaster had had a quickening and vivifying effect, was everywhere at once, an impressive figure of energy. One may be wronging Uncle Chris, but to the eye of the casual observer he seemed in these days of trial to be having the time of his life.

Jill varied the monotony of sitting in her room—which was the only place in the house where one might be sure of not encountering a furniture-broker's man with a note-book and pencil—by taking long walks. She avoided as far as possible the small area which had once made up the whole of London for her, but even so she was not always successful in escaping from old acquaintances. Once, butting through Lennox Gardens on her way to that vast, desolate King's Road which stretches its length out into regions unknown to those whose London is the West End, she happened upon Freddie Rooke, who had been paying a call in his best, and a pair of white spats which would have cut his friend Henry to the quick. It was not an enjoyable meeting. Freddie, keenly alive to the awkwardness of the situation, was scarlet and incoherent; and Jill, who desired nothing less than to talk with one so intimately connected in her mind with all that she had lost, was scarcely more collected. They parted without regret. The only satisfaction that came to Jill from the encounter was the knowledge that Derek was still out of town. He had wired for his things, said Freddie, and had retreated further north. Freddie, it seemed, had been informed of the broken engagement by Lady Underhill in an interview which appeared to have left a lasting impression on his mind. Of Jill's monetary difficulties he had heard nothing.

After this meeting, Jill felt a slight diminution of the oppression which weighed upon her. She could not have borne to have come unexpectedly upon Derek, and, now that there was no danger of that, she found life a little easier. The days passed somehow, and finally there came the morning, when, accompanied by Uncle Chris—voluble and explanatory about the details of what he called "getting everything settled"—she rode in a taxi to take the train for Southampton. Her last impression of London was of rows upon rows of mean houses, of cats wandering in back-yards among groves of home-washed underclothing, and a smoky greyness which gave way, as the train raced on, to the clearer grey of the suburbs and the good green and brown of the open country.

Then the bustle and confusion of the liner; the calm monotony of the journey, when one came on deck each morning to find the vessel so manifestly in the same spot where it had been the morning before that it was impossible to realize that many hundred miles of ocean had really been placed behind one; and finally the Ambrose Channel lightship and the great bulk of New York rising into the sky like a city of fairyland, heartening yet sinister, at once a welcome and a menace.

"There you are, my dear?" said Uncle Chris indulgently, as though it were a toy he had made for her with his own hands. "New York!"

They were standing on the boat-deck, leaning over the rail. Jill caught her breath. For the first time since disaster had come upon her she was conscious of a rising of her spirits. It is impossible to behold the huge buildings which fringe the harbour of New York without a sense of expectancy and excitement. There had remained in Jill's mind from childhood memories a vague picture of what she now saw, but it had been feeble and inadequate. The sight of this towering city seemed somehow to blot out everything that had gone before. The feeling of starting afresh was strong upon her.

Uncle Chris, the old traveller, was not emotionally affected. He smoked placidly and talked in a wholly earthy strain of grapefruit and buckwheat cakes.

It was now, also for the first time, that Uncle Chris touched upon future prospects in a practical manner. On the voyage he had been eloquent but sketchy. With the land of promise within biscuit-throw and the tugs bustling about the great liner's skirts like little dogs about their mistress, he descended to details.

"I shall get a room somewhere," said Uncle Chris, "and start looking about me. I wonder if the old Holland House is still there. I fancy I heard they'd pulled it down. Capital place. I had a steak there in the year . . . But I expect they've pulled it down. But I shall find somewhere to go. I'll write and tell you my address directly I've got one."

Jill removed her gaze from the sky-line with a start.

"Write to me?"

"Didn't I tell you about that?" said Uncle Chris cheerily—

avoiding her eye, however, for he had realized all along that it might be a little bit awkward breaking the news. "I've arranged that you shall go and stay for the time being down at Brookport—on Long Island, you know—over in that direction—with your Uncle Elmer. Daresay you've forgotten you have an Uncle Elmer, eh?" he went on quickly, as Jill was about to speak. "Your father's brother. Used to be in business, but retired some years ago and goes in for amateur farming. Corn and—and corn," said Uncle Chris. "All that sort of thing. You'll like him. Capital chap! Never met him myself, but always heard," said Uncle Chris, who had never to his recollection heard any comments upon Mr. Elmer Mariner whatever, "that he was a splendid fellow. Directly we decided to sail, I cabled to him, and got an answer saying that he would be delighted to put you up. You'll be quite happy there."

Jill listened to this programme with dismay. New York was calling to her, and Brookport held out no attractions at all. She looked down over the side at the tugs puffing their way through the broken blocks of ice that reminded her of a cocoanut candy familiar to her childhood.

"But I want to be with you," she protested.

"Impossible, my dear, for the present. I shall be very busy, very busy indeed for some weeks, until I have found my feet. Really, you would be in the way. He—er—travels the fastest who travels alone! I must be in a position to go anywhere and do anything at a moment's notice. But always remember, my dear," said Uncle Chris, patting her shoulder affectionately, "that I shall be working for you. I have treated you very badly, but I intend to make up for it. I shall not forget that whatever money I may make will really belong to you." He looked at her benignly, like a monarch of finance who has earmarked a million or two for the benefit of a deserving charity. "You shall have it all, Jill."

He had so much the air of having conferred a substantial benefit upon her that Jill felt obliged to thank him. Uncle Chris had always been able to make people grateful for the phantom gold which he showered upon them. He was as lavish a man with the money he was going to get next week as ever borrowed a five-pound note to see him through till Saturday.

"What are you going to do, Uncle Chris?" asked Jill curiously. Apart from a nebulous idea that he intended to saunter through the city picking dollar-bills off the sidewalk, she had no inkling of his plans.

Uncle Chris toyed with his short moustache. He was not quite equal to a direct answer on the spur of the moment. He had a faith in his star. Something would turn up. Something always had turned up in the old days, and doubtless, with the march of civilization, opportunities had multiplied. Somewhere behind those tall buildings the Goddess of Luck awaited him, her hands full of gifts, but precisely what those gifts would be he was not in a position to say.

"I shall—ah—how shall I put it——?"

"Look round?" suggested Jill.

"Precisely," said Uncle Chris gratefully. "Look round. I daresay you have noticed that I have gone out of my way during the voyage to make myself agreeable to our fellow-travellers? I had an object. Acquaintances begun on shipboard will often ripen into useful friendships ashore. When I was a young man I never neglected the opportunities which an ocean voyage affords. The offer of a book here, a steamer-rug there, a word of en-couragement to a chatty bore in the smoke-room—these are small things, but they may lead to much. One meets influential people on a liner. You wouldn't think it to look at him, but that man with the eye-glasses and the thin nose I was talking to just now is one of the richest men in Milwaukee!"

"But's it's not much good having rich friends in Milwaukee when you are in New York!"

"Exactly. There you have put your finger on the very point I have been trying to make. It will probably be necessary for me to travel. And for that I must be alone. I must be a mobile force. I should dearly like to keep you with me, but you can see for yourself that for the moment you would be an encumbrance. Later on, no doubt, when my affairs are more settled . . ."

"Oh, I understand. I'm resigned. But, oh dear! it's going to be very dull down at Brookport."

"Nonsense, nonsense! It's a delightful spot."

"Have you been there?"

"No. But of course everybody knows Brookport. Healthy, invigorating . . . Sure to be. The very name . . . You'll be as happy as the days are long!"

"And how long will the days be!"

"Come, come. You mustn't look on the dark side."

"Is there another?" Jill laughed. "You are an old humbug, Uncle Chris. You know perfectly well what you're condemning me to. I expect Brookport will be like a sort of Southend in winter. Oh, well, I'll be brave. But do hurry and make a fortune, because I want to come to New York."

"My dear," said Uncle Chris solemnly, "if there is a dollar lying loose in this city, rest assured that I shall have it! And, if it's not loose, I will detach it with the greatest possible speed. You have only known me in my decadence, an idle and un-profitable London clubman. I can assure you that, lurking beneath the surface, there is a business acumen given to few men . . ."

"Oh, if you are going to talk poetry," said Jill, "I'll leave you. Anyhow, I ought to be getting below and putting my things together."

II

If Jill's vision of Brookport as a wintry Southend was not entirely fulfilled, neither was Uncle Chris' picture of it as an earthly paradise. At the right time of the year, like most of the summer resorts on the south shore of Long Island, it is not without its attractions; but January is not the month which most people would choose for living in it. It presented itself to Jill on first acquaintance in the aspect of a wind-swept railroad station, dumped down far away from human habitation in the middle of a stretch of flat and ragged country that reminded her a little of parts of Surrey. The station was just a shed on a foundation of planks which lay flush with the rails. From this shed, as the train clanked in, there emerged a tall, shambling man in a weather-beaten overcoat. He had a clean-shaven, wrinkled face, and he looked doubtfully at Jill with small eyes. Something in his expression reminded Jill of her father, as a bad caricature of a public man will recall the original. She introduced herself.

"If you're Uncle Elmer," she said, "I'm Jill."

The man held out a long hand. He did not smile He was as bleak as the east wind that swept the platform.

"Glad to meet you again," he said in a melancholy voice. It was news to Jill that they had met before. She wondered where. Her uncle supplied the information. "Last time I saw you, you were a kiddy in short frocks, running round and shouting to beat the band." He looked up and down the platform "I never heard a child make so much noise!"

"I'm quite quiet now," said Jill encouragingly. The recollection of her infant revelry seemed to her to be distressing her relative.

It appeared, however, that it was not only this that was on his mind.

"If you want to drive home," he said, "we'll have to 'phone to the Durham House for a hack." He brooded a while, Jill remaining silent at his side, loath to break in upon whatever secret sorrow he was wrestling with. "That would be a dollar," he went on. "They're robbers in these parts! A dollar! And it's not over a mile and a half. Are you fond of walking?"

Jill was a bright girl, and could take a hint.

"I love walking," she said. She might have added that she preferred to do it on a day when the wind was not blowing quite so keenly from the East, but her uncle's obvious excitement at the prospect of cheating the rapacity of the sharks at the Durham House restrained her. Her independent soul had not quite adjusted itself to the prospect of living on the bounty of her fellows, relatives though they were, and she was desirous of imposing as light a burden upon them as possible. "But how about my trunk?"

"The expressman will bring that up. Fifty cents!" said Uncle Elmer in a crushed way. The high cost of entertaining seemed to be afflicting this man deeply.

"Oh, yes," said Jill. She could not see how this particular expenditure was to be avoided. Anxious as she was to make herself pleasant, she declined to consider carrying the trunk to their destination. "Shall we start, then?"

Mr. Mariner led the way out into the ice-covered road. The wind welcomed them like a boisterous dog. For some minutes they proceeded in silence.

"Your aunt will be glad to see you," said Mr. Mariner at last in the voice with which one announces the death of a dear friend.

"It's awfully kind of you to have me to stay with you," said Jill. It is a human tendency to think, when crises occur, in terms of melodrama, and unconsciously she had begun to regard herself somewhat in the light of a heroine driven out into the world from the old home, with no roof to shelter her head. The promptitude with which these good people, who, though relatives, were after all complete strangers, had offered her a resting-place touched her. "I hope I shan't be in the way."

"Major Selby was speaking to me on the telephone just now," said Mr. Mariner, "and he said that you might be thinking of settling down in Brookport. I've some nice little places round here which you might like to look at. Rent or buy. It's cheaper to buy. Brookport's a growing place. It's getting known as a summer resort. There's a bungalow down on the shore I'd like to show you to-morrow. Stands in a nice large plot of ground, and if you bought it for twelve thousand you'd be getting a bargain."

Jill was too astonished to speak. Plainly Uncle Chris had made no mention of the change in her fortunes, and this man looked on her as a girl of wealth. She could only think how typical this was of Uncle Chris. There was a sort of boyish impishness about him. She could see him at the telephone, suave and important. He would have hung up the receiver with a complacent smirk, thoroughly satisfied that he had done her an excellent turn.

"I put all my money into real estate when I came to live here," went on Mr. Mariner. "I believe in the place. It's growing all the time."

They had come to the outskirts of a straggling village. The lights in the windows gave a welcome suggestion of warmth, for darkness had fallen swiftly during their walk and the chill of the wind had become more biting. There was a smell of salt in the air now, and once or twice Jill had caught the low booming of waves on some distant beach. This was the Atlantic pounding the sandy shore of Fire Island. Brookport itself lay inside, on the lagoon called the Great South Bay.

They passed through the village, bearing to the right, and found themselves in a road bordered by large gardens in which stood big, dark houses. The spectacle of these stimulated Mr. Mariner to something approaching eloquence. He quoted the price paid for each, the price asked, the price offered, the price that had been paid five years ago. The recital carried them on for another mile, in the course of which the houses became smaller and more scattered, and finally, when the country had become bare and desolate again, they turned down a narrow lane and came to a tall, gaunt house standing by itself in a field.

"This is Sandringham," said Mr. Mariner.

"What!" said Jill. "What did you say?"

"Sandringham. Where we live. I got the name from your father. I remember him telling me there was a place called that in England."

"There is." Jill's voice bubbled. "The King lives there."

"Is that so?" said Mr. Mariner. "Well, I bet he doesn't have the trouble with help that we have here. I have to pay our girl fifty dollars a month, and another twenty for the man who looks after the furnace and chops wood. They're all robbers. And if you kick they quit on you!"

III

Jill endured Sandringham for ten days; and, looking back on that period of her life later, she wondered how she did it. The sense of desolation which had gripped her on the station platform increased rather than diminished as she grew accustomed to her surroundings. The east wind died away, and the sun shone fitfully with a suggestion of warmth, but her uncle's bleakness appeared to be a static quality, independent of weather conditions. Her aunt, a faded woman, with a perpetual cold in the head, did nothing to promote cheerfulness. The rest of the household consisted of a gloomy child, "Tibby," aged eight; a spaniel, probably a few years older, and an intermittent cat, who, when he did put in an appearance, was the life and soul of the party, but whose visits to his home were all too infrequent for Jill.

The picture which Mr. Mariner had formed in his mind of Jill as a wealthy young lady with a taste for house property continued as vivid as ever. It was his practice each morning to conduct her about the neighbourhood, introducing her to the various houses in which he had sunk most of the money he had made in business. Mr. Mariner's life centred around Brookport real estate, and the embarrassed Jill was compelled to inspect sitting-rooms, bathrooms, kitchens, and master's bedrooms till the sound of a key turning in a lock gave her a feeling of nervous exhaustion. Most of her uncle's houses were converted farm-houses, and, as one unfortunate purchaser had remarked, not so darned converted at that. The days she spent at Brookport remained in Jill's memory as a smell of dampness and chill and closeness.

"You want to buy," said Mr. Mariner every time he shut a front-door behind them. "Not rent, Buy. Then, if you don't want to live here, you can always rent in the summer."

It seemed incredible to Jill that the summer would ever come. Winter held Brookport in its grip. For the first time in her life she was tasting real loneliness. She wandered over the snow-patched fields down to the frozen bay, and found the intense stillness, punctuated only by the occasional distant gunshot of some optimist trying for duck, oppressive rather than restful. She looked on the weird beauty of the ice-bound marshes which glittered red and green and blue in the sun with unseeing eyes; for her isolation was giving her time to think, and thought was a torment.

On the eighth day came a letter from Uncle Chris—a cheerful, even rollicking letter. Things were going well with Uncle Chris, it seemed. As was his habit, he did not enter into details, but he wrote in a spacious way of large things to be, of affairs that were coming out right, of prosperity in sight. As tangible evidence of success, he enclosed a present of twenty dollars for Jill to spend in the Brookport shops.

The letter arrived by the morning mail, and two hours later Mr. Mariner took Jill by one of his usual overland routes to see a house nearer the village than most of those which she had viewed. Mr. Mariner had exhausted the supply of cottages belonging to himself, and this one was the property of an acquaintance. There would be an agent's fee for him in the deal, if it went through, and Mr. Mariner was not a man who despised money in small quantities.

There was a touch of hopefulness in his gloom this morning, like the first intimation of sunshine after a wet day. He had been thinking the thing over, and had come to the conclusion that Jill's unresponsiveness when confronted with the houses she had already seen was due to the fact that she had loftier ideas than he had supposed. Something a little more magnificent than the twelve thousand dollar places he had shown her was what she desired. This house stood on a hill looking down on the bay, in several acres of ground. It had its private landing-stage and bath-house, its diary, its sleeping-porches—everything, in fact, that a sensible girl could want. Mr. Mariner could not bring himself to suppose that he would fail again to-day.

"They're asking a hundred and five thousand," he said, "but

I know they'd take a hundred thousand. And, if it was a question of cash down, they would go even lower. It's a fine house. You could entertain there. Mrs. Bruggenheim rented it last summer, and wanted to buy, but she wouldn't go above ninety thousand. If you want it, you'd better make up your mind quick. A place like this is apt to be snapped up in a hurry."

Jill could endure it no longer.

"But, you see," she said gently, "all I have in the world is twenty dollars!"

There was a painful pause. Mr. Mariner shot a swift glance at her in the hope of discovering that she had spoken humorously, but was compelled to decide that she had not.

"Twenty dollars!" he exclaimed.

"Twenty dollars," said Jill.

"But your father was a rich man." Mr. Mariner's voice was high and plaintive. "He made a fortune over here before he went to England."

"It's all gone. I got nipped," said Jill, who was finding a certain amount of humour in the situation, "in Amalgamated Dyes."

"Amalgamated Dyes?"

"They're something," explained Jill, "that people get nipped in."

Mr. Mariner digested this.

"You speculated?" he gasped.

"Yes."

"You shouldn't have been allowed to do it," said Mr. Mariner warmly. "Major Selby, your uncle, ought to have known better than to allow you."

"Yes, oughtn't he?" said Jill demurely.

There was another silence, lasting for about a quarter of a mile.

"Well, it's a bad business," said Mr. Mariner.

"Yes," said Jill. "I've felt that myself."

The result of this conversation was to effect a change in the atmosphere of Sandringham. The alteration in the demeanour of people of parsimonious habit, when they discover that the guest they are entertaining is a pauper and not, as they had supposed, an heiress, is subtle but well marked. In most cases, more well marked than subtle. Nothing was actually said, but there are thoughts that are almost as audible as words. A certain suspense seemed to creep into the air, as happens when a situation has been reached which is too poignant to last. Greek Tragedy affects the reader with the same sense of overhanging doom. Things, we feel, cannot go on as they are.

That night, after dinner, Mrs. Mariner asked Jill to read to her.

"Print tries my eyes so, dear," said Mrs. Mariner.

It was a small thing, but it had the significance of that little cloud that arose out of the sea like a man's hand. Jill appreciated the portent. She was, she perceived, to make herself useful.

"Of course I will," she said cordially. "What would you like me to read?"

She hated reading aloud. It always made her throat sore, and her eye skipped to the end of each page and took the interest out of it long before the proper time. But she proceeded bravely, for her conscience was troubling her. Her sympathy was divided equally between these unfortunate people who had been saddled with an undesired visitor and herself who had been placed in a position at which every independent nerve in her rebelled. Even as a child she had loathed being under obligations to strangers or those whom she did not love.

"Thank you, dear," said Mrs. Mariner, when Jill's voice had roughened to a weary croak. "You read so well." She wrestled ineffectually with her handkerchief against the cold in the head from which she had always suffered. "It would be nice if you would do it every night, don't you think? You have no idea how tired print makes my eyes."

On the following morning after breakfast, at the hour when she had hitherto gone house-hunting with Mr. Mariner, the child Tibby, of whom up till now she had seen little except at meals, presented himself to her, coated and shod for the open and regarding her with a dull and phlegmatic gaze.

"Ma says will you please take me for a nice walk!"

Jill's heart sank. She loved children, but Tibby was not an ingratiating child. He was a Mr. Mariner in little. He had the family gloom. It puzzled Jill sometimes why this branch of the family should look on life with so jaundiced an eye. She remembered her father as a cheerful man, alive to the small humours of life.

"All right, Tibby. Where shall we go?"

"Ma says we must keep on the roads and I mustn't slide."

Jill was thoughtful during the walk. Tibby, who was no conversationalist, gave her every opportunity for meditation. She perceived that in the space of a few hours she had sunk in the social scale. If there was any difference between her position and that of a paid nurse and companion it lay in the fact that she was not paid. She looked about her at the grim countryside, gave a thought to the chill gloom of the house to which she was about to return, and her heart sank.

Nearing home, Tibby vouched his first independent observation.

"The hired man's quit!"

"Has he ?"

"Yep. Quit this morning."

It had begun to snow. They turned and made their way back to the house. The information she had received did not cause Jill any great apprehension. It was hardly likely that her new duties would include the stoking of the furnace. That and cooking appeared to be the only acts about the house which were outside her present sphere of usefulness.

"He killed a rat once in the wood-shed with an axe," said Tibby chattily. "Yessir! Chopped it right in half, and it bled!"

"Look at the pretty snow falling on the trees," said Jill faintly.

At breakfast next morning, Mrs. Mariner having sneezed made a suggestion.

"Tibby, darling, wouldn't it be nice if you and cousin Jill played a game of pretending you were pioneers in the Far West ?"

"What's a pioneer ?" enquired Tibby, pausing in the middle of an act of violence on a plate of oatmeal.

"The pioneers were the early settlers in this country, dear. You have read about them in your history book. They endured a great many hardships, for life was very rough for them, with no railroads or anything. I think it would be a nice game to play this morning."

Tibby looked at Jill. There was doubt in his eye. Jill returned his gaze sympathetically. One thought was in both their minds.

"There is a string to this!" said Tibby's eye.

Mrs. Mariner sneezed again.

"You would have lots of fun," she said.

"What'ud we do ?" asked Tibby cautiously. He had been had this way before. Only last summer, on his mother's suggestion that he should pretend he was a shipwrecked sailor on a desert island, he had perspired through a whole afternoon cutting the grass in front of the house to make a shipwrecked sailor's simple bed.

"I know," said Jill. "We'll pretend we're pioneers stormbound in their log cabin in the woods, and the wolves are howling outside, and they daren't go out, so they make a lovely big fire and sit in front of it and read."

"And eat candy," suggested Tibby, warming to the idea.

"And eat candy," agreed Jill.

Mrs. Mariner frowned.

"I was going to suggest," she said frostily, "that you shovelled snow away from the front steps!"

"Splendid!" said Jill. "Oh, but I forgot. I want to go to the village first."

"There will be plenty of time to do it when you get back."

"All right. I'll do it when I get back."

It was a quarter of an hour's walk to the village. Jill stopped at the post-office.

"Could you tell me," she asked, "when the next train is to New York?"

"There's one at ten-ten," said the woman behind the window. "You'll have to hurry."

"I'll hurry!" said Jill.

★ 8 ★

The Dry-Salters Wing Derek

I

DOCTORS, laying down the law in their usual confident way, tell us that the vitality of the human body is at its lowest at two o'clock in the morning: and that it is then, as a consequence, that the mind is least able to contemplate the present with equanimity, the future with fortitude, and the past without regret. Every thinking man, however, knows that this is not so. The true zero hour, desolate, gloom-ridden, and spectre-haunted, occurs immediately before dinner while we are waiting for that cocktail. It is then that, stripped for a brief moment of our armour of complacency and self-esteem, we see ourselves as we are—frightful chumps in a world where nothing goes right; a grey world in which, hoping to click, we merely get the raspberry; where, animated by the best intentions, we nevertheless succeed in perpetrating the scaliest bloomers and landing our loved ones neck-deep in the gumbo.

So reflected Freddie Rooke, that priceless old bean, sitting disconsolately in an arm-chair at the Drones Club about two weeks after Jill's departure from England, waiting for his friend Algy Martyn to trickle in and give him dinner.

Surveying Freddie, as he droops on his spine in the yielding leather, one is conscious of one's limitations as a writer. Gloom like his calls for the pen of a master. Zola could have tackled it nicely. Gorky might have made a stab at it. Dostoievsky would have handled it with relish. But for oneself the thing is too vast. One cannot wangle it. It intimidates. It would have been bad enough in any case, for Algy Martyn was late as usual and it always gave Freddie the pip to have to wait for dinner: but what made it worse was the fact that the Drones was not one of Freddie's clubs and so, until the blighter Algy arrived, it was impossible for him to get his cocktail. There he sat, surrounded by happy, laughing young men, each grasping a glass of the good old mixture-as-before, absolutely unable to connect. Some of them, casual acquaintances, had nodded to him, waved, and gone on lowering the juice, a spectacle which made Freddie feel much as the wounded soldier would have felt if Sir Philip Sidney, instead of offering him the cup of water, had placed it to his own lips and drained it with a careless "Cheerio!" No wonder Freddie experienced the sort of abysmal soul-sadness which afflicts one of Tolstoi's Russian peasants when, after putting in a heavy day's work strangling his father, beating his wife, and dropping the baby into the city reservoir, he turns to the cupboard, only to find the vodka-bottle empty.

Freddie gave himself up to despondency: and, as always in these days when he was mournful, he thought of Jill. Jill's sad case was a continual source of mental anguish to him. From the first he had blamed himself for the breaking-off of her engagement with Derek. If he had not sent the message to Derek from the police-station, the latter would never have known about their arrest, and all would have been well. And now, a few days ago, had come the news of her financial disaster, with its attendant complications.

It had descended on Freddie like a thunderbolt through the medium of Ronny Devereux.

"I say," Ronny had said, "have you heard the latest? Your pal, Underhill, has broken off his engagement with Jill Mariner."

"I know; rather rotten, what!"

"Rotten? I should say so! It isn't done. I mean to say, chap can't chuck a girl just because she's lost her money. Simply isn't on the board, old man!"

"Lost her money? What do you mean?"

Ronny was surprised. Hadn't Freddie heard? Yes, absolute fact. He had it from the best authority. Didn't know how it had happened and all that, but Jill Mariner had gone completely bust; Underhill had given her the miss-in-baulk; and the poor girl had legged it, no one knew where. Oh, Freddie had met her and she had told him she was going to America? Well, then, legged it to America. But the point was that the swine Underhill had handed her the mitten just because she was broke, and that was what Ronny thought so bally rotten. Broker a girl is, Ronny meant to say, more a fellow should stick to her.

"But——" Freddie rushed to his hero's defence. "But it wasn't that at all. Something quite different. I mean, Derek didn't even know Jill had lost her money. He broke the engagement because . . ." Freddie stopped short. He didn't want everybody to know of that rotten arrest business, as they infallibly would if he confided in Ronny Devereux. Sort of thing he would never hear the last of. "He broke it off because of something quite different."

"Oh, yes!" said Ronny sceptically.

"But he did, really!"

Ronny shook his head.

"Don't you believe it, old son. Don't you believe it. Stands to reason it must have been because the poor girl was broke. You wouldn't have done it and I wouldn't have done it, but Underhill did, and that's all there is to it. I mean, a tick's a tick, and there's nothing more to say. Well, I know he's been a pal of yours, Freddie, but, next time I meet him, by Jove, I'll cut him dead. Only I don't know him to speak to, dash it!" concluded Ronny regretfully.

Ronny's news had upset Freddie. Derek had returned to the

Albany a couple of days ago, moody and silent. They had lunched together at the Bachelors, and Freddie had been pained at the attitude of his fellow-clubmen. Usually, when he lunched at the Bachelors, his table became a sort of social centre. Cheery birds would roll up to pass the time of day, and festive old eggs would toddle over to have coffee and so forth, and all that sort of thing. Jolly! On this occasion nobody had rolled, and all the eggs present had taken their coffee elsewhere. There was an uncomfortable chill in the atmosphere of which Freddie had been acutely conscious, though Derek had not appeared to notice it. The thing had only come home to Derek yesterday at the Albany, when the painful episode of Wally Mason had occurred. It was this way. . . .

"Hullo, Freddie, old top! Sorry to have kept you waiting."

Freddie looked up from his broken meditations, to find that his host had arrived.

"Hullo!"

"A quick bracer," said Algy Martyn, "and then the jolly old food-stuffs. It's pretty late, I see. Didn't notice how time was slipping."

Over the soup, Freddie was still a prey to gloom. For once the healing gin-and-vermouth had failed to do its noble work. He sipped sombrely, so sombrely as to cause comment from his host.

"Pipped?" enquired Algy solicitously.

"Pretty pipped," admitted Freddie.

"Backed a loser?"

"No."

"Something wrong with the old tum?"

"No. . . . Worried."

"Worried?"

"About Derek."

"Derek? Who's . . . ? Oh, you mean Underhill?"

"Yes."

Algy Martyn chased an elusive piece of carrot about his soup plate, watching it interestedly as it slid coyly from the spoon.

"Oh?" he said, with sudden coolness. "What about him?"

Freddie was too absorbed in his subject to notice the change in his friend's tone.

"A dashed unpleasant thing," he said, "happened yesterday morning at my place. I was just thinking about going out to lunch, when the door-bell rang and Barker said a chappie of the name of Mason would like to see me. I didn't remember any Mason, but Barker said the chappie said he knew me when I was a kid. So he loosed him into the room, and it turned out to be a fellow I used to know years ago down in Worcestershire. I didn't know him from Adam at first, but gradually the old bean got to work, and I placed him. Wally Mason his name was. Rummily enough, he had spoken to me at the Leicester that night when the fire was, but not being able to place him, I had given him the miss somewhat. You know how it is. Cove you've never been introduced to says something to you in a theatre, and you murmur something and sheer off. What?"

"Absolutely," agreed Algy Martyn. He thoroughly approved of Freddie's code of etiquette. Sheer off. Only thing to do.

"Well, anyhow, now that he had turned up again and told me who he was, I began to remember. We had been kids together, don't you know. (What's this? Salmon? Oh, right ho.) So I buzzed about and did the jovial host, you know; gave him a drink and a toofer, and all that sort of thing; and talked about the dear old days and what not. And so forth, if you follow me. Then he brought the conversation round to Jill. Of course he knew Jill at the same time when he knew me, down in Worcestershire, you see. We were all pretty pally in those days, if you see what I mean. Well, this man Mason, it seems, had heard somewhere about Jill losing her money, and he wanted to know if it was true. I said absolutely. Hadn't heard any details, but Ronny had told me, and Ronny had had it from some one who had stable information and all that sort of thing. 'Dashed shame, isn't it?' I said. 'She's gone to America, you know.' 'I didn't know,' he said. 'I understood she was going to be married quite soon.' Well, of course, I told him that that was off. He didn't say anything for a bit, then he said 'Off?' I said 'Off.' 'Did she break it off?' asked the chappie. 'Well, no,' I said. 'As a matter of fact Derek broke it off.' He said 'Oh!' (What? Oh yes, a bit of pheasant will be fine.) Where was I? Oh, yes. He said 'Oh!' Now, before this, I ought to tell you, this chappie Mason had asked me to come out and have a bit of lunch. I had told him I was lunching with Derek, and he said 'Right ho,' or words to that effect, 'Bring him along.' Derek had been out for a stroll, you see, and we were waiting for him to come in. Well, just at this point or juncture, if you know what I mean, in he

came, and I said 'Oh, what ho!' and introduced Wally Mason.
'Oh, do you know Underhill?' I said, or something like that.
You know the sort of thing. And then . . ."

Freddie broke off and drained his glass. The recollection of
that painful moment had made him feverish. Social difficulties
always did.

"Then what?" enquired Algy Martyn.

"Well, it was pretty rotten. Derek held out his hand, as a
chappie naturally would, being introduced to a strange chappie,
and Wally Mason, giving it an absolute miss, went on talking to
me just as if we were alone, you know. Look here. Here was I,
where this knife is. Derek over here—this fork—with his hand
out. Mason here—this bit of bread. Mason looks at his watch,
and says 'I'm sorry, Freddie, but I find I've an engagement for
lunch. So long!' and biffed out, without apparently knowing
that Derek was on the earth. I mean . . ." Freddie reached for
his glass. "What I mean is, it was dashed embarrassing. I mean,
cutting a fellow dead in my rooms. I don't know when I've felt
so rotten!"

Algy Martyn delivered judgment with great firmness.

"Chappie was perfectly right!"

"No, but I mean . . ."

"Absolutely correct-o," insisted Algy sternly. "Underhill can't
dash about all over the place giving the girl he's engaged to the
mitten because she's broke, and expect no notice to be taken of
it. If you want to know what I think, old man, your pal Underhill
—I can't imagine what the deuce you see in him, but, school
together and so forth, makes a difference, I suppose—I say, if
you want to know what I think, Freddie, the blighter Underhill
would be well advised either to leg it after Jill and get her to
marry him or else lie low for a goodish while till people have
forgotten the thing. I mean to say, fellows like Ronny and I and
Dick Wimpole and Archie Studd and the rest of our lot—well,
we all knew Jill and thought she was a topper and had danced
with her here and there and seen her about and all that, and
naturally we feel pretty strongly about the whole dashed business.
Underhill isn't in our particular set, but we all know most of the
people he knows, and we talk about this business, and the thing
gets about, and there you are! My sister, who was a great pal of
Jill's, swears that all the girls she knows mean to cut Underhill.
I tell you, Freddie, London's going to get pretty hot for him if

he doesn't do something dashed quick and with great rapidity!"

"But you haven't got the story right, old thing!"

"How not?"

"Well, I mean you think and Ronny thinks and all the rest of you think that Derek broke off the engagement because of the money. It wasn't that at all."

"What was it, then?"

"Well . . . Well, look here, it makes me seem a fearful ass and all that, but I'd better tell you. Jill and I were going down one of those streets near Victoria and a blighter was trying to slay a parrot . . ."

"Parrot-shooting's pretty good in those parts, they tell me," interjected Algy satirically.

"Don't interrupt, old man. This parrot had got out of one of the houses, and a fellow was jabbing at it with a stick, and Jill—you know what she's like; impulsive, I mean, and all that—Jill got hold of the stick and biffed him with some vim, and a policeman rolled up and the fellow made a fuss and the policeman took Jill and me off to chokey. Well, like an ass, I sent round to Derek to bail us out, and that's how he heard of the thing. Apparently he didn't think a lot of it, and the result was that he broke off the engagement."

Algy Martyn has listened to this recital with growing amazement.

"He broke it off because of that?"

"Yes."

"What absolute rot!" said Algy Martyn. "I don't believe a word of it!"

"I say, old man!"

"I don't believe a word of it," repeated Algy firmly. "And nobody else will either. It's dashed good of you, Freddie, to cook up a yarn like that to try and make things look better for the blighter, but it won't work. Such a damn silly story, too!" said Algy with some indignation.

"But it's true!"

"What's the use, Freddie, between old pals?" said Algy protestingly. "You know perfectly well that Underhill's a worm of the most pronounced order, and that, when he found out that Jill hadn't any money, he chucked her."

"But why should Derek care whether Jill was well off or not? He's got enough money of his own."

"Nobody," said Algy judicially, "has got enough money of his own. Underhill thought he was marrying a girl with a sizeable chunk of the ready, and, when the fuse blew out, he decided it wasn't good enough. For Heaven's sake don't let's talk any more about the blighter. It gives me a pain to think of him."

II

Freddie returned to the Albany in a state of gloom and un-easiness. Algy's remarks, coming on top of the Wally Mason episode, had shaken him. The London in which he and Derek moved and had their being is nothing but a village, and it was evident that village gossip was hostile to Derek. People were talking about him. Local opinion had decided that he had behaved badly. Already one man had cut him. Freddie blenched at a sudden vision of streetfuls of men, long Piccadillys of men, all cutting him, one after the other. Something had got to be done.

The subject was not an easy one to broach to his somewhat forbidding friend, as he discovered when the latter arrived about half an hour later. Derek had been attending the semi-annual banquet of the Worshipful Dry-Salters Company down in the City, understudying one of the speakers, a leading member of Parliament, who had been unable to appear; and he was still in the grip of that feeling of degraded repletion which City dinners induce.

Yet, unfavourably disposed as, judging by his silence and the occasional moody grunts he uttered, he appeared to be to a discussion of his private affairs, it seemed to Freddie impossible that the night should be allowed to pass without some word spoken of the subject. He thought of Ronny and what Ronny had said, of Algy and what Algy had said, of Wally Mason and how Wally had behaved in this very room; and he nerved himself to the task.

"Derek, old top."

A grunt.

"I say, Derek, old bean."

Derek roused himself, and looked gloomily across the room to where he stood, warming his legs at the blaze.

"Well?"

Freddie found a difficulty in selecting words. A ticklish

business, this. One that might well have disconcerted a diplomat.
Freddie was no diplomat, and the fact enabled him to find a way
in the present crisis. Equipped by nature with an amiable
tactlessness and a happy gift of blundering, he charged straight
at the main point, and landed on it like a circus elephant alighting
on a bottle.

"I say, you know, about Jill!"

He stooped to rub the backs of his legs, on which the fire was
playing with a little too fierce a glow, and missed his companion's
start and the sudden thickening of his bushy eyebrows.

"Well?" said Derek again.

Freddie nerved himself to proceed. A thought flashed across
his mind that Derek was looking exactly like Lady Underhill.
It was the first time he had seen the family resemblance quite so
marked.

"Ronny Devereux was saying . . ." faltered Freddie.

"Damn Ronny Devereux!"

"Oh, absolutely! But . . ."

"Ronny Devereux! Who the devil *is* Ronny Devereux?"

"Why, old man, you've heard me speak of him, haven't you?
Pal of mine. He came down to the station with Algy and me to
meet your mater that morning."

"Oh, *that* fellow? And he has been saying something
about . . .?"

"It isn't only Ronny, you know," Freddie hastened to interject.
"Algy Martyn's talking about it, too. And lots of other fellows.
And Algy's sister and a lot of people. They're all saying . . ."

"What are they saying?"

Freddie bent down and chafed the back of his legs. He simply
couldn't look at Derek while he had that Lady Underhill
expression on the old map. Rummy he had never noticed before
how extraordinarily like his mother he was. Freddie was conscious
of a faint sense of grievance. He could not have put it into words,
but what he felt was that a fellow had no right to go about looking
like Lady Underhill.

"What are they saying?" repeated Derek grimly.

"Well . . ." Freddie hesitated. "That it's a bit tough . . .
On Jill, you know."

"They think I behaved badly?"

"Well . . . Oh, well, you know!"

Derek smiled a ghastly smile. This was not wholly due to

mental disturbance. The dull heaviness which was the legacy of the Dry-Salters' dinner had begun to change to something more actively unpleasant. A sub-motive of sharp pain had begun to run through it, flashing in and out like lightning through a thunder-cloud. He felt sullen and vicious.

"I wonder," he said with savage politeness, "if, when you chat with your friends, you would mind choosing some other topic than my private affairs."

"Sorry, old man. But they started it, you know."

"And, if you feel you've got to discuss me, kindly keep it to yourself. Don't come and tell me what your damned friends said to each other and to you and what you said to them, because it bores me. I'm not interested. I don't value their opinions as much as you seem to." Derek paused, to battle in silence with the imperious agony within him. "It was good of you to put me up here," he went on, "but I think I won't trespass on your hospitality any longer. Perhaps you'll ask Barker to pack my things to-morrow." Derek moved, as majestically as an ex-guest of the Worshipful Company of Dry-Salters may, in the direction of the door. "I shall go to the Savoy."

"Oh, I say, old man! No need to do that."

"Good night."

"But, I say . . ."

"And you can tell your friend Devereux that, if he doesn't stop poking his nose into my private business, I'll pull it off."

"Well," said Freddie doubtfully, "of course I don't suppose you know, but . . . Ronny's a pretty hefty bird. He boxed for Cambridge in the light-weights the last year he was up, you know. He . . ."

Derek slammed the door. Freddie was alone. He stood rubbing his legs for some minutes, a rueful expression on his usually cheerful face. Freddie hated rows. He liked everything to jog along smoothly. What a rotten place the world was these days! Just one thing after another. First, poor old Jill takes the knock and disappears. He would miss her badly. What a good sort! What a pal! And now—gone. Biffed off. Next, Derek. Together, more or less, ever since Winchester, and now—bing! . . .

Freddie heaved a sigh, and reached out for the *Sporting Times*, his never-failing comfort in times of depression. He lit another cigar and curled up in one of the arm-chairs. He was feeling tired. He had been playing squash all the afternoon, a game at

which he was exceedingly expert and to which he was much
addicted.

Time passed. The paper slipped to the floor. A cold cigar
followed it. From the depths of the chair came a faint snore . . .

A hand on his shoulder brought Freddie with a jerk from
troubled dreams. Derek was standing beside him. A bent,
tousled Derek, apparently in pain.

"Freddie!"

"Hullo!"

A spasm twisted Derek's face.

"Have you got any pepsin?"

Derek uttered a groan. What a mocker of our petty human
dignity is this dyspepsia, bringing low the haughtiest of us, less
than love itself a respecter of persons. This was a different
Derek from the man who had stalked stiffly from the room two
hours before. His pride had been humbled upon the rack.

"Pepsin?"

"Yes. I've got the most damned attack of indigestion."

The mists of sleep rolled away from Freddie. He was awake
again, and became immediately helpful. These were the occasions
when the Last of the Rookes was a good man to have at your side.
It was Freddie who suggested that Derek should recline in the
arm-chair which he had vacated; Freddie who nipped round the
corner to the all-night chemist's and returned with a magic
bottle guaranteed to relieve an ostrich after a surfeit of tenpenny
nails; Freddie who mixed and administered the dose.

His ministrations were rewarded. Presently the agony seemed
to pass. Derek recovered.

One would say that Derek became himself again, but that
the mood of gentle remorse which came upon him as he lay in
the arm-chair was one so foreign to his nature. Freddie had
never seen him so subdued. He was like a convalescent child.
Between them, the all-night chemist and the Dry-Salters seemed
to have wrought a sort of miracle. These temporary softenings of
personality frequently follow City dinners. The time to catch
your Dry-Salter in angelic mood is the day after the semi-annual
banquet. Go to him then and he will give you his watch and
chain.

"Freddie," said Derek.

They were sitting over the dying fire. The clock on the
mantelpiece, beside which Jill's photograph had stood, pointed

to ten minutes past two. Derek spoke in a low, soft voice. Perhaps
the doctors are right after all, and two o'clock is the hour at which
our self-esteem deserts us, leaving in its place regret for past
sins, good resolutions for future behaviour.

"What do Martyn and the others say about . . . you know?"
Freddie hesitated. Pity to start all that again.

"Oh, I know," went on Derek. "They say I behaved like a cad."

"Oh, well . . ."

"They are quite right. I did."

"Oh, I shouldn't say that, you know. Faults on both sides
and all that sort of rot."

"I did!" Derek stared into the fire. Scattered all over London
at the moment, probably a hundred Worshipful Dry-Salters
were equally sleepless and subdued, looking wide-eyed into
black pasts. "Is it true she has gone to America, Freddie?"

"She told me she was going."

"What a fool I've been!"

The clock ticked on through the silence. The fire sputtered
faintly, then gave a little wheeze, like a very old man. Derek
rested his chin on his hands, gazing into the ashes.

"I wish to God I could go over there and find her."

"Why don't you?"

"How can I? There may be an election coming on at any
moment. I can't stir."

Freddie leaped from his seat. The suddenness of the action
sent a red-hot corkscrew of pain through Derek's head.

"What the devil's the matter?" he demanded irritably. Even
the gentle mood which comes with convalescence after a City
dinner is not guaranteed to endure against this sort of thing.

"I've got an idea, old bean!"

"Well, there's no need to dance, is there?"

"I've nothing to keep me here, you know. What's the matter
with my popping over to America and finding Jill?" Freddie
tramped the floor, aglow. Each beat of his foot jarred Derek, but
he made no complaint.

"Could you?" he asked eagerly.

"Of course I could. I was saying only the other day that I
had half a mind to buzz over. It's a wheeze! I'll get on the next
boat and charge over in the capacity of a jolly old ambassador.
Have her back in no time. Leave it to me, old thing! This is
where I come out strong!"

★ 9 ★

Jill in Search of an Uncle

I

NEW YORK welcomed Jill, as she came out of the Pennsylvania Station in Seventh Avenue, with a whirl of powdered snow that touched her cheek like a kiss, the cold, bracing kiss one would expect from this vivid city. She stood at the station entrance, a tiny figure beside the huge pillars, looking round her with eager eyes. A wind was whipping down the avenue. The sky was a clear, brilliant tint of the brightest blue. Energy was in the air, and hopefulness. She wondered if Mr. Elmer Mariner ever came to New York. It was hard to see how even his gloom would contrive to remain unaffected by the exhilaration of the place.

She took Uncle Chris' letter from her bag. He had written from an address on East Fifty-seventh Street. There would be just time to catch him before he went out to lunch. She hailed a taxi-cab which was coming out of the station.

It was a slow ride, halted repeatedly by congestion of the traffic, but a short one for Jill. She was surprised at herself, a Londoner of long standing, for feeling so provincial and being so impressed. But London was far away. It belonged to a life that seemed years ago and a world from which she had parted for ever. Moreover, this was undeniably a stupendous city through which her taxi-cab was carrying her. At Times Square the stream of the traffic plunged into a whirlpool, swinging out of Broadway to meet the rapids which poured in from east, west and north. On Fifth Avenue all the motor-cars in the world were gathered together. On the pavements, pedestrians, muffled against the nipping chill of the crisp air, hurried to and fro. And, above, that sapphire sky spread a rich velvet curtain which made the tops of the buildings stand out like the white minarets of some eastern city of romance.

The cab drew up in front of a stone apartment house; and Jill, getting out, passed under an awning through a sort of mediæval courtyard, gay with potted shrubs, to an inner door. She was impressed. Evidently the tales one heard of fortunes accumulated overnight in this magic city were true, and one of them must have fallen to the lot of Uncle Chris. For nobody to whom money was a concern could possibly afford to live in a place like this. If Crœsus and the Count of Monte Cristo had applied for lodging there, the authorities would probably have looked on them a little doubtfully at first and hinted at the desirability of a month's rent in advance.

In the glass case behind the inner door, reading a newspaper and chewing gum, sat a dignified old man in the rich uniform of a general in the Guatemalan army. He was a brilliant spectacle. He wore no jewellery, but this, no doubt, was due to a private distaste for display. As there was no one else of humbler rank at hand from whom Jill could solicit an introduction and the privilege of an audience, she took the bold step of addressing him directly.

"I want to see Major Selby, please."

The Guatemalan general arrested for a moment the rhythmic action of his jaws, lowered his paper and looked at her with raised eyebrows. At first Jill thought that he was registering haughty contempt, then she saw what she had taken for scorn was surprise.

"Major Selby?"

"Major Selby."

"No Major Selby living here."

"Major Christopher Selby."

"Not here," said the associate of ambassadors and the pampered pet of Guatemala's proudest beauties. "Never heard of him in my life!"

II

Jill had read works of fiction in which at certain crises everything had "seemed to swim" in front of the heroine's eyes, but never till this moment had she experienced that remarkable sensation herself. The Saviour of Guatemala did not actually swim, perhaps, but he certainly flickered. She had to blink to restore his prismatic outlines to their proper sharpness. Already the bustle and noise of New York had begun to induce in her that dizzy condition of unreality which one feels in dreams, and this extraordinary statement added the finishing touch.

Perhaps the fact that she had said "please" to him when she

opened the conversation touched the heart of the hero of a thousand revolutions. Dignified and beautiful as he was to the eye of the stranger, it is unpleasant to have to record that he lived in a world which rather neglected the minor courtesies of speech. People did not often say "please" to him. "Here!" "Hi!" and "Gosh darn you!" yes; but seldom "please." He seemed to approve of Jill, for he shifted his chewing-gum to a position which facilitated speech, and began to be helpful.

"What was the name again?"

"Selby."

"Howja spell it?"

"S-e-l-b-y."

"S-e-l-b-y." Oh, Selby?"

"Yes, Selby."

"What was the first name?"

"Christopher."

"Christopher?"

"Yes, Christopher."

"Christopher Selby? No one of that name living here."

"But there must be."

The veteran shook his head with an indulgent smile.

"You want Mr. Sipperley," he said tolerantly. In Guatemala these mistakes are always happening. "Mr. George Sipperley. He's on the fourth floor. What name shall I say?"

He had almost reached the telephone when Jill stopped him. This is an age of just-as-good substitutes, but she refused to accept any unknown Sipperley as a satisfactory alternative for Uncle Chris.

"I don't want Mr. Sipperley. I want Major Selby."

"Howja spell it once more?"

"S-e-l-b-y."

"S-e-l-b-y. No one of that name living here. Mr. Sipperley"—— he spoke in a wheedling voice, as if determined, in spite of herself, to make Jill see what was in her best interests—"Mr. Sipperley's on the fourth floor. Gentleman in the real estate business," he added insinuatingly. "He's got blond hair and a Boston bull-dog."

"He may be all you say, and he may have a dozen bulldogs..."

"Only one. Jack his name is."

". . . But he isn't the right man. It's absurd. Major Selby wrote to me from this address. This *is* Eighteen East Fifty-seventh Street?"

"This is Eighteen East Fifty-seventh Street," conceded the other cautiously.

"I've got his letter here." She opened her bag, and gave an exclamation of dismay. "It's gone!"

"Mr. Sipperley used to have a friend staying with him last Fall. A Mr. Robertson. Dark-complexioned man with a moustache."

"I took it out to look at the address, and I was sure I put it back. I must have dropped it."

"There's a Mr. Rainsby on the seventh floor. He's a broker down on Wall Street. Short man with an impediment in his speech."

Jill snapped the clasp of her bag.

"Never mind," she said. "I must have made a mistake. I was quite sure that this was the address, but it evidently isn't. Thank you so much. I'm so sorry to have bothered you."

She walked away, leaving the Terror of Paraguay and all points west speechless: for people who said "Thank you so much" to him were even rarer than those who said "please." He followed her with an affectionate eye till she was out of sight, then, restoring his chewing-gum to circulation, returned to the perusal of his paper. A momentary suggestion presented itself to his mind that what Jill had really wanted was Mr. Willoughby on the eighth floor, but it was too late to say so now; and soon, becoming absorbed in the narrative of a spirited householder in Kansas who had run amuck with a hatchet and slain six, he dismissed the matter from his mind.

III

Jill walked back to Fifth Avenue, crossed it, and made her way thoughtfully along the breezy street which, flanked on one side by the Park and on the other by the green-roofed Plaza Hotel and the apartment houses of the wealthy, ends in the humbler and more democratic spaces of Columbus Circle. She perceived that she was in that position, familiar to melodrama, of being alone in a great city. The reflection brought with it a certain discomfort. The bag that dangled from her wrist contained all the money she had in the world, the very broken remains of the twenty dollars which Uncle Chris had sent her at Brookport. She had nowhere to go, nowhere to sleep, and no immediately

obvious means of adding to her capital. It was a situation which
she had not foreseen when she set out to walk to Brookport
station.

She pondered over the mystery of Uncle Chris' disappearance,
and found no solution. The thing was inexplicable. She was as
sure of the address he had given in his letter as she was of
anything in the world. Yet at that address nothing had been
heard of him. His name was not even known. These were deeper
waters than Jill was able to fathom.

She walked on aimlessly. Presently she came to Columbus
Circle, and, crossing Broadway at the point where that street
breaks out into an eruption of automobile shops, found herself,
suddenly hungry, opposite a restaurant whose entire front was
a sheet of plate glass. On the other side of this glass, at marble-
topped tables, apparently careless of their total lack of privacy,
sat the impecunious, lunching, their every mouthful a spectacle
for the passer-by. It reminded Jill of looking at fishes in an
aquarium. In the centre of the window, gazing out in a distrait
manner over piles of apples and grape-fruit, a white-robed
ministrant at a stove juggled ceaselessly with buckwheat cakes.
He struck the final note in the candidness of the establishment,
a priest whose ritual contained no mysteries. Spectators with
sufficient time on their hands to permit them to stand and watch
were enabled to witness a New York midday meal in every stage
of its career, from its protoplasmic beginnings as a stream of
yellowish-white liquid poured on top of the stove to its ultimate
Nirvana in the interior of the luncher in the form of an appetising
cake. It was a spectacle which no hungry girl could resist. Jill
went in, and, as she made her way among the tables, a voice
spoke her name.

"Miss Mariner!"

Jill jumped, and thought for a moment that the thing must
have been an hallucination. It was impossible that anybody in
the place should have called her name. Except for Uncle Chris,
wherever he might be, she knew no one in New York. Then the
voice spoke again, competing valiantly with a clatter of crockery
so uproarious as to be more like something solid than a mere
sound.

"I couldn't believe it was you!"

A girl in blue had risen from the nearest table, and was staring
at her in astonishment. Jill recognized her instantly. Those big,

pathetic eyes, like a lost child's, were unmistakable. It was the parrot girl, the girl whom she and Freddie Rooke had found in the drawing-room at Ovingdon Square that afternoon when the foundations of the world had given way and chaos had begun.

"Good gracious!" cried Jill. "I thought you were in London!"

That feeling of emptiness and panic, the result of her interview with the Guatemalan general at the apartment house, vanished magically. She sat down at this unexpected friend's table with a light heart.

"Whatever are you doing in New York?" asked the girl. "I never knew you meant to come over."

"It was a little sudden. Still, here I am. And I'm starving. What are those things you're eating?"

"Buckwheat cakes."

"Oh, yes. I remember Uncle Chris talking about them on the boat. I'll have some."

"But when did you come over?"

"I landed about ten days ago. I've been down at a place called Brookport on Long Island. How funny running into you like this!"

"I was surprised that you remembered me."

"I've forgotten your name," admitted Jill frankly. "But that's nothing. I always forget names."

"My name's Nelly Bryant."

"Of course. And you're on the stage, aren't you?"

"Yes. I've just got work with Goble and Cohn. . . . Hullo, Phil!"

A young man with a lithe figure and smooth black hair brushed straight back from his forehead had paused at the table on his way to the cashier's desk.

"Hello, Nelly."

"I didn't know you lunched here."

"Don't often. Been rehearsing with Joe up at the Century Roof, and had a quarter of an hour to get a bite. Can I sit down."

"Sure? This is my friend, Miss Mariner."

The young man shook hands with Jill, flashing an approving glance at her out of his dark, restless eyes.

"Pleased to meet you."

"This is Phil Brown," said Nelly. "He plays the straight for

Joe Widgeon. They're the best jazz-and-hokum team on the Keith Circuit."

"Oh, hush!" said Mr. Brown modestly. "You always were a great little booster, Nelly."

"Well, you know you are! Weren't you held over at the Palace last time? Well, then!"

"That's true," admitted the young man. "Maybe we didn't gool 'em, eh? Stop me on the street and ask me! Only eighteen bows second house Saturday!"

Jill was listening, fascinated.

"I can't understand a word," she said. "It's like another language."

"You're from the other side, aren't you?" asked Mr. Brown.

"She only landed a week ago," said Nelly.

"I thought so from the accent," said Mr. Brown. "So our talk sort of goes over the top, does it? Well, you'll learn American soon, if you stick around."

"I've learned some already," said Jill. The relief of meeting Nelly had made her feel very happy. She liked this smooth-haired young man. "A man on the train this morning said to me, 'Would you care for the morning paper, sister?' I said, 'No, thanks, brother, I want to look out of the window and think!'"

"You meet a lot of fresh guys on trains," commented Mr. Brown austerely. "You want to give 'em the cold-storage eye." He turned to Nelly. "Did you go down to Ike, as I told you?"

"Yes."

"Did you cop?"

"Yes. I never felt so happy in my life. I'd waited over an hour on that landing of theirs, and then Johnny Miller came along, and I yelled in his ear that I was after work, and he told me it would be all right. He's awfully good to girls who've worked in shows for him before. If it hadn't been for him I might have been waiting there still."

"Who," enquired Jill, anxious to be abreast of the conversation, "is Ike?"

"Mr. Goble. Where I've just got work. Goble and Cohn, you know."

"I never heard of them!"

The young man extended his hand.

"Put it there!" he said. "They never heard of me! At least,

the fellow I saw when I went down to the office hadn't! Can you beat it!"

"Oh, did you go down there, too?" asked Nelly.

"Sure. Joe wanted to get in another show on Broadway. He'd sort of got tired of vodevil. Say, I don't want to scare you, Nelly, but, if you ask me, that show they're putting out down there is a citron! I don't think Ike's got a cent of his own money in it. My belief is that he's running it for a lot of amateurs. Why, say, listen! Joe and I blow in there to see if there's anything for us, and there's a tall guy in tortoiseshell cheaters sitting in Ike's office. Said he was the author and was engaging the principals. We told him who we were, and it didn't make any hit with him at all. He said he had never heard of us. And, when we explained, he said no, there wasn't going to be any of our sort of work in the show. Said he was making an effort to give the public something rather better than the usual sort of thing. No specialities required. He said it was an effort to restore the Gilbert and Sullivan tradition. Say, who are these Gilbert and Sullivan guys, anyway? They get written up in the papers all the time and I never met any one who'd run across them. If you want my opinion, that show down there is a comic opera!"

"For heaven's sake!" Nelly had the musical comedy performer's horror of the older-established form of entertainment. "Why, comic opera died in the year one!"

"Well, these guys are going to dig it up. That's the way it looks to me." He lowered his voice. "Say, I saw Clarice last night," he said in a confidential undertone. "It's all right."

"It is?"

"We've made it up. It was like this . . ."

His conversation took an intimate turn. He expounded for Nelly's benefit the inner history, with all its ramifications, of a recent unfortunate rift between himself and "the best little girl in Flatbush"—what he had said, what she had said, what her sister had said, and how it all came right in the end. Jill might have felt a little excluded, but for the fact that a sudden and exciting idea had come to her. She sat back, thinking. . . . After all, what else was she to do? She must do something. . . .

She bent forward and interrupted Mr. Brown in his description of a brisk passage of arms between himself and the best little girl's sister, who seemed to be an unpleasant sort of person in every way.

"Mr. Brown."

"Hello?"

"Do you think there would be any chance for me if I asked for work at Goble and Cohn's?"

"You're joking!" cried Nelly.

"I'm not at all."

"But what do you want with work?"

"I've got to find some. And right away, too."

"I don't understand."

Jill hesitated. She disliked discussing her private affairs, but there was obviously no way of avoiding it. Nelly was round-eyed and mystified, and Mr. Brown had manifestly no intention whatever of withdrawing tactfully. He wanted to hear all.

"I've lost my money," said Jill.

"Lost your money! Do you mean . . . ?"

"I've lost it all. Every penny I had in the world."

"Tough!" interpolated Mr. Brown judicially. "I was broke once way out in a tank-town in Oklahoma. The manager skipped with our salaries. Last we saw of him he was doing the trip to Canada in nothing flat."

"But how?" gasped Nelly.

"It happened about the time we met in London. Do you remember Freddie Rooke, who was at our house that afternoon?"

A dreamy look came into Nelly's eyes. There had not been an hour since their parting when she had not thought of that immaculate sportsman. It would have amazed Freddie, could he have known, but to Nelly Bryant he was the one perfect man in an imperfect world.

"Do I!" she sighed ecstatically.

Mr. Brown shot a keen glance at her.

"Aha!" he cried facetiously. "Who is he, Nelly? Who is this blue-eyed boy?"

"If you want to know," said Nelly, defiance in her tone, "he's the fellow who gave me fifty pounds, with no strings tied to it—get that!—when I was broke in London! If it hadn't been for him, I'd be there still."

"Did he?" cried Jill, "Freddie!"

"Yes. Oh, Gee!" Nelly sighed once more. "I suppose I'll never see him again in this world."

"Introduce me to him, if you do," said Mr. Brown. "He sounds just the sort of little pal I'd like to have!"

"You remember hearing Freddie say something about losing money in a slump on the Stock Exchange," proceeded Jill. "Well, that was how I lost mine. It's a long story, and it's not worth talking about, but that's how things stand, and I've got to find work of some sort, and it looks to me as if I should have a better chance of finding it on the stage than anywhere else."

"I'm terribly sorry."

"Oh, it's all right. How much would these people Goble and Cohn give me if I got an engagement?"

"Only forty a week."

"Forty dollars a week! It's wealth! Where are they?"

"Over at the Gotham Theatre in Forty-second Street."

"I'll go there at once."

"But you'll hate it. You don't realize what it's like. You wait hours and hours and nobody sees you."

"Why shouldn't I walk straight in and say that I've come for work?"

Nelly's big eyes grew bigger.

"But you couldn't!"

"Why not?"

"Why, you couldn't!"

"I don't see why."

Mr. Brown intervened with decision.

"You're dead right," he said to Jill approvingly. "If you ask me, that's the only sensible thing to do. Where's the sense of hanging around and getting stalled? Managers are human guys, some of 'em. Probably, if you were to try it, they'd appreciate a bit of gall. It would show 'em you'd got pep. You go down there and try walking straight in. They can't eat you. It makes me sick when I see all those poor devils hanging about outside these offices, waiting to got noticed and nobody ever paying any attention to them. You push the office-boy in the face if he tries to stop you, and go in and make 'em take notice. And, whatever you do, don't leave your name and address! That's the old, motheaten gag they're sure to try to pull on you. Tell 'em there's nothing doing. Say you're out for a quick decision! Stand 'em on their heads!"

Jill got up, fired by this eloquence. She called for her check.

"Good-bye," she said. "I'm going to do exactly as you say. Where can I find you afterwards?" she said to Nelly.

"You aren't really going?"

"I am!"

Nelly scribbled on a piece of paper.

"Here's my address. I'll be in all evening."

"I'll come and see you. Good-bye, Mr. Brown. And thank you."

"You're welcome!" said Mr. Brown.

Nelly watched Jill depart with wide eyes.

"Why did you tell her to do that?" she said.

"Why not?" said Mr. Brown. "I started something didn't I? Well, I guess I'll have to be leaving, too. Got to get back to rehearsal. Say, I like that friend of yours, Nelly. There's no yellow streak about her! I wish her luck!"

* 10 *

Jill Ignores Authority

I

THE offices of Messrs. Goble and Cohn were situated, like everything else in New York that appertains to the drama, in the neighbourhood of Times Square. They occupied the fifth floor of the Gotham Theatre on West Forty-second Street. As there was no lift in the building except the small private one used by the two members of the firm, Jill walked up the stairs, and found signs of a thriving business beginning to present themselves as early as the third floor, where half a dozen patient persons of either sex had draped themselves like roosting fowls upon the banisters. There were more on the fourth floor, and the landing of the fifth, which served the firm as a waiting-room, was quite full. It is the custom of New York theatrical managers—the lowest order of intelligence, with the possible exception of the *limax maximus* or garden slug, known to science—to omit from the calculations the fact that they are likely every day to receive a large number of visitors, whom they will be obliged to keep waiting; and that these people will require somewhere to wait. Such considerations never occur to them. Messrs. Goble and Cohn had provided for those who called to see them one small bench on the landing, conveniently situated at the intersecting point of three draughts, and had let it go at that.

Nobody, except perhaps the night-watchman, had ever seen this bench empty. At whatever hour of the day you happened to call, you would always find three wistful individuals seated side by side with their eyes on the tiny ante-room where sat the office-boy, the telephone-girl, and Mr. Goble's stenographer. Beyond this was the door marked "Private," through which, as it opened to admit some careless, debonair thousand-dollar-a-week comedian who sauntered in with a jaunty "Hello, Ike!" or some furred and scented female star, the rank and file of the profession were greeted, like Moses on Pisgah, with a fleeting glimpse of the promised land, consisting of a large desk and a section of a very fat man with spectacles and a bald head or a younger man with fair hair and a double chin.

The keynote of the mass meeting on the landing was one of determined, almost aggressive smartness. The men wore bright overcoats with bands round the waist, the women those imitation furs which to the uninitiated eye appear so much more expensive than the real thing. Everybody looked very dashing and very young, except about the eyes. Most of the eyes that glanced at Jill were weary. The women were nearly all blondes, blondness having been decided upon in the theatre as the colour that brings the best results. The men were all so much alike that they seemed to be members of one large family—an illusion which was heightened by the scraps of conversation, studded with "dears," "old mans," and "honeys," which came to Jill's ears. A stern fight for supremacy was being waged by a score or so of lively and powerful young scents.

For a moment Jill was somewhat daunted by the spectacle, but she recovered almost immediately. The exhilarating and heady influence of New York still wrought within her. The Berserk spirit was upon her, and she remembered the stimulating words of Mr. Brown, of Brown and Widgeon, the best jazz-and-hokum team on the Keith Circuit. "Walk straight in!" had been the burden of his inspiring address. She pushed her way through the crowd until she came to the small ante-room.

In the ante-room were the outposts, the pickets of the enemy. In one corner a girl was hammering energetically and with great speed on a typewriter; a second girl, seated at a switchboard, was having an argument with Central which was already warm and threatened to descend shortly to personalities; on a chair tilted back so that it rested against the wall, a small boy sat eating sweets and reading the comic page of an evening newspaper. All three were enclosed, like zoological specimens, in a cage formed by a high counter terminating in brass bars.

Beyond these watchers on the threshold was the door marked "Private." Through it, as Jill reached the outer defences, filtered the sound of a piano.

Those who have studied the subject have come to the conclusion that the boorishness of New York theatrical managers' office-boys cannot be the product of mere chance. Somewhere, in some sinister den in the criminal districts of the town, there is a school where small boys are trained for these positions, where their finer instincts are rigorously uprooted and rudeness systematically inculcated by competent professors. Of this school the Cerberus of Messrs. Goble and Cohn had been the star scholar. Quickly seeing his natural gifts, his teachers had given him special attention. When he had graduated, it had been amidst the cordial good wishes of the entire staff. They had taught him all they knew, and they were proud of him. They felt that he would do them credit.

This boy raised a pair of pink-rimmed eyes to Jill, sniffed, bit his thumb-nail, and spoke. He was a snub-nosed boy. His ears and hair were vermilion. His name was Ralph. He had seven hundred and forty-three pimples.

"Woddyerwant?" enquired Ralph, coming within an ace of condensing the question into a word of one syllable.

"I want to see Mr. Goble."

"Zout!" said the Pimple King, and returned to his paper.

There will, no doubt, always be class distinctions. Sparta had her kings and her helots, King Arthur's Round Table its knights and its scullions, America her Simon Legree and her Uncle Tom. But in no nation and at no period of history has any one ever been so brutally superior to any one else as is the Broadway theatrical office-boy to the caller who wishes to see the manager. Thomas Jefferson held these truths to be self-evident, that all men are created equal; that they are endowed by the Creator with certain unalienable rights; that among these rights are life, liberty, and the pursuit of happiness. Theatrical office-boys do not see eye to eye with Thomas. From their pinnacle they look down on the common herd, the *canaille*, and despise them. They coldly question their right to live.

Jill turned pink. Mr. Brown, her guide and mentor, foreseeing this situation, had, she remembered, recommended "pushing the office-boy in the face": and for a moment she felt like following his advice. Prudence, or the fact that he was out of reach behind the brass bars, restrained her. Without further delay she made for the door of the inner room. That was her objective, and she did not intend to be diverted from it. Her fingers were on the handle before any of those present divined her intention. Then the stenographer stopped typing and sat with raised fingers, aghast. The girl at the telephone broke off in mid-sentence and stared round over her shoulder. Ralph, the office-boy, outraged, dropped his paper and constituted himself the spokesman of the invaded force.

"Hey!"

Jill stopped and eyed the lad militantly.

"Were you speaking to me?"

"Yes, I *was* speaking to you!"

"Don't do it again with your mouth full," said Jill, turning to the door.

The belligerent fire in the office-boy's pink-rimmed eyes was suddenly dimmed by a gush of water. It was not remorse that caused him to weep, however. In the heat of the moment he had swallowed a large, jagged sweet, and he was suffering severely.

"You can't go in there!" he managed to articulate, his iron will triumphing over the flesh sufficiently to enable him to speak.

"I *am* going in there!"

"That's Mr. Goble's private room."

"Well, I want a private talk with Mr. Goble."

Ralph, his eyes still moist, felt that the situation was slipping from his grip. This sort of thing had never happened to him before.

"I tell ya he *zout*"'

Jill looked at him sternly.

"You wretched child!" she said, encouraged by a sharp giggle from the neighbourhood of the switchboard. "Do you know where little boys go who don't speak the truth? I can hear him playing the piano. Now he's singing! And it's no good telling me he's busy. If he was busy, he wouldn't have time to sing. If you're as deceitful as this as your age, what do you expect to be when you grow up? You're an ugly little boy, you've got red ears, and your collar doesn't fit! I shall speak to Mr. Goble about you."

With which words Jill opened the door and walked in.

"Good afternoon," she said brightly.

After the congested and unfurnished discomfort of the landing, the room in which Jill found herself had an air of cosiness and almost of luxury. It was a large room, solidly upholstered. Along the further wall, filling nearly the whole of its space, stood a vast and gleaming desk, covered with a litter of papers which rose at one end of it to a sort of mountain of play-scripts in buff covers. There was a bookshelf to the left. Photographs covered the walls. Near the window was a deep leather lounge; to the right of this stood a small piano, the music-stool of which was occupied by a young man with untidy black hair that needed cutting. On top of the piano, taking the eye immediately by reason of its bold brightness, was balanced a large cardboard poster. Much of its surface was filled by a picture of a youth in polo costume bending over a blonde goddess in a bathing-suit. What space was left displayed the legend:

ISAAC GOBLE AND JACOB COHN

PRESENT

THE ROSE OF AMERICA

(A Musical Fantasy)

BOOK AND LYRICS BY OTIS PILKINGTON

MUSIC BY ROLAND TREVIS

Turning her eyes from this, Jill became aware that something was going on at the other side of the desk, and she perceived that a second young man, the longest and thinnest she had ever seen, was in the act of rising to his feet, length upon length like an unfolding snake. At the moment of her entry he had been lying back in an office-chair, so that only a merely nominal section of his upper structure was visible. Now he reared his impressive length until his head came within measurable distance of the ceiling. He had a hatchet face and a receding chin, and he gazed at Jill through what she assumed were the "tortoiseshell cheaters" referred to by her recent acquaintance, Mr. Brown.

"Er . . . ?" said this young man enquiringly in a high flat voice.

Jill, like many other people, had a brain which was under the alternating control of two diametrically opposite forces. It was like a motor-car steered in turn by two drivers, the one a dashing, reckless fellow with no regard for the speed limits, the other a timid novice. All through the proceedings up to this point the dasher had been in command. He had whisked her

along at a break-neck pace, ignoring obstacles and police regula-
tions. Now, having brought her to this situation, he abruptly
abandoned the wheel and turned it over to his colleague, the
shrinker. Jill, greatly daring a moment ago, now felt on overwhelming shyness.

She gulped, and her heart beat quickly. The thin man towered
over her. The black-haired pianist shook his locks at her like
Banquo.

"I . . ." she began.

Then, suddenly, womanly intuition came to her aid. Something
seemed to tell her that these men were just as scared as she was.
And, at the discovery, the dashing driver resumed his post at
the wheel, and she began to deal with the situation with
composure.

"I want to see Mr. Goble."

"Mr. Goble is out," said the long young man, plucking
nervously at the papers on the desk. Jill had affected him
powerfully.

"Out!" She felt she had wronged the pimpled office-boy.

"We are not expecting him back this afternoon. Is there
anything I can do?"

He spoke tenderly. This weak-minded young man was thinking
that he had never seen anything like Jill before. And it was true
that she was looking very pretty, with her cheeks flushed and
her eyes sparkling. She touched a chord in the young man which
seemed to make the world a flower-scented thing, full of soft
music. Often as he had been in love at first sight before in his
time, Otis Pilkington could not recall an occasion on which he
had been in love at first sight more completely than now. When
she smiled at him, it was as if the gates of heaven had opened.
He did not reflect how many times, in similar circumstances,
these same gates had opened before; and that on one occasion
when they had done so it had cost him eight thousand dollars to
settle the case out of court. One does not think of these things
at such times, for they strike a jarring note. Otis Pilkington was
in love. That was all he knew, or cared to know.

"Won't you take a seat, Miss . . ."

"Mariner," prompted Jill. "Thank you."

"Miss Mariner. May I introduce Mr. Roland Trevis?"

The man at the piano bowed. His black hair heaved upon his
skull like seaweed in a ground swell.

"My name in Pilkington. Otis Pilkington."

The uncomfortable silence which always follows introductions was broken by the sound of the telephone-bell on the desk. Otis Pilkington, who had moved out into the room and was nowhere near the desk, stretched forth a preposterous arm and removed the receiver.

"Yes? Oh, will you say, please, that I have a conference at present." Jill was to learn that people in the theatrical business never talked: they always held conferences. "Tell Mrs. Peagrim that I shall be calling later in the afternoon, but cannot be spared just now." He replaced the receiver. "Aunt Olive's secretary," he murmured in a soft aside to Mr. Trevis. "Aunt Olive wanted me to go for a ride." He turned to Jill. "Excuse me. Is there anything I can do for you, Miss Mariner?"

Jill's composure was now completely restored. This interview was turning out so totally different from anything she had expected. The atmosphere was cosy and social. She felt as if she were back in Ovingdon Square, giving tea to Freddie Rooke and Ronny Devereux and the rest of her friends of the London period. All that was needed to complete the picture was a tea-table in front of her. The business note hardly intruded on the proceedings at all. Still, as business was the object of her visit, she felt that she had better approach it.

"I came for work."

"Work!" cried Mr. Pilkington. He, too, appeared to be regarding the interview as purely of a social nature.

"In the chorus," explained Jill.

Mr. Pilkington seemed shocked. He winced away from the word as though it pained him.

"There is no chorus in 'The Rose of America,'" he said.

"I thought it was a musical comedy."

Mr. Pilkington winced again.

"It is a musical *fantasy*'" he said. "But there will be no chorus. We shall have," he added, a touch of rebuke in his voice, "the service of twelve refined ladies of the ensemble."

Jill laughed.

"It does sound much better, doesn't it!" she said. "Well, am I refined enough, do you think?"

"I shall be only too happy if you will join us," said Mr. Pilkington promptly.

The long-haired composer looked doubtful. He struck a note up in the treble, then whirled round on his stool.

"If you don't mind my mentioning it, Otie, we have twelve girls already."

"Then we must have thirteen," said Otis Pilkington firmly.

"Unlucky number," argued Mr. Trevis.

"I don't care. We must have Miss Mariner. You can see for yourself that she is exactly the type we need."

He spoke feelingly. Ever since the business of engaging a company had begun, he had been thinking wistfully of the evening when "The Rose of America" had had its opening performance—at his aunt's house at Newport last summer—with an all-star cast of society favourites and an ensemble recruited entirely from débutantes and matrons of the Younger Set. That was the sort of company he had longed to assemble for the piece's professional career, and until this afternoon he had met with nothing but disappointment. Jill seemed to be the only girl in theatrical New York who came up to the standard he would have liked to demand.

"Thank you very much," said Jill.

There was another pause. The social note crept into the atmosphere again. Jill felt the hostess' desire to keep conversation circulating.

"I hear," she said, "that this piece is a sort of Gilbert and Sullivan opera."

Mr. Pilkington considered the point.

"I confess," he said, "that, in writing the book, I had Gilbert before me as a model. Whether I have in any sense succeeded in . . ."

"The book," said Mr. Trevis, running his fingers over the piano, "is as good as anything Gilbert ever wrote."

"Oh, come, Rolie!" protested Mr. Pilkington modestly.

"Better," insisted Mr. Trevis. "For one thing, it is up-to-date."

"I *do* try to strike the modern note," murmured Mr. Pilkington.

"And you have avoided Gilbert's mistake of being too fanciful."

"He *was* fanciful," admitted Mr. Pilkington. "The music," he added, in a generous spirit of give and take, "has all Sullivan's melody with a newness of rhythm peculiarly its own. You will like the music."

"It sounds," said Jill amiably, "as though the piece is bound to be a tremendous success."

"We hope so," said Mr. Pilkington. "We feel that the time has come when the public is beginning to demand something better than what it has been accustomed to. People are getting tired of the brainless trash and jingly tunes which have been given them by men like Wallace Mason and George Bevan. They want a certain polish. . . . It was just the same in Gilbert and Sullivan's day. They started writing at a time when the musical stage had reached a terrible depth of inanity. The theatre was given over to burlesques of the most idiotic description. The public was waiting eagerly to welcome something of a higher class. It is just the same to-day. But the managers will not see it. 'The Rose of America' went up and down Broadway for months, knocking at managers' doors."

"It should have walked in without knocking, like me," said Jill. She got up. "Well, it was very kind of you to see me when I came in so unceremoniously. But I felt it was no good waiting outside on that landing. I'm so glad everything is settled. Good-bye."

"Good-bye, Miss Mariner." Mr. Pilkington took her out-stretched hand devoutly. "There is a rehearsal called for the ensemble at—when is it, Rolie?"

"Eleven o'clock, day after to-morrow, at Bryant Hall."

"I'll be there, " said Jill. "Good-bye, and thank you very much."

The silence which had fallen upon the room as she left it was broken by Mr. Trevis.

"Some pip!" observed Mr. Trevis.

Otis Pilkington awoke from day-dreams with a start.

"What did you say?"

"That girl . . . I said she was some pippin!"

"Miss Mariner," said Mr. Pilkington icily, "is a most charming, refined, cultured, and vivacious girl, if you mean that."

"Yes," said Mr. Trevis. "That was what I meant!"

II

Jill walked out into Forty-second Street, looking about her with the eye of a conqueror. Very little change had taken place in the aspect of New York since she had entered the Gotham

Theatre, but it seemed a different city to her. An hour ago, she had been a stranger, drifting aimlessly along its rapids. Now she belonged to New York, and New York belonged to her. She had faced it squarely, and forced from it the means of living. She walked on with a new jauntiness in her stride.

The address which Nelly had given her was on the east side of Fifth Avenue. She made her way along Forty-second Street. It seemed the jolliest, alivest street she had ever encountered. The rattle of the Elevated as she crossed Sixth Avenue was music, and she loved the crowds that jostled her with every step she took.

She reached the Fifth Avenue corner just as the policeman out in the middle of the street swung his Stop-and-Go post round to allow the up-town traffic to proceed on its way. A stream of cars which had been dammed up as far as the eye could reach began to flow swiftly past. They moved in a double line, red limousines, blue limousines, mauve limousines, green limousines. She stood waiting for the flood to cease, and, as she did so, there purred past her the biggest and reddest limousine of all. It was a colossal vehicle with a polar-bear at the steering-wheel and another at his side. And in the interior, very much at his ease, his gaze bent courteously upon a massive lady in a mink coat, sat Uncle Chris.

For a moment he was so near to her that, but for the closed window, she could have touched him. Then the polar-bear at the wheel, noting a gap in the traffic, stepped on the accelerator and slipped neatly through. The car moved swiftly on and disappeared.

Jill drew a deep breath. The Stop-and-Go sign swung round again. She crossed the avenue, and set out once more to find Nelly Bryant. It occurred to her, five minutes later, that a really practical and quick-thinking girl would have noted the number of the limousine.

★ 11 ★

Mr. Pilkington's Love Light

I

THE rehearsals of a musical comedy—a term which embraces "musical fantasies"—generally begin in a desultory sort of way at that curious building, Bryant Hall, on Sixth Avenue just off Forty-second Street. There, in a dusty, uncarpeted room, simply furnished with a few wooden chairs and some long wooden benches, the chorus—or, in the case of "The Rose of America," the ensemble—sit round a piano and endeavour, with the assistance of the musical director, to get the words and melodies of the first-act number into their heads. This done, they are ready for the dance director to instil into them the steps, the groupings, and the business for the encores, of which that incurable optimist always seems to expect there will be at least six. Later, the principals are injected into the numbers. And finally, leaving Bryant Hall and dodging about from one unoccupied theatre to another, principals and chorus rehearse together, running through the entire piece over and over again till the opening night of the preliminary road tour.

To Jill, in the early stages, rehearsing was just like being back at school. She could remember her first schoolmistress, whom the musical director somewhat resembled in manner and appearance, hammering out hymns on a piano and leading in a weak soprano an eager, baying pack of children, each anxious from motives of pride to out-bawl her nearest neighbour.

The proceedings began on the first morning with the entrance of Mr. Saltzburg, the musical director, a brisk, busy little man with benevolent eyes behind big spectacles, who bustled over to the piano, sat down, and played a loud chord, designed to act as a sort of bugle blast, rallying the ladies of the ensemble from the corners where they sat in groups, chatting. For the process of making one another's acquaintance had begun some ten minutes before with mutual recognitions between those who knew each other from having been together in previous productions. There followed rapid introductions of friends. Nelly Bryant had been welcomed warmly by a pretty girl with red hair, whom she introduced to Jill as Babe; Babe had a willowy blonde friend, named Lois, and the four of them had seated themselves on one of the benches and opened a conversation; their numbers being added to a moment later by a dark girl with a Southern accent and another blonde. Elsewhere other groups had formed, and the room was filled with a noise like the chattering of starlings. In a body by themselves, rather forlorn and neglected, half a dozen solemn and immaculately dressed young men were propping themselves up against the wall and looking on, like men in a ball-room who do not dance.

Jill listened to the conversation without taking any great part in it herself. She felt as she had done on her first day at school, a little shy and desirous of effacing herself. The talk dealt with clothes, men, and the show business, in that order of importance. Presently one of the young men sauntered diffidently across the room and added himself to the group with the remark that it was a fine day. He was received a little grudgingly, Jill thought, but by degrees succeeded in assimilating himself. A second young man drifted up; reminded the willowy girl that they had worked together in the western company of "You're the One"; was recognized and introduced, and justified his admission to the circle by a creditable imitation of a cat-fight. Five minutes later he was addressing the Southern girl as "honey," and had informed Jill that he had only joined this show to fill in before opening on the three-a-day with the swellest little song-and-dance act which he and a little girl who worked in the cabaret at Geisenheimer's had fixed up.

On this scene of harmony and good-fellowship Mr. Saltzburg's chord intruded jarringly. There was a general movement, and chairs and benches were dragged to the piano. Mr. Saltzburg causing a momentary delay by opening a large brown music-bag and digging in it like a terrier at a rat-hole, conversation broke out again.

Mr. Saltzburg emerged from the bag, with his hands full of papers, protesting.

"Childrun! Chil-*drun!* If you please, less noise and attend to me!" He distributed sheets of paper. "Act One, Opening Chorus. I will play the melody three—four times. Follow attentively. Then we will sing it la-la-la, and after that we will sing the words. So!"

He struck the yellow-keyed piano a vicious blow, producing a tinny and complaining sound. Bending forward with his spectacles almost touching the music, he plodded determinedly through the tune, then encored himself, and after that encored himself again. When he had done this, he removed his spectacles and wiped them. There was a pause.

"Izzy," observed the willowy young lady chattily, leaning across Jill and addressing the Southern girl's blonde friend, "has promised me a sunburst!"

A general stir of interest and a coming close together of heads. "What! Izzy!"

"Sure, Izzy."

"Well!"

"He's just landed the hat-check privilege at the St. Aurea!"

"You don't say!"

"He told me so last night and promised me the sunburst. He was," admitted the willowy girl regretfully, "a good bit tanked at the time, but I guess he'll make good." She mused awhile, a rather anxious expression clouding her perfect profile. She looked like a meditative Greek goddess. "If he doesn't," she added with maidenly dignity, "it's the last time *I* go out with the big stiff. I'd tie a can to him quicker'n look at him!"

A murmur of approval greeted this admirable sentiment.

"Childrun!" protested Mr. Saltzburg. "Chil-drun! Less noise and chatter of conversation. We are here to work! We must not waste time! So! Act One, Opening Chorus. Now, all together. La-la-la . . ."

"La-la-la . . ."

"Tum-tum-tumty-tumty . . ."

"Tum-tum-tumty . . ."

Mr. Saltzburg pressed his hands to his ears in a spasm of pain. "No, no, no! Sour! Sour! Sour! . . . Once again. La-la-la . . ."

A round-face girl with golden hair and the face of a wondering cherub interrupted, speaking with a lisp.

"Mithter Thalzburg."

"Now what is it, Miss Trevor?"

"What sort of a show is this?"

"A musical show," said Mr. Saltzburg severely, "and this is a rehearsal of it, not a conversazione. One more, please."

The cherub was not to be rebuffed.

"Is the music good, Mithter Thalzburg?"

"When you have rehearsed it, you shall judge for yourself. Come now . . ."

"Is there anything in it as good as that waltz of yours you played us when we were rehearthing 'Mind How You Go?' You remember. The one that went . . ."

A tall and stately girl, with sleepy brown eyes and the air of a duchess in the servants' hall, bent forward and took a kindly interest in the conversation.

"Oh, have you composed a varlse, Mr. Saltzburg?" she asked with pleasant condescension. "How interesting, really! Won't you play it for us?"

The sentiment of the meeting seemed to be unanimous in favour of shelving work and listening to Mr. Saltzburg's waltz.

"Oh, Mr. Saltzburg, do!"

"Please!"

"Some one told me it was a pipterino!"

"I certainly do love waltzes!"

"Please, Mr. Saltzburg!"

Mr. Saltzburg obviously weakened. His fingers touched the keys irresolutely.

"But, childrun!"

"I am sure it would be a great pleasure to all of us," said the duchess graciously, "if you would play it. There is nothing I enjoy more than a good varlse."

Mr. Saltzburg capitulated. Like all musical directors he had in his leisure moments composed the complete score of a musical play and spent much of his time waylaying librettists on the Rialto and trying to lure them to his apartment to listen to it, with a view to business. The eternal tragedy of a musical director's life is comparable only to that of the waiter who, himself fasting, has to assist others to eat. Mr. Saltzburg had lofty ideas on music, and his soul revolted at being compelled perpetually to rehearse and direct the inferior compositions of other men. Far less persuasion than he had received to-day was usually required to induce him to play the whole of his score.

"You wish it?" he said. "Well, then! This waltz, you will understand, is the theme of a musical romance which I have composed. It will be sung once in the first act by the heroine, then in the second act as a duet for heroine and hero. I weave it into the finale of the second act, and we have an echo of it, sung off stage, in the third act. What I play you now is the second act duet. The verse is longer. So! The male voice begins."

A pleasant time was had by all for ten minutes.

"Ah, but this is not rehearsing, childrun!" cried Mr. Saltzburg remorsefully at the end of that period. "This is not business. Come now, the opening chorus of Act One, and please this time keep on the key. Before, it was sour, sour. Come! La-la-la . . ."

"Mr. Thalzburg!"

"Miss Trevor?"

"There was an awfully thweet fox-trot you used to play us. I do wish . . ."

"Some other time, some other time! Now we must work. Come! La-la-la . . ."

"I wish you could have heard it, girls" said the cherub regretfully. "Honetht, it was lalapalootha!"

The pack broke into full cry.

"Oh, Mr. Saltzburg!"

"Please, Mr. Saltzburg!"

"Do play the fox-trot, Mr. Saltzburg!"

"If it is as good as the varlse," said the duchess, stooping once more to the common level, "I am sure it must be very good indeed." She powdered her nose. "And one so rarely hears musicianly music nowadays, does one?"

"Which fox-trot?" asked Mr. Saltzburg weakly.

"Play 'em all!" decided a voice on the left.

"Yes, play 'em all," bayed the pack.

"I am sure that that would be charming," agreed the duchess, replacing her powder-puff.

Mr. Saltzburg played 'em all. This man by now seemed entirely lost to shame. The precious minutes that belonged to his employers and should have been earmarked for "The Rose of America" flitted by. The ladies and gentlemen of the ensemble, who should have been absorbing and learning to deliver the melodies of Roland Trevis and the lyrics of Otis Pilkington, lolled back in their seats. The yellow-keyed piano rocked beneath an unprecedented onslaught. The proceedings had begun to resemble not so much a rehearsal as a happy home evening, and grateful glances were cast at the complacent cherub. She had, it was felt, shown tact and discretion.

Pleasant conversation began again.

". . . And I walked a couple of blocks, and there was exactly the same model in Schwartz and Gulderstein's window at twenty-six fifty . . ."

". . . He got on Forty-second Street, and he was kinda fresh from the start. At Sixty-sixth he came sasshaying right down the car and said 'Hello, patootie!' Well, I drew myself up . . ."

". . . . 'Even if you are my sister's husband,' I said to him. Oh, I suppose I got a temper. It takes a lot to arouse it, y'know, but I c'n get pretty mad . . ."

". . . You don't know the half of it, dearie, you don't know the half of it! A one-piece bathing suit! Well, you could call it that, but the cop of the beach said it was more like a baby's sock. And when . . ."

". . . So I said 'Listen, Izzy, that'll be about all from you! My father was a gentleman, though I don't suppose you know what that means, and I'm not accustomed . . .' "

"Hey!"

A voice from the neighbourhood of the door had cut into the babble like a knife into butter; a rough, rasping voice, loud and compelling, which caused the conversation of the members of the ensemble to cease on the instant. Only Mr. Saltzburg, now in a perfect frenzy of musicianly fervour, continued to assault the decrepit piano, unwitting of an unsympathetic addition to his audience.

"What I play you now is the laughing trio from my second act. It is a building number. It is sung by tenor, principal comedian, and soubrette. On the second refrain four girls will come out and two boys. The girls will dance with the two men, the boys with the soubrette. So! On the encore four more girls and two more boys. Third encore, solo-dance for specialty dancer, all on stage beating time by clapping their hands. On repeat, all sing refrain once more, and off. Last encore, the three principals and specialty dancer dance the dance with entire chorus. It is a great building number, you understand. It is enough to make the success of any musical play, but can I get a hearing? No! If I ask managers to listen to my music, they are busy! If I beg them to give me a libretto to set, they laugh—ha! ha!" Mr. Saltzburg gave a spirited and lifelike representation of a manager laughing ha-ha when begged to disgorge a libretto. "Now I play it once more!"

"Like hell you do!" said the voice. "Say, what is this, anyway? A concert?"

Mr. Saltzburg swung round on the music-stool, a startled and apprehensive man, and nearly fell off it. The divine afflatus left him like air oozing from a punctured toy-balloon, and, like such a balloon, he seemed to grow suddenly limp and flat. He stared with fallen jaw at the new arrival.

Two men had entered the room. One was the long Mr. Pilkington. The other, who looked shorter and stouter than he really was beside his giraffe-like companion, was a thick-set, fleshy man in the early thirties with a blond, clean-shaven, double-chinned face. He had smooth, yellow hair, an unwholesome complexion, and light green eyes, set close together. From the edge of the semi-circle about the piano, he glared menacingly over the heads of the chorus at the unfortunate Mr. Saltzburg.

"Why aren't these girls working?"

Mr. Saltzburg, who had risen nervously from his stool, backed away apprehensively from his gaze, and, stumbling over the stool, sat down abruptly on the piano, producing a curious noise like Futurist music.

"I—We—Why, Mr. Goble . . ."

Mr. Goble turned his green gaze on the concert audience, and spread discomfort as if it were something liquid which he was spraying through a hose. The girls who were nearest looked down flutteringly at their shoes: those further away concealed themselves behind their neighbours. Even the duchess, who prided herself on being the possessor of a stare of unrivalled haughtiness, before which the fresh quailed and those who made breaks subsided in confusion, was unable to meet his eyes: and the willowy friend of Izzy, for all her victories over that monarch of the hat-checks, bowed before it like a slim tree before a blizzard.

Only Jill returned the manager's gaze. She was seated on the outer rim of the semi-circle, and she stared frankly at Mr. Goble. She had never seen anything like him before, and he fascinated her. This behaviour on her part singled her out from the throng, and Mr. Goble concentrated his attention on her.

For some seconds he stood looking at her; then, raising a stubby finger, he let his eye travel over the company, and seemed to be engrossed in some sort of mathematical calculation.

"Thirteen," he said at length. "I make it thirteen." He rounded on Mr. Pilkington. "I told you we were going to have a chorus of twelve."

Mr. Pilkington blushed and stumbled over his feet.

"Ah, yes . . . yes," he murmured vaguely. "Yes!"

"Well, there are thirteen here. Count 'em for yourself." He whipped round on Jill. "What's *your* name? Who engaged you?"

A croaking sound from the neighbourhood of the ceiling indicated the clearing of Mr. Pilkington's throat.

"I—er—*I* engaged Miss Mariner, Mr. Goble."

"Oh, *you* engaged her?"

He stared again at Jill. The inspection was long and lingering, and affected Jill with a sense of being inadequately clothed. She returned the gaze as defiantly as she could, but her heart was beating fast. She had never yet been frightened of any man, but there was something reptilian about this fat, yellow-haired individual which disquieted her, much as cockroaches had done in her childhood. A momentary thought flashed through her mind that it would be horrible to be touched by him. He looked soft and glutinous.

"All right," said Mr. Goble at last, after what seemed to Jill many minutes. He nodded to Mr. Saltzburg. "Get on with it! And try working a little this time! I don't hire you to give musical entertainments."

"Yes, Mr. Goble, yes. I mean no, Mr. Goble!"

"You can have the Gotham stage this afternoon," said Mr. Goble. "Call the rehearsal for two sharp."

Outside the door, he turned to Mr. Pilkington.

"That was a fool trick of yours, hiring that girl. Thirteen! I'd as soon walk under a ladder on a Friday as open in New York with a chorus of thirteen. Well, it don't matter. We can sack one of 'em after we've opened on the road." He mused for a moment. "Darned pretty girl, that!" he went on meditatively. "Where did you get her?"

"She—ah—came into the office, when you were out. She struck me as being essentially the type we required for our ensemble, so I—er—engaged her. She——" Mr. Pilkington gulped. "She is a charming, refined girl!"

"She's darned pretty," admitted Mr. Goble, and went on his way wrapped in thought, Mr. Pilkington following timorously. It was episodes like the one that had just concluded which made Otis Pilkington wish that he possessed a little more assertion. He regretted wistfully that he was not one of those men who can put their hat on the side of their heads and shoot out their chins and say to the world "Well, what about it!" He was bearing the financial burden of this production. If it should be a failure, his would be the loss. Yet somehow this coarse, rough person in front of him never seemed to allow him a word in the executive policy of the piece. He treated him as a child. He domineered and he shouted, and behaved as if he were in sole command. Mr. Pilkington sighed. He rather wished he had never gone into this undertaking.

Inside the room, Mr. Saltzburg wiped his forehead, his spectacles, and his hands. He had the aspect of one who wakes from a dreadful dream.

"Childrun!" he whispered brokenly. "Childrun! If you please, once more. Act One, Opening Chorus. Come! La-la-la!"

"La-la-la!" chanted the subdued members of the ensemble.

II

By the time the two halves of the company, ensemble and principals, melted into one complete whole, the novelty of her new surroundings had worn off, and Jill was feeling that there had never been a time when she had not been one of a theatrical troupe, rehearsing. The pleasant social gatherings round Mr. Saltzburg's piano gave way in a few days to something far less agreeable and infinitely more strenuous, the breaking-in of the dances under the supervision of the famous Johnson Miller. Johnson Miller was a little man with snow-white hair and the india-rubber physique of a juvenile acrobat. Nobody knew actually how old he was, but he certainly looked much too advanced in years to be capable of the feats of endurance which he performed daily. He had the untiring enthusiasm of a fox-terrier, and had bullied and scolded more companies along the rocky road that leads to success than any half-dozen dance-directors in the country, in spite of his handicap in being almost completely deaf. He had an almost miraculous gift of picking up the melodies for which it was his business to design dances, without apparently hearing them. He seemed to absorb them through the pores. He had a blunt and arbitrary manner, and invariably spoke his mind frankly and honestly—a habit which made him strangely popular in a profession where the language of equivoque is cultivated almost as sedulously as in the circles of international diplomacy. What Johnson Miller said to your face was official, not subject to revision as soon as your back was turned, and people appreciated this.

Izzy's willowy friend summed him up one evening when the ladies of the ensemble were changing their practice-clothes after a particularly strenuous rehearsal, defending him against the Southern girl, who complained that he made her tired.

"You bet he makes you tired," she said. "So he does me. I'm losing my girlish curves, and I'm so stiff I can't lace my shoes. But he know his business and he's on the level, which is more than you can say of most of these guys in the show business."

"That's right," agreed the Southern girl's blonde friend. "He does know his business. He's put over any amount of shows which would have flopped like dogs without him to stage the numbers."

The duchess yawned. Rehearsing always bored her, and she had not been greatly impressed by what she had seen of "The Rose of America."

"One will be greatly surprised if he can make a success of *this* show! I confess I find it perfectly ridiculous."

"Ithn't it the limit, honetht!" said the cherub, arranging her golden hair at the mirror. "It maketh me thick! Why on earth ith Ike putting it on?"

The girl who knew everything—there is always one in every company—hastened to explain.

"I heard all about that. Ike hasn't any of his own money in the thing. He's getting twenty-five per cent of the show for running it. The angel is the long fellow you see jumping around. Pilkington his name is."

"Well, it'll need to be Rockefeller later on," said the blonde.

"Oh, they'll get thomebody down to fixth it after we've been out on the road a couple of days," said the cherub, optimistically. "They alwayth do. I've seen worse shows than this turned into hits. All it wants ith a new book and lyrics and a different thcore."

"And a new set of principals," said the red-headed Babe. "Did you ever see such a bunch?"

The duchess, with another tired sigh, arched her well-shaped eyebrows and studied the effect in the mirror.

"One wonders where they pick these persons up," she assented languidly. "They remind me of a headline I saw in the paper this morning—'Tons of Hams Unfit for Human Consumption.' Are any of you girls coming my way? I can give two or three of you a lift in my limousine."

"Thorry, old dear, and thanks ever so much," said the cherub, "but I instructed Clarence, my man, to have the street-car waiting on the corner, and he'll be too upset if I'm not there."

Nelly had an engagement to go and help one of the other girls buy a Spring suit, a solemn rite which it is impossible to conduct by oneself: and Jill and the cherub walked to the corner together. Jill had become very fond of the little thing since rehearsals began. She reminded her of a London sparrow. She was so small and perky and so absurdly able to take care of herself.

"Limouthine!" snorted the cherub. The duchess' concluding speech evidently still rankled. "She gives me a pain in the gizthard!"

"Hasn't she got a limousine?" asked Jill.

"Of course she hasn't. She's engaged to be married to a demonstrator in the Speedwell Auto Company, and he thneaks off when he can get away and gives her joy-rides. That's all the limouthine she's got. It beats me why girls in the show business are alwayth tho crazy to make themselves out vamps with a dozen millionaires on a string. If Mae wouldn't four-flush and act like the Belle of the Moulin Rouge, she'd be the nithest girl you ever met. She's mad about the fellow she's engaged to, and wouldn't look at all the millionaires in New York if you brought 'em to her on a tray. She's going to marry him as thoon as he's thaved enough to buy the furniture, and then she'll thettle down in Harlem thomewhere and cook and mind the baby and regularly be one of the lower middle classes. All that's wrong with Mae ith that she's read Gingery Stories and thinkth that's the way a girl has to act when she'th in the chorus."

"That's funny," said Jill. "I should never have thought it. I swallowed the limousine whole."

The cherub looked at her curiously. Jill puzzled her. Jill had, indeed, been the subject of much private speculation among her colleagues.

"This is your first show, ithn't it?" she asked.

"Yes."

"Thay, what are you doing in the chorus, anyway?"

"Getting scolded by Mr. Miller mostly, it seems to me."

"Thcolded by Mr. Miller! Why didn't you say 'bawled out by Johnny'? That'th what any of the retht of us would have said."

"Well, I've lived most of my life in England. You can't expect me to talk the language yet."

"I thought you were English. You've got an acthent like the fellow who plays the dude in thith show. Thay, why did you ever get into the show business?"

"Well . . . well, why did you? Why does anybody?"

"Why did I? Oh, I belong there. I'm a regular Broadway rat. I wouldn't be happy anywhere elthe. I was born in the show business. I've got two thithters in the two-a-day and a brother in thtock in California and dad's one of the betht comedians on the burlethque wheel. But any one can thee you're different. There's no reathon why you should be sticking around in the chorus."

"But there is. I've no money, and I can't do anything to make it."

"Honetht?"

"Honest."

"That's tough." The cherub pondered, her round eyes searching Jill's face. "Why don't you get married?"

Jill laughed.

"Nobody's asked me."

"Somebody thoon will. At least, if he's on the level, and I think he is. You can generally tell by the look of a guy, and, if you ask me, friend Pilkington's got the licence in hith pocket and the ring all ordered and everything."

"Pilkington!" cried Jill aghast.

She remembered certain occasions during rehearsals, when, while the chorus idled in the body of the theatre and listened to the principals working at their scenes, the elongated Pilkington had suddenly appeared in the next seat and conversed sheepishly in a low voice. Could this be love? If so, it was a terrible nuisance. Jill had had her experience in London of enamoured young men who, running true to national form, declined to know when they were beaten, and she had not enjoyed the process of cooling their ardour. She had a kind heart, and it distressed her to give pain. It also got on her nerves to be dogged by stricken males who tried to catch her eye in order that she might observe their broken condition. She recalled one house-party in Wales where it rained all the time and she had been cooped up with a victim who kept popping out from obscure corners and beginning all his pleas with the words "I say, you know . . .!" She trusted that Otis Pilkington was not proposing to conduct a wooing on those lines. Yet he had certainly developed a sinister habit of popping out at the theatre. On several occasions he had startled her by appearing at her side as if he had come up out of a trap.

"Oh, no!" cried Jill.

"Oh, yeth!" insisted the cherub, waving imperiously to an approaching street-car. "Well, I must be getting up-town. I've got a date. Thee you later."

"I'm sure you're mistaken."

"I'm not."

"But what makes you think so ?"

The cherub placed a hand on the rail of the car, preparatory to swinging herself on board.

"Well, for one thing," she said, "he'th been stalking you like an Indian ever since we left the theatre! Look behind you. Good-bye, honey. Thend me a piece of the cake!"

The street-car bore her away. The last that Jill saw of her was a wide and amiable grin. Then, turning, she beheld the snake-like form of Otis Pilkington towering at her side.

Mr. Pilkington seemed nervous but determined. His face was half hidden by the silk scarf that muffled his throat, for he was careful of his health and had a fancied tendency to bronchial trouble. Above the scarf a pair of mild eyes gazed down at Jill through their tortoiseshell-rimmed spectacles. It was hopeless for Jill to try to tell herself that the tender gleam behind the glass was not the love light in Otis Pilkington's eyes. The truth was too obvious.

"Good evening, Miss Mariner," said Mr. Pilkington, his voice sounding muffled and far away through the scarf. "Are you going up-town ?"

"No, down-town," said Jill quickly.

"So am I," said Mr. Pilkington.

Jill felt annoyed, but helpless. It is difficult to bid a tactful farewell to a man who has stated his intention of going in the same direction as yourself. There was nothing for it but to accept the unspoken offer of Otis Pilkington's escort. They began to walk down Broadway together.

"I suppose you are tired after the rehearsal ?" enquired Mr. Pilkington in his precise voice. He always spoke as if he were weighing each word and clipping it off a reel.

"A little. Mr. Miller is very enthusiastic."

"About the piece ?" Her companion spoke eagerly.

"No; I meant hard-working."

"Has he said anything about the piece ?"

"Well, no. You see, he doesn't confide in us a great deal, except to tell us his opinion of the way we do the steps. I don't think we impress him very much, to judge from what he says. But the girls say he always tells every chorus he rehearses that it is the worst he ever had anything to do with."

"And the chor—the—er—ladies of the ensemble ? What do they think of the piece ?"

"Well, I don't suppose they are very good judges, are they?" said Jill diplomatically.

"You mean they do not like it?"

"Some of them don't seem quite to understand it."

Mr. Pilkington was silent for a moment.

"I am beginning to wonder myself whether it may not be a little over the heads of the public," he said ruefully. "When it was first performed . . ."

"Oh, has it been done before?"

"By amateurs, yes, at the house of my aunt, Mrs. Waddesleigh Peagrim, at Newport, last summer. In aid of the Armenian orphans. It was extraordinarily well received on that occasion. We nearly made our expenses. It was such a success that—I feel I can confide in you. I should not like this repeated to your—your—the other ladies—it was such a success that, against my aunt's advice, I decided to give it a Broadway production. Between ourselves, I am shouldering practically all the expenses of the undertaking. Mr. Goble has nothing to do with the financial arrangements of 'The Rose of America.' Those are entirely in my hands. Mr. Goble, in return for a share in the profits, is giving us the benefit of his experience as regards the management and booking of the piece. I have always had the greatest faith in it. Trevis and I wrote it when we were in college together, and all our friends thought it exceptionally brilliant. My aunt, as I say, was opposed to the venture. She holds the view that I am not a good man of business. In a sense, perhaps, she is right. Temperamentally, no doubt, I am more the artist. But I was determined to show the public something superior to the so-called Broadway successes, which are so terribly trashy. Unfortunately, I am beginning to wonder whether it is possible, with the crude type of actor at one's disposal in this country, to give a really adequate performance of such a play as 'The Rose of America.' These people seem to miss the spirit of the piece, its subtle topsy-turvy humour, its delicate whimsicality. This afternoon," Mr. Pilkington choked. "This afternoon I happened to overhear two of the principals, who were not aware that I was within earshot, discussing the play. One of them—these people express themselves curiously—one of them said that he thought it a quince: and the other described it as a piece of gorgonzola cheese! That is not the spirit that wins success!"

Jill was feeling immensely relieved. After all, it seemed, this poor young man merely wanted sympathy, not romance. She had been mistaken, she felt, about that gleam in his eyes. It was not the lovelight: it was the light of panic. He was the author of the play. He had sunk a large sum of money in its production, he had heard people criticizing it harshly, and he was suffering from what her colleagues in the chorus would have called cold feet. It was such a human emotion and he seemed so like an overgrown child pleading to be comforted that her heart warmed to him. Relief melted her defences. And when, on their arrival at Thirty-fourth Street Mr. Pilkington suggested that she partake of a cup of tea at his apartment, which was only a couple of blocks away off Madison Avenue, she accepted the invitation without hesitating.

On the way to his apartment Mr. Pilkington continued in the minor key. He was a great deal more communicative than she herself would have been to such a comparative stranger as she was, but she knew that men were often like this. Over in London, she had frequently been made the recipient of the most intimate confidences by young men whom she had met for the first time the same evening at a dance. She had been forced to believe that there was something about her personality that acted on a certain type of man like the crack in the dam, setting loose the surging flood of their eloquence. To this class Otis Pilkington evidently belonged, for, once started, he withheld nothing.

"It isn't that I'm dependent on Aunt Olive or anything like that," he vouchsafed, as he stirred the tea in his Japanese-print-hung studio. "But you know how it is. Aunt Olive is in a position to make it very unpleasant for me if I do anything foolish. At present, I have reason to know that she intends to leave me practically all that she possesses. Millions!" said Mr. Pilkington, handing Jill a cup. "I assure you, millions! But there is a hard commercial strain in her. It would have the most prejudicial effect upon her if, especially after she had expressly warned me against it, I were to lose a great deal of money over this production. She is always complaining that I am not a business man like my late uncle. Mr. Waddesleigh Peagrim made a fortune in smoked hams." Mr. Pilkington looked at the Japanese prints, and shuddered slightly. "Right up to the time of his death he was urging me to go into the business. I could not have endured it. But, when I heard those two men discussing the play, I almost wished that I had done so."

Jill was now completely disarmed. She would almost have patted this unfortunate young man's head, if she could have reached it.

"I shouldn't worry about the piece," she said. "I've read somewhere or heard somewhere that it's the surest sign of a success when actors don't like a play."

Mr. Pilkington drew his chair an imperceptible inch nearer.

"How sympathetic you are!"

Jill perceived with chagrin that she had been mistaken after all. It *was* the love light. The tortoiseshell-rimmed spectacles sprayed it all over her like a couple of searchlights. Otis Pilkington was looking exactly like a sheep, and she knew from past experience that that was the infallible sign. When young men looked like that, it was time to go.

"I'm afraid I must be off," she said. "Thank you so much for giving me tea. I shouldn't be a bit afraid about the play. I'm sure it's going to be splendid. Good-bye."

"You aren't going already?"

"I must. I'm very late as it is. I promised . . ."

Whatever fiction Jill might have invented to the detriment of her soul was interrupted by a ring at the bell. The steps of Mr. Pilkington's Japanese servant crossing the hall came faintly to the sitting-room.

"Mr. Pilkington in?"

Otis Pilkington motioned pleadingly to Jill.

"Don't go!" he urged. "It's only a man I know. He has probably come to remind me that I am dining with him to-night. He won't stay a minute. Please don't go."

Jill sat down. She had no intention of going now. The cheery voice at the front door had been the cheery voice of her long-lost uncle, Major Christopher Selby.

★ 12 ★

Uncle Chris Borrows a Flat

I

UNCLE CHRIS walked breezily into the room, flicking a jaunty glove. He stopped short on seeing that Mr. Pilkington was not alone.

"Oh, I beg your pardon! I understood . . ." He peered at Jill uncertainly. Mr. Pilkington affected a dim, artistic lighting-system in his studio, and people who entered from the great outdoors generally had to take time to accustom their eyes to it. "If you're engaged . . ."

"Er—allow me . . . Miss Mariner . . . Major Selby."

"Hullo, Uncle Chris!" said Jill.

"God bless my soul!" ejaculated that startled gentleman adventurer, and collapsed on to a settee as if his legs had been mown from under him.

"I've been looking for you all over New York," said Jill.

Mr. Pilkington found himself unequal to the intellectual pressure of the conversation.

"Uncle Chris?" he said with a note of feeble enquiry in his voice.

"Major Selby is my uncle."

"Are you sure?" said Mr. Pilkington. "I mean . . ."

Not being able to ascertain, after a moment's self-examination, what he did mean, he relapsed into silence.

"Whatever are you doing here?" asked Uncle Chris.

"I've been having tea with Mr. Pilkington."

"But . . . but why Mr. Pilkington?"

"Well, he invited me."

"But how do you know him?"

"We met at the theatre."

"Theatre?"

Otis Pilkington recovered his power of speech.

"Miss Mariner is rehearsing with a little play in which I am interested," he explained.

Uncle Chris half rose from the settee. He blinked twice in rapid succession. Jill had never seen him so shaken from his customary poise.

"Don't tell me you have gone on the stage, Jill!"

"I have. I'm in the chorus . . ."

"Ensemble," corrected Mr. Pilkington softly.

"I'm in the ensemble of a piece called 'The Rose of America.' We've been rehearsing for ever so long."

Uncle Chris digested this information in silence for a moment. He pulled at his short moustache.

"Why, of course!" he said at length. Jill, who knew him so well, could tell by the restored ring of cheeriness in his tone that he was himself again. He had dealt with this situation in his mind and was prepared to cope with it. The surmise was confirmed the next instant when he rose and stationed himself in front of the fire. Mr. Pilkington detested steam-heat and had scoured the city till he had found a studio apartment with an open fireplace. Uncle Chris spread his legs and expanded his chest. "Of course," he said. "I remember now that you told me in your letter that you were thinking of going on the stage. My niece," explained Uncle Chris to the attentive Mr. Pilkington, "came over from England on a later boat. I was not expecting her for some weeks. Hence my surprise at meeting her here. Of course. You told me that you intended to go on the stage, and I strongly recommended you to begin at the bottom of the ladder and learn the ground-work thoroughly before you attempted higher flights."

"Oh, that was it ?" said Mr. Pilkington. He had been wondering.

"There is no finer training," resumed Uncle Chris, completely at his ease once more, "than the chorus. How many of the best-known actresses in America began in that way! Dozens. Dozens. If I were giving advice to any young girl with theatrical aspirations, I should say 'Begin in the chorus!' On the other hand," he proceeded, turning to Mr. Pilkington, "I think it would be just as well if you would not mention the fact of my niece being in that position to Mrs. Waddesleigh Peagrim. She might not understand."

"Exactly," assented Mr. Pilkington.

"The term 'chorus' . . ."

"I dislike it intensely myself."

"It suggests . . ."

"Precisely."

Uncle Chris inflated his chest again, well satisfied.

"Capital!" he said. "Well, I only dropped in to remind you, my boy, that you and your aunt are dining with me to-night. I was afraid a busy man like you might forget."

"I was looking forward to it," said Mr. Pilkington, charmed at the description.

"You remember the address ? Nine East Forty-first Street. I have moved, you remember."

"So that was why I couldn't find you at the other place," said Jill "The man at the door said he had never heard of you."

"Stupid idiot!" said Uncle Chris testily. "These New York hall-porters are recruited entirely from homes for the feeble-minded. I suppose he was a new man. Well, Pilkington, my boy, I shall expect you at seven o'clock. Good-bye till then. Come, Jill."

"Good-bye, Mr. Pilkington," said Jill.

"Good-bye for the present, Miss Mariner," said Mr. Pilkington bending down to take her hand. The tortoise-shell spectacles shot a last soft beam at her.

As the front door closed behind them, Uncle Chris heaved a sigh of relief.

"Whew! I think I handled that little contretemps with diplomacy! A certain amount of diplomacy, I think!"

"If you mean," said Jill severely, "that you told some disgraceful fibs . . ."

"Fibs, my dear—or shall we say, artistic mouldings of the unshapely clay of truth—are the . . . how shall I put it ? . . . Well, anyway, they come in dashed handy. It would never have done for Mrs. Peagrim to have found out that you were in the chorus. If she discovered that my niece was in the chorus, she would infallibly suspect me of being an adventurer. And while," said Uncle Chris meditatively, "of course I *am*, it is nice to have one's little secrets. The good lady has had a rooted distaste for girls in that perfectly honourable but maligned profession ever since our long young friend back there was sued for breach of promise by a member of a touring company in his second year at college. We all have our prejudices. That is hers. However, I think, we may rely on our friend to say nothing about the matter. . . . But why did you do it ? My dear child, whatever induced you to take such a step ?"

Jill laughed.

"That's practically what Mr. Miller said to me when we were rehearsing one of the dances this afternoon, only he put it differently." She linked her arm in his. "What else could I do ? I was alone in New York with the remains of that twenty dollars you sent me and no more in sight."

"But why didn't you stay down at Brookport with your Uncle Elmer ?"

"Have you ever seen my Uncle Elmer ?"

"No. Curiously enough, I never have."

"If you had, you wouldn't ask. Brookport! Ugh! I left when

they tried to get me to understudy the hired man, who had resigned."

"What!"

"Yes, they got tired of supporting me in the state to which I was accustomed—I don't blame them!—so they began to find ways of making me useful about the home. I didn't mind reading to Aunt Julia, and I could just stand taking Tibby for walks. But, when it came to shovelling snow, I softly and silently vanished away."

"But I can't understand all this. I suggested to your uncle—diplomatically—that you had large private means."

"I know you did. And he spent all his time showing me over houses and telling me I could have them for a hundred thousand dollars cash down." Jill bubbled. "You should have seen his face when I told him that twenty dollars was all I had in the world!"

"You didn't tell him that!"

"I did."

Uncle Chris shook his head, like an indulgent father disappointed in a favourite child.

"You're a dear girl, Jill, but really you do seem totally lacking in . . . how shall I put it?—finesse. Your mother was just the same. A sweet woman, but with no diplomacy, no notion of *handling* a situation. I remember her as a child giving me away hopelessly on one occasion after we had been at the jam-cupboard. She did not mean any harm, but she was constitutionally incapable of a tactful negative at the right time." Uncle Chris brooded for a moment on the past. "Oh, well, it's a very fine trait, no doubt, though inconvenient. I don't blame you for leaving Brookport if you weren't happy there. But I wish you had consulted me before going on the stage."

"Shall I strike this man?" asked Jill of the world at large. "How could I consult you? My darling, precious uncle, don't you realize that you had vanished into thin air, leaving me penniless? I had to do something. And, now that we are on the subject, perhaps you will explain your movements. Why did you write to me from that place on Fifty-seventh Street if you weren't there?"

Uncle Chris cleared his throat.

"In a sense . . . when I wrote . . . I *was* there."

"I suppose that means something, but it's beyond me. I'm

not nearly as intelligent as you think, Uncle Chris, so you'll have to explain."

"Well, it was this way, my dear. I was in a peculiar position you must remember. I had made a number of wealthy friends on the boat and it is possible that—unwittingly—I gave them the impression that I was as comfortably off as themselves. At any rate, that is the impression they gathered, and it hardly seemed expedient to correct it. For it is a deplorable trait in the character of the majority of rich people that they only—er—expand—they only show the best and most companionable side of themselves to those whom they imagine to be as wealthy as they are. Well, of course, while one was on the boat, the fact that I was sailing under what a purist might have termed false colours did not matter. The problem was how to keep up the—er—innocent deception after we had reached New York. A woman like Mrs. Waddesleigh Peagrim—a ghastly creature, my dear, all front teeth and exuberance, but richer than the Sub-Treasury—looks askance at a man, however agreeable, if he endeavours to cement a friendship begun on board ship from a cheap boarding-house on Amsterdam Avenue. It was imperative that I should find something in the nature of what I might call a suitable base of operations. Fortune played into my hands. One of the first men I met in New York was an old soldier-servant of mine, to whom I had been able to do some kindnesses in the old days. In fact—it shows how bread cast upon the waters returns to us after many days—it was with the assistance of a small loan from me that he was enabled to emigrate to America. Well, I met this man, and, after a short conversation, he revealed the fact that he was the hall-porter at that apartment-house which you visited, the one on Fifty-Seventh Street. At this time of the year, I knew, many wealthy people go south, to Florida and the Carolinas, and it occurred to me that there might be a vacant apartment in his building. There was. I took it."

"But how on earth could you afford to pay for an apartment in a place like that?"

Uncle Chris coughed.

"I didn't say I paid for it. I said I took it. That is, as one might say, the point of my story. My old friend, grateful for favours received and wishing to do me a good turn, consented to become my accomplice in another—er—innocent deception.

I gave my friends the address and telephone number of the apartment-house, living the while myself in surroundings of a somewhat humbler and less expensive character. I called every morning for letters. If anybody rang me up on the telephone, the admirable man answered in the capacity of my servant, took a message, and relayed it on to me at my boarding-house. If anybody called, he merely said that I was out. There wasn't a flaw in the whole scheme, my dear, and its chief merit was its beautiful simplicity."

"Then what made you give it up? Conscience?"

"Conscience never made me give up *anything*," said Uncle Chris firmly. "No, there were a hundred chances to one against anything going wrong, and it was the hundredth that happened. When you have been in New York longer, you will realize that one peculiarity of the place is that the working-classes are in a constant state of flux. On Monday you meet a plumber. Ah! you say, a plumber! Capital! On the following Thursday you meet him again, and he is a car-conductor. Next week he will be squirting soda in a drug-store. It's the fault of these dashed magazines, with their advertisements of correspondence courses— Are You Earning All You Should?—Write To Us and Learn Chicken-Farming By Mail . . . It puts wrong ideas into the fellows' heads. It unsettles them. It was so in this case. Everything was going swimmingly, when my man suddenly conceived the idea that destiny had intended him for a chauffeur-gardener, and he threw up his position!"

"Leaving you homeless!"

"As you say, homeless—temporarily. But, fortunately—I have been amazingly lucky all through; it really does seem as if you cannot keep a good man down—fortunately my friend had a friend who was janitor at a place on East Forty-first Street, and by a miracle of luck the only apartment in the building was empty. It is an office building, but, like some of these places, it has one small bachelor's apartment on the top floor."

"And you are the small bachelor?"

"Precisely. My friend explained matters to his friend—a few financial details were satisfactorily arranged—and here I am, perfectly happy with the cosiest little place in the world, rent free. I am even better off than I was before, as a matter of fact, for my new ally's wife is an excellent cook, and I have been enabled to give one or two very pleasant dinners at my new

home. It lends verisimilitude to the thing if you can entertain a
little. If you are never in when people call, they begin to wonder.
I am giving dinner to your friend Pilkington and Mrs. Peagrim
there to-night. Homey, delightful, and infinitely cheaper than a
restaurant."

"And what will you do when the real owner of the place walks
in in the middle of dinner?"

"Out of the question. The janitor informs me that he left for
England some weeks ago, intending to make a stay of several
months."

"Well, you certainly think of everything."

"Whatever success I may have achieved," replied Uncle Chris,
with the dignity of a Captain of Industry confiding in an inter-
viewer, "I attribute to always thinking of everything."

Jill gurgled with laughter. There was that about her uncle
which always acted on her moral sense like an opiate, lulling it
to sleep and preventing it from rising up and becoming critical.
If he had stolen a watch and chain, he would somehow have
succeeded in convincing her that he had acted for the best under
the dictates of a benevolent altruism.

"What success *have* you achieved?" she asked, interested.
"When you left me, you were on your way to find a fortune.
Did you find it?"

"I have not actually placed my hands on it yet," admitted
Uncle Chris. "But it is hovering in the air all round me. I
can hear the beating of the wings of the dollar-bills as they
flutter to and fro, almost within reach. Sooner or later I shall
grab them. I never forget, my dear, that I have a task before
me—to restore to you the money of which I deprived you. Some
day—be sure—I shall do it. Some day you will receive a letter
from me, containing a large sum—five thousand—ten thousand
—twenty thousand—whatever it may be, with the simple words
'First Instalment.' " He repeated the phrase, as if it pleased him.
"First Instalment!"

Jill hugged his arm. She was in the mood in which she used
to listen to him ages ago telling her fairy stories.

"Go on!" she cried. "Go on! It's wonderful! Once upon a
time Uncle Chris was walking along Fifth Avenue, when he
happened to meet a poor old woman gathering sticks for fire-
wood. She looked so old and tired that he was sorry for her, so
he gave her ten cents which he had borrowed from the janitor,

and suddenly she turned into a beautiful girl and said 'I am a fairy! In return for your kindness I grant you three wishes!' And Uncle Chris thought for a moment, and said, 'I want twenty thousand dollars to send to Jill!' And the fairy said, 'It shall be attended to. And the next article?' "

"It is all very well to joke," protested Uncle Chris, pained by this flippancy, "but let me tell you that I shall not require magic assistance to become a rich man. Do you realize that at houses like Mrs. Waddesleigh Peagrim's I am meeting men all the time who have only to say one little word to make me a millionaire? They are fat, grey men with fishy eyes and large waistcoats, and they sit smoking cigars and brooding on what they are going to do to the market next day. If I were a mind-reader I could have made a dozen fortunes by now. I sat opposite that old pirate, Bruce Bishop, for over an hour the very day before he and his gang sent Consolidated Pea-Nuts down twenty points! If I had known what was in the wind, I doubt if I could have restrained myself from choking his intentions out of the fellow. Well, what I am trying to point out is that one of these days one of these old oysters will have a fleeting moment of human pity and disgorge some tip on which I can act. It is that reflection that keeps me so constantly at Mrs. Peagrim's house." Uncle Chris shivered slightly. "A fearsome woman, my dear! Weighs a hundred and eighty pounds and as skittish as a young lamb in springtime! She makes me dance with her!" Uncle Chris' lips quivered in a spasm of pain, and he was silent for a moment. "Thank Heaven I was once a footballer!" he said reverently.

"But what do you live on?" asked Jill. "I know you are going to be a millionaire next Tuesday week, but how are you getting along in the meantime?"

Uncle Chris coughed.

"Well, as regards actual living expenses. I have managed by a shrewd business stroke to acquire a small but sufficient income. I live in a boarding-house—true—but I contrive to keep the wolf from its door—which, by the by, badly needs a lick of paint. Have you ever heard of Nervino?"

"I don't think so. It sounds like a patent medicine."

"It *is* a patent medicine." Uncle Chris stopped and looked anxiously at her. "Jill, you're looking pale, my dear."

"Am I? We had rather a tiring rehearsal."

"Are you sure," said Uncle Chris seriously, "that it is only that? Are you sure that your vitality has not become generally lowered by the fierce rush of Metropolitan life? Are you aware of the things that can happen to you if you allow the red corpuscles of your blood to become devitalised? I had a friend . . ."

"Stop! You're scaring me to death!"

Uncle Chris gave his moustache a satisfied twirl.

"Just what I meant to do, my dear. And, when I had scared you sufficiently—you wouldn't wait for the story of my consumptive friend. Pity! It's one of my best!—I should have mentioned that I had been having much the same trouble myself until lately, but the other day I happened to try Nervino, the great specific . . . I was giving you an illustration of myself in action, my dear. I went to these Nervino people—happened to see one of their posters and got the idea in a flash—I went to them and said, 'Here am I, a presentable man of persuasive manners and a large acquaintance among the leaders of New York Society. What would it be worth to you to have me hint from time to time at dinner parties and so forth that Nervino is the rich man's panacea?' I put the thing lucidly to them. I said, 'No doubt you have a thousand agents in the city, but have you one who does not look like an agent and won't talk like an agent? Have you one who is inside the houses of the wealthy, at their very dinner-tables, instead of being on the front step, trying to hold the door open with his foot? That is the point you have to consider.' They saw the idea at once. We arranged terms—not as generous as I could wish, perhaps, but quite ample. I receive a tolerably satisfactory salary each week, and in return I spread the good word about Nervino in the gilded palaces of the rich. Those are the people to go for, Jill. They have been so busy wrenching money away from the widow and the orphan that they haven't had time to look after their health. You catch one of them after dinner, just as he is wondering if he was really wise in taking two helpings of the lobster Newburg, and he is clay in your hands. I draw my chair up to his and become sympathetic and say that I had precisely the same trouble myself until recently, and mention a dear old friend of mine who died of indigestion, and gradually lead the conversation round to Nervino. I don't force it on them. I don't even ask them to try it. I merely point to myself, rosy with health, and say that I owe everything to it, and the thing is done. They thank me profusely and scribble the name down on their shirt-cuffs. And there you are! I don't suppose," said Uncle Chris philosophically, "that the stuff can do them any actual harm."

They had come to the corner of Forty-first Street. Uncle Chris felt in his pocket and produced a key.

"If you want to go and take a look at my little nest, you can let yourself in. It's on the twenty-second floor. Don't fail to go out on the roof and look at the view. It's worth seeing. It will give you some idea of the size of the city. A wonderful, amazing city, my dear, full of people who need Nervino. I shall go on and drop in at the club for half an hour. They have given me a fortnight's card at the Avenue. Capital place. Here's the key."

Jill turned down Forty-first Street, and came to a mammoth structure of steel and stone which dwarfed the modest brown houses beside it into nothingness. It was curious to think of a private flat nestling on the summit of this mountain. She went in, and the lift shot her giddily upwards to the twenty-second floor. She found herself facing a short flight of stone steps, ending in a door. She mounted the steps, tried the key, and, turning it, entered a hall-way. Proceeding down the passage, she reached a sitting-room.

It was a small room, but furnished with a solid comfort which soothed her. For the first time since she had arrived in New York, she had the sense of being miles away from the noise and bustle of the city. There was a complete and restful silence. She was alone in a nest of books and deep chairs, on which a large grandfather-clock looked down with that wide-faced benevolence peculiar to its kind. So peaceful was this eyrie, perched high up above the clamour and rattle of civilization, that ever nerve in her body seemed to relax in a delicious content. It was like being in Peter Pan's house in the tree-tops.

II

Jill possessed in an unusual degree that instinct for exploration which is implanted in most of us. She was frankly inquisitive, and could never be two minutes in a strange room without making a tour of it and examining its books, pictures, and photographs. Almost at once she began to prowl.

The mantelpiece was her first objective. She always made for

other people's mantelpieces, for there, more than anywhere
else, is the character of a proprietor revealed. This mantelpiece
was sprinkled with photographs, large, small, framed and
unframed. In the centre of it, standing all alone and looking
curiously out of place among its large neighbours, was a little
snapshot.

It was dark by the mantelpiece. Jill took the photograph to
the window, where the fading light could fall on it. Why, she
could not have said, but the thing interested her. There was
mystery about it. It seemed in itself so insignificant to have the
place of honour.

The snapshot had evidently been taken by an amateur, but it
was one of those lucky successes which happen at rare intervals
to amateur photographers to encourage them to proceed with
their hobby. It showed a small girl in a white dress cut short
above slim, black legs, standing in the porch of an old house,
one hand swinging a sun-bonnet, the other patting an Irish
terrier which had planted its front paws against her waist and
was looking up into her face with that grave melancholy characteristic of Irish terriers. The sunlight was evidently strong, for the
child's face was puckered in a twisted though engaging grin.
Jill's first thought was "What a jolly kid!" And then, with a
leaping of the heart that seemed to send something big and
choking into her throat she saw that it was a photograph of herself.

With a swooping bound memory raced back over the years.
She could feel the hot sun on her face, hear the anxious voice of
Freddie Rooke—then fourteen and for the first time the owner
of a camera—imploring her to stand just like that because he
wouldn't be half a minute only some rotten thing had stuck or
something. Then the sharp click, the doubtful assurance of
Freddie that he thought it was all right if he hadn't forgotten to
shift the film (in which case she might expect to appear in
combination with a cow which he had snapped on his way to
the house), and the relieved disappearance of Pat, the terrier,
who didn't understand photography. How many years ago had
that been ? She could not remember. But Freddie had grown to
long-legged manhood, she to an age of discretion and full-length
frocks, Pat had died, the old house was inhabited by strangers
. . . and here was the silent record of that sun-lit afternoon, three
thousand miles away from the English garden in which it had
come into existence.

The shadows deepened. The top of the great building swayed gently, causing the pendulum of the grandfather-clock to knock against the sides of its wooden case. Jill started. The noise, coming after the dead silence, frightened her till she realized what it was. She had a nervous feeling of not being alone. It was as if the shadows held goblins that peered out at the intruder. She darted to the mantelpiece and replaced the photograph. She felt like some heroine of a fairy-story meddling with the contents of the giant's castle. Soon there would come the sound of a great footstep thud—thud . . .

Thud.

Jill's heart gave another leap. She was perfectly sure she had heard a sound. It had been just like the banging of a door. She braced herself, listening, every muscle tense. And then, cleaving the stillness, came a voice from down the passage—

" Just see them Pullman porters,
    Dolled up with scented waters
    Bought with their dimes and quarters!
        See, here they come! Here they come!"

For an instant Jill could not have said whether she was relieved or more frightened than ever. True, that numbing sense of the uncanny had ceased to grip her, for Reason told her that spectres do not sing rag-time songs. On the other hand, owners of apartments do, and she would almost as readily have faced a spectre as the owner of this apartment. Dizzily, she wondered how in the world she was to explain her presence. Suppose he turned out to be some awful-choleric person who would listen to no explanations.

" Oh, see those starched-up collars!
    Hark how their captain hollers
        'Keep time! Keep time!'
    It's worth a thousand dollars
    To see those tip-collectors. . . ."

Very near now. Almost at the door.

" Those upper-berth inspectors,
    Those Pullman porters on parade!"

A dim, shapeless figure in the black of the doorway. The scrabbling of fingers on the wall.

"Where are you, dammit?" said the voice, apparently addressing the electric-light switch.

Jill shrank back, desperate fingers pressing deep into the back of an arm-chair. Light flashed from the wall at her side. And there, in the doorway, stood Wally Mason in his shirt-sleeves.

⋆ 13 ⋆

The Ambassador Arrives

I

IN these days of rapid movement, when existence has become little more than a series of shocks of varying intensity, astonishment is the shortest-lived of all the emotions. There was an instant in which Jill looked at Wally and Wally at Jill with the eye of total amazement, and then, almost simultaneously, each began—the process was subconscious—to regard this meeting not as an isolated and inexplicable event, but as something resulting from a perfectly logical chain of circumstances.

"Hullo!" said Wally.

"Hullo!" said Jill.

It was not a very exalted note on which to pitch the conversation, but it had the merit of giving each of them a little more time to collect themselves.

"This is . . . I wasn't expecting you!" said Wally.

"I wasn't expecting *you!*" said Jill.

There was another pause, in which Wally, apparently examining her last words and turning them over in his mind, found that they did not square with his preconceived theories.

"You weren't expecting me?"

"I certainly was not!"

"But . . . but you knew I lived here?"

Jill shook her head. Wally reflected for an instant, and then put his finger, with a happy inspiration, on the very heart of the mystery.

"Then how on earth did you get here?"

He was glad he had asked that. The sense of unreality which had come to him in the first startling moment of seeing her and vanished under the influence of logic had returned as strong as ever. If she did not know he lived in this place, how in the name of everything uncanny had she found her way here? A momentary wonder as to whether all this was not mixed up with telepathy and mental suggestion and all that sort of thing came to him. Certainly he had been thinking of her all the time since their parting at the Savoy Hotel that night three weeks and more back . . . No, that was absurd. There must be some sounder reason for her presence. He waited for her to give it.

Jill for the moment felt physically incapable of giving it. She shrank from the interminable explanation which confronted her as a weary traveller shrinks from a dusty, far-stretching desert. She simply could not go into all that now. So she answered with a question.

"When did you land in New York?"

"This afternoon. We were supposed to dock this morning but the boat was late." Wally perceived that he was being pushed away from the main point, and jostled his way back to it. "But what are you doing here?"

"It's such a long story."

Her voice was plaintive. Remorse smote Wally. It occurred to him that he had not been sufficiently sympathetic. Not a word had he said on the subject of her change of fortunes. He had just stood and gaped and asked questions. After all, what the devil did it matter how she came to be here? He had anticipated a long and tedious search for her through the labyrinth of New York, and here Fate had brought her to his very door, and all he could do was to ask why, instead of being thankful. He perceived that he was not much of a fellow.

"Never mind," he said. "You can tell me when you feel like it." He looked at her eagerly. Time seemed to have wiped away that little misunderstanding under the burden of which they had parted. "It's too wonderful finding you like this!" He hesitated. "I heard about—everything," he said awkwardly.

"My——" Jill hesitated too. "My smash?"

"Yes. Freddie Rooke told me. I was terribly sorry."

"Thank you," said Jill.

There was a pause. They were both thinking of that other disaster which had happened. The presence of Derek Underhill seemed to stand like an unseen phantom between them. Finally Wally spoke at random, choosing the first words that came into his head in his desire to break the silence.

"Jolly place, this, isn't it?"

Jill perceived that an opening for those tedious explanations had been granted her.

"Uncle Chris thinks so," she said demurely.

Wally looked puzzled.

"Uncle Chris ? Oh, your uncle ?"

"Yes."

"But—he has never been here."

"Oh, yes. He's giving a dinner-party here to-night!"

"He's . . . what did you say ?"

"It's all right. I only began at the end of the story instead of the beginning. I'll tell you the whole thing. And then . . . then I suppose you will be terribly angry and make a fuss."

"I'm not much of a lad, as Freddie Rooke would say, for making fusses. And I can't imagine being terribly angry with you."

"Well, I'll risk it. Though, if I wasn't a brave girl, I should leave Uncle Chris to explain for himself and simply run away."

"Anything is better than that. It's a miracle meeting you like this, and I don't want to be deprived of the fruits of it. Tell me anything, but don't go."

"You'll be furious."

"Not with you."

"I should hope not with me. I've done nothing. I am the innocent heroine. But I'm afraid you will be very angry with Uncle Chris."

"If he's your uncle, that passes him. Besides, he once licked the stuffing out of me with a whangee. That forms a bond. Tell me all."

Jill considered. She had promised to begin at the beginning, but it was difficult to know what was the beginning.

"Have you ever heard of Captain Kidd ?" she asked at length.

"You're wandering from the point, aren't you ?"

"No, I'm not. *Have* you heard of Captain Kidd ?"

"The pirate ? Of course."

"Well, Uncle Chris is his direct lineal descendant. That really explains the whole thing."

Wally looked at her enquiringly.

"Could you make it a little easier ?" he said.

"I can tell you everything in half a dozen words, if you like. But it will sound awfully abrupt."

"Go ahead."

"Uncle Chris has stolen your apartment."

Wally nodded slowly.

"I see. Stolen my apartment."

"Of course you can't possibly understand. I shall have to tell you the whole thing, after all."

Wally listened with flattering attention as she began the epic of Major Christopher Selby's doings in New York. Whatever his emotions, he certainly was not bored.

"So that's how it all happened," concluded Jill.

For a moment Wally said nothing. He seemed to be digesting what he had heard.

"I see," he said at last. "It's a variant of those advertisements they print in the magazines. 'Why pay rent? Own somebody else's home!'"

"That *does* rather sum it up," said Jill.

Wally burst into a roar of laughter.

"He's a corker!"

Jill was immensely relieved. For all her courageous bearing, she had not relished the task of breaking the news to Wally. She knew that he had a sense of humour, but a man may have a sense of humour and yet not see anything amusing in having his home stolen in his absence.

"I'm so glad you're not angry."

"Of course not."

"Most men would be."

"Most men are chumps."

"It's so wonderful that it happened to be you. Suppose it had been an utter stranger! What could I have done?"

"It would have been the same thing. You would have won him over in two minutes. Nobody could resist you."

"That's very sweet of you."

"I can't help telling the truth. Washington was just the same."

"Then you don't mind Uncle Chris giving his dinner-party here to-night?"

"He has my blessing."

"You really are an angel," said Jill gratefully. "From what he said, I think he looks on it as rather an important function. He had invited a very rich woman, who has been showing him a lot of hospitality—a Mrs. Peagrim . . ."

"Mrs. Waddesleigh Peagrim?"

"Yes? Why, do you know her?"

"Quite well. She goes in a good deal for being Bohemian and knowing people who write and paint and act and so on. That reminds me. I gave Freddie Rooke a letter of introduction to her."

"Freddie Rooke!"

"Yes. He suddenly made up his mind to come over. He came to me for advice about the journey. He sailed a couple of days before I did. I suppose he's somewhere in New York by now, unless he was going on to Florida. He didn't tell me what his plans were."

Jill was conscious of a sudden depression. Much as she liked Freddie, he belonged to a chapter in her life which was closed and which she was trying her hardest to forget. It was impossible to think of Freddie without thinking of Derek, and to think of Derek was like touching an exposed nerve. The news that Freddie was in New York shocked her. New York had already shown itself a city of chance encounters. Could she avoid meeting Freddie?

She knew Freddie so well. There was not a dearer or a better-hearted youth in the world, but he had not that fine sensibility which pilots a man through the awkwardnesses of life. He was a blunderer. Instinct told her that, if she met Freddie, he would talk of Derek, and, if thinking of Derek was touching an exposed nerve, talking of him would be like pressing on that nerve with a heavy hand. She shivered.

Wally was observant.

"There's no need to meet him if you don't want to," he said.

"No," said Jill doubtfully.

"New York's a large place. By the way," he went on, "to return once more to the interesting subject of my lodger, does your uncle sleep here at nights, do you know?"

Jill looked at him gratefully. He was no blunderer. Her desire to avoid Freddie Rooke was, he gave her tacitly to understand, her business, and he did not propose to intrude on it. She liked him for dismissing the subject so easily.

"No, I think he told me he doesn't."

"Well, that's something, isn't it! I call that darned nice of him! I wonder if I could drop back here somewhere about eleven o'clock. Are the festivities likely to be over by then? If I know Mrs. Peagrim, she will insist on going off to one of the hotels to dance directly after dinner. She's a confirmed trotter."

"I don't know how to apologize," began Jill remorsefully.

"Please don't. It's absolutely all right." His eye wandered to the mantelpiece, as it had done once or twice during the conversation. In her hurry Jill had replaced the snapshot with its back to the room, and Wally had the fidgety air of a man whose most cherished possession is maltreated. He got up now and, walking across, turned the photograph round. He stood for a moment, looking at it.

Jill had forgotten the snapshot. Curiosity returned to her.

"Where *did* you get that?" she asked.

Wally turned.

"Oh, did you see this?"

"I was looking at it just before you nearly frightened me to death by appearing so unexpectedly."

"Freddie Rooke sold it to me fourteen years ago."

"Fourteen years ago?"

"Next July," added Wally. "I gave him five shillings for it."

"Five shillings! The little brute!" cried Jill indignantly. "It must have been all the money you had in the world!"

"A trifle more, as a matter of fact. All the money I had in the world was three-and-six. But by a merciful dispensation of Providence the curate had called that morning and left a money-box for subscriptions to the village organ-fund. . . . It's wonderful what you can do with a turn for crime and the small blade of a pocket-knife! I don't think I have ever made money quicker!" He looked at the photograph again. "Not that it seemed quick at the moment. I died at least a dozen agonizing deaths in the few minutes I was operating. Have you ever noticed how slowly time goes when you are coaxing a shilling and a sixpence out of somebody's money-box? Centuries! But I was forgetting. Of course you've had no experience."

"You poor thing!"

"It was worth it."

"And you've had it ever since!"

"I wouldn't part with it for all Mrs. Waddesleigh Peagrim's millions," said Wally with sudden and startling vehemence, "if she offered me them." He paused. "She hasn't, as a matter of fact."

There was a silence. Jill looked at Wally furtively as he returned to his seat. She was seeing him with new eyes. It was as if this trifling incident had removed some sort of a veil. He had suddenly become more alive. For an instant she had seen right into him, to the hidden deeps of his soul. She felt shy and embarrassed.

"Pat died," she said at length. She felt the necessity of saying something.

"I liked Pat."

"He picked up some poison, poor darling . . . How long ago those days seem, don't they?"

"They are always pretty vivid to me. I wonder who has that old house of yours now."

"I heard the other day," said Jill more easily. The odd sensation of embarrassment was passing. "Some people called . . . what was the name? . . . Debenham, I think."

Silence fell again. It was broken by the front-door bell, like an alarm-clock that shatters a dream.

Wally got up.

"Your uncle," he said.

"You aren't going to open the door?"

"That was the scheme."

"But he'll get such a shock when he sees you."

"He must look on it in the light of rent. I don't see why I shouldn't have a little passing amusement from this business."

He left the room. Jill heard the front door open. She waited breathlessly. Pity for Uncle Chris struggled with the sterner feeling that it served him right.

"Hullo!" she heard Wally say.

"Hullo-ullo-ullo!" replied an exuberant voice. "Wondered if I'd find you in, and all that sort of thing. I say, what a deuce of a way it is here. Sort of get a chappie into training for going to heaven, what? I mean, what?"

Jill looked about her like a trapped animal. It was absurd, she felt, but every nerve in her body cried out against the prospect of meeting Freddie. His very voice had opened old wounds and set them throbbing.

She listened in the doorway. Out of sight down the passage, Freddie seemed by the sounds to be removing his overcoat. She stole out and darted like a shadow down the corridor that led to Wally's bedroom. The window of the bedroom opened on to the wide roof which Uncle Chris had eulogized. She slipped noiselessly out, closing the window behind her.

II

"I say, Mason, old top," said Freddie, entering the sitting-room, "I hope you don't mind my barging in like this, but the fact is things are a bit thick. I'm dashed worried, and I didn't know another soul I could talk it over with. As a matter of fact, wasn't sure you were in New York at all, but I remembered hearing you say in London that you were popping back almost at once, so I looked you up in the telephone book and took a chance. I'm dashed glad you *are* back. When did you arrive?"

"This afternoon."

"I've been here two or three days. Well, it's a bit of luck catching you. You see, what I want to ask your advice about . . ."

Wally looked at his watch. He was not surprised to find that Jill had taken to flight. He understood her feelings perfectly, and was anxious to get rid of the inopportune Freddie as soon as possible.

"You'll have to talk quick, I'm afraid," he said. "I've lent this place to a man for the evening, and he's having some people to dinner. What's the trouble?"

"It's about Jill."

"Jill?"

"Jill Mariner, you know. You remember Jill? You haven't forgotten my telling you all that? About her losing her money and coming over to America?"

"No. I remember you telling me that."

Freddie seemed to miss something in his companion's manner, some note of excitement and perturbation.

"Of course," he said, as if endeavouring to explain this to himself, "you hardly knew her, I suppose. Only met once since you were kids and all that sort of thing. But I'm a pal of hers and I'm dashed upset by the whole business, I can tell you. It worries me, I mean to say. Poor girl, you know, landed on her uppers in a strange country. Well, I mean, it worries me. So the first thing I did when I got here was to try to find her. That's why I came over, really, to try to find her. Apart from anything else, you see, poor old Derek is dashed worried about her."

"Need we bring Underhill in?"

"Oh, I know you don't like him and think he behaved rather rummily and so forth, but that's all right now."

"It is, is it?" said Wally drily.

"Oh, absolutely. It's all on again."

"What's all on again?"

"Why, I mean he wants to marry Jill. I came over to find her and tell her so."

Wally's eyes glowed.

"If you have come over as an ambassador . . ."

"That's right. Jolly old ambassador. Very word I used myself."

"I say, if you have come over as an ambassador with the idea of reopening negotiations with Jill on behalf of that infernal swine . . ."

"Old man!" protested Freddie, pained. "Pal of mine, you know."

"If he is, after what's happened, your mental processes are beyond me."

"My what, old son?"

"Your mental processes."

"Oh, ah!" said Freddie, learning for the first time that he had any.

Wally looked at him intently. There was a curious expression on his rough-hewn face.

"I can't understand you, Freddie. If ever there was a fellow who might have been expected to take the only possible view of Underhill's behaviour in this business, I should have said it was you. You're a public-school man. You've mixed all the time with decent people. You wouldn't do anything that wasn't straight yourself to save your life. Yet it seems to have made absolutely no difference in your opinion of this man Underhill that he behaved like an utter cad to a girl who was one of your best friends. You seem to worship him just as much as ever. And you have travelled three thousand miles to bring a message from him to Jill—Good God! *Jill !*—to the effect, as far as I can understand it, that he has thought it over and come to the conclusion that after all she may possibly be good enough for him!"

Freddie recovered the eye-glass which the raising of his eyebrows had caused to fall, and polished it in a crushed sort of way. Rummy, he reflected, how chappies stayed the same all their lives as they were when they were kids. Nasty, tough sort of chap Wally Mason had been as a boy, and here he was, apparently, not altered a bit. At least the only improvement he could detect was that, whereas in the old days Wally, when in an ugly mood like this, would undoubtedly have kicked him, he now seemed content with mere words. All the same, he was being dashed unpleasant. And he was all wrong about

poor Derek. This last fact he endeavoured to make clear.
"You don't understand," he said. "You don't realize. You've never met Lady Underhill, have you?"

"What has she got to do with it?"

"Everything, old bean, everything. If it hadn't been for her, there wouldn't have been any trouble of any description, sort, or order. But she barged in and savaged poor old Derek till she absolutely made him break off the engagement."

"If you call him 'poor old Derek' again, Freddie," said Wally viciously, "I'll drop you out of the window and throw your hat after you! If he's such a gelatine-backboned worm that his mother can . . ."

"You don't know her, old thing! She's *the* original hell-hound!"

"I don't care what . . ."

"Must be seen to be believed," mumbled Freddie.

"I don't care what she's like! Any man who could . . ."

"Once seen, never forgotten!"

"Damn you! Don't interrupt every time I try to get a word in!"

"Sorry, old man! Shan't occur again!"

Wally moved to the window, and stood looking out. He had had much more to say on the subject of Derek Underhill, but Freddie's interruptions had put it out of his head, and he felt irritated and baffled.

"Well, all I can say is," he remarked savagely, "that, if you have come over here as an ambassador to try and effect a re-conciliation between Jill and Underhill, I hope to God you'll never find her."

Freddie emitted a weak cough, like a very far-off asthmatic old sheep. He was finding Wally more overpowering every moment. He had rather forgotten the dear old days of his childhood, but this conversation was beginning to refresh his memory: and he was realizing more vividly with every moment that passed how very Wallyish Wally was—how extraordinarily like the Wally who had dominated his growing intellect when they were both in Eton suits. Freddie in those days had been all for peace, and he was all for peace now. He made his next observation diffidently.

"I *have* found her!"

Wally spun round.

"What!"

"When I say that, I don't absolutely mean I've seen her. I mean I know where she is. That's what I came round to see you about. Felt I must talk it over, you know. The situation seems to me dashed rotten and not a little thick. The fact is, old man, she's gone on the stage. In the chorus, you know. And, I mean to say, well, if you follow what I'm driving at, what, what?"

"In the chorus?"

"In the chorus!"

"How do you know?"

Freddie gropped for his eyeglass, which had fallen again. He regarded it a trifle sternly. He was fond of the little chap, but it was always doing that sort of thing. The whole trouble was that, if you wanted to keep it in its place, you simply couldn't register any sort of emotion with the good old features: and, when you were chatting with a fellow like Wally Mason, you had to be registering something all the time.

"Well, that was a bit of luck, as a matter of fact. When I first got here, you know, it seemed to me the only thing to do was to round up a merry old detective and put the matter in his hands, like they do in stories. *You* know! Ring at the bell. 'And this, if I mistake not, Watson, is my client now.' And then in breezes client and spills the plot. I found a sleuth in the classified telephone directory, and toddled round. Rummy chaps, detectives! Ever met any? I always thought they were lean, hatchet-faced Johnnies with inscrutable smiles. This one looked just like my old Uncle Ted, the one who died of apoplexy. Jovial, puffy-faced bird, who kept bobbing up behind a fat cigar. Have you ever noticed what whacking big cigars these fellows over here smoke? Rummy country, America. You ought to have seen the way this blighter could shift his cigar right across his face with moving his jaw-muscles. Like a flash! Most remarkable thing you ever saw, I give you my honest word! He . . ."

"Couldn't you keep your Impressions of America for the book you're going to write, and come to the point?" said Wally rudely.

'Sorry, old chap," said Freddie meekly. "Glad you reminded me. Well . . . Oh, yes. We had got as far as the jovial old human bloodhound, hadn't we? Well, I put the matter before this chappie. Told him I wanted to find a girl, showed him a photograph, and so forth. I say," said Freddie, wandering off once

more into speculation, "why is it that coves like that always talk
of a girl as 'the little lady' ? This chap kept saying 'We'll find the
little lady for you!' Oh, well, that's rather off the rails, isn't it ?
It just floated across my mind and I thought I'd mention it.
Well, this blighter presumably nosed about and made enquiries
for a couple of days, but didn't effect anything that you might
call substantial. I'm not blaming him, mind you. I shouldn't
care to have a job like that myself. I mean to say, when you
come to think of what a frightful number of girls there are in
this place, to have to . . . well, as I say, he did his best but didn't
click; and then this evening, just before I came here, I met a girl
I had known in England—she was in a show over there—a girl
called Nelly Bryant . . ."

"Nelly Bryant ? I know her."

"Yes ? Fancy that! She was in a thing called 'Follow the Girl'
in London. Did you see it by any chance ? Topping show! There
was one scene where the . . ."

"Get on! Get on! I wrote it."

"You wrote it ?" Freddie beamed simple-hearted admiration.
"My dear old chap, I congratulate you! One of the ripest and
most all-wool musical comedies I've ever seen. I went twenty-
four times. Rummy I don't remember spotting that you wrote it.
I suppose one never looks at the names on the programme.
Yes, I went twenty-four times. The first time I went was with
a couple of chappies from . . ."

"Listen, Freddie!" said Wally feverishly. "On some other
occasion I should dearly love to hear the story of your life, but
just now . . ."

"Absolutely, old man. You're perfectly right. Well, to cut a
long story short, Nelly Bryant told me that she and Jill were
rehearsing with a piece called 'The Rose of America.' "

" 'The Rose of America!' "

"I think that was the name of it."

"That's Ike Goble's show. He called me up on the phone
about it half an hour ago. I promised to go and see a rehearsal
of it to-morrow or the day after. And Jill's in that?"

"Yes. How about it ? I mean, I don't know much about this
sort of thing, but do you think it's the sort of thing Jill ought
to be doing ?"

Wally was moving restlessly about the room. Freddie's news
had disquieted him. Mr. Goble had a reputation.

"I know a lot about it," he replied, "and it certainly isn't."
He scowled at the carpet. "Oh, damn everybody!"

Freddie paused to allow him to proceed, if such should be
his wish, but Wally had apparently said his say. Freddie went
on to point out an aspect of the matter which was troubling him
greatly.

"I'm sure poor old Derek wouldn't like her being in the
chorus!"

Wally started so violently that for a moment Freddie was
uneasy.

"I mean Underhill," he corrected himself hastily.

"Freddie," said Wally, "you're an awfully good chap, but I
wish you would exit rapidly now! Thanks for coming and telling
me, very good of you. This way out!"

"But, old man . . .!"

"Now what?"

"I thought we were going to discuss this binge and decide
what to do and all that sort of thing."

"Some other time. I want to think about it."

"Oh, you will think about it?"

"Yes, I'll think about it."

"Topping! You see, you're a brainy sort of fellow, and you'll
probably hit something."

"I probably shall, if you don't go."

"Eh? Oh, ah, yes!" Freddie struggled into his coat. More
than ever did the adult Wally remind him of the dangerous
stripling of years gone by. "Well, cheerio!"

"Same to you!"

"You'll let me know if you scare up some devilish fruity
wheeze, won't you? I'm at the Biltmore."

"Very good place to be. Go there now."

"Right ho! Well, toodle-oo!"

"The elevator is at the foot of the stairs," said Wally. "You
press the bell and up it comes. You hop in and down you go!
It's a great invention! Good night!"

"Oh, I say. One moment . . ."

"Good *night!*" said Wally.

He closed the door, and ran down the passage.

"Jill!" he called. He opened the bedroom window and stepped
out. "Jill!"

There was no reply.

"Jill!" called Wally once again, but again there was no answer. Wally walked to the parapet, and looked over. Below him the vastness of the city stretched itself in a great triangle, its apex the harbour, its sides the full silver of the East and Hudson Rivers. Directly before him, crowned with its white lantern, the Metropolitan Tower reared its graceful height to the stars. And all around, in the windows of the tall buildings that looked from this bastion on which he stood almost squat, a million lights stared up at him, the unsleeping eyes of New York. It was a scene of which Wally, always sensitive to beauty, never tired: but to-night it had lost its appeal. A pleasant breeze from the Jersey shore greeted him with a quickening whisper of spring-time and romance, but it did not lift the heaviness of his heart. He felt depressed and apprehensive.

★ 14 ★

Mr. Goble Makes the Big Noise

I

SPRING, whose coming the breeze had heralded to Wally as he smoked upon the roof, floated graciously upon New York two mornings later. The city awoke to a day of blue and gold and to a sense of hard times over and good times to come. In his apartment on Park Avenue, Mr. Isaac Goble, sniffing the gentle air from the window of his breakfast-room, returned to his meal and his *Morning Telegraph* with a resolve to walk to the theatre for rehearsal: a resolve which had also come to Jill and Nelly Bryant, eating stewed prunes in their boarding-house in the Forties. On the summit of his sky-scraper, Wally Mason, performing Swedish exercises to the delectation of various clerks and stenographers in the upper windows of neighbouring buildings, felt young and vigorous and optimistic, and went in to his shower-bath thinking of Jill. And it was of Jill, too, that young Pilkington thought, as he propped his long form up against the pillows and sipped his morning cup of tea. For the first time in several days a certain moodiness which had affected Otis Pilkington left him, and he dreamed happy day-dreams.

The gaiety of Otis was not, however, entirely or even primarily

due to the improvement in the weather. It had its source in a
conversation which had taken place between himself and Jill's
Uncle Chris on the previous night. Exactly how it had come
about, Mr. Pilkington was not entirely clear, but, somehow,
before he was fully aware of what he was saying, he had begun
to pour into Major Selby's sympathetic ears the story of his
romance. Encouraged by the other's kindly receptiveness, he
had told him all—his love for Jill, his hopes that some day it
might be returned, the difficulties complicating the situation
owing to the known prejudices of Mrs. Waddesleigh Peagrim
concerning girls who formed the personnel of musical comedy
ensembles. To all these outpourings Major Selby had listened
with keen attention, and finally had made one of those luminous
suggestions, so simple yet so shrewd, which emanate only from
your man of the world. It was Jill's girlish ambition, it seemed
from Major Selby's statement, to become a force in the motion-
picture world. The movies were her objective.

What, he broke off to ask, did Pilkington think of the idea?

Pilkington thought the idea splendid. Miss Mariner, with her
charm and looks, would be wonderful in the movies.

There was, said Uncle Chris, a future for the girl in the
movies.

Mr. Pilkington agreed cordially. A great future indeed.

"Observe," proceeded Uncle Chris, gathering speed and
expanding his chest as he spread his legs before the fire, "how
it would simplify the whole matter if Jill were to become a
motion-picture artist and win fame and wealth in her profession.
You go to your excellent aunt and announce that you are engaged
to be married to Jill Mariner. There is a momentary pause.
'Not *the* Jill Mariner?' falters Mrs. Peagrim. 'Yes, the famous
Miss Mariner!' you reply. Well, I ask you, my boy, can you see
her making any objection? Such a thing would be absurd. No,
I can see no flaw in the project whatsoever." Here Uncle Chris,
as he had pictured Mrs. Peagrim doing, paused for a moment.
"Of course, there would be the preliminaries."

"The preliminaries?"

Uncle Chris' voice became a melodious coo. He beamed upon
Mr. Pilkington.

"Well, think for yourself, my boy! These things cannot be
done without money. I do not propose to allow my niece to
waste her time and her energy in the rank and file of the pro-

fession, waiting years for a chance that might never come. There is plenty of room at the top, and that, in the motion-picture profession, is the place to start. If Jill is to become a motion-picture artist, a special company must be formed to promote her. She must be made a feature, a star, from the beginning. Whether," said Uncle Chris, smoothing the crease of his trousers, "you would wish to take shares in the company yourself . . ."

"Oo . . .!"

". . . is a matter," proceeded Uncle Chris, ignoring the interruption, "for you yourself to decide. Possibly you have other claims on your purse. Possibly this musical play of yours has taken all the cash you are prepared to lock up. Possibly you may consider the venture too speculative. Possibly . . . there are a hundred reasons why you may not wish to join us. But I know a dozen men—I can go down Wall Street to-morrow and pick out twenty men—who will be glad to advance the necessary capital. I can assure you that I personally shall not hesitate to risk—if one can call it risking—any loose cash which I may have lying idle at my banker's."

He rattled the loose cash which he had lying idle in his trouser pocket—fifteen cents in all—and stopped to flick a piece of fluff off his coat-sleeve. Mr. Pilkington was thus enabled to insert a word.

"How much would you want?" he enquired.

"That," said Uncle Chris meditatively, "is a little hard to say. I should have to look into the matter more closely in order to give you the exact figures. But let us say for the sake of argument that you put up—what shall we say?—a hundred thousand? fifty thousand? . . . no, we will be conservative. Perhaps you had better not begin with more than ten thousand. You can always buy more shares later. I don't suppose I shall begin with more than ten thousand myself."

"I could manage ten thousand all right."

"Excellent. We make progress, we make progress. Very well, then. I go to my Wall Street friends and tell them about the scheme, and say 'Here is ten thousand dollars! What is your contribution?' It puts the affair on a business-like basis, you understand. Then we really get to work. But use your own judgment, my boy, you know. Use your own judgment. I would not think of persuading you to take such a step, if you felt at all doubtful. Think it over. Sleep on it. And, whatever you decide

to do, on no account say a word about it to Jill. It would be cruel
to raise her hopes until we are certain that we are in a position
to enable her to realize them. And, of course, not a word to
Mrs. Peagrim."

"Of course."

"Very well, then, my boy," said Uncle Chris affably. "I will
leave you to turn the whole thing over in your mind. Act entirely
as you think best. How is your insomnia, by the way? Did you
try Nervino? Capital! There's nothing like it. It did wonders
for *me*! Good night, good night!"

Otis Pilkington had been turning the thing over in his mind,
with an interval for sleep, ever since. And the more he thought
of it, the better the scheme appeared to him. He winced a little
at the thought of the ten thousand dollars, for he came of prudent
stock and had been brought up in habits of parsimony, but,
after all, he reflected, the money would be merely a loan. Once
the company found its feet, it would be returned to him a
hundred-fold. And there was no doubt that this would put a
completely different aspect on his wooing of Jill, as far as Aunt
Olive was concerned. Why, a cousin of his—young Brewster
Philmore—had married a movie-star only two years ago, and
nobody had made the slightest objection. Brewster was to be
seen with his bride frequently beneath Mrs. Peagrim's roof.
Against the higher strata of Bohemia Mrs. Peagrim had no
prejudice at all. Quite the reverse, in fact. She liked the society
of those whose names were often in the papers and much in the
public mouth. It seemed to Otis Pilkington, in short, that Love
had found a way. He sipped his tea with relish, and when the
Japanese valet brought in the toast all burned on one side,
chided him with a gentle sweetness which, one may hope,
touched the latter's Oriental heart and inspired him with a
desire to serve his best of employers more efficiently.

At half-past ten, Otis Pilkington removed his dressing-gown
and began to put on his clothes to visit the theatre. There was a
rehearsal-call for the whole company at eleven. As he dressed,
his mood was as sunny as the day itself.

And the day, by half-past ten, was as sunny as ever Spring day
had been in a country where Spring comes early and does its best
from the very start. The blue sky beamed down on a happy city.
To and fro the citizenry bustled, aglow with the perfection of
the weather. Everywhere was gaiety and good cheer, except on

the stage of the Gotham Theatre, where an early rehearsal, preliminary to the main event, had been called by Johnson Miller in order to iron some of the kinks out of the "My Heart and I" number, which, with the assistance of the male chorus, the leading lady was to render in Act One.

On the stage of the Gotham gloom reigned—literally, because the stage was wide and deep and was illumined only by a single electric light; and figuratively, because things were going even worse than usual with the "My Heart and I" number, and Johnson Miller, always of an emotional and easily stirred temperament, had been goaded by the incompetence of his male chorus to a state of frenzy. At about the moment when Otis Pilkington shed his flowered dressing-gown and reached for his trousers (the heather-mixture with the red twill), Johnson Miller was pacing the gangway between the orchestra pit and the first row of the orchestra chairs, waving one hand and clutching his white locks with the other, his voice raised the while in agonized protest.

"Gentlemen, you silly idiots," complained Mr. Miller loudly, "you've had three weeks to get these movements into your thick heads, and you haven't done a damn thing right! You're all over the place! You don't seem able to turn without tumbling over each other like a lot of Keystone Kops! What's the matter with you? You're not doing the movements I showed you; you're doing some you have invented yourselves, and they are rotten! I've no doubt you think you can arrange a number better than I can, but Mr. Goble engaged me to be the director, so kindly do exactly as I tell you. Don't try to use your own intelligence, because you haven't any. I'm not blaming you for it. It wasn't your fault that your nurses dropped you on your heads when you were babies. But it handicaps you when you try to think."

Of the seven gentlemanly members of the male ensemble present, six looked wounded by this tirade. They had the air of good men wrongfully accused. They appeared to be silently calling on Heaven to see justice done between Mr. Miller and themselves. The seventh, a long-legged young man in faultlessly fitting tweeds of English cut, seemed, on the other hand, not so much hurt as embarrassed. It was this youth who now stepped down to the darkened footlights and spoke in a remorseful and conscience-stricken manner.

"I say!"

Mr. Miller, that martyr to deafness, did not hear the pathetic bleat. He had swung off at right angles and was marching in an overwrought way up the central aisle leading to the back of the house, his india-rubber form moving in convulsive jerks. Only when he had turned and retraced his steps did he perceive the speaker and prepare to take his share in the conversation.

"What?" he shouted, "Can't hear you!"

"I say, you know, it's my fault, really."

"What?"

"I mean to say, you know . . ."

"What? Speak up, can't you?"

Mr. Saltzburg, who had been seated at the piano, absently playing a melody from his unproduced musical comedy, awoke to the fact that the services of an interpreter were needed. He obligingly left the music-stool and crept, crab-like, along the ledge of the stage-box. He placed his arm about Mr. Miller's shoulders and his lips to Mr. Miller's left ear, and drew a deep breath.

"He says it is his fault!"

Mr. Miller nodded adhesion to this admirable sentiment.

"I know they're not worth their salt!" he replied.

Mr. Saltzburg patiently took a fresh stock of breath.

"This young man says it is his fault that the movement went wrong!"

"Tell him I only signed on this morning, laddie," urged the tweed-clad young man.

"He only joined the company this morning!"

This puzzled Mr. Miller.

"How do you mean, warning?" he asked.

Mr. Saltzburg, purple in the face, made a last effort.

"This young man is new," he bellowed carefully, keeping to words of one syllable. "He does not yet know the steps. He says this is his first day here, so he does not yet know the steps. When he has been here some more time he will know the steps. But now he does not know the steps."

"What he means, " explained the young man in tweeds helpfully, "is that I don't know the steps."

"He does not know the steps!" roared Mr. Saltzburg.

"I know he doesn't know the steps," said Mr. Miller. "Why doesn't he know the steps? He's had long enough to learn them"

"He is new!"

"Hugh ?"

"New!"

"Oh, new ?"

"Yes, new!"

"Why the devil is he new ?" cried Mr. Miller, awaking suddenly to the truth and filled with a sense of outrage. "Why didn't he join with the rest of the company ? How can I put on chorus numbers if I am saddled every day with new people to teach ? Who engaged him ?"

"Who engaged you ?" enquired Mr. Saltzburg of the culprit.

"Mr. Pilkington."

"Mr. Pilkington," shouted Mr. Saltzburg.

"When ?"

"When ?"

"Last night."

"Last night."

Mr. Miller waved his hands in a gesture of divine despair, spun round, darted up the aisle, turned, and bounded back.

"What can I do ?" he wailed. "My hands are tied! I am hampered! I am handicapped! We open in two weeks, and every day I find somebody new in the company to upset everything I have done. I shall go to Mr. Goble and ask to be released from my contract. I shall . . . Come along, come along, come along now!" he broke off suddenly. "Why are we wasting time ? The whole number once more. The whole number once more from the beginning!"

The young man tottered back to his gentlemanly colleagues, running a finger in an agitated manner round the inside of his collar. He was not used to this sort of thing. In a large experience of amateur theatricals he had never encountered anything like it. In the breathing-space afforded by the singing of the first verse and refrain by the lady who played the heroine of "The Rose of America," he found time to make an enquiry of the artist on his right.

"I say! Is he always like this ?"

"Who ? Johnny ?"

"The sportsman with the hair that turned white in a single night. The barker on the skyline. Does he often get the wind up like this ?"

His colleague smiled tolerantly.

"Why, that's nothing!" he replied. "Wait till you see him really cut loose! That was just a gentle whisper!"

"My God!" said the newcomer, staring into a bleak future.

The leading lady came to the end of her refrain, and the gentlemen of the ensemble, who had been hanging about upstage, began to curvet nimbly down towards her in a double line; the new arrival, with an eye on his nearest neighbour, endeavouring to curvet as nimbly as the others. A clapping of hands from the dark auditorium indicated—inappropriately—that he had failed to do so. Mr. Miller could be perceived—dimly—with all his fingers entwined in his hair.

"Clear the stage!" yelled Mr. Miller. "Not you!" he shouted, as the latest addition to the company began to drift off with the others. "You stay!"

"Me?"

"Yes, you. I shall have to teach you the steps by yourself, or we shall get nowhere. Go up-stage. Start the music again, Mr. Saltzburg. Now, when the refrain begins, come down. Gracefully! Gracefully!"

The young man, pink but determined, began to come down gracefully. And it was while he was thus occupied that Jill and Nelly Bryant, entering the wings which were beginning to fill up as eleven o'clock approached, saw him.

"Whoever is that?" said Nelly.

"New man," replied one of the chorus gentlemen. "Came this morning."

Nelly turned to Jill.

"He looks just like Mr. Rooke!" she exclaimed.

"He *is* Mr. Rooke!" said Jill.

"He can't be!"

"He *is!*"

"But what is he doing here?"

Jill bit her lip.

"That's just what I'm going to ask him myself," she said.

II

The opportunity for a private conversation with Freddie did not occur immediately. For ten minutes he remained alone on the stage, absorbing abusive tuition from Mr. Miller: and at the end of that period a further ten minutes was occupied with the rehearsing of the number with the leading lady and the rest of

the male chorus. When, finally, a roar from the back of the
auditorium announced the arrival of Mr. Goble and at the same
time indicated Mr. Goble's desire that the stage should be
cleared and the rehearsal proper begin, a wan smile of recognition
and a faint "What ho!" was all that Freddie was able to bestow
upon Jill, before, with the rest of the ensemble, they had to go
and group themselves for the opening chorus. It was only when
this had been run through four times and the stage left vacant
for two of the principals to play a scene that Jill was able to
draw the Last of the Rookes aside in a dark corner and put him
to the question.

"Freddie, what are you doing here?"

Freddie mopped his streaming brow. Johnson Miller's idea
of an opening chorus was always strenuous. On the present
occasion, the ensemble were supposed to be guests at a Long
Island house-party, and Mr. Miller's conception of the gathering
suggested that he supposed house-party guests on Long Island
to consist exclusively of victims of St. Vitus' dance. Freddie
was feeling limp, battered, and exhausted; and, from what he
had gathered, the worst was yet to come.

"Eh?" he said feebly.

"What are you doing here?"

"Oh, ah, yes! I see what you mean! I suppose you're surprised
to find me in New York, what?"

"I'm not surprised to find you in New York. I knew you had
come over. But I am surprised to find you on the stage, being
bullied by Mr. Miller."

"I say," said Freddie in an awed voice. "He's a bit of a nut,
that lad, what? He reminds me of the troops of Midian in the
hymn. The chappies who prowled and prowled around. I'll bet
he's worn a groove in the carpet. Like a jolly old tiger at the
Zoo at feeding time. Wouldn't be surprised at any moment to
look down and find him biting a piece out of my leg!"

Jill seized his arm and shook it.

"Don't *ramble*, Freddie! Tell me how you got here."

"Oh, that was pretty simple. I had a letter of introduction to
this chappie Pilkington who's running this show, and, we having
got tolerably pally in the last few days, I went to him and asked him
to let me join the merry throng. I said I didn't want any money,
and the little bit of work I would do wouldn't make any difference
so he said 'Right ho!' or words to that effect, and here I am."

"But why? You can't be doing this for fun, surely?"

"Fun!" A pained expression came into Freddie's face. "My idea of fun isn't anything in which jolly old Miller, the bird with the snowy hair, is permitted to mix. Something tells me that that lad is going to make it his life-work picking on me. No, I didn't do this for fun. I had a talk with Wally Mason the night before last, and he seemed to think that being in the chorus wasn't the sort of thing you ought to be doing, so I thought it over and decided that I ought to join the troupe too. Then I could always be on the spot, don't you know, if there was any trouble. I mean to say, I'm not much of a chap and all that sort of thing, but still I might come in handy one of these times. Keep a fatherly eye on you, don't you know, and what not!"

Jill was touched. "You're a dear, Freddie!"

"I thought, don't you know, it would make poor old Derek a bit easier in his mind."

Jill froze.

"I don't want to talk about Derek, Freddie, please."

"Oh, I know what you must be feeling, Pretty sick, I'll bet, what? But if you could see him now . . ."

"I don't want to talk about him!"

"He's pretty cut up, you know. Regrets bitterly and all that sort of thing. He wants you to come back again."

"I see! He sent you to fetch me?"

"That was more or less the idea."

"It's a shame that you had all the trouble. You can get messenger-boys to go anywhere and do anything nowadays. Derek ought to have thought of that."

Freddie looked at her doubtfully.

"You're spoofing, aren't you? I mean to say, you wouldn't have liked it!"

"I shouldn't have disliked it any more than his sending you."

"Oh, but I wanted to pop over. Keen to see America and so forth."

Jill looked past him at the gloomy stage. Her face was set, and her eyes sombre.

"Can't you understand, Freddie? You've known me a long time. I should have thought that you would have found out by now that I have a certain amount of pride. If Derek wanted me back, there was only one thing for him to do—come over and find me himself."

"Rummy! That's what Mason said, when I told him. You two don't realize how dashed busy Derek is these days."

"Busy!"

Something in her face seemed to tell Freddie that he was not saying the right thing, but he stumbled on.

"You've no notion how busy he is. I mean to say, elections coming on and so forth. He daren't stir from the metrop."

"Of course I couldn't expect him to do anything that might interfere with his career, could I ?"

"Absolutely not. I knew you would see it!" said Freddie charmed at her reasonableness. All rot, what you read about women being unreasonable. "Then I take take it it's all right, eh ?"

"All right ?"

"I mean you will toddle home with me at the earliest opp. and make poor old Derek happy ?"

Jill laughed discordantly.

"Poor old Derek!" she echoed. "He has been badly treated, hasn't he ?"

"Well, I wouldn't say that," said Freddie doubtfully. "You see, coming down to it, the thing was more or less his fault, what ?"

"More or less!"

"I mean to say . . ."

"More or less!"

Freddie glanced at her anxiously. He was not at all sure now that he liked the way she was looking or the tone in which she spoke. He was not a keenly observant young man, but there did begin at this point to seep through to his brain-centres a suspicion that all was not well.

"Let me pull myself together!" said Freddie warily to his immortal soul. "I believe I'm getting the raspberry!" And there was silence for a space.

The complexity of life began to weigh upon Freddie. Life was like one of those shots at squash which seem so simple till you go to knock the cover off the ball, when the ball sort of edges away from you and you miss it. Life, Freddie began to perceive, was apt to have a nasty back-spin on it. He had never had any doubt when he had started, that the only difficult part of this expedition to America would be the finding of Jill. Once found, he had presumed that she would be delighted to hear his good news and would joyfully accompany him home on the next boat.

It appeared now, however, that he had been too sanguine. Optimist as he was, he had to admit that, as far as could be ascertained with the naked eye, the jolly old binge might be said to have sprung a leak.

He proceeded to approach the matter from another angle.

"I say!"

"Yes?"

"You do love old Derek, don't you? I mean to say you know what I mean, *love* him and all that sort of rot?"

"I don't know!"

"You don't know! Oh, I say, come now! You must *know!* Pull up your socks, old thing . . . I mean, pull yourself together! You either love a chappie or you don't."

Jill smiled painfully.

"How nice it would be if everything were as simple and straightforward as that. Haven't you ever heard that the dividing line between love and hate is just a thread? Poets have said so a great number of times."

"Oh, poets!" said Freddie, dismissing the genus with a wave of the hand. He had been compelled to read Shakespeare and all that sort of thing at school, but it had left him cold, and since growing to man's estate he had rather handed the race of bards the mitten. He liked Doss Chiderdoss' stuff in the *Sporting Times*, but beyond that he was not much of a lad for poets.

"Can't you understand a girl in my position not being able to make up her mind whether she loves a man or despises him?"

Freddie shook his head.

"No," he said. "It sounds dashed silly to me!"

"Then what's the good of talking?" cried Jill. "It only hurts."

"But—won't you come back to England?"

"No."

"Oh, I say! Be a sport! Take a stab at it!"

Jill laughed again—another of those grating laughs which afflicted Freddie with a sense of foreboding and failure. Something had undoubtedly gone wrong with the works. He began to fear that at some point in the conversation—just where he could not say—he had been less diplomatic than he might have been.

"You speak as if you were inviting me to a garden-party! No, I won't take a stab at it. You've a lot to learn about women, Freddie!"

"Women *are* rum!" conceded that perplexed ambassador.

Jill began to move away.

"Don't go!" urged Freddie.

"Why not? What's the use of talking any more? Have you ever broken an arm or a leg, Freddie?"

"Yes," said Freddie, mystified. "As a matter of fact, my last year at Oxford, playing soccer for the college in a friendly game, some blighter barged into me and I came down on my wrist. But . . ."

"It hurt?"

"Like the deuce!"

"And then it began to get better, I suppose. Well, used you to hit it, and twist it, and prod it, or did you leave it alone to try and heal? I won't talk any more about Derek! I simply won't! I'm all smashed up inside, and I don't know if I'm ever going to get well again, but at least I'm going to give myself a chance. I'm working as hard as ever I can, and I'm forcing myself not to think of him. I'm in a sling, Freddie, like your wrist, and I don't want to be prodded. I hope we shall see a lot of each other while you're over here—you always were the greatest dear in the world—but you mustn't mention Derek again, and you mustn't ask me to go home. If you avoid those subjects, we'll be as happy as possible. And now I'm going to leave you to talk to poor Nelly. She has been hovering round for the last ten minutes, waiting for a chance to speak to you. She worships you, you know!"

Freddie started violently.

"Oh, I say! What rot!"

Jill had gone, and he was still gaping after her, when Nelly Bryant moved towards him—shyly, like a worshipper approaching a shrine.

"Hello, Mr. Rooke!" said Nelly.

"Hullo-ullo-ullo!" said Freddie.

Nelly fixed her large eyes on his face. A fleeting impression passed through Freddie's mind that she was looking unusually pretty this morning: nor was the impression unjustified. Nelly was wearing for the first time a Spring suit which was the outcome of hours of painful selection among the wares of a dozen different stores, and the knowledge that the suit was just right seemed to glow from her like an inner light. She felt happy, and her happiness had lent an unwonted colour to her face and a soft brightness to her eyes.

"How nice it is, your being here!"

Freddie waited for the inevitable question, the question with which Jill had opened their conversation; but it did not come. He was surprised, but relieved. He hated long explanations, and he was very doubtful whether loyalty to Jill could allow him to give them to Nelly. His reason for being where he was had to do so intimately with Jill's most private affairs. A wave of gratitude to Nelly swept through him when he realized that she was either incurious or else too delicate-minded to show inquisitiveness.

As a matter of fact, it was delicacy that kept Nelly silent. Seeing Freddie here at the theatre, she had, as is not uncommon with fallible mortals, put two and two together and made the answer four when it was not four at all. She had been deceived by circumstantial evidence. Jill, whom she had left in England wealthy and secure, she had met again in New York penniless as the result of some Stock Exchange cataclysm in which, she remembered with the vagueness with which one recalls once-heard pieces of information, Freddie Rooke had been involved. True, she seemed to recollect hearing that Freddie's losses had been comparatively slight, but his presence in the chorus of "The Rose of America" seemed to her proof that after all they must have been devastating. She could think of no other reason except loss of money which could have placed Freddie in the position in which she now found him, so she accepted it; and, with the delicacy which was innate in her and which a hard life had never blunted, decided, directly she saw him, to make no allusion to the disaster.

Such was Nelly's view of the matter, and sympathy gave to her manner a kind of maternal gentleness which acted on Freddie, raw from his late encounter with Mr. Johnson Miller and disturbed by Jill's attitude in the matter of poor old Derek, like a healing balm. His emotions were too chaotic for analysis, but one thing stood out clear from the welter—the fact that he was glad to be with Nelly as he had never been glad to be with a girl before, and found her soothing as he had never supposed a girl could be soothing.

They talked desultorily of unimportant things, and every minute found Freddie more convinced that Nelly was not as other girls. He felt that he must see more of her.

"I say," he said. "When this binge is over . . . when the rehearsal finishes, you know, how about a bite to eat?"

"I should love it. I generally go to the Automat."

"The how-much ? Never heard of it."

"In Times Square. It's cheap, you know."

"I was thinking of the Cosmopolis."

"But that's so expensive."

"Oh, I don't know. Much the same as any of the other places, isn't it ?"

. Nelly's manner became more motherly than ever. She bent forward and touched his arm affectionately.

"You haven't to keep up any front with me," she said gently. "I don't care whether you're rich or poor or what. I mean, of course I'm awfully sorry you've lost your money, but it makes it all the easier for us to be real pals, don't you think so ?"

"Lost my money ?"

"Well, I know you wouldn't be here if you hadn't. I wasn't going to say anything about it, but, when you talked of the Cosmopolis, I just had to. You lost your money in the same thing Jill Mariner lost hers, didn't you ? I was sure you had, the moment I saw you here. Who cares ? Money isn't everything!"

Astonishment kept Freddie silent for an instant: after that he refrained from explanations of his own free will. He accepted the situation and rejoiced in it. Like many other wealthy and modest young men, he had always had a sneaking suspicion at the back of his mind that any girl who was decently civil to him was so from mixed motives—or, more likely, motives that were not even mixed. Well, dash it, here was a girl who seemed to like him although under the impression that he was broke to the wide. It was an intoxicating experience. It made him feel a better chap. It fortified his self-respect.

"You know," he said, stammering a little, for he found a sudden difficulty in controlling his voice. "You're a dashed good sort!"

"I'm awfully glad you think so."

There was a silence—as far, at least, as he and she were concerned. In the outer world, beyond the piece of scenery under whose shelter they stood, stirring things, loud and exciting things, seemed to be happening. Some sort of an argument appeared to be in progress. The rasping voice of Mr. Goble was making itself heard from the unseen auditorium. These things they sensed vaguely, but they were too occupied with each other to ascertain details.

"What was the name of that place again?" asked Freddie.

"The what-ho-something?"

"The Automat?"

"That's the little chap! We'll go there, shall we?"

"The food's quite good. You go and help yourself out of slot-machines, you know."

"My favourite indoor sport!" said Freddie with enthusiasm. "Hullo! What's up? It sounds as if there were dirty work at the cross-roads!"

The voice of the assistant stage-manager was calling, sharply excited, agitation in every syllable.

"All the gentlemen of the chorus on the stage, please! Mr. Goble wants all the chorus-gentlemen on the stage!"

"Well, cheerio for the present," said Freddie. "I suppose I'd better look into this."

He made his way on to the stage.

III

There is an insidious something about the atmosphere of a rehearsal of a musical play which saps the finer feelings of those connected with it. Softened by the gentle beauty of the Spring weather, Mr. Goble had come to the Gotham Theatre that morning in an excellent temper, firmly intending to remain in an excellent temper all day. Five minutes of "The Rose of America" had sent him back to the normal; and at ten minutes past eleven he was chewing his cigar and glowering at the stage with all the sweetness gone from his soul. When Wally Mason arrived at a quarter past eleven and dropped into the seat beside him, the manager received him with a grunt and even omitted to offer him a cigar. And when a New York theatrical manager does that, it is a certain sign that his mood is of the worst.

One may find excuses for Mr. Goble. "The Rose of America" would have tested the equanimity of a far more amiable man: and on Mr. Goble what Otis Pilkington had called its delicate whimsicality jarred profoundly. He had been brought up in the lower-browed school of musical comedy, where you shelved the plot after the opening number and filled in the rest of the evening by bringing on the girls in a variety of exotic costumes, with some good vaudeville specialists to get the laughs. Mr. Goble's idea of a musical piece was something embracing trained seals, acrobats, and two or three teams of skilled buck-and-wing dancers, with nothing on the stage, from a tree to a lamp-shade, which could not suddenly turn into a chorus-girl. The austere legitimateness of "The Rose of America" gave him a pain in the neck. He loathed plot, and "The Rose of America" was all plot.

Why, then, had the earthy Mr. Goble consented to associate himself with the production of this intellectual play? Because he was subject, like all other New York managers, to intermittent spasms of the idea that the time is ripe for a revival of comic opera. Sometimes, lunching in his favourite corner in the Cosmopolis grill-room, he would lean across the table and beg some other manager to take it from him that the time was ripe for a revival of comic opera—or, more cautiously, that pretty soon the time was going to be ripe for a revival of comic opera. And the other manager would nod his head and thoughtfully stroke his three chins and admit that, sure as God made little apples, the time was darned soon going to be ripe for a revival of comic opera. And then they would stuff themselves with rich food and light big cigars and brood meditatively.

With most managers these spasms, which may be compared to twinges of conscience, pass as quickly as they come, and they go back to coining money with rowdy musical comedies, quite contented. But Otis Pilkington, happening along with the script of "The Rose of America" and the cash to back it, had caught Mr. Goble in the full grip of an attack, and all the arrangements had been made before the latter emerged from the influence. He now regretted his rash act.

"Say, listen," he said to Wally, his gaze on the stage, his words proceeding from the corner of his mouth, "you've got to stick around with this show after it opens on the road. We'll talk terms later. But we've got to get it right, don't care what it costs. See?"

"You think it will need fixing?"

Mr. Goble scowled at the unconscious artists, who were now going through a particularly arid stretch of dialogue.

"Fixing! It's all wrong! It don't add up right! You'll have to rewrite it from end to end."

"Well, I've got some idea about it. I saw it played by amateurs last summer, you know. I could make a quick job of it, if you want me to. But will the author stand for it?"

Mr. Goble allowed a belligerent eye to stray from the stage, and twisted it round in Wally's direction.

"Say, listen! He'll stand for anything I say. I'm the little guy that gives orders round here. I'm the big noise!"

As if in support of this statement he suddenly emitted a terrific bellow. The effect was magical. The refined and pains-taking artists on the stage stopped as if they had been shot. The assistant stage-director bent sedulously over the footlights, which had now been turned up, shading his eyes with the prompt script.

"Take that over again!" shouted Mr. Goble. "Yes, that speech about life being like a water-melon. It don't sound to me as though it meant anything." He cocked his cigar at an angle, and listened fiercely. He clapped his hands. The action stopped again. "Cut it!" said Mr. Goble tersely.

"Cut the speech, Mr. Goble?" queried the obsequious assistant stage-director.

"Yes. Cut it. It don't mean nothing!"

Down the aisle, springing from a seat at the back, shimmered Mr. Pilkington, wounded to the quick.

"Mr. Goble! Mr. Goble!"

"Well?"

"That is the best epigram in the play."

"The best what?"

"Epigram. The best epigram in the play."

Mr. Goble knocked the ash off his cigar. "The public don't want epigrams. The public don't like epigrams. I've been in the show business fifteen years, and I'm telling you! Epigrams give them a pain under the vest. All right, get on."

Mr. Pilkington fluttered agitatedly. This was his first experience of Mr. Goble in the capacity of stage-director. It was the latter's custom to leave the early rehearsals of the pieces with which he was connected to a subordinate producer, who did what Mr. Goble called the breaking-in. This accomplished, he would appear in person, undo most of the other's work, make cuts, tell the actors how to read their lines, and generally enjoy himself. Producing plays was Mr. Goble's hobby. He imagined himself to have a genius in that direction, and it was useless to try to induce him to alter any decision to which he might have come. He regarded those who did not agree with him with the lofty contempt of an Eastern despot.

Of this Mr. Pilkington was not yet aware.

"But, Mr. Goble . . .!"

The potentate swung irritably round on him.

"What is it ? What *is* it ? Can't you see I'm busy ?"

"That epigram . . ."

"It's out!"

"But . . .!"

"It's out!"

"Surely," protested Mr. Pilkington almost tearfully, "I have a voice . . ."

"Sure you have a voice," retorted Mr. Goble, "and you can use it any old place you want, except in my theatre. Have all the voice you like! Go round the corner and talk to yourself! Sing in your bath! But don't come using it here, because I'm the little guy that does all the talking in this theatre! That fellow makes me tired," he added complainingly to Wally, as Mr. Pilkington withdrew like a foiled python. "He don't know nothing about the show business, and he keeps butting in and making fool suggestions. He ought to be darned glad he's getting his first play produced and not trying to teach me how to direct it." He clapped his hands imperiously. The assistant stage-manager bent over the footlights. "What was that that guy said ? Lord Finchley's last speech. Take it again."

The gentleman who was playing the part of Lord Finchley, an English character actor who specialized in London "nuts," raised his eyebrows, annoyed. Like Mr. Pilkington, he had never before come into contact with Mr. Goble as stage-director, and, accustomed to the suaver methods of his native land, he was finding the experience trying. He had not yet recovered from the agony of having that water-melon line cut out of his part. It was the only good line, he considered, that he had. Any line that is cut out of an actor's part is always the only good line he-has.

"The speech about Omar Khayyam ?" he enquired with suppressed irritation.

"I thought that was the way you said it. All wrong! It's Omar *of* Khayyam."

"I think you will find that Omar Khayyam is the—ah—generally accepted version of the poet's name," said the portrayer of Lord Finchley, adding beneath his breath. "You silly ass!"

"You say Omar *of* Khayyam," bellowed Mr. Goble. "Who's running this show, anyway ?"

"Just as you please."

Mr. Goble turned to Wally.

"These actors . . ." he began, when Mr. Pilkington appeared again at his elbow.

"Mr. Goble! Mr. Goble!"

"What is it *now* ?"

"Omar Khayyam was a Persian poet. His *name* was Khayyam."

"That wasn't the way *I* heard it," said Mr. Goble doggedly. "Did *you* ?" he enquired of Wally. "I thought he was born at Khayyam."

"You're probably quite right," said Wally, "but, if so, everybody else has been wrong for a good many years. It's usually supposed that the gentleman's name was Omar Khayyam. Khayyam, Omar J. Born A.D. 1050, educated privately and at Bagdad University. Represented Persia in the Olympic Games of 1072, winning the sitting high-jump and the egg-and-spoon race. The Khayyams were quite a well-known family in Bagdad, and there was a lot of talk when Omar, who was Mrs. Khayyam's pet son, took to drink and writing poetry. They had had it all fixed for him to go into his father's date business."

Mr. Goble was impressed. He had a respect for Wally's opinion, for Wally had written "Follow the Girl" and look what a knock-out that had been. He stopped the rehearsal again.

"Go back to that Khayyam speech!" he said interrupting Lord Finchley in mid-sentence.

The actor whispered a hearty English oath beneath his breath. He had been up late last night, and, in spite of the fair weather, he was feeling a trifle on edge.

" 'In the words of Omar of Khayyam ' . . ."

Mr. Goble clapped his hands.

"Cut that 'of,' " he said. "The show's too long, anyway."

And, having handled a delicate matter in masterly fashion, he leaned back in his chair and chewed the end off another cigar.

For some minutes after this the rehearsal proceeded smoothly. If Mr. Goble did not enjoy the play, at least he made no criticisms except to Wally. To him he enlarged from time to time on the pain which "The Rose of America" caused him.

"How I ever came to put on junk like this beats me," confessed Mr. Goble frankly.

"You probably saw that there was a good idea at the back of

it," suggested Wally. "There is, you know. Properly handled, it's an idea that could be made into a success."

"What would you do with it?"

"Oh, a lot of things," said Wally warily. In his younger and callower days he had sometimes been rash enough to scatter views on the reconstruction of plays broadcast, to find them gratefully absorbed and acted upon and treated as a friendly gift. His affection for Mr. Goble was not so overpowering as to cause him to give him ideas for nothing now. "Any time you want me to fix it for you, I'll come along. About one and a half per cent of the gross would meet the case, I think."

Mr. Goble faced him, registering the utmost astonishment and horror.

"One and a half per cent for fixing a show like this? Why, darn it, there's hardly anything to do to it! It's—it's *in!*"

"You called it junk just now."

"Well, all I meant was that it wasn't the sort of thing I cared for myself. The public will eat it. Take it from me, the time is just about ripe for a revival of comic opera."

"This one will want all the reviving you can give it. Better use a pulmotor."

"But that long boob, that Pilkington . . . he would never stand for my handing you one and a half per cent."

"I thought *you* were the little guy who arranged things round here."

"But he's got money in the show."

"Well, if he wants to get any out, he'd better call in somebody to rewrite it. You don't have to engage me if you don't want to. But I know I could make a good job of it. There's just one little twist the thing needs and you would have quite a different piece."

"What's that?" enquired Mr. Goble casually.

"Oh, just a little . . . what shall I say? . . . a little touch of what-d'you-call-it and a bit of thingummy. You know the sort of thing! That's all it wants."

Mr. Goble gnawed his cigar, baffled.

"You think so, eh?" he said at length.

"And perhaps a suspicion of *je-ne-sais-quoi*," added Wally.

Mr. Goble worried his cigar, and essayed a new form of attack. "You've done a lot of work for me," he said. "Good work!"

"Glad you liked it," said Wally.

"You're a good kid. I like having you around. I was half
thinking of giving you a show to do this Fall. Corking book.
French farce. Ran two years in Paris. But what's the good, if
you want the earth?"

"Always useful, the earth. Good thing to have."

"See here, if you'll fix up this show for half of one per cent, I'll
give you the other to do."

"You shouldn't slur your words so. For a moment I thought
you said 'half of one per cent.' One and a half of course you
really said.

"If you won't take half, you don't get the other."

"All right," said Wally. "There are lots of other managers in
New York. Haven't you seen them popping about? Rich,
enterprising men, and all of them love me like a son."

"Make it one per cent," said Mr. Goble, "and I'll see if I can
fix it with Pilkington."

"One and a half."

"Oh, damn it, one and a half, then," said Mr. Goble morosely.
"What's the good of splitting straws?"

"Forgotten Sports of the Past—Splitting the Straw. All right.
If you drop me a line to that effect, legibly signed with your
name, I'll wear it next my heart. I shall have to go now. I have a
date. Good-bye. Glad everything's settled and everybody's happy."

For some moments after Wally had left, Mr. Goble sat hunched
up in his orchestra-chair, smoking sullenly, his mood less sunny
than ever. Living in a little world of sycophants, he was galled
by the off-hand way in which Wally always treated him. There
was something in the latter's manner which seemed to him
sometimes almost contemptuous. He regretted the necessity of
having to employ him. There was, of course, no real necessity
why he should have employed Wally. New York was full of
librettists who would have done the work equally well for half
the money, but, like most managers, Mr. Goble had the mental
processes of a sheep. "Follow the Girl" was the last outstanding
musical success in New York theatrical history: Wally had written
it, therefore nobody but Wally was capable of re-writing "The
Rose of America." The thing had for Mr. Goble the inevitability
of Fate. Except for deciding mentally that Wally had swelled
head, there was nothing to be done.

Having decided that Wally had swelled head, and not feeling
much better, Mr. Goble concentrated his attention on the stage.

A good deal of action had taken place there during the recently concluded business talk, and the unfortunate Lord Finchley was back again, playing another of his scenes. Mr. Goble glared at Lord Finchley. He did not like him, and he did not like the way he was speaking his lines.

The part of Lord Finchley was a non-singing role. It was a type part. Otis Pilkington had gone to the straight stage to find an artist, and had secured the not uncelebrated Wentworth Hill, who had come over from London to play in an English comedy which had just closed. The newspapers had called the play thin, but had thought that Wentworth Hill was an excellent comedian. Mr. Hill thought so, too, and it was consequently a shock to his already disordered nerves when a bellow from the auditorium stopped him in the middle of one of his speeches and a rasping voice informed him that he was doing it all wrong.

"I beg your pardon?" said Mr. Hill, quietly but dangerously, stepping to the footlights.

"All wrong!" repeated Mr. Goble.

"Really?" Wentworth Hill, who a few years earlier had spent several terms at Oxford University before being sent down for aggravated disorderliness, had brought little away with him from that seat of learning except the Oxford manner. This he now employed upon Mr. Goble with an icy severity which put the last touch to the manager's fermenting state of mind. "Perhaps you would be kind enough to tell me just how you think that part should be played?"

Mr. Goble marched down the aisle.

"Speak out to the audience," he said, stationing himself by the orchestra pit. "You're turning your head away all the darned time."

"I may be wrong," said Mr. Hill, "but I have played a certain amount, don't you know, in pretty good companies, and I was always under the impression that one should address one's remarks to the person one was speaking to, not deliver a recitation to the gallery. I was taught that that was the legitimate method."

The word touched off all the dynamite in Mr. Goble. Of all things in the theatre he detested most the "legitimate method." His idea of producing was to instruct the cast to come down to the footlights and hand it to 'em. These people who looked up-stage and talked to the audience through the backs of their necks revolted him.

"Legitimate! That's a hell of a thing to be! Where do you get that legitimate stuff? You aren't playing Ibsen!"

"Nor am I playing a knockabout vaudeville sketch."

"Don't talk back at me!"

"Kindly don't shout at *me*! Your voice is unpleasant enough without your raising it."

Open defiance was a thing which Mr. Goble had never encountered before, and for a moment it deprived him of breath. He recovered it, however, almost immediately.

"You're fired!"

"On the contrary," said Mr. Hill, "I'm resigning." He drew a greeen-covered script from his pocket and handed it with an air to the pallid assistant stage-director. Then, more gracefully than ever Freddie Rooke had managed to move down-stage under the tuition of Johnson Miller, he moved up-stage to the exit. "I trust that you will be able to find someone who will play the part according to your ideas!"

"I'll find," bellowed Mr. Goble at his vanishing back, "a chorus-man who'll play it a damned sight better than you!" He waved to the assistant stage-director. "Send the chorus-men on the stage!"

"All the gentlemen of the chorus on the stage, please!" shrilled the assistant stage-director, bounding into the wings like a retriever. "Mr. Goble wants all the chorus-gentlemen on the stage!"

There was a moment, when the seven male members of "The Rose of America" ensemble lined up self-consciously before his gleaming eyes, when Mr. Goble repented of his brave words. An uncomfortable feeling passed across his mind that Fate had called his bluff and that he would not be able to make good. All chorus-men are exactly alike, and they are like nothing else on earth. Even Mr. Goble, anxious as he was to overlook their deficiencies, could not persuade himself that in their ranks stood even an adequate Lord Finchley.

And then, just as a cold reaction from his fervid mood was about to set in, he perceived that Providence had been good to him. There, at the extreme end of the line, stood a young man who, as far as appearance went, was the ideal Lord Finchley— as far as appearance went, a far better Lord Finchley than the late Mr. Hill. He beckoned imperiously.

"You at the end!"

"Me?" said the young man.

"Yes, you. What's your name?"

"Rooke. Freddie Rooke, don't you know."

"You're English, aren't you?"

"Eh? Oh, yes, absolutely!"

"Ever played a part before?"

"Part? Oh, I see what you mean. Well, in amateur theatricals, you know, and all that sort of rot."

His words were music to Mr. Goble's ears. He felt that his Napoleonic action had justified itself by success. His fury left him. If he had been capable of beaming, one would have said that he beamed at Freddie.

"Well, you play the part of Lord Finchley from now on. Come to my office this afternoon for your contract. Clear the stage. We've wasted enough time."

Five minutes later, in the wings, Freddie, receiving congratulations from Nelly Bryant, asserted himself.

"*Not* the Automat to-day, I *think*, what? Now that I'm a jolly old star and all that sort of thing, it can't be done. Directly this is over we'll roll round to the Cosmopolis. A slight celebration is indicated, what? Right ho! Rally round, dear heart, rally round!"

* 15 *

Jill Explains

I

THE lobby of the Hotel Cosmopolis is the exact centre of New York, the spot where at certain hours one is sure of meeting everybody one knows. The first person that Nelly and Freddie saw, as they passed through the swing doors, was Jill. She was seated on the chair by the big pillar in the middle of the hall.

"What ho!" said Freddie. "Waiting for someone?"

"Hullo, Freddie. Yes, I'm waiting for Wally Mason. I got a note from him this morning, asking me to meet him here. I'm a little early. I haven't congratulated you yet. You're wonderful!"

"Thanks, old girl. Our young hero *is* making pretty hefty strides in his chosen profesh, what? Mr. Rooke, who appears quite

simple and unspoiled by success, replied to our representative's
enquiry as to his future plans, that he proposed to stagger into
the grill-room and imbibe about eighteen dollars' worth of
lunch. Yes, it *is* a bit of all right, taking it by and large, isn't it ?
I mean to say, the salary, the jolly old salary, you know . . .
quite a help when a fellow's lost all his money!"

Jill was surprised to observe that the Last of the Rookes was
contorting his face in an unsightly manner that seemed to be
an attempt at a wink, pregnant with hidden meaning. She took
her cue dutifully, though without understanding.

"Oh, yes," she replied.

Freddie seemed grateful. With a cordial "Cheerio!" he led
Nelly off to the grill-room.

"I didn't know Jill knew Mr. Mason," said Nelly, as they sat
down at their table.

"No ?" said Freddie absently, running an experienced eye over
the bill of fare. He gave an elaborate order. "What was that ?
Oh, absolutely! Jill and I and Wally were children together."

"How funny you should all be together again like this."

"Yes. Oh, good Lord!"

"What's the matter ?"

"It's nothing. I meant to send a cable to a pal of mine in
England. I'll send it after lunch."

Freddie took out his handkerchief, and tied a knot in it. He
was slightly ashamed of the necessity of taking such a precaution,
but it was better to be on the safe side. His interview with Jill
at the theatre had left him with the conviction that there was
only one thing for him to do, and that was to cable poor old
Derek to forget impending elections and all the rest of it and
pop over to America at once. He knew that he would never
have the courage to re-open the matter with Jill himself. As an
ambassador he was a spent force. If Jill was to be wooed from her
mood of intractability, Derek was the only man to do it. Freddie
was convinced that, seeing him in person, she would melt and
fall into his arms. Too dashed absurd, Freddie felt, two loving
hearts being separated like this and all that sort of thing. He
replaced his handkerchief in his pocket, relieved, and concentrated himself on the entertainment of Nelly. A simple task, for
the longer he was with this girl, the easier did it seem to talk to
her.

Jill, left alone in the lobby, was finding the moments pass

quite pleasantly. She liked watching the people as they came in. One or two of the girls of the company fluttered in like birds, were swooped upon by their cavaliers, and fluttered off to the grill-room. The red-headed Babe passed her with a genial nod, and, shortly after, Lois Denham, the willowy recipient of sunbursts from her friend Izzy of the hat-checks, came by in company with a sallow, hawk-faced young man with a furtive eye, whom Jill took—correctly—to be Izzy himself. Lois was looking pale and proud, and, from the few words which came to Jill's ears as they neared her, seemed to be annoyed at having been kept waiting.

It was immediately after this that the swing-doors revolved rather more violently than usual, and Mr. Goble burst into view.

There was a cloud upon Mr. Goble's brow, seeming to indicate that his grievance against life had not yet been satisfactorily adjusted; but it passed as he saw Jill, and he came up to her with what he would probably have claimed to be an ingratiating smile.

"Hullo!" said Mr. Goble. "All alone?"

Jill was about to say that the condition was merely temporary when the manager went on.

"Come and have a bit of lunch."

"Thank you very much," said Jill, with the politeness of dislike, "but I'm waiting for someone."

"Chuck him!" advised Mr. Goble cordially.

"No, thanks, I couldn't really."

The cloud began to descend again upon Mr. Goble's brow. He was accustomed to having these invitations of his treated as royal commands.

"Come along!"

"I'm afraid it's impossible."

Mr. Goble subjected her to a prolonged stare, seemed about to speak, changed his mind, and swung off moodily in the direction of the grill-room. He was not used to this sort of treatment.

He had hardly gone, when Wally appeared.

"What was he saying to you?" demanded Wally abruptly, without preliminary greeting.

"He was asking me to lunch."

Wally was silent for a moment. His good-natured face wore an unwonted scowl.

"He went in there, of course?" he said, pointing to the grill-room.

"Yes."

"Then let's go into the other room," said Wally. He regained his good humour. "It was awfully good of you to come. I didn't know whether you would be able to."

"It was very nice of you to invite me."

Wally grinned.

"How perfect our manners are! It's a treat to listen! How did you know that that was the one hat in New York I wanted you to wear?"

"Oh, these things get about. Do you like it?"

"It's wonderful. Let's take this table, shall we?"

II

They sat down. The dim, tapestry-hung room soothed Jill. She was feeling a little tired after the rehearsal. At the far end of the room an orchestra was playing a tune that she remembered and liked. Her mind went back to the last occasion on which she and Wally had sat opposite each other at a restaurant. How long ago it seemed! She returned to the present to find Wally speaking to her.

"You left very suddenly the other night," said Wally.

"I didn't want to meet Freddie."

Wally looked at her commiseratingly.

"I don't want to spoil your lunch," he said, "but Freddie knows all. He has tracked you down. He met Nelly Bryant, whom he seems to have made friends with in London, and she told him where you were and what you were doing. For a girl who fled at his mere approach the night before last, you don't seem very agitated by the news," he said, as Jill burst into a peal of laughter.

"You haven't heard?"

"Heard what?"

"Freddie got Mr. Pilkington to put him in the chorus of the piece. He was rehearsing when I arrived at the theatre this morning, and having a terrible time with Mr. Miller. And, later on, Mr. Goble had a quarrel with the man who was playing the Englishman, and the man threw up his part, and Mr. Goble said he could get anyone in the chorus to play it just as well.

and he chose Freddie. So now Freddie is one of the principals, and bursting with pride!"

Wally threw his head back and uttered a roar of appreciation which caused a luncher at a neighbouring table to drop an oyster which he was poising in mid-air.

"Don't make such a noise!" said Jill severely. "Everyone's looking at you."

"I must! It's the most priceless thing I ever heard. I've always maintained and I always will maintain that for pure lunacy nothing can touch the musical comedy business. There isn't anything that can't happen in musical comedy. 'Alice in Wonderland' is nothing to it."

"Have you felt that, too? That's exactly how I feel. It's like a perpetual 'Mad Hatter's Tea-Party.'"

"But what on earth made Freddie join the company at all?"

A sudden gravity descended upon Jill. The words had reminded her of the thing which she was perpetually striving to keep out of her thoughts.

"He said he wanted to be there to keep an eye on me."

Gravity is infectious. Wally's smile disappeared. He, too, had been recalled to thoughts which were not pleasant.

Wally crumbled his roll. There was a serious expression on his face.

"Freddie was quite right. I didn't think he had so much sense."

"Freddie was not right," flared Jill. The recollection of her conversation with that prominent artist still had the power to fire her independent soul. "I'm not a child. I can look after myself. What I do is my own business."

"I'm afraid you're going to find that your business is several people's business. I am interested in it myself. I don't like your being on the stage. Now bite my head off!"

"It's very kind of you to bother about me . . ."

"I said 'Bite my head off!' I didn't say 'Freeze me!' I take the licence of an old friend who in his time has put worms down your back, and I repeat—I don't like your being on the stage."

"I shouldn't have thought you would have been so"—Jill sought for a devastating adjective—"so mid-Victorian!"

"As far as you are concerned, I'm the middest Victorian in existence. Mid is my middle name." Wally met her indignant gaze squarely. "I—do—not—like—your—being—on—the—

stage! Especially in any company which Ike Goble is running."

"Why Mr. Goble particularly?"

"Because he is not the sort of man you ought to be coming in contact with."

"What nonsense!"

"It isn't nonsense at all. I suppose you've read a lot about the morals of theatrical managers . . ."

"Yes. And it seemed to be exaggerated and silly."

"So it is. There's nothing wrong with most of them. As a general thing, they are very decent fellows—extraordinarily decent if you think of the position they are in. I don't say that in a business way there's much they won't try to put over on you. In the theatre, when it comes to business, everything goes except biting and gouging. 'There's never a law of God or man runs north of fifty-three.' If you alter that to 'north of Forty-first Street' it doesn't scan as well, but it's just as true. Perhaps it would be more accurate to say that the Golden Rule is suspended there. You get used to it after you have been in the theatre for a while, and, except for leaving your watch and pocket-book at home when you have to pay a call on a manager and keeping your face to him so that he can't get away with your back collar-stud, you don't take any notice of it. It's all a game. If a manager swindles you, he wins the hole and takes the honour. If you foil him, you are one up. In either case, it makes no difference to the pleasantness of your relations. You go on calling him by his first name, and he gives you a couple of cigars out of his waistcoat pocket and says you're a good kid. There is nothing personal in it. He has probably done his best friend out of a few thousand dollars the same morning, and you see them lunching together after the ceremony as happily as possible. You've got to make allowances for managers. They are the victims of heredity. When a burglar marries a hat-check girl, their offspring goes into the theatrical business automatically, and he can't shake off the early teaching which he imbibed at his father's knee. But morals . . ."

Wally broke off to allow the waiter to place a fried sole before him. Waiters always select the moment when we are talking our best to intrude themselves.

"As regards morals," resumed Wally, "that is a different matter. Most managers are respectable, middle-aged men with wives and families. They are in the business to make money, and they don't want anything else out of it. The girls in their companies are like so many clerks to them, just machines that help to bring the money in. They don't know half a dozen of them to speak to. But our genial Ike is not like that." Wally consumed a mouthful of sole. "Ike Goble is a bad citizen. He paws! He's a slinker and a prowler and a leerer. He's a pest and a worm! He's fat and soft and flabby. He has a greasy soul, a withered heart, and an eye like a codfish. Not knocking him, of course!" added Wally magnanimously. "Far be it from me to knock anyone! But, speaking with the utmost respect and viewing him in the most favourable light, he is a combination of tom-cat and the things you see when you turn over a flat stone! Such are the reasons why I am sorry that you are in his company."

Jill had listened to this diatribe with a certain uneasiness. Her brief encounters with Mr. Goble told her that every word was probably true. She could still feel the unpleasant sensation of being inspected by the eye which Wally had compared—quite justly—to that of a codfish. But her pride forbade any admission of weakness.

"I can take care of myself," she said.

"I don't doubt it," said Wally. "And you could probably take care of yourself if you fell into a muddy pond. But I shouldn't like to stand on the bank and watch you doing it. I know what girls in the chorus have to go through. Hanging about for hours in draughts, doing nothing, while the principals go through their scenes, and yelled at if they try to relieve the tedium of captivity with a little light conversation . . ."

"Yes," admitted Jill. "There has been a good lot of that."

"There always is. I believe if the stage-carpenter was going to stick a screw in a flat, they would call a chorus-rehearsal to watch him to do it . . . Jill, you must get out of it. It's no life for you. The work . . ."

"I like the work."

"While it's new, perhaps, but . . ."

Jill interrupted him passionately.

"Oh, can't you understand!" she cried. "I want the work. I need it. I want something to do, something to occupy my mind. I hate talking about it, but you know how things are with me. Freddie must have told you. Even if he didn't, you must have guessed, meeting me here all alone and remembering how things were when we last met. You must understand! Haven't you ever had a terrible shock or a dreadful disappointment that seemed to smash up the whole world? And didn't you find that the only possible thing to do was to work and work and work as hard as ever you could? When I first came to America, I nearly went mad. Uncle Chris sent me down to a place on Long Island, and I had nothing to do all day but think. I couldn't stand it. I ran away and came to New York and met Nelly Bryant and got this work to do. It saved me. It kept me busy all day and tired me out and didn't give me time to think. The harder it is, the better it suits me. It's an antidote. I simply wouldn't give it up now. As for what you were saying, I must put up with that. The other girls do, so why shouldn't I?"

"They are toughened to it."

"Then I must get toughened to it. What else is there for me to do? I must do something."

"Marry me!" said Wally, reaching across the table and putting his hand on hers. The light in his eyes lit up his homely face like a lantern.

III

The suddenness of it startled Jill into silence. She snatched her hand away and drew back, looking at him in wonderment. She was confusedly aware of a babble of sound—people talking, people laughing, the orchestra playing a lively tune. All her senses seemed to have become suddenly more acute. She was intensely alive to small details. Then, abruptly, the whole world condensed itself into two eyes that were fastened upon hers—compelling eyes which she felt a panic desire to avoid.

She turned her head away, and looked out into the restaurant. It seemed incredible that all these people, placidly intent upon their food and their small talk, should not be staring at her, wondering what she was going to say; nudging each other and speculating. Their detachment made her feel alone and helpless. She was nothing to them and they did not care what happened to her, just as she had been nothing to those frozen marshes down at Brookport. She was alone in an indifferent world, with her own problems to settle for herself.

Other men had asked Jill to marry them—a full dozen of them, here and there in country houses and at London dances, before she had met and loved Derek Underhill; but nothing that she had had in the way of experience had prepared her for Wally. These others had given her time to marshal her forces, to collect herself, to weigh them thoughtfully in the balance. Before speaking, they had signalled their devotion in a hundred perceptible ways—by their pinkness, their stammering awkwardness, by the glassy look in their eyes. They had not shot a proposal at her like a bullet from out of the cover of a conversation that had nothing to do with their emotions at all.

Yet, now that the shock of it was dying away, she began to remember signs she would have noticed, speeches which ought to have warned her . . .

"Wally!" she gasped.

She found that he affected her in an entirely different fashion from the luckless dozen of those London days. He seemed to matter more, to be more important, almost—though she rebelled at the word—more dangerous.

"Let me take you out of it all! You aren't fit for this sort of life. I can't bear to see you . . ."

Jill bent forward and touched his hand. He started as though he had been burned. The muscles of his throat were working.

"Wally, it's——" She paused for a word. "Kind" was horrible. It would have sounded cold, almost supercilious. "Sweet" was the sort of thing she could imagine Lois Denham saying to her friend Izzy. She began her sentence again. "You're a dear to say that, but . . ."

Wally laughed chokingly.

"You think I'm altruistic? I'm not. I'm just as selfish and self-centred as any other man who wants a thing very badly. I'm as altruistic as a child crying for the moon. I want you to marry me because I love you, because there never was anybody like you, because you're the whole world, because I always have loved you. I've been dreaming about you for a dozen years, thinking about you, wondering about you—wondering where you were, what you were doing, how you looked. I used to think that it was just sentimentality, that you merely stood for a time of my life when I was happier than I have ever been since. I used to think that you were just a sort of peg on which I was hanging a pleasant sentimental regret for days which could never come back. You were a memory that seemed to personify

all the other memories of the best time of my life. You were the
goddess of old associations. Then I met you in London, and it
was different. I wanted you—*you!* I didn't want you because
you recalled old times and were associated with dead happiness,
I wanted *you!* I knew I loved you directly you spoke to me at
the theatre that night of the fire. I loved your voice and your
eyes and your smile and your courage. And then you told me
you were engaged. I might have expected it, but I couldn't keep
my jealousy from showing itself, and you snubbed me as I
deserved. But now . . . things are different now. Everything's
different, except my love."

Jill turned her face to the wall beside her. A man at the next
table, a corpulent, red-faced man, had begun to stare. He could
have heard nothing, for Wally had spoken in a low voice; but
plainly he was aware that something more interesting was
happening at their table than at any of the other tables, and he
was watching with a bovine inquisitiveness which affected Jill
with a sense of outrage. A moment before, she had resented the
indifference of the outer world. Now, this one staring man
seemed like a watching multitude. There were tears in her
eyes, and she felt that the red-faced man suspected it.

"Wally . . ." Her voice broke. "It's impossible."

"Why? Why, Jill?"

"Because . . . Oh, it's impossible!"

There was a silence.

"Because . . ." He seemed to find a difficulty in speaking.
"Because of Underhill?"

Jill nodded. She felt wretched. The monstrous incongruity of
her surroundings oppressed her. The orchestra had dashed into
a rollicking melody, which set her foot tapping in spite of herself.
At a near-by table somebody was shouting with laughter. Two
waiters at a service-stand were close enough for her to catch
snatches of their talk. They were arguing about an order of fried
potatoes. Once again her feelings veered round, and she loathed
the detachment of the world. Her heart ached for Wally. She
could not look at him, but she knew exactly what she would see
if she did—honest, pleading eyes searching her face for something which she could not give.

"Yes," she said.

The table creaked. Wally was leaning further forward. He
seemed like something large and pathetic—a big dog in trouble.

She hated to be hurting him. And all the time her foot tapped accompaniment to the rag-time tune.

"But you can't live all your life with a memory," said Wally.

Jill turned and faced him. His eyes seemed to leap at her, and they were just as she had pictured them.

"You don't understand," she said gently. "You don't understand."

"It's ended. It's over."

Jill shook her head.

"You can't still love him, after what has happened!"

"I don't know," said Jill unhappily.

The words seemed to bewilder Wally as much as they had bewildered Freddie.

"You don't know?"

Jill shut her eyes tight. Wally quivered. It was a trick she had had as a child. In perplexity, she had always screwed up her eyes just like that, as if to shut herself up in herself.

"Don't talk for a minute, Wally," she said. "I want to think."

Her eyes opened.

"It's like this," she said. He had seen her look at him in exactly the same way a hundred times. "I don't suppose I can make you understand, but this is how it is. Suppose you had a room, and it was full—of things. Furniture. And there wasn't any space left. You—you couldn't put anything else in till you had taken all that out, could you? It might not be worth anything, but it would still be there, taking up all the room."

Wally nodded.

"Yes," he said. "I see."

"My heart's full, Wally dear. I know it's just lumber that's choking it up, but it's difficult to get it out. It takes time getting it out. I put it in, thinking it was wonderful furniture, the most wonderful in the world, and—I was cheated. It was just lumber. But it's there. It's still there. It's there all the time. And what am I to do?"

The orchestra crashed, and was silent. The sudden stillness seemed to break a spell. The world invaded the little island where they sat. A chattering party of girls and men brushed past them. The waiter, judging that they had been there long enough, slipped a strip of paper, decorously turned upside down, in front of Wally. He took the money, and went away to get change.

Wally turned to Jill.

"I understand," he said. "All this hasn't happened, and we're just as good pals as before?"

"Yes."

"But . . ." He forced a laugh . . . "mark my words, a time may come, and then . . . !"

"I don't know," said Jill.

"A time may come," repeated Wally. "At any rate, let me think so. It has nothing to do with me. It's for you to decide, absolutely. I'm not going to pursue you with my addresses! If ever you get that room of yours emptied, you won't have to hang out a 'To Let' sign. I shall be waiting, and you will know where to find me. And, in the meantime, yours to command, Wallace Mason. Is that clear?"

"Quite clear." Jill looked at him affectionately. "There's nobody I'd rather open that room to than you, Wally. You know that."

"Is that the solemn truth?"

"The solemn truth."

"Then," said Wally, "in two minutes you will see a startled waiter. There will be about fourteen dollars change out of that twenty he took away. I'm going to give it all to him."

"You mustn't!"

"Every cent!" said Wally firmly. "And the young Greek brigand who stole my hat at the door is going to get a dollar! That, as our ascetic and honourable friend Goble would say, is the sort of little guy *I* am!"

The red-faced man at the next table eyed them as they went out, leaving behind them a waiter who clutched totteringly for support at the back of a chair.

"Had a row," he decided, "but made it up."

He called for a toothpick.

★ 16 ★

Mr. Goble Plays with Fate

I

ON the broadwalk at Atlantic City, that much-enduring seashore resort which has been the birthplace of so many musical plays, there stands an all-day and all-night restaurant, under the same management and offering the same hospitality as the one in Columbus Circle at which Jill had taken her first meal on arriving in New York. At least, its hospitality is noisy during the waking and working hours of the day; but there are moments when it has an almost cloistral peace, and the customer, abashed by the cold calm of its snowy marble and the silent gravity of the white-robed attendants, unconsciously lowers his voice and tries to keep his feet from shuffling, like one in a temple. The members of the chorus of "The Rose of America," dropping in by ones and twos at six o'clock in the morning about two weeks after the events recorded in the last chapter, spoke in whispers and gave their orders for breakfast in a subdued undertone.

The dress-rehearsal had just dragged its weary length to a close. It is the custom of the dwellers in Atlantic City, who seem to live entirely by pleasure, to attend a species of vaudeville performances—incorrectly termed a sacred concert—on Sunday nights, and it had been one o'clock in the morning before the concert scenery could be moved out of the theatre and the first act set of "The Rose of America" moved in. And, as by some unwritten law of the drama no dress-rehearsal can begin without a delay of at least an hour and a half, the curtain had not gone up on Mr. Miller's opening chorus till half-past two. There had been dress-parades, conferences, interminable arguments between the stage-director and a mysterious man in shirt-sleeves about the lights, more dress-parades, further conferences, hitches with regard to the sets, and another outbreak of debate on the subject of blues, ambers, and the management of the "spot," which was worked by a plaintive voice, answering to the name of Charlie, at the back of the family circle. But by six o'clock a complete, if ragged, performance had been given, and the chorus, who had partaken of no nourishment since dinner on the previous night, had limped off round the corner for a bite of breakfast before going to bed.

They were a battered and a draggled company, some with dark circles beneath their eyes, others blooming with the unnatural scarlet of the make-up which they had been too tired to take off. The Duchess, haughty to the last, had fallen asleep with her head on the table. The red-headed Babe was lying back in her chair, staring at the ceiling. The Southern girl blinked like an owl at the morning sunshine out on the boardwalk.

The Cherub, whose triumphant youth had brought her

almost fresh through a sleepless night, contributed the only
remark made during the interval of waiting for the meal.

"The fascination of a thtage life! Why girls leave home!"
She looked at her reflection in the little mirror of her vanity-bag.
"It *is* a face!" she murmured reflectively. "But I should hate to
have to go around with it long!"

A sallow young man, with the alertness peculiar to those who
work on the night-shifts of restaurants, dumped a tray down on
the table with a clatter. The Duchess woke up. Babe took her
eyes off the ceiling. The Southern girl ceased to look at the
sunshine. Already, at the mere sight of food, the extraordinary
recuperative powers of the theatrical worker had begun to
assert themselves. In five minutes these girls would be feeling
completely restored and fit for anything.

Conversation broke out with the first sip of coffee, and the
calm of the restaurant was shattered. Its day had begun.

"It's a great life if you don't weaken," said the Cherub hungrily
attacking her omelette. "And the wortht is yet to come! I
thuppose all you old dears realithe that this show will have to be
rewritten from end to end, and we'll be reharthing day and
night all the time we're on the road."

"Why?" Lois Denham spoke with her mouth full. "What's
wrong with it?"

The Duchess took a sip of coffee.

"Don't make me laugh!" she pleaded. "What's wrong with
it? What's right with it, one would feel more inclined to ask!"

"One would feel thtill more inclined," said the Cherub, "to
athk why one was thuch a chump as to let oneself in for this sort
of thing when one hears on all sides that waitresses earn thixty
dollars a month."

"The numbers are all right," argued Babe. "I don't mean
the melodies, but Johnny has arranged some good business."

"He always does," said the Southern girl. "Some more
buckwheat cakes, please. But what about the book?"

"I never listen to the book."

The Cherub laughed.

"You're too good to yourself! I listened to it right along, and
take it from me it's sad! Of courthe they'll have it fixed. We
can't open in New York like this. My professional reputation
wouldn't thtand it! Didn't you thee Wally Mason in front,
making notes? They've got him down to do the rewriting."

Jill, who had been listening in a dazed way to the conversation, fighting against the waves of sleep which flooded over her, woke up.

"Was Wally—was Mr. Mason there?"

"Sure. Sitting at the back."

Jill could not have said whether she was glad or sorry. She had not seen Wally since that afternoon when they had lunched together at the Cosmopolis, and the rush of the final weeks of rehearsals had given her little opportunity for thinking of him. At the back of her mind had been the feeling that sooner or later she would have to think of him, but for two weeks she had been tired and too busy to re-examine him as a factor in her life. There had been times when the thought of him had been like the sunshine on a winter day, warming her with almost an impersonal glow in moments of depression. And then some sharp, poignant memory of Derek would come to blot him out.

She came out of her thoughts to find that the talk had taken another turn.

"And the worth of it is," the Cherub was saying, "we shall rehearthe all day and give a show every night and work ourselves to the bone, and then, when they're good and ready, they'll fire one of us!"

"That's right!" agreed the Southern girl.

"They couldn't!" Jill cried.

"You wait!" said the Cherub. "They'll never open in New York with thirteen girls. Ike's much too thuperstitious."

"But they wouldn't do a thing like that after we've all worked so hard!"

There was a general burst of sardonic laughter. Jill's opinion of the chivalry of theatrical managers seemed to be higher than that of her more experienced colleagues.

"They'll do anything," the Cherub assured her.

"You don't know the half of it, dearie," scoffed Lois Denham. "You don't know the half of it!"

"Wait till you've been in as many shows as I have," said Babe, shaking her red locks. "The usual thing is to keep a girl slaving her head off all through the road-tour and then fire her before the New York opening."

"But it's a shame! It isn't fair!"

"If one is expecting to be treated fairly," said the Duchess with a prolonged yawn, "one should not go into the show-business."

And, having uttered this profoundly true maxim, she fell asleep again.

The slumber of the Duchess was the signal for a general move. Her somnolence was catching. The restorative effects of the meal were beginning to wear off. There was a call for a chorus rehearsal at four o'clock, and it seemed the wise move to go to bed and get some sleep while there was time. The Duchess was roused from her dreams by means of a piece of ice from one of the tumblers; bills were paid; and the company poured out, yawning and chattering, into the sunlight of the empty boardwalk.

Jill detached herself from the group, and made her way to a seat facing the sea. Tiredness had fallen upon her like a leaden weight, crushing all the power out of her limbs, and the thought of walking to the boarding-house where, from motives of economy, she was sharing a room with the Cherub, paralysed her.

It was a perfect morning, clear and cloudless, with the warm freshness of a day that means to be hotter later on. The sea sparkled in the sun. Little waves broke lazily on the grey sand. Jill closed her eyes, for the brightness of sun and water was trying; and her thoughts went back to what the Cherub had said.

If Wally was really going to rewrite the play, they would be thrown together. She would be obliged to meet him, and she was not sure that she was ready to meet him. Still, he would be somebody to talk to on subjects other than the one eternal topic of the theatre, somebody who belonged to the old life. She had ceased to regard Freddie Rooke in this light; for Freddie, solemn with his new responsibilities as a principal, was the most whole-hearted devotee of "shop" in the company. Freddie nowadays declined to consider any subject for conversation that did not have to do with "The Rose of America" in general and his share in it in particular. Jill had given him up, and he had paired off with Nelly Bryant. The two were inseparable. Jill had taken one or two meals with them, but Freddie's professional monologues, of which Nelly seemed never to weary, were too much for her. As a result she was now very much alone. There were girls in the company whom she liked, but most of them had their own intimate friends, and she was always conscious of not being really wanted. She was lonely, and, after examining the matter as clearly as her tired mind would allow, she found herself curiously soothed by the thought that Wally would be near to mitigate her loneliness.

She opened her eyes, blinking. Sleep had crept upon her with an insidious suddenness, and she had almost fallen over on the seat. She was bracing herself to get up and begin the long tramp to the boarding-house, when a voice spoke at her side.

"Hullo! Good morning!"

Jill looked up.

"Hullo, Wally!"

"Surprised to see me?"

"No. Milly Trevor said she had seen you at the rehearsal last night."

Wally came round the bench and seated himself at her side. His eyes were tired, and his chin dark and bristly.

"Had breakfast?"

"Yes, thanks. Have you?"

"Not yet. How are you feeling?"

"Rather tired."

"I wonder you're not dead. I've been through a good many dress-rehearsals, but this one was the record. Why they couldn't have had it comfortably in New York and just have run through the piece without scenery last night, I don't know, except that in musical comedy it's eitiquette always to do the most inconvenient thing. They know perfectly well that there was no chance of getting the scenery into the theatre till the small hours. You must be worn out. Why aren't you in bed?"

"I couldn't face the walk. I suppose I ought to be going, though."

She half rose, then sank back again. The glitter of the water hypnotized her. She closed her eyes again. She could hear Wally speaking, then his voice grew suddenly faint and far off, and she ceased to fight the delicious drowsiness.

Jill awoke with a start. She opened her eyes, and shut them again at once. The sun was very strong now. It was one of those prematurely warm days of early Spring which have all the languorous heat of late summer. She opened her eyes once more, and found that she was feeling greatly refreshed. She also discovered that her head was resting on Wally's shoulder.

"Have I been asleep?"

Wally laughed.

"You have been having what you might call a nap." He massaged his left arm vigorously. "You needed it. Do you feel more rested now?"

"Good gracious! Have I been squashing your poor arm all the time? Why didn't you move?"

"I was afraid you would fall over. You just shut your eyes and toppled sideways."

"What's the time?"

Wally looked at his watch.

"Just on ten."

"Ten!" Jill was horrified. "Why, I have been giving you cramp for about three hours! You must have had an awful time!"

"Oh, it was all right. I think I dozed off myself. Except that the birds didn't come and cover us with leaves it was rather like the Babes in the Wood."

"But you haven't had any breakfast! Aren't you starving?"

"Well, I'm not saying I wouldn't spear a fried egg with some vim if it happened to float past. But there's plenty of time for that. Lots of doctors say you ought to eat breakfast, and Indian fakirs go without food for days at a time in order to develop their souls. Shall I take you back to wherever you're staying? You ought to get a proper sleep in bed."

"Don't dream of taking me. Go off and have something to eat."

"Oh, that can wait. I'd like to see you safely home."

Jill was conscious of a renewed sense of his comfortingness. There was no doubt about it, Wally was different from any other man she had known. She suddenly felt guilty, as if she were obtaining something valuable under false pretences.

"Wally!"

"Hullo?"

"You—you oughtn't to be so good to me!"

"Nonsense! Where's the harm in lending a hand—or, rather, an arm—to a pal in trouble?"

"You know what I mean. I can't . . . that is to say . . . it isn't as though . . . I mean . . ."

Wally smiled a tired, friendly smile.

"If you're trying to say what I think you're trying to say, don't! We had all that out two weeks ago. I quite understand the position. You mustn't worry yourself about it." He took her arm, and they crossed the boardwalk. "Are we going in the

right direction? You lead the way. I know exactly how you feel.
We're old friends, and nothing more. But, as an old friend, I
claim the right to behave like an old friend. If an old friend can't
behave like an old friend, how *can* an old friend behave? And
now we'll rule the whole topic out of the conversation. But
perhaps you're too tired for conversation?"

"Oh, no."

"Then I will tell you about the sad death of young Mr.
Pilkington."

"What!"

"Well, when I say death, I use the word in a loose sense. The
human giraffe still breathes, and I imagine, from the speed with
which he legged it back to his hotel when we parted, that he still
takes nourishment. But really he is dead. His heart is broken. We
had a conference after the dress-rehearsal, and our friend Mr.
Goble told him in no uncertain words—in the whole course of
my experience I have never heard words less uncertain—that
his damned rotten high-brow false-alarm of a show—I am
quoting Mr. Goble—would have to be rewritten by alien hands.
And these are them! On the right, alien right hand. On the left,
alien left hand. Yes, I am the instrument selected for the murder
of Pilkington's artistic aspirations. I'm going to rewrite the show.
In fact, I have already rewritten the first act and most of the
second. Goble foresaw this contingency and told me to get busy
two weeks ago, and I've been working hard ever since. We shall
start rehearsing the new version to-morrow and open in
Baltimore next Monday with practically a different piece. And
it's going to be a pippin, believe *me*, said our hero modestly. A
gang of composers has been working in shifts for two weeks,
and, by chucking out nearly all of the original music, we shall
have a good score. It means a lot of work for you, I'm afraid. All
the business of the numbers will have to be re-arranged.'

"I like work," said Jill. "But I'm sorry for Mr. Pilkington."

"He's all right. He owns seventy per cent of the show. He
may make a fortune. He's certain to make a comfortable sum.
That is, if he doesn't sell out his interest in pique—or dudgeon,
if you prefer it. From what he said at the close of the proceedings,
I fancy he would sell out to anybody who asked him. At least,
he said that he washed his hands of the piece. He's going back
to New York this afternoon—won't even wait for the opening.
Of course, *I'm* sorry for the poor chap in a way, but he had no

right, with the excellent central idea which he got, to turn out such a rotten book. Oh, by the way!"

"Yes?"

"Another tragedy! Unavoidable, but pathetic. Poor old Freddie! He's out!"

"Oh, no!"

"Out!" repeated Wally firmly.

"But didn't you think he was good last night?"

"He was awful! But that isn't why. Goble wanted his part rewritten as a Scotchman, so as to get McAndrew, the fellow who made such a hit last season in 'Hoots, Mon!' That sort of thing is always happening in musical comedy. You have to fit parts to suit whatever good people happen to be available at the moment. My heart bleeds for Freddie, but what can one do? At any rate he isn't so badly off as a fellow was in one of my shows. In the second act he was supposed to have escaped from an asylum, and the management, in a passion for realism, insisted that he should shave his head. The day after he shaved it, they heard that a superior comedian was disengaged and fired him. It's a ruthless business."

"The girls were saying that one of us would be dismissed."

"Oh, I shouldn't think that's likely."

"I hope not."

"So do I. What are we stopping for?"

Jill had halted in front of a shabby-looking house, one of those depressing buildings which spring up overnight at seashore resorts and start to decay the moment the builders have left them.

"I live here."

"Here?" Wally looked at her in consternation. "But . . ."

Jill smiled.

"We working-girls have got to economize. Besides, it's quite comfortable—fairly comfortable—inside, and it's only for a week." She yawned. "I believe I'm falling asleep again. I'd better hurry in and go to bed. Good-bye, Wally dear. You've been wonderful. Mind you go and get a good breakfast."

II

When Jill arrived at the theatre at four o'clock for the chorus rehearsal, the expected blow had not fallen. No steps had apparently been taken to eliminate the thirteenth girl whose presence in the cast preyed on Mr. Goble's superstitious mind. But she found her colleagues still in a condition of pessimistic foreboding. "Wait!" was the gloomy watchword of "The Rose of America" chorus.

The rehearsal passed off without event. It lasted until six o'clock, when Jill, the Cherub, and two or three of the other girls went to snatch a hasty dinner before returning to the theatre to make up. It was not a cheerful meal. Reaction had set in after the over-exertion of the previous night, and it was too early for first-night excitement to take its place. Everybody, even the Cherub, whose spirits seldom failed her, was depressed, and the idea of an overhanging doom had grown. It seemed now to be merely a question of speculating on the victim, and the conversation gave Jill, as the last addition to the company, and so the cause of swelling the ranks of the chorus to the unlucky number, a feeling of guilt. She was glad when it was time to go back to the theatre.

The moment she and her companions entered the dressing-room, it was made clear to them that the doom had fallen. In a chair in the corner, all her pretence and affectation swept away in a flood of tears, sat the unhappy Duchess, the centre of a group of girls anxious to console, but limited in their ideas of consolation to an occasional pat on the back and an offer of a fresh pocket-handkerchief.

"It's tough, honey!" somebody was saying as Jill came in.

Somebody else said it was fierce, and a third girl declared it to be the limit. A fourth girl, well-meaning but less helpful than she would have liked to be, was advising the victim not to worry.

The story of the disaster was brief and easily told. The Duchess, sailing in at the stage-door, had paused at the letter-box to see if Cuthbert, her faithful auto-salesman, had sent her a good-luck telegram. He had, but his good wishes were unfortunately neutralized by the fact that the very next letter in the box was one from the management, crisp and to the point, informing the Duchess that her services would not be required that night or thereafter. It was the subtle meanness of the blow that roused the indignation of "The Rose of America" chorus, the cunning villainy with which it had been timed.

"Poor Mae, if she'd opened to-night, they'd have had to give her two weeks' notice or her salary. But they can fire her without a cent just because she's only been rehearsing and hasn't given a show!"

The Duchess burst into a fresh flood of tears.

"Don't you worry, honey!" advised the well-meaning girl who would have been in her element looking in on Job with Bildad the Shuhite and his friends. "Don't you worry!"

"It's tough!" said the girl, who had adopted that form of verbal consolation.

"It's fierce!" said the girl who preferred that adjective.

The other girl, with an air of saying something new, repeated her statement that it was the limit. The Duchess cried forlornly throughout. She had needed this engagement badly. Chorus salaries are not stupendous, but it is possible to save money by means of them during a New York run, especially if you have spent three years in a milliner's shop and can make your own clothes, as the Duchess, in spite of her air of being turned out by Fifth Avenue modistes, could and did. She had been looking forward, now that this absurd piece was to be rewritten by someone who knew his business and had a good chance of success, to putting by just those few dollars that make all the difference when you are embarking on married life. Cuthbert, for all his faithfulness, could not hold up the financial end of the establishment unsupported for at least another eighteen months; and this disaster meant that the wedding would have to be postponed again. So the Duchess, abandoning that aristocratic manner criticized by some of her colleagues as "up-stage" and by others as "Ritz-y," sat in her chair and consumed pocket-handkerchiefs as fast as they were offered to her.

Jill had been the only girl in the room who had spoken no word of consolation. This was not because she was not sorry for the Duchess. She had never been sorrier for any one in her life. The pathos of that swift descent from haughtiness to misery had bitten deep into her sensitive heart. But she revolted at the idea of echoing the banal words of the others. Words were no good, she thought, as she set her little teeth and glared at an absent management—a management just about now presumably distending itself with a luxurious dinner at one of the big hotels. Deeds were what she demanded. All her life she had been a girl of impulsive action, and she wanted to act impulsively now. She was in much the same Berserk mood as had swept her, raging, to the defence of Bill the parrot on the occasion of his dispute with Henry of London. The fighting spirit which had been drained from her by the all-night rehearsal had come back in full measure.

"What are you going to *do* ? she cried. "Aren't you going to *do* something ?"

Do ? The members of "The Rose of America" ensemble looked doubtfully at one another. Do ? It had not occurred to them that there was anything to be done. These things happened, and you regretted them, but as for doing anything, well, what *could* you do ?

Jill's face was white and her eyes were flaming. She dominated the roomful of girls like a little Napoleon. The change in her startled them. Hitherto they had always looked on her as rather an unusually quiet girl. She had always made herself unobtrusively pleasant to them all. They all liked her. But they had never suspected her of possessing this militant quality. Nobody spoke, but there was a general stir. She had flung a new idea broadcast, and it was beginning to take root. Do something ? Well, if it came to that, why not ?

"We ought all to refuse to go on to-night unless they let her go on!" Jill declared.

The stir became a movement. Enthusiasm is catching, and every girl is at heart a rebel. And the idea was appealing to the imagination. Refuse to give a show on the opening night! Had a chorus ever done such a thing ? They trembled on the verge of making history.

"Strike ?" quavered somebody at the back.

"Yes, strike!" cried Jill.

"Hooray! That's the thtuff!" shouted the Cherub, and turned the scale. She was a popular girl, and her adherence to the Cause confirmed the doubters. "Thtrike!"

"Strike! Strike!"

Jill turned to the Duchess, who had been gaping amazedly at the demonstration. She no longer wept, but she seemed in a dream.

"Dress and get ready to go on," Jill commanded. "We'll all dress and get ready to go on. Then I'll go and find Mr. Goble and tell him what we mean to do. And, if he doesn't give in, we'll stay here in this room, and there won't be a performance!"

III

Mr. Goble, with a Derby hat on the back of his head and an unlighted cigar in the corner of his mouth, was superintending the erection of the first act set when Jill found him. He was standing with his back to the safety-curtain glowering at a blue canvas, supposed to represent one of those picturesque summer skies which you get at the best places on Long Island. Jill, coming down-stage from the staircase that led to the dressing-room, interrupted his line of vision.

"Get out of the light!" bellowed Mr. Goble, always a man of direct speech, adding "Damn you!" for good measure.

"Please move to one side," interpreted the stage-director. "Mr. Goble is looking at the set."

The head carpenter, who completed the little group, said nothing. Stage carpenters always say nothing. Long association with fussy directors has taught them that the only policy to pursue on opening nights is to withdraw into the silence, wrap themselves up in it, and not emerge until the enemy has grown tired and gone off to worry somebody else.

"It don't look right!" said Mr. Goble, cocking his head on one side.

"I see what you mean, Mr. Goble," assented the stage-director obsequiously. "It has perhaps a little too much—er—not quite enough—yes, I see what you mean!"

"It's too—damn—BLUE!" rasped Mr. Goble, impatient of the vacillating criticism. "That's what's the matter with it."

The head carpenter abandoned the silent policy of a lifetime. He felt impelled to utter. He was a man who, when not at the theatre, spent most of his time in bed, reading all-fiction magazines; but it so happened that once, last summer, he had actually seen the sky; and he considered that this entitled him to speak almost as a specialist on the subject.

"Ther sky *is* blue!" he observed huskily. "Yessir! I seen it!"

He passed into the silence again, and, to prevent a further lapse, stopped up his mouth with a piece of chewing-gum.

Mr. Goble regarded the silver-tongued orator wrathfully. He was not accustomed to chatterboxes arguing with him like this. He would probably had said something momentous and crushing, but at this point Jill intervened.

"Mr. Goble."

The manager swung round on her.

"What *is* it?"

It is sad to think how swiftly affection can change to dislike in this world. Two weeks before, Mr. Goble had looked on Jill

with favour. She had seemed good in his eyes. But that refusal
of hers to lunch with him, followed by a refusal some days later
to take a bit of supper somewhere, had altered his views on
feminine charm. If it had been left to him, as most things were
about this theatre, to decide which of the thirteen girls should
be dismissed, he would undoubtedly have selected Jill. But at
this stage in the proceedings there was the unfortunate necessity
of making concessions to the temperamental Johnson Miller.
Mr. Goble was aware that the dance-director's services would
be badly needed in the re-arrangement of the numbers during
the coming week or so, and he knew that there were a dozen
managers waiting eagerly to welcome him if he threw up his
present job, so he had been obliged to approach him in quite a
humble spirit and enquire which of his female chorus could be
most easily spared. And, as the Duchess had a habit of carrying
her haughty languor on to the stage and employing it as a
substitute for the chorea which was Mr. Miller's ideal, the dance-
director had chosen her. To Mr. Goble's dislike of Jill, therefore,
was added now something of the fury of the baffled potentate.

" 'Jer want ?" he demanded.

"Mr. Goble is extremely busy," said the stage-director.
"Extremely."

A momentary doubt as to the best way of approaching her
subject had troubled Jill on her way downstairs, but, now that
she was on the battlefield confronting the enemy, she found herself cool, collected, and full of a cold rage which steeled her
nerves without confusing her mind.

"I came to ask you to let Mae D'Arcy go on to-night."

"Who the hell's Mae D'Arcy ?" Mr. Goble broke off to
bellow at a scene-shifter who was depositing the wall of Mrs.
Stuyvesant van Dyke's Long Island residence too far down
stage. "Not there, you fool! Higher up!"

"You gave her notice this evening," said Jill.

"Well, what about it ?"

"We want you to withdraw it."

"Who's 'we' ?"

"The other girls and myself."

Mr. Goble jerked his head so violently that the Derby hat
flew off, to be picked up, dusted, and restored by the stage-director.

"Oh, so you don't like it ? Well, you know what you can
do . . ."

"Yes," said Jill, "we do. We are going to strike."

"What?"

"If you don't let Mae go on, we shan't go on. There won't be a performance to-night, unless you like to give one without a chorus."

"Are you crazy?"

"Perhaps. But we're quite unanimous."

Mr. Goble, like most theatrical managers, was not good at words over two syllables.

"You're what?"

"We've talked it over, and we've all decided to do what I said."

Mr. Goble's hat shot off again, and gambolled away into the wings, the the stage-director bounding after it like a retriever.

"Whose idea's this?" demanded Mr. Goble. His eyes were a little foggy, for his brain was adjusting itself but slowly to the novel situation.

"Mine."

"Oh, yours! I thought as much!"

"Well," said Jill, "I'll go back and tell them that you will not do what we ask. We will keep our make-up on in case you change your mind."

She turned away.

"Come back!"

Jill proceeded toward the staircase. As she went, a husky voice spoke in her ear.

"Go to it, kid! You're all right!"

The head-carpenter had broken his Trappist vows twice in a single evening, a thing which had not happened to him since the night three years ago, when, sinking wearily into a seat in a dark corner for a bit of a rest, he found that one of his assistants had placed a pot of red paint there.

IV

To Mr. Goble, fermenting and full of strange oaths, entered Johnson Miller. The dance-director was always edgy on first nights, and during the foregoing conversation had been flitting about the stage like a white-haired moth. His deafness had kept him in complete ignorance that there was anything untoward afoot, and he now approached Mr. Goble with his watch in his hand.

"Eight twenty-five," he observed. "Time those girls were on stage."

Mr. Goble, glad of a concrete target for his wrath, cursed him in about two hundred and fifty rich and well-selected words.

"Huh?" said Miller, hand to ear.

Mr. Goble repeated the last hundred and eleven words, the pick of the bunch.

"Can't hear!" said Mr. Miller regretfully. "Got a cold."

The grave danger that Mr. Goble, a thick-necked man, would undergo some sort of a stroke was averted by the presence of mind of the stage-director, who, returning with the hat, presented it like a bouquet to his employer, and then, his hands being now unoccupied, formed them into a funnel and through this flesh-and-blood megaphone endeavoured to impart the bad news.

"The girls say they won't go on!"

Mr. Miller nodded.

"I *said* it was time they were on."

"They're on strike!"

"It's not," said Mr. Miller austerely, "what they *like*, it's what they're paid for. They ought to be on stage. We should be ringing up in two minutes."

The stage-director drew another breath, then thought better of it. He had a wife and children, and, if dadda went under with apoplexy, what became of the home, civilization's most sacred product? He relaxed the muscles of his diaphragm, and reached for pencil and paper.

Mr. Miller inspected the message, felt for his spectacle-case, found it, opened it, took out his glasses, replaced the spectacle-case, felt for his handkerchief, polished the glasses, replaced the handkerchief, put the glasses on, and read. A blank look came into his face.

"Why?" he enquired.

The stage-director, with a nod of the head intended to imply that he must be patient and all would come right in the future, recovered the paper, and scribbled another sentence. Mr. Miller perused it.

"Because Mae D'Arcy has got her notice?" he queried, amazed. "But the girl can't dance a step."

The stage-director, by means of a wave of the hand, a lifting of both eyebrows, and a wrinkling of the nose, replied that the situation, unreasonable as it might appear to the thinking man,

was as he had stated and must be faced. What, he enquired—
through the medium of a clever drooping of the mouth and a
shrug of the shoulders—was to be done about it?

Mr. Miller remained for a moment in meditation.

"I'll go and talk to them," he said.

He flitted off, and the stage-director leaned back against the
asbestos curtain. He was exhausted, and his throat was in
agony, but nevertheless he was conscious of a feeling of quiet
happiness. His life had been lived in the shadow of the constant
fear that some day Mr. Goble might dismiss him. Should that
disaster occur, he felt there was always a future for him in the
movies.

Scarcely had Mr. Miller disappeared on his peace-making
errand, when there was a noise like a fowl going through a
quickset hedge, and Mr. Saltzburg, brandishing his baton as if
he were conducting an unseen orchestra, plunged through the
scenery at the left upper entrance and charged excitedly down
the stage. Having taken his musicians twice through the overture,
he had for ten minutes been sitting in silence, waiting for the
curtain to go up. At last, his emotional nature cracking under
the strain of this suspense, he had left his conductor's chair and
plunged down under the stage by way of the musician's bolthole
to ascertain what was causing the delay.

"What is it? What is it? What is it? What is it?" enquired
Mr. Saltzburg. "I wait and wait and wait and wait and wait . . .
We cannot play the overture again. What is it? What has
happened?"

Mr. Goble, that overwrought soul, had betaken himself to the
wings where he was striding up and down with his hands behind
his back, chewing his cigar. The stage-director braced himself
once more to the task of explanation.

"The girls have struck!"

Mr. Saltzburg blinked through his glasses.

"The girls?" he repeated blankly.

"Oh, damn it!" cried the stage-director, his patience at last
giving way. "You know what a girl is, don't you?"

"They have what?"

"Struck! Walked out on us! Refused to go on!"

Mr. Saltzburg reeled under the blow.

"But it is impossible! Who is to sing the opening chorus?"

In the presence of one to whom he could relieve his mind without fear of consequences, the stage-director became savagely jocular.

"That's all arranged," he said. "We're going to dress the carpenters in skirts. The audience won't notice anything wrong."

"Should I speak to Mr. Goble?" queried Mr. Saltzburg doubtfully.

"Yes, if you don't value your life," returned the stage-director. Mr. Saltzburg pondered.

"I will go and speak to the childrun," he said. "I will talk to them. They know *me!* I will make them be reasonable."

He bustled off in the direction taken by Mr. Miller, his coat-tails flying behind him. The stage-director, with a tired sigh, turned to face Wally, who had come in through the iron pass-door from the auditorium.

"Hullo!" said Wally cheerfully. "Going strong? How's everybody at home? Fine? So am I! By the way, am I wrong or did I hear something about a theatrical entertainment of some sort here to-night?" He looked about him at the empty stage. In the wings, on the prompt side, could be discerned the flannel-clad forms of the gentlemanly members of the male ensemble, all dressed up for Mrs. Stuyvesant van Dyke's tennis party. One or two of the principals were standing perplexedly in the lower entrance. The O.P. side had been given over by general consent to Mr. Goble for his perambulations. Every now and then he would flash into view through an opening in the scenery. "I understood that to-night was the night for the great revival of comic opera. Where are the comics, and why aren't they opping?"

The stage-director repeated his formula once more.

"The girls have struck!"

"So have the clocks," said Wally. "It's past nine."

"The chorus refuse to go on."

"No really! Just artistic loathing of the rotten piece or is there some other reason?"

"They're sore because one of them has been given her notice and they say they won't give a show unless she's taken back. They've struck. That Mariner girl started it."

"She did!" Wally's interest became keener. "She would!" he said approvingly. "She's a heroine!"

"Little devil! I never liked that girl!"

"Now there," said Wally, "is just the point on which we differ. I have always liked her, and I've known her all my life.

So, shipmate, if you have any derogatory remarks to make about Miss Mariner, keep them where they belong—*there!*" He prodded the other sharply in the stomach. He was smiling pleasantly, but the stage-director, catching his eye, decided that his advice was good and should be followed. It is just as bad for the home if the head of the family gets his neck broken as if he succumbs to apoplexy.

"You surely aren't on their side?" he said.

"Me!" said Wally. "Of course I am. I'm always on the side of the down-trodden and oppressed. If you know of a dirtier trick than firing a girl just before the opening, so that they won't have to pay her two weeks' salary, mention it. Till you do, I'll go on believing that it is the limit. Of course I'm on the girls' side. I'll make them a speech if they want me to, or head the procession with a banner if they are going to parade down the boardwalk. I'm for 'em, Father Abraham, a hundred thousand strong. And then a few! If you want my considered opinion, our old friend Goble has asked for it and got it. And I'm glad— glad—glad, if you don't mind my quoting Pollyanna for a moment. I hope it chokes him!"

"You'd better not let him hear you talking like that!"

"*Au contraire*, as we say in the Gay City, I'm going to make a point of letting him hear me talk like that! Adjust the impression that I fear any Goble in shining armour, because I don't. I propose to speak my mind to him. I would beard him in his lair, if he had a beard. Well, I'll clean-shave him in his lair. That will be just as good. But hist! whom have we here? Tell me, do you see the same thing I see?"

Like the vanguard of a defeated army, Mr. Saltzburg was coming dejectedly across the stage.

"Well?" said the stage-director.

"They would not listen to me," said Mr. Saltzburg brokenly. "The more I talked the more they did not listen!" He winced at a painful memory. "Miss Trevor stole my baton, and then they all lined up and sang the 'Star-Spangled Banner'!"

"Not the words?" cried Wally incredulously. "Don't tell me they knew the words!"

"Mr. Miller is still up there, arguing with them. But it will be of no use. What shall we do?" asked Mr. Saltzburg helplessly. "We ought to have rung up half an hour ago. What shall we do-oo-oo?"

"We must go and talk to Goble," said Wally. "Something has got to be settled quick. When I left, the audience was getting so impatient that I thought he was going to walk out on us. He's one of those nasty, determined-looking men. So come along!"

Mr. Goble, intercepted as he was about to turn for another walk up-stage, eyed the deputation sourly and put the same question that the stage-director had put to Mr. Saltzburg.

"Well?"

Wally came briskly to the point.

"You'll have to give in," he said, "or else go and make a speech to the audience, the burden of which will be that they can have their money back by applying at the box-office. These Joans of Arc have got you by the short hairs!"

"I won't give in!"

"Then give out!" said Wally. "Or pay out, if you prefer it. Trot along and tell the audience that the four dollars fifty in the house will be refunded."

Mr. Goble gnawed his cigar.

"I've been in the show business fifteen years . . ."

"I know. And this sort of thing has never happened to you before. One gets new experiences."

Mr. Goble cocked his cigar at a fierce angle, and glared at Wally. Something told him that Wally's sympathies were not wholly with him.

"They can't do this sort of thing to *me!*" he growled.

"Well, they are doing it to someone, aren't they," said Wally, "and, if it's not you, who is it?"

"I've a damned good mind to fire them all!"

"A corking idea! I can't see a single thing wrong with it except that it would hang up the production for another five weeks and lose you your bookings and cost you a week's rent of this theatre for nothing and mean having all the dresses made over and lead to all your principals going off and getting other jobs. These trifling things apart, we may call the suggestion a bright one."

"You talk too damn much!" said Mr. Goble, eyeing him with distaste.

"Well, go on, *you* say something. Something sensible."

"It is a very serious situation . . ." began the stage-director.

"Oh, shut up!" said Mr. Goble.

The stage-director subsided into his collar.

"I cannot play the overture again," protested Mr. Saltzburg. "I cannot!"

At this point Mr. Miller appeared. He was glad to see Mr. Goble. He had been looking for him, for he had news to impart.

"The girls," said Mr. Miller, "have struck! They won't go on!"

Mr. Goble, with the despairing gesture of one who realizes the impotence of words, dashed off for his favourite walk up stage. Wally took out his watch.

"Six seconds and a bit," he said approvingly, as the manager returned. "A very good performance. I should like to time you over the course in running-kit."

The interval for reflection, brief as it had been, had apparently enabled Mr. Goble to come to a decision.

"Go," he said to the stage-director, "and tell 'em that fool of a D'Arcy girl can play. We've got to get that curtain up."

"Yes, Mr. Goble."

The stage-director galloped off.

"Get back to your place," said the manager to Mr. Saltzburg, "and play the overture again."

"Again!"

"Perhaps they didn't hear it the first two times," said Wally.

Mr. Goble watched Mr. Saltzburg out of sight. Then he turned to Wally.

"That damned Mariner girl was at the bottom of this! She started the whole thing! She told me so. Well, I'll settle *her!* She goes to-morrow!"

"Wait a minute," said Wally, "Wait one minute! Bright as it is, that idea is *out!*"

"What the devil has it got to do with you?"

"Only this, that if you fire Miss Mariner, I take that neat script which I've prepared and I tear it into a thousand fragments. Or nine hundred. Anyway, I tear it. Miss Mariner opens in New York, or I pack up my work and leave."

Mr. Goble's green eyes glowed.

"Oh, you're stuck on her, are you?" he sneered. "I see!"

"Listen, dear heart," said Wally, gripping the manager's arm, "I can see that you are on the verge of introducing personalities into this very pleasant little chat. Resist the impulse! Why not let your spine stay where it is instead of having it kicked up through your hat? Keep to the main issue. Does Miss Mariner open in New York or does she not?"

There was a tense silence. Mr. Goble permitted himself a swift review of his position. He would have liked to do many things to Wally, beginning with ordering him out of the theatre, but prudence restrained him. He wanted Wally's work. He needed Wally in his business: and, in the theatre, business takes precedence of personal feelings.

"All right!" he growled reluctantly.

"That's a promise," said Wally. "I'll see that you keep it." He looked over his shoulder. The stage was filled with gaily-coloured dresses. The mutineers had returned to duty. "Well, I'll be getting along. I'm rather sorry we agreed to keep clear of personalities, because I should have like to say that, if ever they have a skunk-show at Madison Square Garden, you ought to enter—and win the blue ribbon. Still, of course, under our agreement my lips are sealed, and I can't event hint at it. Good-bye. See you later, I suppose?"

Mr. Goble, giving a creditable imitation of a living statue, was plucked from his thoughts by a hand upon his arm. It was Mr. Miller, whose unfortunate ailment had prevented him from keeping abreast of the conversation.

"What did he say?" enquired Mr. Miller, interested. "I didn't hear what he said!"

Mr. Goble made no effort to inform him.

★ 17 ★

The Cost of a Row

I

OTIS PILKINGTON had left Atlantic City two hours after the conference which had followed the dress-rehearsal, firmly resolved never to go near "The Rose of America" again. He had been wounded in his finest feelings. There had been a moment, when Mr. Goble had given him the choice between having the piece rewritten and cancelling the production altogether, when he had inclined to the heroic course. But for one thing Mr. Pilkington would have defied the manager, refused to allow his script to be touched, and removed the play from his hands. That one thing was the fact that, up to the day of the dress-rehearsal, the expenses of the production had amounted to the appalling sum of thirty-two thousand eight hundred and fifty-nine dollars, sixty-eight cents, all of which had to come out of Mr. Pilkington's pocket. The figures, presented to him in a neatly typewritten column stretching over two long sheets of paper, had stunned him. He had had no notion that musical plays cost so much. The costumes alone had come to ten thousand six hundred and sixty-three dollars and fifty cents, and somehow that odd fifty cents annoyed Otis Pilkington as much as anything on the list. A dark suspicion that Mr. Goble, who had seen to all the executive end of the business, had a secret arrangement with the costumier whereby he received a private rebate, deepened his gloom. Why, for ten thousand six hundred and sixty-three dollars and fifty cents you could dress the whole female population of New York State and have a bit left over for Connecticut. So thought Mr. Pilkington, as he read the bad news in the train. He only ceased to brood upon the high cost of costuming when in the next line but one there smote his eye an item of four hundred and ninety-eight dollars for "Clothing." Clothing! Weren't costumes clothing? Why should he have to pay twice over for the same thing? Mr. Pilkington was just raging over this, when something lower down in the column caught his eye.

It was the words:—

Clothing 187.45

At this Otis Pilkington uttered a stifled cry, so sharp and so anguished that an old lady in the next seat, who was drinking a glass of milk, dropped it and had to refund the railway company thirty-five cents for breakages. For the remainder of the journey she sat with one eye warily on Mr. Pilkington, waiting for his next move.

This adventure quieted Otis Pilkington down, if it did not soothe him. He returned blushingly to a perusal of his bill of costs, nearly every line of which contained some item that infuriated and dismayed him. "Shoes" ($213.50) he could understand, but what on earth was "Academy. Rehl. $105.50"? What was "Cut . . . $15"? And what in the name of everything infernal was this item for "Frames," in which mysterious luxury he had apparently indulged to the extent of ninety-four dollars and fifty cents? "Props" occurred on the list no fewer than seventeen times. Whatever his future, at whatever poorhouse he might spend his declining years, he was supplied with enough props to last his liftime.

Otis Pilkington stared blankly at the scenery that flitted past the train windows. (Scenery! There had been two charges for scenery! "Friedmann, Samuel . . . Scenery . . . $3711" and "Unitt and Wickes . . . Scenery . . . $2120"). He was suffering the torments of the ruined gamester at the roulette-table. Thirty-two thousand eight hundred and fifty nine dollars, six-eight cents! And he was out of pocket ten thousand in addition from the cheque he had handed over two days ago to Uncle Chris as his share of the investment of starting Jill in the motion-pictures. It was terrible! It deprived one of the power of thought.

The power of thought, however, returned to Mr. Pilkington almost immediately, for, remembering suddenly that Roland Trevis had assured him that no musical production, except one of those elaborate girl-shows with a chorus of ninety, could possibly cost more than fifteen thousand dollars at an outside figure, he began to think about Roland Trevis, and continued to think about him until the train pulled into the Pennsylvania Station.

For a week or more the stricken financier confined himself mostly to his rooms, where he sat smoking cigarettes, gazing at Japanese prints, and trying not to think about "props" and "rehl." Then, gradually, the almost maternal yearning to see his brain-child once more, which can never be wholly crushed out of a young dramatist, returned to him—faintly at first, then getting stronger by degrees till it could no longer be resisted. Otis Pilkington, having instructed his Japanese valet to pack a few simple necessaries in a suit-case, took a cab to the Grand Central Station and caught an afternoon train for Rochester, where his recollection of the route planned for the tour told him "The Rose of America" would now be playing.

Looking into his club on the way, to cash a cheque, the first person he encountered was Freddie Rooke.

"Good gracious!" said Otis Pilkington. "What are you doing here?"

Freddie looked up dully from his reading. The abrupt stoppage of his professional career—his life-work, one might almost say—had left Freddie at a very loose end; and so hollow did the world seem to him at the moment, so uniformly futile all its so-called allurements, that, to pass the time, he had just been trying to read the *National Geographic Magazine*.

"Hullo!" he said. "Well, might as well be here as anywhere, what?" he replied to the other's question.

"But why aren't you playing?"

"They sacked me! They've changed my part to a bally Scotchman! Well, I mean to say, I couldn't play a bally Scotchman!"

Mr. Pilkington groaned in spirit. Of all the characters in his musical fantasy on which he prided himself, that of Lord Finchley was his pet. And he had been burked, murdered, blotted out, in order to make room for a bally Scotchman.

"The character's called 'The McWhustle of McWhustle' now!" said Freddie sombrely.

The McWhustle of McWhustle! Mr. Pilkington almost abandoned his trip to Rochester on receiving this devastating piece of information.

"He comes on in Act One in kilts!"

"In kilts! At Mrs. Stuyvesant van Dyke's garden-party! On Long Island!"

"It isn't Mrs. Stuyvesant van Dyke any longer, either," said Freddie. "She's been changed to the wife of a pickle manufacturer."

"A pickle manufacturer!"

"Yes. They said it ought to be a comedy part."

If agony had not caused Mr. Pilkington to clutch for support at the back of a chair, he would undoubtedly have wrung his hands.

"But it *was* a comedy part!" he wailed. "It was full of the subtlest, most delicate satire on Society. They were delighted with it at Newport! Oh, this is too much! I shall make a strong protest! I shall insist on these parts being kept as I wrote them! I shall . . . I must be going at once, or I shall miss my train." He paused at the door. "How was business in Baltimore?"

"Rotten!" said Freddie, and returned to his *National Geographic Magazine*.

Otis Pilkington tottered into his cab. He was shattered by what he had heard. They had massacred his beautiful play and, doing so had not even made a success of it by their own sordid commercial lights. Business at Baltimore had been rotten! That meant more expense, further columns of figures with "frames" and "rehl." in front of them! He staggered into the station.

"Hey!" cried the taxi-driver.

Otis Pilkington turned.

"Sixty-five cents, mister, if *you* please! Forgetting I'm not your private shovoor, wasn't you?"

Mr. Pilkington gave him a dollar. Money—money! Life was just one long round of paying out and paying out.

II

The day which Mr. Pilkington had selected for his visit to the provinces was a Tuesday. "The Rose of America" had opened at Rochester on the previous night, after a week at Atlantic City in its original form and a week at Baltimore in what might be called its second incarnation. Business had been bad in Atlantic City and no better in Baltimore, and a meagre first-night house at Rochester had given the piece a cold reception, which had put the finishing touches to the depression of the company in spite of the fact that the Rochester critics, like those of Baltimore, had written kindly of the play. One of the maxims of the theatre is that "out-of-town notices don't count," and the company had refused to be cheered by them.

It is to be doubted, however, if even crowded houses would have aroused much response from the principals and chorus of "The Rose of America." For two weeks without a break they had been working under forced draught, and they were weary in body and spirit. The new principals had had to learn parts in exactly half the time usually given for that purpose, and the chorus, after spending five weeks assimilating one set of steps and groupings, had been compelled to forget them and rehearse an entirely new set. From the morning after the first performance at Atlantic City, they had not left the theatre except for sketchy half-hour meals.

Jill, standing listlessly in the wings while the scene-shifters arranged the Second Act set, was aware of Wally approaching from the direction of the pass-door.

"Miss Mariner, I believe?" said Wally. "I suppose you know you look perfectly wonderful in that dress? All Rochester's talking about it, and there is some idea of running excursion trains from Troy and Utica. A great stir it has made!"

Jill smiled. Wally was like a tonic to her during these days of overwork. He seemed to be entirely unaffected by the general depression, a fact which he attributed himself to the happy

accident of being in a position to sit back and watch the others
toil. But in reality Jill knew that he was working as hard as any
one. He was working all the time, changing scenes, adding lines,
tinkering with lyrics, smoothing over principals whose nerves
had become strained by the incessant rehearsing, keeping within
bounds Mr. Goble's passion for being the big noise about the
theatre. His cheerfulness was due to the spirit that was in him,
and Jill appreciated it. She had come to feel very close to Wally
since the driving rush of making over "The Rose of America"
had begun.

"They seemed quite calm to-night," she said. "I believe half
of them were asleep."

"They're always like that in Rochester. They cloak their
deeper feelings. They wear the mask. But you can tell from the
glassy look in their eyes that they are really seething inwardly.
But what I came round about was—(a)—to give you this
letter . . ."

Jill took the letter, and glanced at the writing. It was from
Uncle Chris. She placed it on the axe over the fire-buckets for
perusal later.

"The man at the box-office gave it to me," said Wally, "when
I looked in there to find out how much money there was in the
house to-night. The sum was so small that he had to whisper
it."

"I'm afraid the piece isn't a success."

"Nonsense! Of course it is! We're doing fine. That brings
me to section (b) of my discourse. I met poor old Pilkington in
the lobby, and he said exactly what you have just said, only at
greater length."

"Is Mr. Pilkington here?"

"He appears to have run down on the afternoon train to have
a look at the show. He is catching the next train back to New
York! Whenever I meet him, he always seems to be dashing off
to catch the next train back to New York! Poor chap! Have you
ever done a murder? If you haven't, don't! I know exactly what
it feels like, and it feels rotten! After two minutes' conversation
with Pilkington, I could sympathize with Macbeth when he
chatted with Banquo. He said I had killed his play. He nearly
wept, and he drew such a moving picture of a poor helpless
musical fantasy being lured into a dark alley by thugs and there
slaughtered that he almost had me in tears too. I felt like a

beetle-browed brute with a dripping knife and hands imbrued with innocent gore."

"Poor Mr. Pilkington!"

"Once more you say exactly what he said, only more crisply. I comforted him as well as I could, told him all was for the best and so on, and he flung the box-office receipts in my face and said that the piece was as bad a failure commercially as it was artistically. I couldn't say anything to that, seeing what a house we've got to-night, except to bid him look out to the horizon where the sun will shortly shine. In other words, I told him that business was about to buck up and that later on he would be going about the place with a sprained wrist from clipping coupons. But he refused to be cheered, cursed me some more for ruining his piece, and ended by begging me to buy his share of it cheap."

"You aren't going to?"

"No, I am not—but simply and solely for the reason that, after that fiasco in London, I raised my right hand—thus—and swore an oath that never, as long as I lived, would I again put up a cent for a production, were it the most obvious cinch on earth. I'm gun-shy. But if he does happen to get hold of anyone with a sporting disposition and a few thousands to invest, that person will make a fortune. This piece is going to be a gold-mine."

Jill looked at him in surprise. With anybody else but Wally she would have attributed this confidence to author's vanity. But with Wally, she felt, the fact that the piece, as played now, was almost entirely his own work did not count. He viewed it dispassionately, and she could not understand why, in the face of half-empty houses, he should have such faith in it.

"But what makes you think so? We've been doing awfully badly so far."

Wally nodded.

"And we shall do awfully badly in Syracuse the last half of this week. And why? For one thing, because the show isn't a show at all at present. Why should people flock to pay for seats for what are practically dress-rehearsals of an unknown play? Half the principals have had to get up in their parts in two weeks, and they haven't had time to get anything out of them. They are groping for their lines all the time. The girls can't let themselves go in the numbers, because they are wondering if they are going to remember the steps. The show hasn't had time

to click together yet. It's just ragged. Take a look at it in another
two weeks! I *know*! I don't say musical comedy is a very lofty
form of art, but still there's a certain amount of science about it.
If you go in for it long enough, you learn the tricks, and take it
from me that, if you have a good cast and some catchy numbers,
it's almost impossible not to have a success. We've got an
excellent cast now, and the numbers are fine. I tell you—as I
tried to tell Pilkington, only he wouldn't listen—that this show
is all right. There's a fortune in it for somebody. But I suppose
Pilkington is now sitting in the smoking-car of an east-bound
train, trying to get the porter to accept his share in the piece
instead of a tip!"

If Otis Pilkington was not actually doing that, he was doing
something like it. Sunk in gloom, he bumped up and down on
an uncomfortable seat, wondering why he had ever taken the
trouble to make the trip to Rochester. He had found exactly what
he had expected to find, a mangled caricature of his brain-child
playing to a house half empty and wholly indifferent. The only
redeeming feature, he thought vindictively, as he remembered
what Roland Trevis had said about the cost of musical productions, was the fact that the new numbers were undoubtedly
better than those which his collaborator had originally
supplied.

And "The Rose of America," after a disheartening Wednesday
matinée and a not much better reception on the Wednesday night,
packed its baggage and moved to Syracuse, where it failed just
as badly. Then for another two weeks it wandered on from one
small town to another, up and down New York State and through
the doldrums of Connecticut, tacking to and fro like a storm-
battered ship, till finally the astute and discerning citizens of
Hartford welcomed it with such a reception that hardened
principals stared at each other in a wild surmise, wondering if
these things could really be: and a weary chorus forgot its
weariness and gave encore after encore with a snap and vim
which even Mr. Johnson Miller was obliged to own approximated
to something like it. Nothing to touch the work of his choruses
of the old days, of course, but nevertheless fair, quite fair.

The spirits of the company revived. Optimism reigned.
Principals smiled happily and said they had believed in the thing
all along. The ladies and gentlemen of the ensemble chattered
contentedly of a year's run in New York. And the citizens of

Hartford fought for seats, and, if they could not get seats, stood up at the back.

Of these things Otis Pilkington was not aware. He had sold his interest in the piece two weeks ago for ten thousand dollars to a lawyer acting for some client unknown, and was glad to feel that he had saved something out of the wreck.

* 18 *

Jill Receives Notice

I

THE violins soared to one last high note; the bassoon uttered a final moan; the pensive person at the end of the orchestra-pit just under Mrs. Waddesleigh Peagrim's box, whose duty it was to slam the drum at stated intervals, gave that much-enduring instrument a concluding wallop; and, laying aside his weapons, allowed his thoughts to stray in the direction of cooling drinks. Mr. Saltzburg lowered the baton which he had stretched quivering towards the roof and sat down and mopped his forehead. The curtain fell on the first act of "The Rose of America," and simultaneously tremendous applause broke out from all over the Gotham Theatre, which was crammed from floor to roof with that heterogeneous collection of humanity which makes up the audience of a New York opening performance. The applause continued like the breaking of waves on a stony beach. The curtain rose and fell, rose and fell, rose and fell again. An usher, stealing down the central aisle, gave to Mr. Saltzburg an enormous bouquet of American Beauty roses, which he handed to the prima donna, who took it with a brilliant smile and a bow, nicely combining humility with joyful surprise. The applause, which had begun to slacken, gathered strength again. It was a superb bouquet, nearly as big as Mr. Saltzburg himself. It had cost the prima donna close on a hundred dollars that morning at Thorley's, but it was worth every cent of the money.

The house-lights went up. The audience began to move up the aisles to stretch its legs and discuss the piece during the intermission. There was a general babble of conversation. Here, a composer who had not got an interpolated number in the show was explaining to another composer who had not got an interpolated number in the show the exact source from which a third composer who had got an interpolated number in the show had stolen the number which he had got interpolated. There, two musical comedy artists who were temporarily resting were agreeing that the prima donna was a dear thing but that, contrary as it was to their life-long policy to knock anybody, they must say that she was beginning to show the passage of years a trifle and ought to be warned by some friend that her career as an *ingénue* was a thing of the past. Dramatic critics, slinking in twos and threes into dark corners, were telling each other that "The Rose of America" was just another of those things but it had apparently got over. The general public was of the opinion that it was a knock-out.

"Otie, darling," said Mrs. Waddesleigh Peagrim, leaning her ample shoulder on Uncle Chris' perfectly fitting sleeve and speaking across him to young Mr. Pilkington, "I do congratulate you, dear. It's perfectly delightful! I don't know when I have enjoyed a musical piece so much. Don't you think it's perfectly darling, Major Selby?"

"Capital!" agreed that suave man of the world, who had been bored as near extinction as makes no matter. "Congratulate you, my boy!"

"You clever, clever thing!" said Mrs. Peagrim, skittishly striking her nephew on the knee with her fan. "I'm proud to be your aunt! Aren't you proud to know him, Mr. Rooke?"

The fourth occupant of the box awoke with a start from the species of stupor into which he had been plunged by the spectacle of the McWhustle of McWhustle in action. There had been other dark moments in Freddie's life. Once, back in London, Parker had sent him out into the heart of the West End without his spats and he had not discovered their absence till he was half-way up Bond Street. On another occasion, having taken on a stranger at squash for a quid a game, he had discovered too late that the latter was an ex-public-school champion. He had felt gloomy when he had learned of the breaking-off of the engagement between Jill Mariner and Derek Underhill, and sad when it had been brought to his notice that London was giving Derek the cold shoulder in consequence. But never in his whole career had he experienced such gloom and such sadness as had come to him that evening while watching this unspeakable person in kilts murder that part that should have been his. And the audience, confound them, had roared with laughter at every damn silly thing the fellow had said!

"Eh?" he replied. "Oh, yes, rather, absolutely!"

"We're *all* proud of you, Otie darling," proceeded Mrs. Peagrim. "The piece is a wonderful success. You will make a fortune out of it. And just think, Major Selby, I tried my best to argue the poor, dear boy out of putting it on! I thought it was so rash to risk his money in a theatrical venture. But then," said Mrs. Peagrim in extenuation, "I had only seen the piece when it was done at my house at Newport, and of course it really was rather dreadful nonsense then! I might have known that you would change it a great deal before you put it on in New York. As I always say, plays are not written, they are rewritten! Why, you have improved this piece a hundred per cent, Otie! I wouldn't know it was the same play!"

She slapped him smartly once more with her fan, ignorant of the gashes she was inflicting. Poor Mr. Pilkington was suffering twin torments, the torture of remorse and the agonized jealousy of the unsuccessful artist. It would have been bad enough to have to sit and watch a large audience rocking in its seats at the slapstick comedy which Wally Mason had substituted for his delicate social satire: but, had this been all, at least he could have consoled himself with the sordid reflection that he, as owner of the piece, was going to make a lot of money out of it. Now, even this material balm was denied him. He had sold out, and he was feeling like the man who parts for a song with shares in an apparently goldless gold mine, only to read in the papers next morning that a new reef has been located. Into each life some rain must fall. Quite a shower was falling now into young Mr. Pilkington's.

"Of course," went on Mrs. Peagrim, "when the play was done at my house, it was acted by amateurs. And you know what amateurs are! The cast to-night is perfectly splendid. I do think that Scotchman is the most killing creature! Don't you think he is wonderful, Mr. Rooke?"

We may say what we will against the upper strata of Society, but it cannot be denied that breeding tells. Only by falling back for support on the traditions of his class and the solid support of a gentle up-bringing was the Last of the Rookes able to crush down the words that leaped to his lips and to substitute for them a politely conventional agreement. If Mr. Pilkington was feeling like a too impulsive seller of gold mines, Freddie's emotions were akin to those of the Spartan boy with the fox under his vest. Nothing but Winchester and Magdalen could have produced the smile which, though twisted and confined entirely to his lips, flashed on to his face and off again at his hostess' question.

"Oh, rather! Priceless!"

"Wasn't that part an Englishman before?" asked Mrs. Peagrim. "I thought so. Well, it was a stroke of genius changing it. This Scotchman is too funny for words. And such an artist!"

Freddie rose shakily. One can stand just so much.

"Think," he mumbled, "I'll be pushing along and smoking a cigarette."

He groped his way to the door.

"I'll come with you, Freddie my boy," said Uncle Chris, who felt an imperative need of five minutes' respite from Mrs. Peagrim. "Let's get out into the air for a moment. Uncommonly warm it is here."

Freddie assented. Air was what he felt he wanted most.

Left alone in the box with her nephew, Mrs. Peagrim continued for some moments in the same vein, innocently twisting the knife in the open wound. It struck her from time to time that darling Otie was perhaps a shade unresponsive, but she put this down to the nervous strain inseparable from a first night of a young author's first play.

"Why," she concluded, "you will make thousands and thousands of dollars out of this piece. I am sure it is going to be another 'Merry Widow.' "

"You can't tell from a first night audience," said Mr. Pilkington sombrely, giving out a piece of theatrical wisdom he had picked up at rehearsals.

"Oh, but you can. It's so easy to distinguish polite applause from the real thing. No doubt many of the people down here have friends in the company or other reasons for seeming to enjoy the play, but look how the circle and the gallery were enjoying it! You can't tell me that that was not genuine. They love it. How hard," she proceeded commiseratingly, "you must have worked, poor boy, during the tour on the road to improve the piece so much! I never liked to say so before but even you must agree with me now that that original version of yours, which was done down at Newport, was the most terrible non-sense! And how hard the company must have worked too! Otie," cried Mrs. Peagrim, aglow with the magic of a brilliant idea, "I will tell you what you must really do. You must give a supper and dance to the whole company on the stage to-morrow night after the performance."

"What!" cried Otis Pilkington, startled out of his lethargy by this appalling suggestion. Was he, the man who, after planking down thirty-two thousand eight hundred and fifty-nine dollars, sixty-eight cents for "props" and "frames" and "rehl," had sold out for a paltry ten thousand, to be still further victimized?

"They do deserve it, don't they, after working so hard?"

"It's impossible," said Otis Pilkington vehemently. "Out of the question."

"But, Otie, darling, I was talking to Mr. Mason when he came down to Newport to see the piece last summer, and he told me that the management nearly always gives a supper to the company, especially if they have had a lot of extra rehearsing to do."

"Well, let Goble give them a supper if he wants to."

"But you know that Mr. Goble, though he had his name on the programme as the manager, has really nothing to do with it. You own the piece, don't you?"

For a moment Mr. Pilkington felt an impulse to reveal all, but refrained. He knew his Aunt Olive too well. If she found out that he had parted at a heavy loss with this valuable property, her whole attitude towards him would change—or, rather it would revert to her normal attitude, which was not unlike that of a severe nurse to a weak-minded child. Even in his agony there had been a certain faint consolation, due to the entirely unwonted note of respect in the voice with which she had addressed him since the fall of the curtain. He shrank from forfeiting this respect, unentitled though he was to it.

"Yes," he said in his precise voice. "That, of course, is so."

"Well, then!" said Mrs. Peagrim.

"But it seems so unnecessary! And think what it would cost."

This was a false step. Some of the reverence left Mrs. Peagrim's voice, and she spoke a little coldly. A gay and gallant spender herself, she had often had occasion to rebuke a tendency to over-parsimony in her nephew.

"We must not be mean, Otie!" she said.

Mr. Pilkington keenly resented her choice of pronouns. "We" indeed! Who was going to foot the bill? Both of them, hand in hand, or he alone, the chump, the boob, the easy mark who got this sort of thing wished on him!

"I don't think it would be possible to get the stage for a supper-party," he pleaded, shifting his ground. "Goble wouldn't give it to us."

"As if Mr. Goble would refuse you anything after you have written a wonderful success for this theatre! And isn't he getting his share of the profits? Directly after the performance you must go round and ask him. Of course he will be delighted to give you the stage. I will be hostess," said Mrs. Peagrim radiantly. "And now, let me see, whom shall we invite?"

Mr. Pilkington stared gloomily at the floor, too bowed down by his weight of cares to resent the "we," which had plainly come to stay. He was trying to estimate the size of the gash which this preposterous entertainment would cleave in the Pilkington bank-roll. He doubted if it was possible to go through with it under five hundred dollars; and, if, as seemed only too probable, Mrs. Peagrim took the matter in hand and gave herself her head, it might get into four figures.

"Major Selby, of course," said Mrs. Peagrim musingly, with a cooing note in her voice. Long since had that polished man of affairs made a deep impression upon her. "Of course Major Selby, for one. And Mr. Rooke. Then there are one or two of my friends who would be hurt if they were left out. How about Mr. Mason? Isn't he a friend of yours?"

Mr. Pilkington snorted. He had endured much and was prepared to endure more, but he drew the line at squandering his money on the man who had sneaked up behind his brain-child with a hatchet and chopped its precious person into little bits.

"He is *not* a friend of mine," he said stiffly, "and I do not wish him to be invited!"

Having attained her main objective, Mrs. Peagrim was prepared to yield minor points.

"Very well, if you do not like him," she said. "But I thought he was quite an intimate of yours. It was you who asked me to invite him to Newport last summer."

"Much," said Mr. Pilkington coldly, "has happened since last summer."

"Oh, very well," said Mrs. Peagrim again. "Then we will not

include Mr. Mason. Now, directly the curtain has fallen, Otie dear, pop right round and find Mr. Goble and tell him what you want."

II

It is not only twin-souls in this world who yearn to meet each other. Between Otis Pilkington and Mr. Goble there was little in common, yet, at the moment when Otis set out to find Mr. Goble, the thing which Mr. Goble desired most in the world was an interview with Otis. Since the end of the first act, the manager had been in a state of mental upheaval. Reverting to the gold-mine simile again, Mr. Goble was in the position of a man who has had a chance of purchasing such a mine and now, learning too late of the discovery of the reef, is feeling the truth of the poet's dictum that "of all sad words of tongue or pen, the saddest are these: 'It might have been.' " The electric success of "The Rose of America" had stunned Mr. Goble; and realizing, as he did, that he might have bought Otis Pilkington's share dirt cheap at almost any point of the preliminary tour, he was having a bad half hour with himself. The only ray in the darkness which brooded on his indomitable soul was the thought that it might still be possible, by getting hold of Mr. Pilkington before the notices appeared, and shaking his head sadly and talking about the misleading hopes which young authors so often draw from an enthusiastic first-night reception and impressing upon him that first-night receptions do not deceive your expert who has been fifteen years in the show-business and mentioning gloomily that he had heard a coupla the critics roastin' the show to beat the band . . . by doing all these things, it might still be possible to depress Mr. Pilkington's young enthusiasm and induce him to sell his share at a sacrifice price to a great-hearted friend who didn't think the thing would run a week but was willing to buy as a sporting speculation, because he thought Mr. Pilkington a good kid, and after all these shows that flop in New York sometimes have a chance on the road.

Such were the meditations of Mr. Goble, and, on the final fall of the curtain, amid unrestrained enthusiasm on the part of the audience, he had dispatched messengers in all directions with instructions to find Mr. Pilkington and conduct him to the presence. Meanwhile, he waited impatiently on the empty stage.

The sudden advent of Wally Mason, who appeared at this

moment, upset Mr. Goble terribly. Wally was a factor in the situation which he had not considered. An infernal, tactless fellow, always trying to make mischief and upset honest merchants, Wally, if present at the interview with Otis Pilkington, would probably try to act in restraint of trade and would blurt out some untimely truth about the prospects of the piece. Not for the first time, Mr. Goble wished Wally a sudden stroke of apoplexy.

"Went well, eh?" said Wally amiably. He did not like Mr. Goble, but on the first night of a successful piece personal antipathies may be sunk. Such was his effervescent good humour at the moment that he was prepared to treat Mr. Goble as a man and a brother.

"H'm!" replied Mr. Goble doubtfully, paving the way.

"What are you h'ming about?" demanded Wally, astonished. "The thing's a riot."

"You never know," responded Mr. Goble in the minor key.

"Well!" Wally stared. "I don't know what more you want. The audience sat up on its hind legs and squealed, didn't they?"

"I've an idea," said Mr. Goble, raising his voice as the long form of Mr. Pilkington crossed the stage towards them, "that the critics will roast it. If you ask *me*," he went on loudly, "it's just the sort of show the critics will pan the life out of. I've been fifteen years in the . . ."

"Critics!" cried Wally. "Well, I've just been talking to Alexander of the *Times*, and he said it was the best musical piece he had ever seen and that all the other men he had talked to thought the same."

Mr. Goble turned a distorted face to Mr. Pilkington. He wished that Wally would go. But Wally, he reflected, bitterly, was one of those men who never go. He faced Mr. Pilkington and did the best he could.

"Of course it's got a *chance*," he said gloomily. "Any show has got a *chance*! But I don't know . . . I don't know . . ."

Mr. Pilkington was not interested in the future prospects of "The Rose of America." He had a favour to ask, and he wanted to ask it, have it refused if possible, and get away. It occurred to him that, by substituting for the asking of a favour a peremptory demand, he might save himself a thousand dollars.

"I want the stage after the performance to-morrow night, for a supper to the company," he said brusquely.

He was shocked to find Mr. Goble immediately complaisant.

"Why, sure," said Mr. Goble readily. "Go as far as you like!"
He took Mr. Pilkington by the elbow and drew him up-stage,
lowering his voice to a confidential undertone. "And now, listen,"
he said, "I've something I want to talk to you about. Between
you and I and the lamp-post, I don't think this show will last a
month in New York. It don't add up right! There's something
all wrong about it."

Mr. Pilkington assented with an emphasis which amazed
the manager. "I quite agree with you! If you had kept it the
way it was originally . . ."

"Too late for that!" sighed Mr. Goble, realizing that his
star was in the ascendant. He had forgotten for the moment
that Mr. Pilkington was an author. "We must make the best of
a bad job! Now, you're a good kid and I wouldn't like you to go
around town saying that I had let you in. It isn't business,
maybe, but, just because I don't want you to have any kick
coming, I'm ready to buy your share of the thing and call it a
deal. After all, it may get money on the road. It ain't likely, but
there's a chance, and I'm willing to take it. Well, listen. I'm
probably robbing myself, but I'll give you fifteen thousand if
you want to sell."

A hated voice spoke at his elbow.

"I'll make you a better offer than that," said Wally. "Give
me your share of the show for three dollars in cash and I'll
throw in a pair of sock-suspenders and an Ingersoll. Is it a go?"

Mr. Goble regarded him balefully.

"Who told you to butt in?" he enquired sourly.

"Conscience!" replied Wally. "Old Henry W. Conscience!
I refuse to stand by and see the slaughter of the innocents.
Why don't you wait till he's dead before you skin him!" He
turned to Mr. Pilkington. "Don't you be a fool!" he said
earnestly. "Can't you see the thing is the biggest hit in years?
Do you think Jesse James here would be offering you a cent
for your share if he didn't know there was a fortune in it? Do
you imagine . . . ?"

"It is immaterial to me," interrupted Otis Pilkington loftily,
"what Mr. Goble offers. I have already sold my interest!"

"What!" cried Mr. Goble.

"When?" cried Wally.

"I sold it half-way through the road-tour, "said Mr. Pilkington,
"to a lawyer, acting on behalf of a client whose name I did not learn."

In the silence which followed this revelation, another voice spoke.

"I should like to speak to you for a moment, Mr. Goble, if I may," It was Jill, who had joined the group unperceived.

Mr. Goble glowered at Jill, who met his gaze composedly.

"I'm busy!" snapped Mr. Goble. "See me to-morrow!"

"I would prefer to see you know."

"You would prefer!" Mr. Goble waved his hands despairingly, as if calling on heaven to witness the persecution of a good man.

Jill exhibited a piece of paper stamped with the letter-heading of the management.

"It's about this," she said. "I found it in the box as I was going out."

"What's that?"

"It seems to be a fortnight's notice."

"And that," said Mr. Goble," is what it *is* !"

Wally uttered an exclamation.

"Do you mean to say . . . ?"

"Yes, I do!" said the manager, turning on him. He felt that he had out-manœuvred Wally. "I agreed to let her open in New York, and she's done it, hasn't she ? Now she can get out. I don't want her. I wouldn't have her if you paid me. She's a nuisance in the company, always making trouble, and she can go."

"But I would prefer not to go," said Jill

"You would prefer!" The phrase infuriated Mr. Goble. "And what has what you would prefer got to do with it ?"

"Well, you see," said Jill, "I forgot to tell you before, but I own the piece!"

III

Mr. Goble's jaw fell. He had been waving his hands in another spacious gesture, and he remained frozen with outstretched arms, like a semaphore. This evening had been a series of shocks for him, but this was the worst shock of all.

"You—what!" he stammered.

"I own the piece," repeated Jill. "Surely that gives me authority to say what I want done and what I don't want done."

There was a silence, Mr. Goble, who was having difficulty with his vocal chords, swallowed once or twice. Wally and Mr. Pilkington stared dumbly. At the back of the stage, a belated scene-shifter, homeward bound, was whistling as much as he could remember of the refrain of a popular song.

"What do you mean you own the piece?" Mr. Goble at length gurgled.

"I bought it."

"You bought it?"

"I bought Mr. Pilkington's share through a lawyer for ten thousand dollars."

"Ten thousand dollars! Where did you get ten thousand dollars?" Light broke upon Mr. Goble. The thing became clear to him. "Damn it!" he cried. "I might have known you had some man behind you! You'd never have been so darned fresh if you hadn't had some John in the background, paying the bills! Well, of all the . . ."

He broke off abruptly, not because he had said all that he wished to say, for he had only touched the fringe of his subject, but because at this point Wally's elbow smote him in the parts about the third button of his waistcoat and jarred all the breath out of him.

"Be quiet!" said Wally dangerously. He turned to Jill "Jill, you don't mind telling me how you got ten thousand dollars, do you?"

"Of course not, Wally. Uncle Chris sent it to me. Do you remember giving me a letter from him at Rochester? The cheque was in that."

Wally stared.

"Your uncle! But he hasn't any money!"

"He must have made it somehow."

"But he couldn't! How could he?"

Otis Pilkington suddenly gave tongue. He broke in on them with a loud noise that was half a snort and half a yell. Stunned by the information that it was Jill who had bought his share in the piece, Mr. Pilkington's mind had recovered slowly and then had begun to work with a quite unusual rapidity. During the preceding conversation he had been doing some tense thinking, and now he saw all.

"It's a swindle! It's a deliberate swindle!" shrilled Mr. Pilkington. The tortoise-shell-rimmed spectacles flashed sparks. "I've been made a fool of! I've been swindled! I've been robbed!"

Jill regarded him with wide eyes.

"What do you mean?"

"You know what I mean!"

"I certainly do not! You were perfectly willing to sell the piece."

"I'm not talking about that! You know what I mean! I've been robbed!"

Wally snatched at his arm as it gyrated past him in a gesture of anguish which rivalled the late efforts in that direction of Mr. Goble, who was now leaning against the safety-curtain trying to get his breath back.

"Don't be a fool," said Wally curtly. "Talk sense! You know perfectly well that Miss Mariner wouldn't swindle you."

"She may not have been in it," conceded Mr. Pilkington. "I don't know whether she was or not. But that uncle of hers swindled me out of ten thousand dollars! The smooth old crook!"

"Don't talk like that about Uncle Chris!" said Jill, her eyes flashing. "Tell me what you mean."

"Yes, come on, Pilkington," said Wally grimly. "You've been scattering some pretty serious charges about. Let's hear what you base them on. Be coherent for a couple of seconds."

Mr. Goble filled his depleted lungs.

"If you ask me . . ." he began.

"We don't, said Wally curtly. "This has nothing to do with you. Well," he went on, "we're waiting to hear what this is all about."

Mr. Pilkington gulped. Like most men of weak intellect who are preyed on by the wolves of the world, he had ever a strong distaste for admitting that he had been deceived. He liked to regard himself as a shrewd young man who knew his way about and could take care of himself.

"Major Selby," he said, adjusting his spectacles, which emotion had caused to slip down his nose, "came to me a few weeks ago with a proposition. He suggested the formation of a company to start Miss Mariner in the motion-pictures."

"What!" cried Jill.

"In the motion-pictures," repeated Mr. Pilkington. "He wished to know if I cared to advance any capital towards the venture. I thought it over carefully and decided that I was favourably disposed towards the scheme. I . . ." Mr. Pilkington gulped again. "I gave him a cheque for ten thousand dollars!"

"Of all the fools!" said Mr. Goble with a sharp laugh. He caught Wally's eye and subsided once more.

Mr. Pilkington's fingers strayed agitatedly to his spectacles.

"I may have been a fool," he cried shrilly, "though I was perfectly willing to risk the money had it been applied to the object for which I gave it. But when it comes to giving ten thousand dollars just to have it paid back to me in exchange for a very valuable piece of theatrical property . . . my own money . . . handed back to me . . .!"

Words failed Mr. Pilkington.

"I've been deliberately swindled!" he added, after a moment, harking back to the main motive.

Jill's heart was like lead. She could not doubt for an instant the truth of what the victim had said. Woven into every inch of the fabric, plainly hall-marked on its surface, she could perceive the signature of Uncle Chris. If he had come and confessed to her himself, she could not have been more certain that he had acted precisely as Mr. Pilkington had charged. There was that same impishness, that same bland unscrupulousness, that same pathetic desire to do her a good turn however it might affect anybody else which, if she might compare the two things, had caused him to pass her off on unfortunate Mr. Mariner of Brookport as a girl of wealth with tastes in the direction of real estate.

Wally was not so easily satisfied.

"You've no proof whatever . . ."

Jill shook her head.

"It's true, Wally. I know Uncle Chris. It must be true."

"But Jill . . .!"

"It must be. How else could Uncle Chris have got the money ?"

Mr. Pilkington, much encouraged by this ready acquiescence in his theories, got under way once more.

"The man's a swindler! A swindler! He's robbed me! I have been robbed! He never had any intention of starting a motion-picture company. He planned it all out . . .!"

Jill cut into the babble of his denunciations. She was sick at heart, and she spoke almost listlessly.

"Mr. Pilkington!" The victim stopped. "Mr. Pilkington, if what you say is true, and I'm afraid there is no doubt that it is, the only thing I can do is to give you back your property. So will you please try to understand that everything is just as it was before you gave my uncle the money. You've got back your ten thousand dollars and you've got back your piece, so there's nothing more to talk about."

Mr. Pilkington, dimly realizing that the financial aspect of the affair had been more or less satisfactorily adjusted, was nevertheless conscious of a feeling that he was being thwarted. He had much more to say about Uncle Chris and his methods of doing business, and it irked him to be cut short like this.

"Yes, but I do not think. . . . That's all very well, but I have by no means finished . . ."

"Yes, you have," said Wally.

"There's nothing more to talk about," repeated Jill. "I'm sorry this should have happened, but you've nothing to complain about now, have you? Good night."

And she turned quickly away, and walked towards the door.

"But I hadn't *finished!*" wailed Mr. Pilkington, clutching at Wally. He was feeling profoundly aggrieved. If it is bad to be all dressed up and no place to go, it is almost worse to be full of talk and to have no one to talk it to. Otis Pilkington had at least another twenty minutes of speech inside him on the topic of Uncle Chris, and Wally was the nearest human being with a pair of ears.

Wally was in no mood to play the part of confidant. He pushed Mr. Pilkington earnestly in the chest and raced after Jill. Mr. Pilkington, with the feeling that the world was against him, tottered back into the arms of Mr. Goble, who had now recovered his breath and was ready to talk business.

"Have a good cigar," said Mr. Goble, producing one. "Now, see here, let's get right down to it. If you'd care to sell out for twenty thousand . . ."

"I would *not* care to sell out for twenty thousand!" yelled the overwrought Mr. Pilkington. "I wouldn't sell out for a million! You're a swindler! You want to rob me! You're a crook!"

"Yes, yes," assented Mr. Goble gently. "But, all joking aside, suppose I was to go up to twenty-five thousand . . .?" He twined his fingers lovingly in the slack of Mr. Pilkington's coat. "Come now! You're a good kid! Shall we say twenty-five thousand?"

"We will *not* say twenty-five thousand! Let me go!"

"Now, now, *now!*" pleaded Mr. Goble. "Be sensible! Don't get all worked up! Say, *do* have a good cigar!"

"I *won't* have a good cigar!" shouted Mr. Pilkington.

He detached himself with a jerk, and stalked with long strides up the stage. Mr. Goble watched him go with a lowering gaze. A heavy sense of the unkindness of fate was oppressing Mr. Goble. If you couldn't gyp a bone-headed amateur out of a piece of property, whom could you gyp? Mr. Goble sighed. It hardly seemed to him worth while going on.

IV

Out in the street Wally had overtaken Jill, and they faced one another in the light of a street lamp. Forty-first Street at midnight is a quiet oasis. They had it to themselves.

Jill was pale, and she was breathing quickly, but she forced a smile.

"Well, Wally," she said. "My career as a manager didn't last long, did it?"

"What are you going to do?"

Jill looked down the street.

"I don't know," she said. "I suppose I shall have to start trying to find something."

"But . . ."

Jill drew him suddenly into the dark alley-way leading to the stage-door of the Gotham Theatre's nearest neighbour, and, as she did so, a long, thin form, swathed in an overcoat and surmounted by an opera-hat, flashed past.

"I don't think I could have gone through another meeting with Mr. Pilkington," said Jill. "It wasn't his fault, and he was quite justified, but what he said about Uncle Chris rather hurt."

Wally, who had ideas of his own similar to those of Mr. Pilkington on the subject of Uncle Chris and had intended to express them, prudently kept them unspoken.

"I suppose," he said, "there is no doubt . . .?"

"There can't be. Poor Uncle Chris! He is like Freddie. He means well!"

There was a pause. They left the alley and walked down the street.

"Where are you going now?" asked Wally.

"I'm going home."

"Where's home?"

"Forty-ninth Street. I live in a boarding-house there."

A sudden recollection of the boarding-house at which she had lived in Atlantic City smote Wally, and it turned the scale. He had not intended to speak, but he could not help himself.

"Jill!" he cried. "It's no good. I *must* say it! I want to get you out of all this. I want to take care of you. Why should you go on living this sort of life, when . . . Why won't you let me . . .?"

He stopped. Even as he spoke, he realized the futility of what he was saying. Jill was not a girl to be won with words.

They walked on in silence for a moment. They crossed Broadway, noisy with night traffic, and passed into the stillness on the other side.

"Wally," said Jill at last.

She was looking straight in front of her. Her voice was troubled.

"Yes?"

Jill hesitated.

"Wally, you wouldn't want me to marry you if you knew you weren't the only man in the world that mattered to me, would you?"

They had reached Sixth Avenue before Wally replied.

"No!" he said.

For an instant, Jill could not have said whether the feeling that shot through her like the abrupt touching of a nerve was relief or disappointment. Then suddenly she realized that it was disappointment. It was absurd to her to feel disappointed, but at that moment she would have welcomed a different attitude in him. If only this problem of hers could be taken forcefully out of her hands, what a relief it would be. If only Wally, masterfully insistent, would batter down her hesitations and *grab* her, knock her on the head and carry her off like a caveman, care less about her happiness and concentrate on his own, what a solution it would be. . . . But then he wouldn't be Wally. . . . Nevertheless, Jill gave a little sigh. Her new life had changed her already. It had blunted the sharp edge of her independence. To-night she was feeling the need of some one to lean on—some one strong and cosy and sympathetic who would treat her like a little girl and shield her from all the roughness of life. The fighting spirit had gone out of her, and she was no longer the little warrior facing the world with a brave eye and a tilted chin. She wanted to cry and be petted.

"No!" said Wally again. There had been the faintest suggestion of a doubt when he had spoken the word before, but now it shot out like a bullet. "And I'll tell you why. I want *you*—and, if you married me feeling like that, it wouldn't be you. I want Jill, the whole Jill, and nothing but Jill, and, if I can't have that, I'd rather not have anything. Marriage isn't a motion-picture close-up with slow fade-out on the embrace. It's a partnership, and what's the good of a partnership if your heart's not in it? It's like collaborating with a man you dislike. . . . I believe you wish sometimes—not often, perhaps, but when you're feeling lonely and miserable—that I would pester and bludgeon you into marrying me. . . . What's the matter?"

Jill had started. It was disquieting to have her thoughts read with such accuracy.

"Nothing," she said.

"It wouldn't be any good," Wally went on, "because it wouldn't be *me*. I couldn't keep that attitude up, and I know I should hate myself for ever having tried it. There's nothing in the world I wouldn't do to help you, though I know it's no use offering to do anything. You're a fighter, and you mean to fight your own battle. It might happen that, if I kept after you and badgered you and nagged you, one of these days, when you were feeling particularly all alone in the world and tired of fighting for yourself, you might consent to marry me. But it wouldn't do. Even if you reconciled yourself to it, it wouldn't do. I suppose the cave-woman sometimes felt rather relieved when everything was settled for her with a club, but I'm sure the caveman must have had a hard time ridding himself of the thought that he had behaved like a cad and taken a mean advantage. I don't want to feel like that. I couldn't make you happy if I felt like that. Much better to have you go on regarding me as a friend . . . knowing that, if ever your feelings do change, that I am right there, waiting. . . ."

"But by that time *your* feelings will have changed!"

Wally laughed.

"Never!"

"You'll meet some other girl . . ."

"I've met every girl in the world! None of them will do!" The lightness came back into Wally's voice. "I'm sorry for the poor things, but they won't do! Take 'em away! There's only one girl in the world for me—oh, confound it! why is it that one always thinks in song-titles! Well, there it is. I'm not going to bother you. We're pals. And, as a pal, may I offer you my bank-roll?"

"No!" said Jill. She smiled up at him. "I believe you would give me your coat if I asked you for it!"

Wally stopped.

"Do you want it? Here you are!"

"Wally, behave! There's a policeman looking at you!"

"Oh, well, if you won't! It's a good coat, all the same."

They turned the corner and stopped before a brown-stone

house, with a long ladder of untidy steps running up to the front door.

"Is this where you live?" Wally asked. He looked at the gloomy place disapprovingly. "You do choose the most awful places!"

"I don't choose them. They're thrust on me. Yes, this is where I live. If you want to know the exact room, it's the third window up there over the front door. Well, good night."

"Good night," said Wally. He paused. "Jill."

"Yes?"

"I know it's not worth mentioning, and it's breaking our agreement to mention it, but you *do* understand, don't you?"

"Yes, Wally dear, I understand."

"I'm round the corner, you know, waiting! And if you ever *do* change, all you've got to do is just to come to me and say 'It's all right!' . . ."

Jill laughed a little shakily.

"That doesn't sound very romantic!"

"Not sound romantic? If you can think of any three words in the language that sound more romantic, let me have them! Well, never mind how they sound, just say them, and watch the result! But you must get to bed. Good night."

"Good night, Wally."

She passed in through the dingy door. It closed behind her, and Wally stood for some moments staring at it with a gloomy repulsion. He thought he had never seen a dingier door.

Then he started to walk back to his apartment. He walked very quickly, with clenched hands. He was wondering if after all there was not something to be said for the methods of the caveman when he went a-wooing. Twinges of conscience the caveman may have had when all was over, but at least he had established his right to look after the woman he loved.

★ 19 ★

Mrs. Peagrim Burns Incense

I

"THEY tell me . . . I am told . . . I am informed . . . No, one moment, Miss Frisby."

Mrs. Peagrim wrinkled her fair forehead. It has been truly

said that there is no agony like the agony of literary composition, and Mrs. Peagrim was having rather a bad time getting the requisite snap and ginger into her latest communication to the Press. She bit her lip, and would have passed her twitching fingers restlessly through her hair but for the thought of the damage which such an action must do to her coiffure. Miss Frisby, her secretary, an anæmic and negative young woman, waited patiently, pad on knee, and tapped her teeth with her pencil.

"Please do not make that tapping noise, Miss Frisby," said the sufferer querulously. "I cannot think. Otie, dear, can't you suggest a good phrase ? You ought to be able to, being an author."

Mr. Pilkington, who was strewn over an arm-chair by the window, awoke from his meditations, which, to judge from the furrow just above the bridge of his tortoise-shell spectacles and the droop of his weak chin, were not pleasant. It was the morning after the production of "The Rose of America," and he had passed a sleepless night, thinking of the harsh words he had said to Jill. Could she ever forgive him ? Would she have the generosity to realize that a man ought not to be held accountable for what he says in the moment when he discovers that he has been cheated, deceived, robbed—in a word, hornswoggled ? He had been brooding on this all night, and he wanted to go on brooding now. His aunt's question interrupted his train of thought.

"Eh ?" he said vaguely, gaping.

"Oh, don't be so absent-minded!" snapped Mrs. Peagrim, not unjustifiably annoyed. "I am trying to compose a paragraph for the papers about our party to-night, and I can't get the right phrase . . . Read what you've written, Miss Frisby."

Miss Frisby, having turned a pale eye on the pothooks and twiddleys in her note-book, translated them in a pale voice.

" 'Surely of all the leading hostesses in New York Society there can be few more versatile than Mrs. Waddesleigh Peagrim. I am amazed every time I go to her delightful home on West End Avenue to see the scope and variety of her circle of intimates. Here you will see an ambassador with a fever . . .' "

"With a *what ?*" demanded Mrs. Peagrim sharply.

" 'Fever,' I thought you said," replied Miss Frisby stolidly. "I wrote 'fever.' "

" 'Diva.' Do use your intelligence, my good girl. Go on."

"Here you will see an ambassador with a diva from the opera, exchanging the latest gossip from the chancelleries for intimate news of the world behind the scenes. There, the author of the latest novel talking literature to the newest débutante. Truly one may say that Mrs. Peagrim has revived the saloon.' "

Mrs. Peagrim bit her lip.

" 'Salon.' "

" 'Salon,' " said Miss Frisby unemotionally. " They tell me, I am told, I am informed . . . ' " She paused. " That's all I have."

" Scratch out those last words," said Mrs. Peagrim irritably. " You really are hopeless, Miss Frisby! Couldn't you see that I had stopped dictating and was searching for a phrase ? Otie, what is a good phrase for ' I am told ' ? "

Mr. Pilkington forced his wandering attention to grapple with the problem.

" ' I hear,' " he suggested at length.

"Tchah!" ejaculated his aunt. Then her face brightened. "I have it. Take dictation, please, Miss Frisby. 'A little bird whispers to me that there were great doings last night on the stage of the Gotham Theatre after the curtain had fallen on "The Rose of America," which, as everybody knows, is the work of Mrs. Peagrim's clever young nephew, Otis Pilkington.' " Mrs. Peagrim shot a glance at her clever young nephew, to see how he appreciated the boost, but Otis' thoughts were far away once more. He was lying on his spine, brooding, brooding. Mrs. Peagrim resumed her dictation. " 'In honour of the extraordinary success of the piece, Mrs. Peagrim, who certainly does nothing by halves, entertained the entire company to a supper-dance after the performance. A number of prominent people were among the guests, and Mrs. Peagrim was a radiant and vivacious hostess. She has never looked more charming. The high jinks were kept up to an advanced hour, and every one agreed that they had never spent a more delightful evening.' There! Type as many copies as are necessary, Miss Frisby, and send them out this afternoon with photographs."

Miss Frisby having vanished in her pallid way, the radiant and vivacious hostess turned on her nephew again.

"I must say, Otie," she began complainingly, "that, for a man who has had a success like yours, you are not very cheerful. I should have thought the notices of the piece would have made you the happiest man in New York."

There was once a melodrama where the child of the persecuted heroine used to dissolve the gallery in tears by saying "Happiness? What *is* happiness, moth-aw?" Mr. Pilkington did not use these actual words, but he reproduced the stricken infant's tone with great fidelity.

"Notices! What are notices to me?"

"Oh, don't be so affected!" cried Mrs. Peagrim. "Don't pretend that you don't know every word of them by heart!"

"I have not seen the notices, Aunt Olive," said Mr. Pilkington dully.

Mrs. Peagrim looked at him with positive alarm. She had never been overwhelmingly attached to her long nephew, but since his rise to fame something resembling affection had sprung up in her, and his attitude now disturbed her.

"You can't be well, Otie!" she said solicitously. "Are you ill?"

"I have a severe headache," replied the martyr. "I passed a wakeful night."

"Let me go and mix you a dose of the most wonderful mixture," said Mrs. Peagrim maternally. "Poor boy! I don't wonder, after all the nervousness and excitement . . . You sit quite still and rest. I will be back in a moment."

She bustled out of the room, and Mr. Pilkington sagged back into his chair. He had hardly got his meditations going once more, when the door opened and the maid announced "Major Selby."

"Good morning," said Uncle Chris breezily, sailing down the fairway with outstretched hand. "How are—oh!"

He stopped abruptly, perceiving that Mrs. Peagrim was not present and—a more disturbing discovery—that Otis Pilkington was. It would be exaggeration to say that Uncle Chris was embarrassed. That master-mind was never actually embarrassed. But his jauntiness certainly ebbed a little, and he had to pull his moustache twice before he could face the situation with his customary *aplomb*. He had not expected to find Otis Pilkington here, and Otis was the last man he wished to meet. He had just parted from Jill, who had been rather plain-spoken with regard to the recent financial operations; and, though possessed only of a rudimentary conscience, Uncle Chris was aware that his next interview with young Mr. Pilkington might have certain aspects bordering on awkwardness and he would have liked time to prepare a statement for the defence. However, here the man was, and the situation must be faced.

"Pilkington!" he cried. "My dear fellow! Just the man I wanted to see! I'm afraid there has been a little misunderstanding. Of course, it has all been cleared up now, but still I must insist on making a personal explanation, really I must insist. The whole matter was a most absurd misunderstanding. It was like this . . ."

Here Uncle Chris paused in order to devote a couple of seconds to thought. He had said it was "like this," and he gave his moustache another pull as though he were trying to drag inspiration out of it. His blue eyes were as frank and honest as ever, and showed no trace of the perplexity in his mind, but he had to admit to himself that, if he managed to satisfy his hearer that all was for the best and that he had acted uprightly and without blame, he would be doing well.

Fortunately, the commercial side of Mr. Pilkington was entirely dormant this morning. The matter of the ten thousand dollars seemed trivial to him in comparison with the weightier problems which occupied his mind.

"Have you seen Miss Mariner?" he asked eagerly.

"Yes. I have just parted from her. She was upset, poor girl, of course, exceedingly upset."

Mr. Pilkington moaned hollowly.

"Is she very angry with me?"

For a moment the utter inexplicability of the remark silenced Uncle Chris. Why Jill should be angry with Mr. Pilkington for being robbed of ten thousand dollars he could not understand, for Jill had told him nothing of the scene that had taken place on the previous night. But evidently this point was to Mr. Pilkington the nub of the matter, and Uncle Chris, like the strategist he was, rearranged his forces to meet the new development.

"Angry?" he said slowly. "Well, of course . . ."

He did not know what it was all about, but no doubt if he confined himself to broken sentences which meant nothing light would shortly be vouchsafed to him.

"In the heat of the moment," confessed Mr. Pilkington, "I'm afraid I said things to Miss Mariner which I now regret."

Uncle Chris began to feel on solid ground again.

"Dear, dear!" he murmured regretfully.

"I spoke hastily."

"Always think before you speak, my boy."

"I considered that I had been cheated . . ."

"My dear boy!" Uncle Chris' blue eyes opened wide. "Please! Haven't I said that I could explain all that? It was a pure misunderstanding . . ."

"Oh, I don't care about that part of it . . ."

"Quite right," said Uncle Chris cordially. "Let bygones be bygones. Start with a clean slate. You have your money back, and there's no need to say another word about it. Let us forget it," he concluded generously. "And, if I have any influence with Jill, you may count on me to use it to dissipate any little unfortunate rift which may have occurred between you."

"You think there's a chance that she might overlook what I said?"

"As I say, I will use any influence I may possess to heal the breach. I like you, my boy. And I am sure that Jill likes you. She will make allowances for any ill-judged remarks you may have uttered in a moment of heat."

Mr. Pilkington brightened, and Mrs. Peagrim, returning with a medicine-glass, was pleased to see him looking so much better.

"You are a positive wizard, Major Selby," she said archly. "What have you been saying to the poor boy to cheer him up so? He has a bad headache this morning."

"Headache?" said Uncle Chris, starting like a war-horse that had heard the bugle. "I don't know if I have ever mentioned it, but *I* used to suffer from headaches at one time. Extraordinarily severe headaches. I tried everything, until one day a man I knew recommended a thing called—don't know if you have ever heard of it . . ."

Mrs. Peagrim, in her role of ministering angel, was engrossed with her errand of mercy. She was holding the medicine-glass to Mr. Pilkington's lips, and the seed fell on stony ground.

"Drink this, dear," urged Mrs. Peagrim.

"Nervino," said Uncle Chris.

"There!" said Mrs. Peagrim. "That will make you feel much better. How well *you* always look, Major Selby!"

"And yet at one time," said Uncle Chris perseveringly, "I was a martyr . . ."

"I can't remember if I told you last night about the party. We are giving a little supper-dance to the company of Otie's play after the performance this evening. Of course you will come?"

Uncle Chris philosophically accepted his failure to secure the ear of his audience. Other opportunities would occur.

"Delighted," he said. "Delighted."

"Quite a simple, Bohemian little affair," proceeded Mrs. Peagrim. "I thought it was only right to give the poor things a little treat after they have all worked so hard."

"Certainly, certainly. A capital idea."

"We shall be quite a small party. If I once started asking anybody outside our *real* friends, I should have to ask everybody."

The door opened.

"Mr. Rooke," announced the maid.

Freddie, like Mr. Pilkington, was a prey to gloom this morning. He had read one or two of the papers, and they had been disgustingly lavish in their praise of The McWhustle of McWhustle. It made Freddie despair of the New York Press. In addition to this, he had been woken up at seven o'clock, after going to sleep at three, by the ringing of the telephone and the announcement that a gentleman wished to see him: and he was weighed down with that heavy-eyed languor which comes to those whose night's rest is broken.

"Why, how do you do, Mr. Rooke!" said Mrs. Peagrim.

"How-de-do," replied Freddie, blinking in the strong light from the window. "Hope I'm not barging in and all that sort of thing? I came round about this party to-night, you know."

"Oh, yes?"

"Was wondering," said Freddie, "if you would mind if I brought a friend of mine along? Popped in on me from England this morning. At seven o'clock," said Freddie plaintively. "Ghastly hour, what? Didn't do a thing to the good old beauty sleep! Well, what I mean to say is, I'd be awfully obliged if you'd let me bring him along."

"Why, of course," said Mrs. Peagrim. "Any friend of yours, Mr. Rooke . . ."

"Thanks awfully. Special reason why I'd like him to come, and all that. He's a fellow named Underhill. Sir Derek Underhill. Been a pal of mine for years and years."

Uncle Chris started.

"Underhill! Is Derek Underhill in America?"

"Landed this morning. Routed me out of bed at seven o'clock."

"Oh, do you know him, too, Major Selby?"said Mrs. Peagrim. "Then I'm sure he must be charming!"

"Charming," began Uncle Chris in measured tones, "is an adjective which I cannot . . ."

"Well, thanks most awfully," interrupted Freddie. "It's fearfully good of you to let me bring him along. I must be staggering off now. Lot of things to do."

"Oh, must you go already?"

"Absolutely must. Lots of things to do."

Uncle Chris extended a hand to his hostess.

"I think I will be going along, too, Mrs. Peagrim. I'll walk a few yards with you, Freddie, my boy. There are one or two things I would like to talk over. Till to-night, Mrs. Peagrim."

"Till to-night, Major Selby." She turned to Mr. Pilkington as the door closed. "What charming manners Major Selby has. So polished. A sort of old-world courtesy. So smooth!"

"Smooth," said Mr. Pilkington dourly, "is right!"

II

Uncle Chris confronted Freddie sternly outside the front door.

"What does this mean? Good God, Freddie, have you no delicacy?"

"Eh?" said Freddie blankly.

"Why are you bringing Underhill to this party? Don't you realize that poor Jill will be there? How do you suppose she will feel when she sees that blackguard again? The cad who threw her over and nearly broke her heart!"

Freddie's jaw fell. He groped for his fallen eyeglass.

"Oh, my aunt! Do you think she will be pipped?"

"A sensitive girl like Jill?"

"But, listen. Derek wants to marry her."

"What?"

"Oh, absolutely. That's why he's come over."

Uncle Chris shook his head.

"I don't understand this. I saw the letter myself which he wrote to her, breaking off the engagement."

"Yes, but he's dashed sorry about all that now. Wishes he had never been such a mug, and all that sort of thing. As a matter of fact, that's why I shot over here in the first place. As an ambassador, don't you know. I told Jill all about it directly I saw her, but she seemed inclined to give it a miss rather, so I cabled old Derek to pop here in person. Seemed to me, don't you know, that Jill might be more likely to make it up and all that if she saw old Derek."

Uncle Chris nodded, his composure restored.

"Very true. Yes, certainly, my boy, you acted most sensibly. Badly as Underhill behaved, she undoubtedly loved him. It would be the best possible thing that could happen if they could be brought together. It is my dearest wish to see Jill comfortably settled. I was half hoping that she might marry young Pilkington."

"Good God! The Pilker!"

"He is quite a nice young fellow," argued Uncle Chris. "None too many brains, perhaps, but Jill would supply that deficiency. Still, of course, Underhill would be much better."

"She ought to marry someone," said Freddie earnestly. "I mean, all rot a girl like Jill having to knock about and rough it like this."

"You're perfectly right."

"Of course," said Freddie thoughtfully, "the catch in the whole dashed business is that she's such a bally independent sort of girl. I mean to say, it's quite possible she may hand Derek the mitten, you know."

"In that case, let us hope that she will look more favourably on young Pilkington."

"Yes," said Freddie. "Well, yes. But—well, I wouldn't call the Pilker a very ripe sporting proposition. About sixty to one against is the way I should figure it if I were making a book. It may be just because I'm feeling a bit pipped this morning— got turfed out of bed at seven o'clock and all that—but I have an idea that she may give both of them the old razz. May be wrong, of course."

"Let us hope that you are, my boy," said Uncle Chris gravely. "For in that case I should be forced into a course of action from which I confess that I shrink."

"I don't follow."

"Freddie, my boy, you are a very old friend of Jill's and I am her uncle. I feel that I can speak plainly to you. Jill is the dearest thing to me in the world. She trusted me, and I failed her. I was responsible for the loss of her money, and my one object in life is to see her by some means or other in a position equal to the one of which I deprived her. If she married a rich man, well and good. That, provided she marries him because she is fond of him, will be the very best thing that can happen. But if she does not, there is another way. It may be possible for me to marry a rich woman."

Freddie stopped, appalled.

"Good God! You don't mean . . . you aren't thinking of marrying Mrs. Peagrim!"

"I wouldn't have mentioned names, but, as you have guessed . . . Yes, if the worst comes to the worst, I shall make the supreme sacrifice. To-night will decide. Good-bye, my boy. I want to look in at my club for a few minutes. Tell Underhill that he has my best wishes."

"I'll bet he has!" gasped Freddie.

* 20 *

Derek Loses One Bird and Secures Another

I

IT is safest for the historian, if he values accuracy, to wait till a thing has happened before writing about it. Otherwise he may commit himself to statements which are not borne out by the actual facts. Mrs. Peagrim, recording in advance the success of her party at the Gotham Theatre, had done this. It is true that she was a "radiant and vivacious hostess," and it is possible, her standard not being very high, that she had "never looked more charming." But, when she went on to say that all present were in agreement that they had never spent a more delightful evening, she deceived the public. Uncle Chris, for one; Otis Pilkington, for another, and Freddie Rooke, for a third, were so far from spending a delightful evening that they found it hard to mask their true emotions and keep a smiling face to the world.

Otis Pilkington, indeed, found it impossible, and, ceasing to try, left early. Just twenty minutes after the proceedings had begun, he seized his coat and hat, shot out into the night, made off blindly up Broadway, and walked twice round Central Park before his feet gave out and he allowed himself to be taken back to his apartment in a taxi. Jill had been very kind and very sweet and very regretful, but it was only too manifest that on the question of becoming Mrs. Otis Pilkington her mind was made up. She was willing to like him, to be a sister to him, to watch his future progress with considerable interest, but she would not marry him.

One feels sorry for Otis Pilkington in his hour of travail. This was the fifth or sixth time that this sort of thing had happened to him, and he was getting tired of it. If he could have looked into the future—five years almost to a day from that evening—and seen himself walking blushfully down the aisle of St. Thomas' with Roland Trevis' sister Angela on his arm, his gloom might have been lightened. More probably, however, it would have been increased. At the moment, Roland Trevis' sister Angela was fifteen, frivolous, and freckled and, except that he rather disliked her and suspected her—correctly—of laughing at him, amounted to just *nil* in Mr. Pilkington's life. The idea of linking his lot with hers would have appalled him, enthusiastically though he was in favour of it five years later.

However, Mr. Pilkington was unable to look into the future, so his reflections on this night of sorrow were not diverted from Jill. He thought sadly of Jill till two-thirty, when he fell asleep in his chair and dreamed of her. At seven o'clock his Japanese valet, who had been given the night off, returned home, found him, and gave him breakfast. After which, Mr. Pilkington went to bed, played three games of solitaire, and slept till dinner-time, when he awoke to take up the burden of life again. He still brooded on the tragedy which had shattered him. Indeed, it was only two weeks later, when at a dance he was introduced to a red-haired girl from Detroit, that he really got over it.

The news was conveyed to Freddie Rooke by Uncle Chris. Uncle Chris, with something of the emotions of a condemned man on the scaffold waiting for a reprieve, had watched Jill and Mr. Pilkington go off together into the dim solitude at the back of the orchestra chairs, and, after an all too brief interval, had observed the latter whizzing back, his every little movement having a meaning of its own—and that meaning one which convinced Uncle Chris that Freddie, in estimating Mr. Pilkington as a sixty to one chance, had not erred in his judgment of form.

Uncle Chris found Freddie in one of the upper boxes, talking to Nelly Bryant. Dancing was going on down on the stage, but

Freddie, though normally a young man who shook a skilful shoe, was in no mood for dancing to-night. The return to the scenes of his former triumphs and the meeting with the companions of happier days, severed from him by a two-weeks' notice, had affected Freddie powerfully. Eyeing the happy throng below, he experienced the emotions of that Peri who, in the poem, "at the gate of Eden stood disconsolate."

Excusing himself from Nelly and following Uncle Chris into the passage-way outside the box, he heard the other's news listlessly. It came as no shock to Freddie. He had never thought Mr. Pilkington anything to write home about, and had never supposed that Jill would accept him. He said as much. Sorry for the chap in a way, and all that, but had never imagined for an instant that he would click.

"Where is Underhill?" asked Uncle Chris agitated.

"Derek? Oh, he isn't here yet."

"But why isn't he here? I understood that you were bringing him with you."

"That was the scheme, but it seems he had promised some people he met on the boat to go to a theatre and have a bit of supper with them afterwards. I only heard about it when I got back this morning."

"Good God, boy! Didn't you tell him that Jill would be here to-night?"

"Oh, rather. And he's coming on directly he can get away from these people. Ought to be here any moment now."

Uncle Chris plucked at his moustache gloomily. Freddie's detachment depressed him. He had looked for more animation and a greater sense of the importance of the issue.

"Well, pip-pip for the present," said Freddie, moving toward the box. "Have to be getting back. See you later."

He disappeared, and Uncle Chris turned slowly to descend the stairs. As he reached the floor below, the door of the stage-box opened, and Mrs. Peagrim came out.

"Oh, Major Selby!" cried the radiant and vivacious hostess "I couldn't think where you had got to. I have been looking for you everywhere."

Uncle Chris quivered slightly, but braced himself to do his duty.

"May I have the pleasure . . .?" he began, then broke off as he saw the man who had come out of the box behind his hostess. "Underhill!" He grasped his hand and shook it warmly.

"My dear fellow! I had no notion that you had arrived!"

"Sir Derek came just a moment ago," said Mrs. Peagrim.

"How are you, Major Selby?" said Derek. He was a little surprised at the warmth of his reception. He had not anticipated this geniality.

"My dear fellow, I'm delighted to see you," cried Uncle Chris. "But, as I was saying, Mrs. Peagrim, may I have the pleasure of this dance?"

"I don't think I will dance this one," said Mrs. Peagrim surprisingly. "I'm sure you two must have ever so much to talk about. Why don't you take Sir Derek and give him a cup of coffee?"

"Capital idea!" said Uncle Chris. "Come this way, my dear fellow. As Mrs. Peagrim says, I have ever so much to talk about. Along this passage, my boy. Be careful. There's a step. Well, well, well! It's delightful to see you again!" He massaged Derek's arm affectionately. Every time he had met Mrs. Peagrim that evening he had quailed inwardly at what lay before him, should some hitch occur to prevent the re-union of Derek and Jill: and now that the other was actually here, handsomer than ever and more than ever the sort of man no girl could resist, he declined to admit the possibility of a hitch. His spirits soared. "You haven't seen Jill yet, of course?"

"No." Derek hesitated. "Is Jill . . . Does she . . . I mean . . ."

Uncle Chris resumed his osteopathy. He kneaded his companion's coat-sleeve with a jovial hand.

"My dear fellow, of course! I am sure that a word or two from you will put everything right. We all make mistakes. I have made them myself. I am convinced that everything will be perfectly all right. . . . Ah, there she is. Jill, my dear, here is an old friend to see you!"

II

Since the hurried departure of Mr. Pilkington, Jill had been sitting in the auditorium, lazily listening to the music and watching the couples dancing on the stage. She found herself drifting into a mood of gentle contentment, and was at a loss to account for this. She was happy—quietly and peacefully happy, when she was aware that she ought to have been both agitated and apprehensive. When she had anticipated the recent interview with Otis Pilkington, which she had known was bound to come sooner or later, it had been shrinkingly and with foreboding. She hated hurting people's feelings, and, though she read Mr. Pilkington's character accurately enough to know that time would heal any anguish which she might cause him, she had had no doubt that the temperamental surface of that long young man, when he succeeded in getting her alone, was going to be badly bruised. And it had fallen out just as she had expected. Mr. Pilkington had said his say and departed, a pitiful figure, a spectacle which should have wrung her heart. It had not wrung her heart. Except for one fleeting instant when she was actually saying the fatal words, it had not interferred with her happiness at all; and already she was beginning to forget that the incident had ever happened.

And, if the past should have depressed her, the future might have been expected to depress her even more. There was nothing in it, either immediate or distant, which could account for her feeling gently contented. And yet, as she leaned back in her seat, her heart was dancing in time to the dance-music of Mrs. Peagrim's hired orchestra. It puzzled Jill.

And then, quite suddenly, yet with no abruptness or sense of discovery, just as if it were something which she had known all along, the truth came upon her. It was Wally, the thought of Wally, the knowledge that Wally existed, that made her happy. He was a solid, comforting, reassuring fact in a world of doubts and perplexities. She did not need to be with him to be fortified, it was enough just to think of him. Present or absent, his personality heartened her like fine weather or music or a sea-breeze—or like that friendly, soothing nightlight which they used to leave in her nursery when she was little, to scare away the goblins and see her safely over the road that led to the gates of the city of dreams.

Suppose there were no Wally . . . ?

Jill gave a sudden gasp, and sat up, tingling. She felt as she had sometimes felt as a child, when, on the edge of sleep, she had dreamed that she was stepping off a precipice and had woken, tense and alert, to find that there was no danger after all. But there was a difference between that feeling and this. She had woken, but to find that there was danger. It was as though some inner voice was calling to her to be careful, to take thought. Suppose there were no Wally? . . . And why

should there always be Wally? He had said confidently enough
that there would never be another girl . . . But there were
thousands of other girls, millions of other girls, and could she
suppose that one of them would not have the sense to snap up a
treasure like Wally? A sense of blank desolation swept over Jill.
Her quick imagination, leaping ahead, had made the vague
possibility of a distant future an accomplished fact. She felt,
absurdly, a sense of overwhelming loss.

Into her mind, never far distant from it, came the thought of
Derek. And, suddenly, Jill made another discovery. She was
thinking of Derek, and it was not hurting. She was thinking
of him quite coolly and clearly and her heart was not aching.

She sat back and screwed her eyes tight, as she had always
done when puzzled. Something had happened to her, but how
it had happened and when it had happened and why it had
happened she could not understand. She only knew that now
for the first time she had been granted a moment of clear vision
and was seeing things truly.

She wanted Wally. She wanted him in the sense that she
could not do without him. She felt nothing of the fiery tumult
which had come upon her when she first met Derek. She and
Wally would come together with a smile and build their life on
an enduring foundation of laughter and happiness and good
fellowship. Wally had never shaken and never would shake her
senses as Derek had done. If that was love, then she did not
love Wally. But her clear vision told her that it was not love.
It might be the blazing and crackling of thorns, but it was not
the fire. She wanted Wally. She needed him as she needed the
air and the sunlight.

She opened her eyes and saw Uncle Chris coming down the
aisle towards her. There was a man with him, and, as they moved
closer in the dim light, Jill saw that it was Derek.

"Jill, my dear," said Uncle Chris, "here is an old friend to
see you!"

And, having achieved their bringing together, he proceeded
to withdraw delicately whence he had come. It is pleasant to be
able to record that he was immediately seized upon by Mrs.
Peagrim, who had changed her mind about not dancing, and
led off to be her partner in a fox-trot, in the course of which
she trod on his feet three times.

"Why, Derek!" said Jill cheerfully. Except for a mild wonder

how he came to be there, she found herself wholly unaffected
by the sight of him. "Whatever are *you* doing here?"

Derek sat down beside her. The cordiality of her tone had
relieved, yet at the same time disconcerted him. Man seldom
attains to perfect contentment in this world, and Derek, while
pleased that Jill apparently bore him no ill-will, seemed to miss
something in her manner which he would have been glad to
find there.

"Jill!" he said huskily.

It seemed to Derek only decent to speak huskily. To his
orderly mind this situation could be handled only in one way.
It was a plain, straight issue of the strong man humbling himself
—not too much of course, but sufficiently: and it called, in his
opinion, for the low voice, the clenched hand, and the broken
whisper. Speaking as he had spoken, he had given the scene
the right key from the start—or would have done if she had not
got in ahead of him and opened it on a note of absurd cheeriness?
Derek found himself resenting her cheeriness. Often as he had
attempted during the voyage from England to visualize to himself
this first meeting, he had never pictured Jill smiling brightly at
him. It was a jolly smile, and made her look extremely pretty,
but it jarred upon him. A moment before he had been half
relieved, half disconcerted: now he was definitely disconcerted.
He searched in his mind for a criticism of her attitude, and came
to the conclusion that what was wrong with it was that it was
too friendly. Friendliness is well enough in its way, but in
what should have been a tense clashing of strong emotions it
did not seem to Derek fitting.

"Did you have a pleasant trip?" asked Jill. "Have you come
over on business?"

A feeling of bewilderment came upon Derek. It was wrong, it
was all wrong. Of course, she might be speaking like this to
cloak intense feeling, but, if so, she had certainly succeeded.
From her manner, he and she might be casual acquaintances. A
pleasant trip! In another minute she would be asking him how
he had come out on the sweepstake on the ship's run. With a
sense of putting his shoulder to some heavy weight and heaving
at it, he sought to lift the conversation to a higher plane.

"I came to find *you!*" he said; still huskily but not so huskily
as before. There are degrees of huskiness, and Derek's was
sharpened a little by a touch of irritation.

"Yes ?" said Jill.

Derek was now fermenting. What she ought to have said, he did not know, but he knew that it was not "Yes ?"

"Yes ?" in the circumstances was almost as bad as "Really ?"

There was a pause. Jill was looking at him with a frank and unembarrassed gaze which somehow deepened his sense of annoyance. Had she looked at him coldly, he could have understood and even appreciated it. He had been expecting coldness, and had braced himself to combat it. He was still not quite sure in his mind whether he was playing the role of a penitent or a King Cophetua, but in either character he might have anticipated a little temporary coldness, which it would have been his easy task to melt. But he had never expected to be looked at as if he were a specimen in a museum, and that was how he was feeling now. Jill was not looking at him—she was inspecting him, examining him, and he chafed under the process.

Jill, unconscious of the discomfort she was causing, continued to gaze. She was trying to discover in just what respect he had changed from the god he had been. Certainly not in looks. He was as handsome as ever—handsomer, indeed, for the sunshine and clean breezes of the Atlantic had given him an exceedingly becoming coat of tan. And yet he must have changed, for now she could look upon him quite dispassionately and criticize him without a tremor. It was like seeing a copy of a great painting. Everything was there, except the one thing that mattered, the magic and the glamour. It was like . . . She suddenly remembered a scene in the dressing-room when the company had been in Baltimore. Lois Denham, duly the recipient of the sunburst which her friend Izzy had promised her, had unfortunately, in a spirit of girlish curiosity, taken it to a jeweller to be priced, and the jeweller had blasted her young life by declaring it a paste imitation. Jill recalled how the stricken girl—previous to calling Izzy on the long distance and telling him a number of things which, while probably not news to him, must have been painful hearing—had passed the vile object round the dressing-room for inspection. The imitation was perfect. It has been impossible for the girls to tell that the stones were not real diamonds. Yet the jeweller, with his sixth sense, had seen through them in a trifle under ten seconds. Jill came to the conclusion that her newly-discovered love for Wally Mason had equipped her with a sixth sense, and that by its aid she was really for the first time seeing Derek as he was.

Derek had not the privilege of being able to read Jill's thoughts. All he could see was the outer Jill, and the outer Jill, as she had always done, was stirring his emotions. Her daintiness afflicted him. Not for the first, the second, or the third time since they had come into each other's lives, he was astounded at the strength of the appeal which Jill had for him when they were together, as contrasted with its weakness when they were apart. He made another attempt to establish the scene on a loftier plane.

"What a fool I was!" he sighed. "Jill! Can you ever forgive me ?"

He tried to take her hand. Jill skilfully eluded him.

"Why, of course I've forgiven you, Derek, if there was anything to forgive."

"Anything to forgive!" Derek began to get into his stride. These were the lines on which he had desired the interview to develop. "I was a brute! A cad!"

"Oh, no!"

"I was. Oh, I have been through hell!"

Jill turned her head away. She did not want to hurt him, but nothing could have kept her from smiling. She had been so sure that he would say that sooner or later.

"Jill!" Derek had misinterpreted the cause of her movement, and had attributed it to emotion. "Tell me that everything is as it was before."

Jill turned.

"I'm afraid I can't say that, Derek."

"Of course not!" agreed Derek in a comfortable glow of manly remorse. He liked himself in the character of the strong man abashed. "It would be too much to expect, I know. But, when we are married . . ."

"Do you really want to marry me ?"

"Jill!"

"I wonder!"

"How can you doubt it ?"

Jill looked at him.

"Have you thought what it would mean ?"

"What it would mean ?"

"Well, your mother . . ."

"Oh!" Derek dismissed Lady Underhill with a grand gesture.

"Yes," persisted Jill, "but, if she disapproved of your marrying

me before, wouldn't she disapprove a good deal more now, when
I haven't a penny in the world and am just in the chorus . . ."

A sort of strangled sound proceeded from Derek's throat.

"In the chorus!"

"Didn't you know? I thought Freddie must have told you."

"In the chorus!" Derek stammered. "I thought you were
here as a guest of Mrs. Peagrim's."

"So I am—like the rest of the company."

"But . . . But . . ."

"You see, it would be bound to make everything a little
difficult," said Jill. Her face was grave, but her lips were twitching.
"I mean, you are rather a prominent man, aren't you, and if you
married a chorus-girl . . ."

"Nobody would know," said Derek limply.

Jill opened her eyes.

"Nobody would *know*!" She laughed. "But, of course, you've
never met our Press-agent. If you think that nobody would
know that a girl in the company had married a baronet who
was a member of parliament and expected to be in the Cabinet
in a few years, you're wronging him! The news would be on
the front page of all the papers the very next day—columns of
it, with photographs. There would be articles about it in the
Sunday papers. Illustrated! And then it would be cabled to
England and would appear in the papers there . . . You see,
you're a very important person, Derek."

Derek sat clutching the arms of his chair. His face was chalky.
Though he had never been inclined to underestimate his
importance as a figure in the public eye, he had overlooked the
disadvantages connected with such an eminence. He gurgled
wordlessly. He had been prepared to brave Lady Underhill's
wrath and assert his right to marry whom he pleased, but this
was different.

Jill watched him curiously and with a certain pity. It was so
easy to read what was passing in his mind. She wondered what
he would say, how he would flounder out of his unfortunate
position. She had no illusions about him now. She did not even
contemplate the possibility of chivalry winning the battle which
was going on within him.

"It would be very awkward, wouldn't it?" she said.

And then pity had its way with Jill. He had treated her badly;
for a time she had thought that he had crushed all the heart out

of her: but he was suffering, and she hated to see anybody suffer.

"Besides," she said. "I'm engaged to somebody else."

As a suffocating man, his lips to the tube of oxygen, gradually comes back to life, Derek revived—slowly as the meaning of her words sank into his mind, then with a sudden abruptness.

"What?" he cried.

"I'm going to marry somebody else. A man named Wally Mason."

Derek swallowed. The chalky look died out of his face, and he flushed hotly. His eyes, half relieved, half indignant, glowed under their pent-house of eyebrow. He sat for a moment in silence.

"I think you might have told me before!" he said huffily.

Jill laughed.

"Yes, I suppose I ought to have told you before."

"Leading me on . . .!"

Jill patted him on the arm.

"Never mind, Derek! It's all over now. And it was great fun, wasn't it!"

"Fun!"

"Shall we go and dance? The music is just starting."

"I *won't* dance!"

Jill got up.

"I must," she said. "I'm so happy I can't keep still. Well, good-bye, Derek, in case I don't see you again. It was nice meeting after all this time. You haven't altered a bit!"

Derek watched her flit down the aisle, saw her jump up the little ladder on to the stage, watched her vanish into the swirl of the dance. He reached for a cigarette, opened his case, and found it empty. He uttered a mirthless, Byronic laugh. The thing seemed to him symbolic.

III

Not having a cigarette of his own, Derek got up and went to look for the only man he knew who could give him one: and after a search of a few minutes came upon Freddie all alone in a dark corner, apart from the throng. It was a very different Freddie from the moody youth who had returned to the box after his conversation with Uncle Chris. He was leaning against a piece of scenery with his head tilted back and a beam of startled happiness on his face. So rapt was he in his reflections that he did not become aware of Derek's approach until the latter spoke.

"Got a cigarette, Freddie?"

Freddie withdrew his gaze from the roof.

"Hullo, old son! Cigarette? Certainly and by all means. Cigarettes? Where are the cigarettes? Mr. Rooke, forward! Show cigarettes." He extended his case to Derek, who helped himself in sombre silence, finding his boyhood's friend's exuberance hard to bear. "I say, Derek, old scream, the most extraordinary thing has happened! You'll never guess. To cut a long story short and come to the blow-out of the scenario, I'm engaged! Engaged, old crumpet! You know what I mean—engaged to be married!"

"Ugh!" said Derek gruffly, frowning over his cigarette.

"Don't wonder you're surprised," said Freddie, looking at him a little wistfully, for his friend had scarcely been gushing, and he would have welcomed a bit of enthusiasm. "Can hardly believe it myself."

Derek awoke to a sense of the conventions.

"Congratulate you," he said. "Do I know her?"

"Not yet, but you will soon. She's a girl in the company—in the chorus as a matter of fact. Girl named Nelly Bryant. An absolute corker. I'll go further—a topper. You'll like her, old man."

Derek was looking at him, amazed.

"Good Heavens!" he said.

"Extraordinary how these things happen," proceeded Freddie. "Looking back, I can see, of course, that I always thought her a topper, but the idea of getting engaged—I don't know—sort of thing that doesn't occur to a chappie, if you know what I mean. What I mean to say is, we had always been the greatest of pals and all that, but it never struck me that she would think it much of a wheeze getting hooked up for life with a chap like me. We just sort of drifted along and so forth. All very jolly and what not. And then this evening—I don't know. I had a bit of a hump, what with one thing and another, and she was most dashed sweet and patient and soothing and—and—well, and what not, don't you know, and suddenly—deuced rummy sensation—the jolly old scales seemed to fall, if you follow me, from my good old eyes; I don't know if you get the idea. I suddenly seemed to look myself squarely in the eyeball and say to myself, 'Freddie, old top, how do we go? Are we not missing a good thing?' And, by Jove, thinking it over, I found that I was absolutely correct-o! You've no notion how dashed sympathetic she is, old man! I mean to say, I had this hump, you know, owing to one thing and another, and was feeling that life was more or less of a jolly old snare and delusion, and she bucked me up and all that, and suddenly I found myself kissing her and all that sort of rot, and she was kissing me and so on and so forth, and she's got the most ripping eyes, and there was nobody about, and the long and the short of it was, old boy, that I said, 'Let's get married!' and she said, 'When?' and that was that, if you see what I mean. The scheme now is to pop down to the City Hall and get a licence, which it appears you have to have if you want to bring this sort of binge off with any success and vim, and then what ho for the padre! Looking at it from every angle, a bit of a good egg, what? Happiest man in the world, and all that sort of thing."

At this point in his somewhat incoherent epic Freddie paused. It had occurred to him that he had perhaps laid himself open to a charge of monopolising the conversation.

"I say! You'll forgive my dwelling a bit on this thing, won't you? Never found a girl who would look twice at me before, and it's rather unsettled the old bean. Just occurred to me that I may have been talking about my own affairs a bit. Your turn now, old thing. Sit down, as the blighters in the novels used to say, and tell me the story of your life. You've seen Jill, of course?"

"Yes," said Derek shortly.

"And it's all right, eh? Fine! We'll make a double wedding of it, what? Not a bad idea, that! I mean to say, the man of God might make a reduction for quantity and shade his fee a bit. Do the job half price!"

Derek threw down the end of his cigarette, and crushed it with his heel. A closer observer than Freddie would have detected long ere this the fact that his demeanour was not that of a happy and successful wooer.

"Jill and I are not going to be married," he said.

A look of blank astonishment came into Freddie's cheerful face. He could hardly believe that he had heard correctly. It is true that, in gloomier mood, he had hazarded the theory to

Uncle Chris that Jill's independence might lead her to refuse Derek, but he had not really believed in the possibility of such a thing even at the time, and now, in the full flood of optimism consequent on his own engagement, it seemed even more incredible.

"Great Scott!" he cried. "Did she give you the raspberry?"

It is to be doubted whether the pride of the Underhills would have permitted Derek to reply in the affirmative, even if Freddie had phrased his question differently; but the brutal directness of the query made such a course impossible for him. Nothing was dearer to Derek than his self-esteem, and, even at the expense of the truth, he was resolved to shield it from injury. To face Freddie and confess that any girl in the world had given him, Derek Underhill, what he coarsely termed the raspberry was a task so revolting as to be utterly beyond his powers.

"Nothing of the kind!" he snapped. "It was because we both saw that the thing would be impossible. Why didn't you tell me that Jill was in the chorus of this damned piece?"

Freddie's mouth slowly opened. He was trying not to realize the meaning of what his friend was saying. His was a faithful soul, and for years—to all intents and purposes for practically the whole of his life—he had looked up to Derek and reverenced him. He absolutely refused to believe that Derek was intending to convey what he seemed to be trying to convey; for, if he was, well . . . by Jove . . . it was too rotten and Algy Martyn had been right after all and the fellow was simply . . .

"You don't mean, old man," said Freddie with an almost pleading note in his voice, "that you're going to back out of marrying Jill because she's in the chorus?"

Derek looked away, and scowled. He was finding Freddie, in the capacity of inquisitor, as trying as he had found him in the role of exuberant fiancé. It offended his pride to have to make explanations to one whom he had always regarded with a patronizing tolerance as not a bad fellow in his way but in every essential respect negligible.

"I have to be sensible," he said, chafing as the indignity of his position intruded itself more and more. "You know what it would mean . . . Paragraphs in all the papers . . . photographs . . . the news cabled to England . . . everybody reading it and misunderstanding . . . I've got my career to think of . . . It would cripple me . . ."

His voice trailed off, and there was silence for a moment. Then Freddie burst into speech. His good-natured face was hard with unwonted scorn. Its cheerful vacuity had changed to stony contempt. For the second time in the evening the jolly old scales had fallen from Freddie's good old eyes, and, as Jill had done, he saw Derek as he was.

"My sainted aunt!" he said slowly. "So that's it, what? Well, I've always thought a dashed lot of you, as you know. I've always looked up to you as a bit of a nib and wished I was like you. But, great Scott! if that's the sort of a chap you are, I'm deuced glad I'm not! I'm going to wake up in the middle of the night and think how unlike you I am and pat myself on the back! Ronny Devereux was perfectly right. A tick's a tick, and that's all there is to say about it. Good old Ronny told me what you were, and, like a silly ass, I wasted a lot of time trying to make him believe you weren't that sort of chap at all. It's no good standing there looking like your mother," said Freddie firmly. "This is where we jolly well part brass-rags! If we ever meet again, I'll trouble you not to speak to me, because I've a reputation to keep up! So there you have it in a bally nutshell!"

Scarcely had Freddie ceased to administer it to his former friend in a bally nutshell, when Uncle Chris, warm and dishevelled from the dance as interpreted by Mrs. Waddesleigh Peagrim, came bustling up, saving Derek the necessity of replying to the harangue.

"Well, Underhill, my dear fellow," began Uncle Chris affably, attaching himself to the other's arm, "what . . .?"

He broke off, for Derek, freeing his arm with a wrench, turned and walked rapidly away. Derek had no desire to go over the whole thing again with Uncle Chris. He wanted to be alone, to build up, painfully and laboriously, the ruins of his self-esteem. The pride of the Underhills had had a bad evening.

Uncle Chris turned to Freddie.

"What is the matter?" he asked blankly.

"I'll tell you what's the jolly old matter!" cried Freddie. "The blighter isn't going to marry poor Jill after all! He's changed his rotten mind! It's off!"

"Off?"

"Absolutely off!"

"Absolutely off?"

"Napoo!" said Freddie. "He's afraid of what will happen to

his blasted career if he marries a girl who's been in the chorus."

"But, my dear boy!" Uncle Chris blinked. "But, my dear boy! This is ridiculous . . . Surely, if I were to speak a word . . ."

"You can if you like. *I* wouldn't speak to the man again if you paid me! But it won't do any good, so what's the use?"

Slowly Uncle Chris adjusted his mind to the disaster.

"Then you mean . . . ?"

"It's off!" said Freddie.

For a moment Uncle Chris stood motionless. Then, with a sudden jerk, he seemed to stiffen his backbone. His face was bleak, but he pulled at his moustache jauntily.

"*Morituri te salutant!*" he said. "Good-bye, Freddie, my boy."

He turned away, gallant and upright, the old soldier.

"Where are you going? asked Freddie.

"Over the top!" said Uncle Chris.

"What do you mean?"

"I am going," said Uncle Chris steadily, "to find Mrs. Peagrim!"

"Good God!" cried Freddie. He followed him, protesting weakly, but the other gave no sign that he had heard. Freddie saw him disappear into the stage-box, and, turning, found Jill at his elbow.

"Where did Uncle Chris go?" asked Jill. "I want to speak to him."

"He's in the stage-box, with Mrs. Peagrim."

"With Mrs. Peagrim?"

"Proposing to her," said Freddie solemnly.

Jill stared.

"Proposing to Mrs. Peagrim? What do you mean?"

Freddie drew her aside, and began to explain.

IV

In the dimness of the stage-box, his eyes a little glassy and a dull despair in his soul, Uncle Chris was wondering how to begin. In his hot youth he had been rather a devil of a fellow in between dances, a coo-er of soft phrases and a stealer of never very stoutly withheld kisses. He remembered one time in Bangalore . . . but that had nothing to do with the case. The point was, how to begin with Mrs. Peagrim. The fact that twenty-five years ago he had crushed in his arms beneath the shadows of the deodars a girl whose name he had forgotten, though he remembered that she had worn a dress of some pink stuff, was immaterial and irrelevant. Was he to crush Mrs. Peagrim in his arms? Not, thought Uncle Chris to himself, on a bet. He contented himself for the moment with bending an intense gaze upon her and asked if she was tired.

"A little," panted Mrs. Peagrim, who, though she danced often and vigorously, was never in the best of condition, owing to her habit of neutralizing the beneficent effects of exercise by surreptitious candy-eating. "I'm a little out of breath."

Uncle Chris had observed this for himself, and it had not helped him to face his task. Lovely woman loses something of her queenly dignity when she puffs. Inwardly, he was thinking how exactly his hostess resembled the third from the left of a troupe of performing sea-lions which he had seen some years ago on one of his rare visits to a vaudeville house.

"You ought not to tire yourself," he said with a difficult tenderness.

"I *am* so fond of dancing," pleaded Mrs. Peagrim. Recovering some of her breath, she gazed at her companion with a sort of short-winded archness. "You are always so sympathetic, Major Selby."

"Am I?" said Uncle Chris. "Am I?"

"You know you are!"

Uncle Chris swallowed quickly.

"I wonder if you have ever wondered," he began, and stopped. He felt that he was not putting it as well as he might. "I wonder if it has ever struck you that there's a reason." He stopped again. He seemed to remember reading something like that in an advertisement in a magazine, and he did not want to talk like an advertisement. "I wonder if it has ever struck you, Mrs. Peagrim," he began again, "that any sympathy on my part might be due to some deeper emotion which . . . Have you never suspected that you have never suspected . . ." Uncle Chris began to feel that he must brace himself up. Usually a man of fluent speech, he was not at his best to-night. He was just about to try again, when he caught his hostess' eye, and the soft gleam in it sent him cowering back into the silence as if he was taking cover from an enemy's shrapnel.

Mrs. Peagrim touched him on the arm.

"You were saying . . .?" she murmured encouragingly.

Uncle Chris shut his eyes. His fingers pressed desperately into the velvet curtain beside him. He felt as he had felt when a raw lieutenant in India, during his first hill-campaign, when the etiquette of the service had compelled him to rise and walk up and down in front of his men under a desultory shower of jezail-bullets. He seemed to hear the damned things *whop-whopping* now . . . and almost wished that he could really hear them. One or two good bullets just now would be a welcome diversion.

"Yes ?" said Mrs. Peagrim.

"Have you never felt," babbled Uncle Chris, "that, feeling as I feel, I might have felt . . . that is to say, might be feeling a feeling . . . ?"

There was a tap at the door of the box. Uncle Chris started violently. Jill came in.

"Oh, I beg your pardon," she said. "I wanted to speak . . ."

"You wanted to speak to me ?" said Uncle Chris, bounding up. "Certainly, certainly, certainly, of course. If you will excuse me for a moment ?"

Mrs. Peagrim bowed coldly. The interruption had annoyed her. She had no notion who Jill was, and she resented the intrusion at this particular juncture intensely. Not so Uncle Chris, who skipped out into the passage like a young lamb.

"Am I in time ?" asked Jill in a whisper.

"In time ?"

"You know what I mean. Uncle Chris, listen to me! You are not to propose to that awful woman. Do you understand ?"

Uncle Chris shook his head.

"The die is cast!"

"The die isn't anything of the sort," said Jill. "Unless . . ." She stopped, aghast. "You don't mean that you have done it already ?"

"Well, no. To be perfectly accurate, no. But . . ."

"Then that's all right. I know why you were doing it, and it was very sweet of you, but you mustn't."

"But, Jill, you don't understand."

"I do understand."

"I have a motive . . ."

"I know your motive. Freddie told me. Don't you worry yourself about me, dear, because I am all right. I am going to be married."

A look of ecstatic relief came into Uncle Chris' face.

"Then Underhill . . . ?"

"I am not marrying Derek. Somebody else. I don't think you know him, but I love him, and so will you." She pulled his face down and kissed him. "Now you can go back."

Uncle Chris was almost too overcome to speak. He gulped a little.

"Jill," he said shakily, "this is a . . . this is a great relief."

"I knew it would be."

"If you are really going to marry a rich man . . ."

"I didn't say he was rich."

The joy ebbed from Uncle Chris' face.

"If he is not rich, if he cannot give you everything of which I . . ."

"Oh, don't be absurd! Wally has all the money anybody needs. What's money?"

"What's money?" Uncle Chris stared. "Money, my dear child, is . . . is . . . well, you mustn't talk of it in that light way. But, if you think you will really have enough . . . ?"

"Of course we shall. Now you can go back. Mrs. Peagrim will be wondering what has become of you."

"Must I?" said Uncle Chris doubtfully.

"Of course. You must be polite."

"Very well," said Uncle Chris. "But it will be a little difficult to continue the conversation on what you might call general lines. However!"

Back in the box, Mrs. Peagrim was fanning herself with manifest impatience.

"What did that girl want?" she demanded.

Uncle Chris seated himself with composure. The weakness had passed, and he was himself again.

"Oh, nothing, nothing. Some trivial difficulty, which I was able to dispose of in a few words."

Mrs. Peagrim would have liked to continue her researches, but a feeling that it was wiser not to stray too long from the main point restrained her. She bent towards him.

"You were going to say something when that girl interrupted us."

Uncle Chris shot his cuffs with a debonair gesture.

"Was I? Was I? To be sure, yes. I was saying that you ought not to let yourself get tired. Deuce of a thing, getting tired. Plays the dickens with the system."

Mrs. Peagrim was disconcerted. The atmosphere seemed to have changed, and she did not like it. She endeavoured to restore the tone of the conversation.

"You are so sympathetic," she sighed, feeling that she could not do better than to begin again at that point. The remark had produced good results before and it might do so a second time.

"Yes," agreed Uncle Chris cheerily. "You see, I have seen something of all this sort of thing, and I realize the importance of it. I know what all this modern rush and strain of life is for a woman in your position. Parties every night . . . dancing . . . a thousand and one calls on the vitality . . . bound to have an effect sooner or later, unless—*unless*," said Uncle Chris solemnly, "one takes steps. Unless one acts in time. I had a friend——" His voice sank—"I had a very dear friend over in London, Lady Alice—but the name would convey nothing—the point is that she was in exactly the same position as you. On the rush all the time. Never stopped. The end was inevitable. She caught cold, hadn't sufficient vitality to throw it off, went to a dance in mid-winter, contracted pneumonia . . ." Uncle Chris sighed. "All over in three days," he said sadly. "Now at that time," he resumed. "I did not know what I know now. If I had heard of Nervino then . . ." He shook his head. "It might have saved her life. It *would* have saved her life. I tell you, Mrs. Peagrim, that there is nothing, there is no lack of vitality which Nervino cannot set right. I am no physician myself, I speak as a layman, but it acts on the red corpuscles of the blood . . ."

Mrs. Peagrim's face was stony. She had not spoken before, because he had given her no opportunity, but she spoke now in a hard voice.

"Major Selby!"

"Mrs. Peagrim?"

"I am not interested in patent medicines!"

"One can hardly call Nervino that," said Uncle Chris reproachfully. "It is a sovereign specific. You can get it at any drug store. It comes in two sizes, the dollar-fifty—or large—size, and the . . ."

Mrs. Peagrim rose majestically.

"Major Selby, I am tired . . ."

"Precisely. And, as I say, Nervino . . ."

"Please," said Mrs. Peagrim coldly, "go to the stage-door and see if you can find my limousine. It should be waiting in the street."

"Certainly," said Uncle Chris. "Why, certainly, certainly, certainly."

He left the box and proceeded across the stage. He walked with a lissom jauntiness. His eye was bright. One or two of those whom he passed on his way had the idea that this fine-looking man was in pain. They fancied that he was moaning. But Uncle Chris was not moaning. He was humming a gay snatch from the lighter music of the 'nineties.

✶ 21 ✶

Wally Mason Learns a New Exercise

I

UP on the roof of his apartment, far above the bustle and clamour of the busy city, Wally Mason, at eleven o'clock on the morning after Mrs. Peagrim's Bohemian party, was greeting the new day, as was his custom, by going through his ante-breakfast exercises. Mankind is divided into two classes—those who do setting-up exercises before breakfast and those who know they ought to but don't. To the former and more praiseworthy class Wally had belonged since boyhood. Life might be vain and the world a void, but still he touched his toes the prescribed number of times and twisted his muscular body about according to the ritual. He did so this morning a little more vigorously than usual, partly because he had sat up too late the night before and thought too much and smoked too much, with the result that he had risen heavy-eyed, at the present disgraceful hour, and partly because he hoped by wearying the flesh to still the restlessness of the spirit. Spring generally made Wally restless, but never previously had it brought him this distracted feverishness. So he lay on his back and waved his legs in the air, and it was only when he had risen and was about to go still further into the matter that he perceived Jill standing beside him.

"Good Lord!" said Wally.

"Don't stop," said Jill, "I'm enjoying it."

"How long have you been here?"

"Oh, I only just arrived. I rang the bell, and the nice old

lady who is cooking your lunch told me you were out here."

"Not lunch. Breakfast."

"Breakfast! At this hour?"

"Won't you join me?"

"I'll join you. But I had my breakfast long ago."

Wally found his despondency magically dispelled. It was extraordinary how the mere sight of Jill could make the world a different place. It was true the sun had been shining before her arrival, but in a flabby, weak-minded way, not with the brilliance it had acquired immediately he heard her voice.

"If you don't mind waiting for about three minutes while I have a shower and dress . . ."

"Oh, is the entertainment over?" asked Jill, disappointed. "I always arrive too late for everything."

"One of these days you shall see me go through the whole programme, including shadow-boxing and the goose-step. Bring your friends! But at the moment I think it would be more of a treat for you to watch me eat an egg. Go and look at the view. From over there you can see Hoboken."

"I've seen it. I don't think much of it."

"Well, then, on this side we have Brooklyn. There is no stint. Wander to and fro and enjoy yourself. The rendezvous is in the sitting-room in about four moments."

Wally vaulted through the passage-window and disappeared. Then he returned and put his head out.

"I say!"

"Yes?"

"Just occurred to me. Your uncle won't be wanting this place for half an hour or so, will he? I mean, there will be time for me to have a bite of breakfast?"

"I don't suppose he will require your little home till some time in the evening."

"Fine!"

Wally disappeared again, and a few moments later Jill heard the faint splashing of water. She walked to the parapet and looked down. On the windows of the nearer buildings the sun cast glittering beams, but further away a faint, translucent mist hid the city. There was Spring humidity in the air. In the street she had found it oppressive: but on the breezy summit of this steel-and-granite cliff the air was cool and exhilarating. Peace stole into Jill's heart as she watched the boats dropping slowly down the

East River, which gleamed like dull steel through the haze. She had come to Journey's End, and she was happy. Trouble and heartache seemed as distant as those hurrying black ants down on the streets. She felt far away from the world on an enduring mountain of rest. She gave a little sigh of contentment and turned to go in as Wally called.

In the sitting-room her feeling of security deepened. Here, the world was farther away than ever. Even the faint noises which had risen to the roof were inaudible, and only the cosy tick-tock of the grandfather's clock punctuated the stillness.

She looked at Wally with a quickening sense of affection. He had the divine gift of silence at the right time. Yes, this was home. This was where she belonged.

"It didn't take me in, you know," said Jill at length, resting her arms on the table and regarding him severely.

Wally looked up.

"What didn't take you in?"

"That bath of yours. Yes, I know you turned on the cold shower, but you stood at a safe distance and watched it *show!*"

Wally waved his fork.

"As Heaven is my witness. . . . Look at my hair! Still damp! And I can show you the towel."

"Well, then, I'll bet it was the hot water. Why weren't you at Mrs. Peagrim's party last night?"

"It would take too long to explain all my reasons, but one of them was that I wasn't invited. How did it go off?"

"Splendidly, Freddie's engaged!"

Wally lowered his coffee cup.

"Engaged! You don't mean what is sometimes slangily called betrothed?"

"I do. He's engaged to Nelly Bryant. Nelly told me all about it when she got home last night. It seems that Freddie said to her 'What ho!' and she said 'You bet!' and Freddie said 'Pip pip!' and the thing was settled." Jill bubbled. "Freddie wants to go into vaudeville with her!"

"No! The Juggling Rookes? Or Rooke and Bryant, the cross-talk team, a thoroughly refined act, swell dressers on and off?"

"I don't know. But it doesn't matter. Nelly is domestic. She's going to have a little home in the country, where she can grow chickens and pigs."

"Father's in the pigstye, you can tell him by his hat, eh ?''

"Yes. They will be very happy. Freddie will be a father to her parrot."

Wally's cheerfulness diminished a trifle. The contemplation of Freddie's enviable lot brought with it the inevitable contrast with his own. A little home in the country. . . . Oh, well!

II

There was a pause. Jill was looking a little grave.

"Wally!''

"Yes ?''

She turned her face away, for there was a gleam of mischief in her eyes which she did not wish him to observe.

"Derek was at the party!''

Wally had been about to butter a piece of toast. The butter, jerked from the knife by the convulsive start which he gave, popped up in a semi-circle and plumped on to the tablecloth. He recovered himself quickly.

"Sorry!'' he said. "You mustn't mind that. They want me to be second-string for the "Boosting the Butter'' event at the next Olympic Games, and I'm practising all the time. . . . Underhill was there, eh ?''

"Yes.''

"You met him ?''

"Yes.''

Wally fiddled with his knife.

"Did he come over . . . I mean . . . had he come specially to see you ?''

"Yes.''

"I see.''

There was another pause.

"He wants to marry you ?''

"He said he wanted to marry me.''

Wally got up and went to the window. Jill could smile safely now, and she did, but her voice was still grave.

"What ought I to do, Wally ? I thought I would ask you as you are such a friend.''

Wally spoke without turning.

"You ought to marry him, of course.''

"You think so ?''

"You ought to marry him, of course," said Wally doggedly. "You love him, and the fact that he came all the way to America must mean that he still loves you. Marry him!"

"But . . ." Jill hesitated. "You see, there's a difficulty."

"What difficulty ?"

"Well . . . it was something I said to him just before he went away. I said something that made it a little difficult."

Wally continued to inspect the roofs below.

"What did you say ?"

"Well . . . it was something . . . something that I don't believe he liked . . . something that may interfere with his marrying me."

"What did you say ?"

"I told him I was going to marry *you !*"

Wally spun round. At the same time he leaped in the air. The effect of the combination of movements was to cause him to stagger across the room and, after two or three impromptu dance steps which would have interested Mrs. Peagrim, to clutch at the mantelpiece to save himself from falling. Jill watched him with quiet approval.

"Why, that's wonderful, Wally! Is that another of your morning exercises ? If Freddie does go into vaudeville, you ought to get him to let you join the troupe."

Wally was blinking at her from the mantelpiece.

"Jill!"

"Yes ?"

"What—what—what . . .!"

"Now, don't talk like Freddie, even if you are going into vaudeville with him."

"You said you were going to marry *me ?*"

"I said I was going to marry you!"

"But—do you mean . . .?"

The mischief died out of Jill's eyes. She met his gaze frankly and seriously.

"The lumber's gone, Wally," she said. "But my heart isn't empty. It's quite, quite full, and it's going to be full for ever and ever and ever."

Wally left the mantelpiece, and came slowly towards her.

"Jill!" He choked. "Jill!"

Suddenly he pounced on her and swung her off her feet. She gave a little breathless cry.

"Wally! I thought you didn't approve of cavemen!"

"This," said Wally, "is just another new morning exercise I've thought off!"

Jill sat down, gasping.

"Are you going to do that often, Wally?"

"Every day for the rest of my life!"

"Goodness!"

"Oh, you'll get used to it. It'll grow on you."

"You don't think I am making a mistake marrying you?"

"No, no! I've given the matter a lot of thought, and . . . in fact, no, no!"

"No." said Jill thoughtfully. "I think you'll make a good husband. I mean, suppose we ever want the piano moved or something . . . Wally!" she broke off suddenly.

"You have our ear."

"Come out on the roof," said Jill. "I want to show you something funny."

Wally followed her out. They stood at the parapet together, looking down.

"There!" said Jill, pointing.

Wally looked puzzled.

"I see many things, but which is the funny one?"

"Why, all these people. Over there—and there—and there. Scuttering about and thinking they know everything there is to know, and not one of them has the least idea that I am the happiest girl on earth!"

"Or that I'm the happiest man! Their ignorance is—what is the word I want? Abysmal. They don't know what it's like to stand beside you and see that little dimple in your chin. . . . They don't know you've got a little dimple on your chin . . . . They don't know. . . . They don't know. . . . Why, I don't suppose a single one of them even knows that I'm just going to kiss you!"

"Those girls in that window over there do," said Jill. "They are watching us like hawks."

"Let 'em!" said Wally briefly.